The GREATEST MARATHI STORIES EVER TOLD

In the same series

The Greatest Bengali Stories Ever Told (ed.) Arunava Sinha

The Greatest Urdu Stories Ever Told (ed.) Muhammad Umar Memon

The Greatest Odia Stories Ever Told (eds.) Leelawati Mohapatra,
Paul St-Pierre, and K. K. Mohapatra

The Greatest Hindi Stories Ever Told (ed.) Poonam Saxena

The Greatest Tamil Stories Ever Told (eds.) Sujatha Vijayaraghavan
and Mini Krishnan

The Greatest Assamese Stories Ever Told (ed.) Mitra Phukan

The Greatest Gujarati Stories Ever Told (ed.) Rita Kothari

The Greatest Kashmiri Stories Ever Told (ed.) Neerja Mattoo

The Greatest Telugu Stories Ever Told (eds.) Dasu Krishnamoorty
and Tamraparni Dasu

The Greatest Goan Stories Ever Told (ed.) Manohar Shetty

The GREATEST MARATHI STORIES EVER TOLD

Selected and edited by
ASHUTOSH POTDAR

ALEPH BOOK COMPANY
An independent publishing firm
promoted by *Rupa Publications India*

First published in India in 2022
by Aleph Book Company
7/16 Ansari Road, Daryaganj
New Delhi 110 002

This edition copyright © Aleph Book Company 2022
Copyright for individual stories and translations vests in respective authors/translators/proprietors.

Introduction copyright © Ashutosh Potdar
The acknowledgements on pp. 275–77 constitute an extension of the copyright page.

All rights reserved.

This is a work of fiction. Names, characters, places, and incidents are either the product of the authors' imagination or are used fictitiously and any resemblance to any actual persons, living or dead, events, or locales is entirely coincidental.

No part of this publication may be reproduced, transmitted, or stored in a retrieval system, in any form or by any means, without permission in writing from Aleph Book Company.

ISBN: 978-93-93852-06-9

1 3 5 7 9 10 8 6 4 2

Printed in India

This book is sold subject to the condition that it shall not, by way of trade or otherwise, be lent, resold, hired out, or otherwise circulated without the publisher's prior consent in any form of binding or cover other than that in which it is published.

CONTENTS

Introduction ASHUTOSH POTDAR   vii

1. What a Life! SHRIPAD MAHADEV MATE   1
2. Divine Intervention CHINTAMAN VINAYAK JOSHI   8
3. I'll Be Right Back DIGAMBAR BALKRUSHNA MOKASHI   15
4. Manjula ARVIND GOKHALE   26
5. Gold from the Graves ANNA BHAU SATHE   39
6. Hymn of the Deceased GURUNATH ABAJI KULKARNI   47
7. A Faceless Evening GANGADHAR GADGIL   51
8. Morning Glory SHANKAR PATIL   58
9. The Husband BHAU PADHYE   71
10. King Maruti VYANKATESH MADGULKAR   79
11. Sorrow KAMAL DESAI   85
12. Revolt BABURAO BAGUL   92
13. The God of Brahmins HAMID DALWAI   104
14. Vacancy RATNAKAR MATKARI   111
15. A Black Hole JAYANT VISHNU NARLIKAR   116
16. Relationships ASHA BAGE   124
17. Continuity SHYAM MANOHAR   135
18. And Then It Poured GAURI DESHPANDE   143
19. Kalluri's Radio VILAS SARANG   156
20. Crows YOGIRAJ WAGHMARE   168
21. Red Muck BHASKAR CHANDANSHIV   179
22. The Eclipse Shall Pass.... URMILA PAWAR   192
23. The Dust of Vaikuntha RANGANATH PATHARE   209
24. The Boss and his Dog BHARAT SASNE   231

25.	War SANIYA	236
26.	Once there Was a Crow RAJAN GAVAS	246
27.	The Fort MILIND BOKIL	259
28.	Hari's Laughter JAYANT PAWAR	266

Acknowledgements   275
Notes on the Authors   278
Notes on the Translators   290

INTRODUCTION
ASHUTOSH POTDAR

Some stories have left an indelible mark on my life. I remember them because they, more or less, speak to me, and sometimes, touch my heart. Through stories, I learned about worlds beyond my own. They allowed me to see how we relate to others and our world. These unforgettable stories keep coming back to me at different moments in life. They also make me reflect on our surroundings, learn, and envision a future. I have been reading stories ever since I learnt to read Marathi as a child. I often feel that I should read them again and again—I discover new layers each time—and share them with others. This anthology brings together the best of such stories—short, to be read in a brief sitting—drawn from the relentlessly inventive modern Marathi story-writing tradition. This collection is an attempt to give the reader a chance to dip in and out of some of the best creative reflections of human behaviour and the universe. From stories set in the farmland, home, or graveyard, and from the folksy to the formal; each of the stories in this anthology takes the reader into vividly different worlds and times, exploring seen, unseen, and imagined realities. The stories in this collection travel from the era of Tukaram, Tilak, Gandhi, and Ambedkar to that of modern-day villages, small towns, and cities. The characters include young and old men and women speaking a range of Marathi dialects and representing diverse ways of living, worldviews, and values. Whether it is the battles of the oppressed lower classes and castes, the agonies of a debt-ridden farmer, the struggles of a 'happily-married' woman within her middle-class family or the angst of an inward-looking soul, the stories deal with lives both big and small. Everyday life with successes and failures, accomplishments and adversities are briefly illuminated. The secret and hidden worlds of relationships are laid bare. The narrators, omniscient or speaking in first person or third, tell the stories of animals, birds, lands, neighbourhoods, saints, and even the imagined world beyond earth and common people. They are not mere vehicles for propaganda, nor do they represent an ideology. Rather, imbued with artistic sensitivity and reflexivity, the stories explore the vagaries of the form. The stories are sad, melancholic, mischievous, sarcastic, humorous, elegant, and experimental—together, they showcase the range, variety, and vibrancy of the Marathi short story.

Putting this collection together, observing the translators' work in transferring the expressions of one language to the other while they do justice to the landscapes, peoplescapes, and soundscapes in the stories has been fascinating and revelatory. The discussions with the translators have helped me better appreciate the stories in consideration. A native Marathi reader may be aware of the untranslatability of some of the stories originally written in regional varieties of Marathi set within a specific cultural context. The translations don't mimic the dialects, at times, a reader might struggle to understand the complexities of the contexts that carry regional and caste references.

It is possible that these are the greatest Marathi stories. To me, they certainly are the greatest, for me, in my world.

Stories have been told since the beginning of time. Oral or written, heard or read—stories are intrinsic to Marathi culture, too. They have been rooted here for ages in the form of gosht, akhyan, kahani, or katha. They are narrated in different forms, on different occasions. Sometimes they are told on the occasion of a fasting ritual, as a vrata, a vow made in faith in the auspicious month of Shravan. In this ritual, each day of the week would be committed to a moral tale. However, not all forms of the story are a part of the rituals. For example, I grew up hearing stories from people going door-to-door—composed in various forms and styles—narrating family histories or predicting the future of humankind. These stories are arranged in mesmerizing rhythmic patterns built through rhyming words. Sentences are short. Words are suggestive. Whether it's a metaphysical allegory in a bharuda, a philosophical discourse in a keertan, or a poetic world in an abhang or a powada, the lives, deaths, histories, and glories are narrated or performed in the language of the common people. Repetition is expected. Compositions are evocative and easily understood. Stories are not always burdened by gods, goddesses, genders, or castes. Nevertheless, they are not simple tales. The philosophies are explained through parables in *Leelacharitra*, the hagiographic prose text that narrates the life of Chakradhar Swami, guru of Mahanubhav sect, written by Mhaimbhat in 1278 CE. The *Leelacharitra* narrates Chakradhar Swami's leelas or activities on earth; each leela is a separate narrative or conversational form. The leelas contain the narration of the speeches of the real people and the events in their life told in fictional and parabolic forms. These early narrative forms were nourished by elements of wonder while providing entertainment to the readers and giving them knowledge.

The modern Marathi laghu katha, the short story, that we read today emerged from the journals and periodicals published during the nineteenth-century print era. It was around this time that the great Marathi poet Keshavasut (1886–1905) established new conventions of poetry. Marathi theatre flourished through innovations in writing and presentation. The first generation of women storytellers began writing, and Satyashodhak jalsas, inspired by Mahatma Phule, performed the stories of people at the margins of society. At that time, the Marathi short story form was limited to urban, educated, upper-caste people. The writing was influenced by the newly established colonial education system, reformative movements, existing narrative traditions and forms, exposure to Persian, Arabic, and Western storytelling through translations, and the narrative elements of wonder, supernaturalism, and morality.

The urge to bear witness to historic events, share an anecdote, or develop a character-sketch through a narrative was at the heart of the newly introduced literary form of the short story. Shorter than the novel that had first appeared in 1857,[1] the short story, published in magazines, became visible as a modern story form, distinct from the traditionally heard (or read) fables, parables, and mythologies. By publishing short stories by a range of writers like Hari Narayan Apte, V. S. Gurjar, Diwakar Krishna, and others, magazines such as *Karamnuk* (edited by H. N. Apte) and *Manoranjan* (edited by Kashinath Raghunath Mitr) validated the importance of the form. 'Shantabai' is known to have contributed to *Manoranjan* in 1896 with her story 'Bichari Anandibai', the first by a woman writer. However, the publication of the first collection of stories written by a woman writer had to wait until 1915, when Lakshmitanaya (Lakshmibai Abhyankar) came out with her collection, *Sadyasthiti*.[2] Although Vishnu Ghanshyam's 1854 story, published in parts in the magazine *Marathi Dnyanprasarak*, is considered the first short story, it was H. N. Apte's stories that drew readers' attention and helped establish the genre.

As Vijaya Rajadhyaksha has observed in her essay,[3] Apte's stories, full of reformist zeal, played a significant role in transforming the traditional story-listening audience into readers by appealing to them to 'listen' to the story. Thus, inspired by social awakening and reform movements, the short story, like other modern literary forms, remained committed to representing contemporary social reality and describing how one *should* live rather than depicting how one lived. The element of wonder took a backseat with the rise of social realism. Social realism remained a solid creative impulse even among later generations of writers.

---

[1] The first Marathi novel, *Yamunaparyatan*, was written by Baba Padamanji and published in 1857. It was also the year of the great revolt in India.
[2] Anjali Soman, *Marathi Kathechi Sthitigati*, Pune: Pratima Prakashan, 1995.
[3] Vijaya Rajadhyaksha, 'Kathechya Paremparene Mala Kaay Dile', *Kathashatabdi*, Pune: Granthali, 1993.

Women writers living in traditional, educated familial structures began discussing women's personhood and subjectivity through their stories. Janakibai Marathe, in 'Abhagi Yamuna', explored a different narrative structure by telling the story in the form of an epistolary correspondence between Gangu, a young married girl, and Yamu, her eldest widowed sister. Later, another woman writer, Vibhavari Shirurkar, differentiated herself as a significant voice in the printed form of the short story with her compact structure and dynamic language. Gradually, the story freed itself from the bondage of 'telling', and became conscious of the self and the 'other'. However, descriptions of 'reality', outwardly close to the novel form, made the story slow, lengthy, and repetitive. It was also plagued with cumbersome descriptions, artificial sentences, and ornate language.

While the story as a didactic form had been established, Professor N. S. Phadke, a popular writer, proposed 'art for art's sake' and insisted on the storytelling techniques and its purity as a form.[4] According to him, the short story is an impactful narration within a short time with a minimum number of characters, leaving a lasting impression on a reader's mind. While Professor Phadke introduced playfulness, spontaneity, and elegance in the language of short story writing through his love stories, as Anjali Soman observes, he failed to present a deeper and more comprehensive view of life.[5] This 'art for art's sake' style of writing was to entertain general readers, fulfil their unfulfilled desires, and manipulate their sensuality. Countering Professor Phadke's view, V. S. Khandekar, a 1976 Jnanpith awardee, came up with 'art for life's sake' as his vision. The conflicts between the lives of the rich and the poor, the owner and the labourer, and conscience and irrationality became central to Khandekar's fictional endeavours. While depicting human relationships, his stories touched on

---

[4]N. S. Phadke has discussed his view repeatedly, including in his book *Pratibha-Sadhan*, Pune: Venus Prakashan, 1952.
[5]Soman, *Marathi Kathechi Sthitigati*.

contemporary political concerns, India's freedom movement, Gandhianism, and communism, while underscoring heated debates about the purpose of literature. Others, such as S. M. Mate, who was also writing at this time, resonated with the notion of 'art for life's sake'. His story, 'What a Life!'—included in this collection—awakened readers to the glaring lack of attention that society has paid to the basic conditions of human existence.

The Mardhekar era, named after the influential writer and scholar B. S. Mardhekar (1909–56), enabled the rethinking of the relationship between life, values, and literature through his writing. In more than one way, this era, spearheaded by Mardhekar's sensibilities, became a part of the epoch-making consciousness amongst writers of breaking away from existing conventions. The prevailing format of the story naturally seemed inadequate to fictionalize the concerns of urban writers facing a strong sense of alienation, disconnectedness, and disillusionment through emerging urbanization, machine culture, and industrialization. The rethinking of literary forms became inevitable. This resulted in the emergence of the navkatha, in Vilas Sarang's words, 'the most developed and sophisticated form in Marathi'.[6] Navkatha—a new story—remained the hallmark of the new realist mode employed by the generation comprising, by and large, writers born in the 1920s and 1930s. It turned the format of short-story writing inside out. With the stories of writers from the navkatha generation like Gangadhar Gadgil, Arvind Gokhale, and P. B. Bhave, the understanding of the genre changed. Focusing on formal experimentation and style, the navkatha tradition made the story more flexible as a reaction against the establishment and the existing mould. The stories of Gadgil and Gokhale redefined the realistic plot of storytelling to address the contemporary values of the time. The pettiness of human life, the loneliness of individuals,

---

[6]Vilas Sarang, 'Confessions of a Marathi Writer', *World Literature Today*, Vol. 68, No.2 (Spring 1994):310.

and the excitement and anxiety of a past event became recurring themes in the stories of these writers. Giving prominence to the psychoanalysis of a character, it became fashionable to study and write about the different shades of human personality. The complex relationship between an image and its representation became so blurred in navkatha that, at times, it confused the reader. As a result, the navkatha started being equated with an obscure storytelling convention. Literary magazines like *Satyakatha* played a significant role in constructing notions of literariness rooted in formal experimentation during this period. They built momentum in support of the navkatha through critical essays, reviews, and special issues dedicated to the short story. Inspired by new literature and criticism from Europe, America, and other languages in India, the writers became more perceptive of the short story and its position within the literary milieu.

However, over time, the themes of urban despair, frustration, and alienation, which were considered to be the navkatha way of being modern, became recurring and clichéd. While the navkatha challenged the establishment, it was in turn critiqued for approving obscenity, obscurity, frustration, zealotry, ugliness, and obsolescence through the writing practice. Sudha Joshi, in her book on the Marathi short story,[7] draws the reader's attention to the limited scope of the self-absorbed navkatha within the boundaries of its middle-class worldviews.

Nevertheless, story-writing as a form didn't fall simply within the navkatha style in this period. For instance, the writings of C. V. Joshi and D. B. Mokashi, in the same period, deviate from the established navkatha understanding of disillusionment and frustration. Chintaman Vinayak Joshi, fondly known as Chi Vi, was known for his wry, indulgent look at the comic side of common people's lives and magically transforming their pain, without glorifying it, into a telling form. In Mokashi's stories, we

---

[7]Sudha Joshi, *Katha: Sankalpana ani Samiksha*, Mumbai: Mouj Prakashan, 2019.

don't see the disbelief, orphanhood, and loss of values reminiscent of the navkatha tradition. Interestingly, Mokashi criticized the adhunik or modern and younger writers and their tendency to get 'bored' easily; he suggested they read the arya meter poetry of Moropant, an eighteenth-century Marathi poet.[8]

The Marathi navkatha vision of the middle class created protagonists whose backgrounds were, more or less, like those of the writers themselves. The new exploration within Marathi literary culture was, as Sarang writes, 'Hopelessly mired in the stick-in-the-mud middle-class ethos and reflexes.'[9] Not surprisingly, the majority of the readership in this culture was urban, rich, middle class, educated, and upper caste. Casteist and gendered expressions remained outside its worldviews. Obviously, voices of dissent—of farmers, of women, of Adivasis, of the lower-middle classes, and of the underprivileged across urban and rural environs did not find expression. The Dhag (ember) era, as I call it after Uddhav Shelke's critically acclaimed novel *Dhag* (1960) transformed Marathi literature in post-independence modern India. This era gave confidence to the never-before-heard voices of the Shelkes in the emerging democratic nation. Oppressed classes, outcastes, women, Adivasis, and other voices of dissent felt empowered to participate in the nation-building processes through the new reforms of the time and sociopolitical movements inspired by Dr Bhimrao Ambedkar and Mahatma Gandhi. It was a revolt against the oppressive system expressed in the people's dialect and the narrative form of storytelling. With this, a new sense of ownership of the nation emerged among the disadvantaged and underprivileged across public spheres. A large group, which had so far been on the periphery, was now making inroads toward the mainstream, where the majority of the Marathi readership was urban, middle class, and upper caste. Writers like Namdeo Dhasal,

---

[8]Sarojini Vaidya and Madhuri Panashikar, 'Prastavana', *Jara Jaun Yeto*, Pune: Pratima Prakashan, 1997.
[9]Ibid.

Narayan Surve, Arun Kolatkar, and Bhau Padhye questioned the didacticism of idealistic realism and the sentimental individualism of experimental modernism. They responded to contemporary Marathi and broader global sociopolitical and literary thoughts. The navsahitya (new literature) questioned the existing romantic, nostalgic, and hypothetical reality of the earlier Phadke-Khandekar era. This surprised the dogmatists who had a narrow and dichotomized understanding of fiction: either as the 'showing' of social reality or as a world of ornamented prose.

The writings of prolific writers and revolutionary thinkers such as Anna Bhau Sathe and Baburao Bagul challenged the single, monolithic, and linear view of modernity embedded in the straightforward understanding of the relationship between tradition and modernity, and viewed formal experimentation as an impact of colonialism and Western literature. Restless in hierarchical and exploitative social structures, writers like Sathe and Bagul felt empowered by Dr Ambedkar's call for self-respect and self-reliance to revolt against the oppressive system. With the deeply impactful and intense stories penned by Bagul and Sathe, modern Marathi literature went beyond ascribing literary expression only to metaphorical narration and artistic innovation. The stories of these writers echoed the contemporary view that society and literature have to be located within the subaltern practice of challenging existing institutions with a view to annihilating oppressive human conditions. Sathe, Bagul, and other Dalit writers questioned the already decided aesthetic matrix of the 'modern' set within experimental story-writing and its representation among the learned few. Combined with Namdeo Dhasal's revolutionary writings and the vision of the literary journal *Asmitadarsh*, publishing stories by Dalit writers increased manifold and it questioned the existing caste hegemonies and belief systems through a wide range of debates and literary forms. Stories of Shankarrao Kharat, Sharankumar Limbale, Arjun Dangle, Waman Hoval, Keshav Meshram, and Amitabh that exposed hypocrisies and double standards in contemporary society are significant. Also among this cohort was Urmila Pawar from the later years of the Marathi story-writing history. Inspired by Ambedkar's vision, her stories are known for highlighting the violence of the underlying social structure that is oppressive to Dalit women. Going deeper and expanding the scope, her story in this collection is a poignant narration of a dwarf named Sumi. Thus, while depicting the established oppressive structure of the disabled and abled, Pawar pushes her narrative to put the 'one-and-a-half-foot' Sumi in conflict with Suresh, who is missing a forearm since birth, to expose the anomalies and unexplored tensions between individuals at the margins of the society. Pawar is part of a long history of Marathi women's storytelling tradition that goes back to the late nineteenth century. The depiction of open hostility as well as subtle tensions existing within the patriarchal structures of society is at the core of the rich repertoire of women's writing represented by writers like Vibhavari Shirurkar, Sumati Kshetramade, Kusumavati Deshpande, Kamal Desai, Asha Bage, Vijaya Rajyadhyaksh, Gauri Deshpande, Priya Tendulkar, Pratima Ingole, Saniya, and Pratima Joshi. Five elegantly written stories in this collection, by Kamal Desai, Asha Bage, Gauri Deshpande, Urmila Pawar, and Saniya, deal with women's struggles for selfhood within the broader context of changing family structures, power dynamics of human relationships, and society. Seamlessly moving between the characters and the worlds they inhabit, these stories explore the grey and elusive areas of women's lives and shine a light on their inner lives.

As mentioned above, the navsahitya introduced different modes of storytelling. One such mode was of stories set in the rural context—gramin sahitya, or in Rajan Gavas's words, krishijan sanskriti sahitya (literature of agro-community culture) that I grew up reading and listening to. The stories of Vyankatesh Madgulkar, Anand Yadav, Shankar Patil, D. M. Mirasdar, R. R. Borade, Bhaskar Chandanshiv, Yogiraj Waghmare, Charuta Sagar, Rajan Gavas, Mahadev More, and several others explored the complex relationship between the landscape, the people, the community, and the language. The stories of Madgulkar, especially, are credited with having changed conventional gramin sahitya by sidestepping the narration of romantic or sentimental stories of village life. He gave this form a new life through his own unique ways of showing, rather than telling, the intricacies of human life. Many readers are also fascinated by the evergreen stories of Shankar Patil, a dynamic storyteller writing in the simple, fluent speech of common village folk.

Shankar Patil's 'Morning Glory', Bhaskar Chandanshiv's 'Red Muck', and Yogiraj Waghmare's 'Crows', in this collection, represent the complex gramin katha form that depicts the grind of rural poverty. The worlds depicted in these stories are not nostalgia-driven, nor do they approach themes with romantic idealization. They are not being privileged and indifferent to people's needs. Patil, Chandanshiv, and Waghmare enable their readers to step beyond the boundaries of their subjective experience to explore essential human conditions rooted in class and caste. They remind us of human conditions intertwined within the class-caste complexities as opposed to the much-emphasized particularism of a middle-class identity absorbed in alienation and disconnectedness in the post-independence milieu.

Several Marathi writers have predominantly focused, almost exclusively, on urban sensibilities—pictured the black and white world of middle-class domesticity, modern romantic feelings, individual desires and aspirations, and emotional turmoil. However, G. A. Kulkarni, Sadanand Rege, Vilas Sarang, Bhau Padhye, and Shyam Manohar have gone a different route. Their stories have inspired debates on literature's layered relationship to the 'real', or 'reality', the 'social', and notions of 'truth'. They proposed a complex understanding of content and form built on and blending the representational form in response to the existential concerns of diverse identities and relationships. These writers challenged the conventional storytelling genre with omniscient control over characters and an old-fashioned representational style of writing fiction. The subjective contemplation, poetic imagery, and complexities of novel-like experiences of the inevitable and destined tragedy of grief in human life are reflected in the stories of G. A. Kulkarni, who has achieved an iconic status in modern Marathi literature. The context of his stories—imbibing folklore, myths, and symbols in unconventional ways—is not individual or social but eternal human existential questions. Bhau Padhye maintained that no single morality could be held as fixed or superior. Manohar, known for a subtle investigation into human life with his sharp humour and arch tone, levitates everyday occurrences into a narrative of uncommon richness and intensity. 'Kalluri's Radio', included in this collection, is among Sarang's best stories and displays all of his mastery: the effortless shifts in time, the ability to convey evolution in civilizations in a few pages; and the exploration of complex truths about human existence in uncomplicated, robust language. These writers believed in values like truth, beauty, and love, and weren't ideologically rigid and socially or religiously orthodox. Jayant Naralikar, in his sci-fi stories, and Ratnakar Matkari, with horror and supernatural elements, presented an intricate, reflexive, and unusual engagement with the real world. Several other writers, including Vidyadhar Pundalik, Waman Chorghade, Anand Jategaonkar, Sharadchandra Chirmule, H. M. Marathe, Madhu Mangesh Karnik, S. D. Panvalkar, and Sakha Kalal have different ways of creatively looking at individual dreams and desires, family values, cultural decadence, and the inside and outside worlds of human existence.

With the growth in readership through the larger networks of special Diwali issue publications unique to Marathi traditions, the short-story readership went beyond traditional middle-class city dwellers to appeal to the small-town readers sensitive to contemporary debates in culture, politics, and literature. Unlike navkatha writing that concealed engagement with the inequalities of caste, religion, and gender in favour of an individual's sense of un-belonging, the writers in the late twentieth century developed a strong sense of their identities and connection to their roots.

The Marathi story flourished in the liberalization-globalization era—interpreting contemporary realities through the lens of capitalist manipulations, tensions between the village and the city, imperialist violence, postcolonial discontent, the re-evaluation of the past, and many narrative voices. The positions of the author, character, reader, and the authenticity of representation in a writer's personal experience in her writing came to the fore. Some of the writers involved in the politics of representation have pushed for the idea that 'true' representation is validated by lived experience. On the one hand, the writers have proposed a universally inclusive vision of the middle class in response to cultural and political transitions spurred by decolonization. On the other hand, some of them have reinforced the strong connections with their roots and identities. Several short-story writers like Ranganath Pathare, Bharat Sasne, Meghna Pethe, Satish Tambe, Milind Bokil, Rajan Gavas, Rajeev Naik, G. K. Ainapure, and Jayant Pawar didn't focus exclusively on the short story. Some of them explored, rather well, the novel, drama, theatre, poetry, as well as criticism, pedagogy, and anthropology from interdisciplinary perspectives. This has resulted in the interface of a literary form, society, and culture and the literariness that could then be different across genres. Additionally, the long story format became a quintessential form for writers to explore. Although the critically acclaimed and influential writer and Jnanpith awardee Bhalchandra Nemade has dismissed the short story as a literary form, it has provided an exciting window to youthful, creative intellectuals who saw themselves as uniquely poised to interrogate the changing circumstances anew and explore the richness of artistic possibilities. In the last few years, the Marathi story has gone beyond printed pages to attract a new audience through its adaptations in the form of film, television serials, theatre performances, as well as audio books, providing the short story with more visibility and popularity. As a result, a new generation of storytellers from diverse socio-cultural and economic backgrounds has written in unique forms and styles. It would require another anthology to put together Marathi stories written by the younger writers in the last forty-odd years that are not included in this collection. At the same time, unfortunately, writers are being mindlessly boxed and restricted into groups representing a certain region, dialect, caste, class, religion, and gender. Forgetting the possible crossovers across caste, class, and gender, identity politics and the market-driven publishing practices in cities and towns have misconstrued the form of storytelling for the hefty details of personal experiences full of simplified historical and political understanding, nostalgic image-making, narrow and pedantic approaches toward life, soulless experimentation, and easy narrative conclusions. In this context, I hope that readers will enjoy the entertaining, reflective and thought-provoking stories in this collection that present a broad perpective that has outlasted changing tastes.

WHAT A LIFE!
SHRIPAD MAHADEV MATE

Taba was around thirty, thirty-two. Though he was dark-skinned, he was handsome, tall, and vigorous. He must have exercised when he was younger, since his body was compact and well formed, but because of the hard-working life he led, his swagger had slowly diminished. Physical exercise and hard labour are so different! Bodybuilders, after they have done their sit-ups and pull-ups, go for a nice long run. Well, postmen and delivery-men run, too. But a postman's legs never look as shapely as those of a bodybuilder, do they? Gymnasts raise and lower their barbells and dumb-bells hundreds of times. But so does a lumberjack Mahar. He, too, raises and lowers his heavy axe, hundreds of times. But would the arms of a Mahar look as muscular as those of an athlete? An acrobat has ropey and taut muscles, and a labourer's legs are swollen and varicose-veined: the muscles he uses end up looking knotty and tough, and his whole body has a pale shadow of not thriving.

The same had happened to Taba. His body still had the vigour of youth, but when you looked at him closely, it was obvious that this man did not get enough food—at least not nutritious food. Poverty had cast on his face a mask of anxiety and tension.

His world consisted of his wife, his mother, and himself. Some may say that a small family is a good thing. But about this, too, Taba was unhappy. Manjula suited Taba well. Her nose was not at all straight and narrow, it was like anybody else's, nor especially beautiful. Her eyebrows were not arched, they were hairy, like other people's. She just suited Taba well, that's all. Almost as tall as Taba, strong and straightforward, she was around twenty-five, and kept Taba's house capably. What ornaments could they afford for her? But still, even in their scorching poverty, Taba was appreciative towards her, a sentiment born out of his love for her. Manjula herself earned some money, too, but Taba said to her, 'Don't spend your money on essentials. Save your money for yourself.' When he had enough money saved, he bought some jewellery for her: a simple beaded necklace, or a pair of silver bangles, or some such bauble. When she wore the silver and smiled at Taba from behind her veil, he was utterly delighted. He would have got many more things for her, but whenever he bought her something, she went to the market herself and bought a gift for him, maybe a colourful vest or a turban. She was always aware that her husband let her keep her money to spend as she pleased.

They owned a cow and a goat. Taba's mother, in spite of her weak eyesight, took care of the animals. Their house was small, but the front yard was spacious and the old woman kept it sparkling clean: there was nobody in the house to make a mess.

One Sunday, a couple of my students and I were walking near Taba's house. When Taba saw us, he came out to greet us. Seeing his honest but anxious face, I felt great sympathy and respect for him. I told him that we were looking for a place to hold classes for our night school. When I told Taba about our plan, he said, 'Why don't you sit here in my yard! It's not like your students are going to steal the yard!' So right away there was a meeting of minds. When Taba's mother and wife heard us talking, they too, said that they would keep the yard clean for the students to use. Seeing that all three of them liked our plan for a school made me happy too. That was how the school started.

One day I said to Taba, 'Good, now your kids will have a school at home.' To which Manjula, who had been standing by the door, said, 'No, Teacher uncle, God has not given us a child.' Taba looked at her, half-smiling, then looked at me and said, 'Master ji, we don't have a child, true, but I will go to your school instead. I could maybe learn to read and write.' So I introduced Taba to the alphabet, letter by letter, right from the beginning: Shri Ganeshay Namah. In a few days' time he could read a simple Ramayana. He was absolutely thrilled by it, as was I.

But writing and reading was just a small part of our friendship. While the rest of the students practised their alphabet, Taba and I sat to one side and talked about many other things. Because of our mutual respect, I gradually gained Taba's trust, and we started talking about things beyond our day-to-day life. I found out that Taba had no vices. He never drank alcohol. Not only that, he had never touched bidis. The most he did was to take a pinch of tobacco now and then. This man—soft-spoken, honest, generous—had fallen by the wayside, only because of his birth. Behind his dirty shirt was an unblemished heart; under the shapeless turban was an upright mind. Really, our definition of friendship is so narrow! We never transcend beyond clothes like ours, customs like ours, education like ours, likes and dislikes like ours. Do we ever think that our hopes and aspirations could also be found elsewhere? Do we ever realize that we might find our ideals in someone with a different accoutrement? Taba was a labourer and most of his time was spent doing physical work. But I came to see that while his body toiled, his mind, set free from drudgery, occupied itself with other thoughts.

One day, after school, I was on my way home, and as usual, Taba came to see me off. But that day, Manjula joined us, walking a few steps behind Taba. When Taba softly said, 'Go,' she reluctantly turned back.

'Taba! Is something special today? Do you want to tell me something?' I asked. Taba said, 'Master ji, I thought of saying this many times before, but I'll say it today. I earn a living because I work. My wife works too. We can't make ends meet on my wages. What if a time comes when I'm out of action? Then what? Where will I find other work? So the wife has to work, too. Master, we do live a life, but what life is this? We eat because we work, that's about all. But in earning a living, we miss out on life.'

Taba became emotional; my own throat felt constricted. I swallowed hard, stopped walking, and listened. 'Master ji, my wife is more precious to me than my own life, but I don't have any time to spend with her. Early in the morning, at four-thirty, we get up, she cooks some food, we pack some lunch, and get out of the house. After half a mile, she goes one way, I go the other. She works at the Ram Narayan Mill, and I work at the Agriculture College. We, both of us, feel bad to go our separate ways. She stops, turns around and looks at me, and I look at her. A dozen times. It's still early in the morning. This young woman, my wife, has to walk through a slum. What can you say about the men over there! Maybe they will notice her and who knows what might happen then! I worry about her more and more. All day long, she is working somewhere and I am someplace else. I get off work at six. By the time we get home, it's seven, seven-thirty. The two of us get together then, finally! Next day, the same thing happens again, and my inside feels hollow with fear. If I'm late to work, the boss will cuss me. What kind of life is this! Do we ever get a chance to get together, or be sweet to each other?'

As Taba's anxiety and sadness grew, he sighed and stopped. Many people are unhappy because they don't have someone who loves them, but thousands of people are unhappy because they may have someone to love, but no time to love.

Taba collected himself and went on, 'If you want to stay at home, then you must go hungry, and if you don't show up for work, then you're absent, and you lose your job. So where are you going to get another job! So my wife and I—we don't complain and just go to our goddamn jobs—'

Hearing himself, Taba was taken aback. He bowed before me, saying, 'I am sorry, let me please touch your feet.' I grabbed hold of his hands and raised him up.

'But I swear on your feet—why is God so angry with me? In the evenings, when I am coming home, I see men like you and their women out for a walk together. They're smiling at each other, talking, enjoying the air. Then I think—look at our lives, cheaper than dirt. God, you son of a bitch, why did you do this to us?'

He would have gone on like this, but I asked, 'Taba, tell me right now what I can do, right away.'

'Please find jobs for the both of us, here in town, in the same place.'

I said yes, and went home right away. On the way home, my mind was full of Taba's stinging words. It was a small complaint, really, but in it were the seeds of so much of our civic unrest. Those who think about the structure of our society and its economic fallout will certainly see it. Really, what economic structure is this that promulgates family life but doesn't help families live properly?

I felt a deep respect for Taba when I imagined the turmoil he must feel every day, letting his wife walk alone through the slum, and for Manjula, who had to face the daily ordeal, and in the evening had to come home with a smile on her face, ready to please Taba. In our literature we read stories about the virtues and vices of kings, emperors, rich people, and the educated middle class. But even the virtues that we so loudly praise are dependent upon economic stability and traditional ways of life. Poor folk who do not have the above-mentioned stability nevertheless treat each other with respect and honesty. Everyone should examine closely how they spend their day, and they will discover how togetherness brings about happiness. They will also see how hard life must be if a man and his wife cannot get together. Even when their lives are devoid of such pleasure, they are still loyal to each other and enjoy togetherness. Their loyalty deserves a place in our literature.

After I heard Taba's complaint, I searched for a job for them, and Taba was lucky: I found them a job nearby in Budhvar Peth. Taba and Manjula were relieved. Their workday began at eight-thirty in the morning and ended at five-thirty. The main driving force of a happy marriage is for lovers to live together. Taba and Manjula now got that, so they were happy. At work, they ate their lunch together. When the foreman found out that they were man and wife, he stopped his wisecracking. Taba started to pay better attention at night school; he no longer yawned in class. When a person's life is stable he gets more ideas of cleanliness, appreciation, and politeness. The couple had had no time for such luxuries, but now, with the time they spent together, their lives took on a special glow.

Days followed days, months followed months. One night, when I was about to go home, Taba and Manjula came to see me off. I knew they wanted to tell me something. By now we were quite open and friendly with each other. So, half-jokingly, I asked, 'Today you're getting rid of Master ji, are you?' Manjula looked at Taba. I knew she had been unwell recently, but the funny thing was Taba seemed delighted by it. Taba said, 'Master ji, I want to say something. May I?'

I said, 'Don't say anything if you don't trust me.'

'Oh no, it's not like that,' they said. Taba said, 'My wife is pregnant. She is a few weeks gone. And at work, it's very busy. They are pouring concrete for the third floor. She has to carry a basket of concrete mixture on her head, climb two flights of stairs, empty the basket, and come down for the next one. This won't do. Looks like our family will get larger. So how can she do this hard work? Our cow is pregnant too. My mother says, "Feed the cow plenty of grass. A kid is on the way. He will need a lot of milk." But that means Manjula will need to work more. If I say that I'll find a night job, then the wife says "I won't let you work extra for me. Let's have this child first."' Taba looked content with the hope of his future parenthood. Manjula was on cloud nine.

I said, 'Don't worry. I will make sure that Manjula gets a job on the ground floor.' They went back to their house, and I, too, went home, feeling miserable.

There was a storm brewing in my mind. Why do we have pregnant women working? Can't it be arranged that women who are shaping our next generation in their bodies, atom by atom, get proper rest? We make much of pregnancy—the invitations, the dinners, the ceremonies, the worship of a pregnant woman—I think all that is good. It's just that all women should be able to experience them. When that happens, mankind will be truly happy. Until then, poor people will live in an unending cycle of hard work. I went back home thinking these thoughts. The next day I went to see Manjula's supervisor. It was not necessary to explain much. When I told him about the situation, he gladly offered Manjula work on the ground floor. After a few weeks, Manjula stopped going to work.

Nowadays Taba's house is happy. Little Bhairu crawls all over the yard. Taba's mother has the boy all the time—so much so that Manjula doesn't get to play with him. The calf sniffs the boy with his wet nose. Taba and Manjula have the same hard jobs, but somehow they don't feel as hard as they did. Manjula bai is proud to call herself the boy's mother. When Bhairu comes to the classroom, the boys don't yell at him, they pull him closer.

The old lady enjoyed having a grandson, and died soon after. A dried leaf fell and a shiny new leaf took its place.

Translated by Jayant Karve

DIVINE INTERVENTION
CHINTAMAN VINAYAK JOSHI

Sometimes, when a man is unable to complete a task, the gods themselves come at night and do it for him. A poet once wanted to compose a poem. He struggled with paper and pen, but the poem just wouldn't get written. In the middle of his efforts, he fell asleep. That night the goddess Saraswati herself came and wrote it for him. The poet woke up to find the poem was complete. He thought he had woken up in the middle of the night, finished it, and gone back to sleep. Scientists call this a marvel of psychology. But I say it is divine intervention (so says Antoba Gurav). We are told that the gods helped Kabir weave his brocade scarves and Gora Kumbhar shape his clay pots. The *Bhakti Vijay* tells us that God helped Janabai grind the grain. Is it lying? To assume that man accomplishes really difficult tasks without God's blessings would be to deny the truth of God leaving his kanthi, his gold chain, beside Janabai's grinding stone.

Manasshastra sab jhoot hai—psychology is all falsehood. It is entirely God's doing and that is the truth. Marutiraya, the deity of our Osadwadi, came to the aid of one of his devotees and saved him. But people call it a psychological miracle or attribute it to the awakening of man's sixth sense.

Professor Kurlekar's Great Little Circus had come to Wai. It had all the usual circus acts in its repertoire—single bar (gymnastics) trapeze artists, tightrope balancing acts, horses running around in circles making rhythmic patterns, man wrestling with a tiger—but the star attraction of the show was the Malabari performer Iranna. He could imitate the body language of most animals convincingly. Sometimes he would put on a coarse and blotchy sheath like a frog and leap onto a platform ten feet up, his arms and legs held close to his sides. It seemed as if he had no bones in his body. People would be amazed by his flexibility when he scratched his head with his toes. And then, like a frog, he would stick out his long tongue and snap up a fly.

After that he would arch his neck, puff out his chest, and bend down to pick up grain from the ground like a peacock. He would spread his imaginary tail and begin to dance. As the dance ended, a clown would pretend to chase him away. Then Iranna would stretch his arms out and fly up to a plank twelve feet up.

He would then dress like a monkey and make leaps and bounds, long and high. He would sit on a branch and scratch his seat as a monkey does, or look at people and hiss, baring his teeth. But two things Iranna had no control over—his weak tail and the fixed wrinkles on his face. And they were his two shortcomings. Yet, in those days, Kurlekar's circus was entirely dependent on Iranna's tricks for its popularity.

News of Iranna's unbelievable feats had reached the seniormost European officials. One Saturday, the manager of the circus got a message from the governor in Mahabaleshwar stating that they wanted to attend a show on Monday. 'We want to see the monkey tricks,' they said. At that time, Iranna had been unwell and had not performed for five or six days. The manager told him, 'If you come into the ring and do your act on Monday, I will give you a hundred rupees as a reward. If not, I will fire you from your job. If the governor praises the circus, it will receive patronage from the small princely states. The rajas, the rao bahadurs, and the khan bahadurs will support us. Forget about your health and do your act. I will take care of the rest.'

Now Iranna had taken a loan of a hundred rupees from a Pathan and was looking forward to getting the reward that night. But when Monday morning dawned, and his fever showed no signs of abating, Iranna became frightened. His wife, Iravva, was also worried. Someone advised her to go and place a challenge before the Maruti of Osadwadi. Iravva used to perform cycle tricks in the circus. She took one of the cycles and rode straight to the Maruti temple at Osadwadi. Beating her head on the deity's feet, she began to plead, 'Bhimarupi, Maharudra...strong like Bhim, oh Fiery One, how is it you feel no pity for me? Hanumantha, oh son of Anjani, why do you have no sympathy for this orphaned child? If tomorrow that Pathan tries to rob my honour for the sake of a hundred rupees, who will I turn to? Bajaranga, Swami, bless me!' She pleaded with Maruti using every form and epithet she knew.

Seeing the childlike Iravva sitting in front of him, the orange shendur powder started dripping from Maruti's eyes. Iravva saw this as a sign of blessing and she felt hopeful. 'Swami,' she declared, 'until you show me mercy I will not let go of your feet.' So saying she held on tightly to the deity's feet. Now the brahmachari Maruti, a celibate, did not like this gesture at all. But what could he do?

'Oh girl,' the word escaped Maruti's lips. That word appeared to Iravva as a haven, just as a sheltered island would to a ship tossed on the sea of sorrow.

'Ji Bappa,' she said humbly.

'Child, tell me what your pain is. If it is possible for me to alleviate it, I will certainly do so. But first let go of my feet. You are tickling me.' The sounds emerged from Maruti's mouth, but his lips did not move.

'Deva, Bajaranga! My dhani, my husband, is a pehelwan, a wrestler, and a devotee of yours. By mimicking many animals in Kurlekar's circus, he earns his living. His monkey acts are more real than those of a monkey itself.'

Maruti was very pleased to hear this. Learning that she was the wife of a man from his own clan, he felt sympathy for her.

'Girl, what were you saying about the Pathan?' he asked.

'My dhani had taken a loan of a hundred rupees from a Pathan. If the money is not returned within three days, the man will beat up my husband and drag me away. Though my husband is a strong man, he is a debtor. Even a tiger will fear a mouse if he is a debtor.'

'I don't understand this loan business. All I know is that you need a hundred rupees. Tell me how I can obtain them for you,' said Maruti.

'Balabhima, you Mighty One, cure my husband of his fever so he can perform his act in the circus and claim the reward,' Iravva requested.

Now Maruti became thoughtful. 'Look here, beta,' he said. 'Curing someone of a fever is not in my hands. That is the job of the celestial physicians, the twin Ashwini Kumaras. But suppose, instead of your husband, I play his part in the circus. Will that do? As soon as I complete the act I will collect the hundred rupees from the manager. You come to the temple tomorrow morning as soon as the cock crows and take the hundred-rupee note from the gap in the stone beneath my feet and throw it in the Pathan's face,' said Maruti.

Iravva was delighted with this plan. Clasping Maruti's feet tightly once again, she exclaimed, 'Aiyyaiyo Swami! You will take so much trouble for me? I will never be able to repay your favour.'

'But remember one thing, child. Very few people know that we gods go around doing things for our devotees. So no one, not even your husband, must come to know that it was I who did the act. If you tell him, his life will be shortened,' Bajaranga said, blinking.

Noble beings always prefer to grant their favours secretly.

Maruti then told Iravva to shut the door as soon as he left the premises. Why? So that no one would know that the deity had gone out. He would shrink himself and enter through the window on his return, he told her. Full of gratitude, Iravva prostrated before him and took temporary leave of him.

The evening performance of the circus began with the arrival of the governor and his party. The first item was a display of horses making patterns as they galloped in circles. Several acts followed. After watching a few more acts by animals and humans, madam governor began to yawn. On a chair behind the governor saheb sat his ADC (in the sequence of letters in the alphabet, A is followed by B. But why in the case of bodyguards of these bigwigs, D follows A, I don't know!). The ADC summoned the manager and told him, 'Professor Kurlekar, bring on the monkey act now. After watching it, the governor saheb and his entourage will depart for Mahabaleshwar. Lady saheb cannot bear late nights.'

'Yes, sir...I mean, no, sir...showing monkey play, sir...' stuttered the manager and sent for Iranna. After almost ten minutes the messenger returned, flapping his hands. 'Sayeb, Iranna is sick... very sick...cannot speak...' he reported.

The manager thought this was a ploy on Iranna's part to extract more money from him. But it was an emergency. If the monkey act is not performed, the memsaheb, the governor saheb, and all big shots will get annoyed with me. They will increase the tax on my earnings, my animals will be denied their ration, they will impose power cuts and stop our night shows.... Such disheartening thoughts assailed Kurlekar's mind and turned his heart to water.

Just as a pony finished jumping through a ring of fire and was about to disappear behind the curtain, an ear-splitting 'Whooop' was heard. All eyes turned to the top of the central pole of the tent. A huge monkey.... What a monkey! Is a monkey ever this big! It must be a man in the guise of a monkey...it must be Iranna...he must have entered from the back and seated himself on a swing, merrily swaying away, the spectators thought. And then the monkey took a flying leap across eighty feet and landed on a trapeze bar at the opposite end of the tent. He held onto the bar with his tail and swung to and fro. The manager thought it was a new trick Iranna had devised. The monkey jumped down fifty feet, then, in one movement, sprang upwards to the top of the tent. He made several of these enormous leaps, turned somersaults and cartwheels, picked up objects with his tail, clambered up the smooth pole, and then slithered down head first. All these tricks he performed. After such displays of strength and speed, he lifted his whole body off the ground and stood erect, resting on his tail, like a kangaroo! Every act was greeted with thunderous applause. All the big people were thrilled. 'We have not seen such amazing feats even in a European circus!' the governor declared.

Once the monkey act was over the governor and his lady got ready to depart. The manager wanted the monkey-man Iranna to garland the important guests. You must have guessed by now that the monkey act was performed by the Osadwadi Maruti himself. Would this great devotee of Lord Rama ever put a garland around the necks of mere mortals such as these? Anyway, before the manager could say anything, the monkey had scrambled to the top of the pole and vanished. Once the big people had gone, Maruti went to the manager and said, 'Malak, hand over the hundred rupees as promised.' The manager was so happy that he placed one hundred and one rupees in Maruti's palm. One hundred was the promised amount and one rupee, a baksheesh, a tip. Amid the tension and excitement, the manager had not realized that it was not Iranna at all.

As planned, Iranna's wife entered the temple at five o'clock the next morning. She put her hand into the gap in the stone beneath Maruti's feet and pulled out one hundred and one rupees. It is not necessary to mention that with these hundred rupees she would repay the Pathan's loan. After collecting the money, Iravva tried very hard to talk to Maruti. But he had turned into a stone idol once again.

The next morning the manager went and clicked his fingers outside Iranna's tent. Iranna timidly asked him to enter. The manager rushed to Iranna, who was lying on his cot, and grabbed his hands. 'Congratulations, Iranna,' he gushed. 'With your performance yesterday you not only saved my honour, you also did a tremendous service to my company's reputation.' Iranna thought the manager was being sarcastic because he had refused to perform the previous night. He cowered in embarrassment and fear. 'Malak, there was nothing I could do. Only the thermometer will tell you how sick I was. I must have had a fever of at least a hundred and twelve degrees,' he whimpered.

The manager wondered if Iranna was delirious. Just then Iravva barged into the tent. She stopped, alarmed to see the manager there. The manager smiled. 'Akka,' he said, 'wasn't Iranna's act last night extraordinary? How did he manage to give the impression that the tail was strong, that it had come alive?'

Iravva replied, 'That is our own special secret. No one will ever know it.'

'What leaps, what somersaults in the air! The governor was delighted and very impressed. He has given his own handkerchief, with his name on it, as a reward for Iranna. This is what they call the white man's generosity! Iranna, I will make you a partner in the company. Don't leave the company,' the manager exclaimed.

Am I dreaming or what, thought Iranna and looked at his wife. She understood her husband's confusion and said, 'As if you don't know all this! Aho, you got out of bed with the fever, you went there, performed your tricks, then came back and lay down. You don't remember?'

Iranna scratched his head and admitted he didn't recall any of it. The manager thought he had done it all in his sleep. He and Iranna thought it was a psychological miracle. Iravva alone knew the 'andar ki baat'...the inside story.

The two-anna share in the profits of the circus Iranna had got for free. After all, he wouldn't be able to do what Maruti had done, would he? Ordinary people believe that Iranna had proved that he could perform this extraordinary feat in a semi-conscious state, something he could not have done when fully conscious. With this, Antoba finished his story.

Indeed, the act of Osadwadi's Maruti is truly unbelievable.

Translated by Keerti Ramachandra

I'LL BE RIGHT BACK

DIGAMBAR BALKRUSHNA MOKASHI

Ganesh Oak. Age: twenty-five. Science graduate. Height: five foot six. Slim. Healthy. Friendly. Job in a foreign collaboration company. Salary: six hundred and seventy-five. Father: an agent for life insurance. Currently stationed in Akluj. Elder sister married. Younger brother in medical school.

Ganesh Oak was our next-door neighbour. Ten years ago, my sister-in-law's daughter was of marrying age. I had sent the above information to her as a marriage possibility. At that time, I had found all kinds of information about him in great detail, including his salary, how much his life insurance was, which sports teams he followed, whether he smoked, what kinds of illnesses he had had as a child, what kinds of friends he had, everything. I do a thorough job.

Later, Ganesh Oak chose to marry some other girl, but that's a different thing. You need to take these rejections lightly. Ganesh Oak married some other girl, and our niece did not go without marriage either. Ganesh Oak remained our neighbour, and a good neighbour at that. Over the next ten years, our neighbourly friendship got deeper, because when Ganesh's wife had a daughter and a son soon after, my wife's experience helped them a lot. One time, their daughter started to cry. Literally started to choke. So my wife went to their house and gave the girl a mantra. The kid miraculously stopped crying in a matter of minutes. That's just one example. The point is that Ganesh Oak's family and ours became good friends.

Now he is thirty-five. In the past ten years his salary had

increased quite a bit. He bought a steel safe, had a kitchen counter installed, then bought a fridge. I worked in the state government. My salary was much lower than his. But that didn't affect our friendship. When we went to the movies, we left our kids with them, and they did the same. When we celebrated our son's thread ceremony, Ganesh had just returned from overseas. He had bought a transistor there, which he gave us as a gift. It was working till last year. He brought a shaver too. It still works. In short, Ganesh Oak was doing pretty well. Doing very well, in fact. Once, when we were chatting, he said, 'Bhau, my daughter Champa is nine years old. I'm saving enough so that by the time she gets married, she will have twenty thousand rupees. That will be enough—I hope. And if my son shows aptitude, I'll send him to medical school.'

So, at thirty-five, Ganesh Oak was doing very well. One night, around nine o'clock, his wife came to our house looking distressed. Her husband, who should have been home around six, had not come back yet. I got up, changed into street clothes, and from the restaurant on the corner, called his office. No one answered.

I came back, and from Ganesh Oak's wife, took the address of one of his co-workers. Ganesh and this co-worker took the same company bus to and from work. He was surprised when he heard that Ganesh Oak had not come home yet, because he had got off the bus at six-fifteen, as usual. This bus stop was about five hundred steps from where we lived. So he should have reached home in fifteen minutes. This co-worker didn't think it was normal that Ganesh Oak had taken so long to come home. He changed into street clothes and came out with me. He said, 'I know a couple of places. Let me go check, and I'll come back and let you know. He's probably playing cards someplace.' He knew Ganesh Oak was not a card aficionado. I did, too. He was talking to me as if I were a kid. He went to check around. On the way home I thought maybe I should go via the weighing station like Ganesh Oak did—as if by going that way I could retrace his steps. Obviously I was not going to find anything. It's difficult to find a person who does not want to be found. When a man who goes to work at a certain time, comes home a certain time, someone who has long-time friends and unsurprising habits—if he doesn't come home, where do you look? Still, I went by the weighing station. Stood where Ganesh Oak's bus stops, and I thought, it's past ten now. Just four hours ago he got off this bus. He must have looked like the man standing in a circle like in the ad in *Time* magazine. So Ganesh Oak got off the bus and started walking, but in which direction? At six, this part of town is busy. There's a lot of traffic. At ten, most shops were closed. There were just a few customers at the paanwallah's shop. This was where Ganesh Oak and I used to come for a walk after dinner and Ganesh Oak would buy cigarettes. Remembering this, I asked the paanwallah about Ganesh Oak. He said, 'Oak sahib came here after work and left his bag here. He wanted to go someplace and didn't want to carry it. See that bag over there? That's his.'

I asked, 'He left his bag here and then went which way?'

The paanwallah didn't remember.

I had met someone who had talked to Ganesh Oak, I saw his bag—it seemed to explain a lot of things. At least I had a place where I could begin thinking. Why did Ganesh Oak leave his bag? Where did he go? He wanted to go someplace. Where? I went back home asking myself these questions like detectives do in detective novels. The atmosphere in Ganesh Oak's house was desolate. His wife was weeping. My wife was rubbing her back, comforting her. A couple of other women were there. When my wife saw me, she came out. She asked, 'Did you find him?' I shook my head. I didn't say anything about the bag he had left at the paanwallah's shop. Didn't want to give any false hope.

My wife said, 'Do you think he had an affair with some girl at the office?'

I asked, 'Do you think so?'

'Probably not, but you can never tell with men.'

She asked me to stay home and went back to the Oaks' apartment. I stood in the balcony. Men, women, and children went by. Some of them were perhaps jealous of Ganesh Oak's wealth. But I didn't have time to wonder what they thought about Ganesh Oak's disappearance. I heard a scooter. It was Ganesh Oak's co-worker. He came to me and said, 'Nobody knows where he went. I have brought my scooter. Let's go to the police station and let the police know. We know how accidents happen nowadays. And we need to let our factory manager know, too. Our new production is in process. Tomorrow if Ganesh Oak is not there, that'll be a big problem. The time factor is very important for us. A rival company is after the same product.'

One person, but different people have different concerns about him. The wife worries about one thing, the co-workers about something else, the neighbours about something else still. When we were on our way to the police station on the co-worker's scooter, he said, 'Don't mention this to anyone, but I'm afraid our rival company has kidnapped him to hamper our production.'

Then at the police station, the policeman said, 'Do you want to file a report now or later? I suggest waiting for about forty-eight hours. People who go missing often come back. Something goes wrong here'—he tapped his head—'but it's usually temporary.'

But we were not willing to wait. So he took down all the information. I said, 'He may have had an accident. Nowadays you can't tell when some car may hit you.'

The policeman said, 'There's no report of an accident in our district.'

I didn't say anything. I thought Ganesh Oak left his bag at the shop and from there went someplace. Maybe he had an accident at the place he went to. But I didn't tell him about the bag.

We left the police station and went to the bungalow of the factory manager. It was almost midnight. We were waking this important person late at night, which meant Ganesh Oak must be an important person himself. He was important to us not just because he lived in our building. He was probably planning to build a bungalow of his own, instead of paying a huge deposit for an apartment. We went to the gate, rang the bell. The manager, dressed in pyjamas and a nightshirt, came out, rubbing his eyes. The co-worker went to the manager and said, 'Sir, let's go inside. It's important.'

He had already told me what was important. He wanted to show 'the secret' to the manager. The two of them went inside. When they came out, the manager did not look sleepy. He picked up the phone, and said, 'Hello! Commissioner sahib! Good evening! My name is Kelkar, I'm the factory manager for XXX. I'm sorry to call you so late. It's your duty, you say! Great! An employee of ours has not returned home. We have let the police know, but would you please give some attention to this matter? Yes, he's an important employee...yes, every worker is important, I agree...I read your article on traffic control. It's fantastic...revolutionary, I'd say. You must come and speak at our Lions Club....'

I was happy to see that the search for Ganesh Oak had reached the 'upper echelon'. Now the wheels will move faster.

I said, 'Perhaps Mr Oak had an accident.'

The manager dialled again. 'I'll tell our phone operator. She'll call the hospital from her home.'

We were up all night. I took a nap early in the morning, but that's all. My wife stayed awake at the Oaks'. In the morning, she made breakfast for Ganesh Oak's kids. I made tea for us. There was no news in the morning paper. In the afternoon they ran a special bulletin, describing Ganesh Oak and asking the public to report if they saw this person. In the afternoon an inspector came. My wife called me over. The inspector asked Oak's wife various questions in front of me, questions about different aspects. From the questions you could see how many different ways trouble can arise in a person's life. First he asked simple, straightforward questions, like what Ganesh Oak took to office, et cetera. Then he asked, 'Did you two fight?'

'Not at all. We were planning our vacation that's coming up.'

'Had he disappeared like this before?'

'Never. He has always come home on time.'

'Has he left you a note or anything?'

'No.'

'Did you check?'

'Yes.'

The tears she had kept at bay started to flow again. It must have hurt her that after ten years of happy marriage, her husband would leave her without as much as a note. Besides, she had heard other people talk. Also, there was a hidden fear, a possibility of there being 'a woman'. The inspector asked, 'Any chronic diseases?'

'Not at all. He took care of his body—never became overweight. Used to say to me, "You're going to get fat. Watch out."'

The inspector came with me to our apartment. After we sat down, he asked me, 'How is the Oaks' married life?'

I said, 'Ideal. In all these years, I never heard them fight.'

Oak's co-worker came in and I introduced them. The inspector asked him, 'I'm going to visit the factory anyway, but now that I've met you, let me ask you this: Sometimes an officer of a company has a special relationship with the stenographer. Mr Oak's steno....'

The co-worker laughed and said, 'No cause for alarm there. There is a steno in his section, but he is a man. Oak is not into that kind of thing. What do you think?'

I said, 'I think so too. Did you ask around near the bus stop where he got off?'

The inspector replied, 'Yes. We got his bag from the paanwallah. There are papers in it, just routine paperwork. He left the bag with the paanwallah.'

So the bag wasn't a secret after all. And it happened just the way I thought it would. They found the bag but made no progress on the search.

'Was Ganesh Oak responsible for money?'

The inspector had brought up a new angle. It made sense in a way: he had bought things recently, like a TV and fridge, and their clothes and their lifestyle—my wife said Ganesh Oak's wife had at least fifty tolas of gold on her. We were on good terms with Ganesh Oak and his wife, so we didn't pay much attention. But if this money was illicit and if this was to come out into the open, then Ganesh Oak's disappearance made sense.

But the co-worker said, 'There's no connection with money. He is in new product development. And he's a technical man. He never sees a paisa of company money. But there's another angle. When you meet our manager, he'll tell you about it. I'm not at liberty to talk about it.'

The inspector smiled and said, 'We have talked about it already. It's not a secret in your industry. Skilled employees do get stolen. We're looking into that.'

The co-worker said, 'It would be enough for our rival concern to take Ganesh Oak and put him away for a couple of weeks. In two weeks, we'd be behind schedule.'

I said, 'Here's another angle for your consideration. Nowadays they give you a flower or something to smell and they hypnotize you and kidnap you.'

'There have been cases like that. If it is so, then Oak should be back in two or three days.'

The co-worker said, 'You wouldn't believe how fierce the competition is in our industry. Hundreds of thousands of rupees are spent on a project. We do everything possible to complete projects on time.'

That day, Oak's photo was on the TV. I only heard about it later because there is only one television in our building—the Oaks'—and it was turned off. The day after that, the photo and the news were in the newspaper. If the rival concern was up to some mischief, then Ganesh Oak's company was making plenty of noise. On the third day, the police deployed dogs in their search.

Nothing came of that, either. On the fourth day, Ganesh Oak's wife was still crying, the poor thing, and the kids had not gone to school. On the fifth day, I sent them off to school.

All the people in our building were trying to sneak a look. Oak's wife did not sit in their living room. To her, her husband's disappearance was a thing of pain, and bad luck, and sorrow. If Ganesh Oak had died (don't say that), it would've been pure sorrow, and perhaps she would've accepted it. Seven days went by. The coverage on the radio ended. The papers forgot the news item. Slowly the atmosphere in the building normalized. After a couple of weeks, relatives stopped coming. It was almost a month later when I stopped calling the police every other day. Ganesh Oak's company put him on leave and sent home his salary for half a day. How much longer they would do this remains to be seen.

After Ganesh Oak's disappearance, I constantly had this feeling as if someone who was walking with me had suddenly disappeared. I kept thinking, how could he go? Where could he be? What was he doing? It was a scary feeling. It was as if I was in a battle and the soldier standing next to me got hit by a bullet. It was worse than that, because in a battle you know bullets are coming. He was younger than me, I kept ruminating about that too.

Does he have a woman on the side? Has he stolen company money? Has a competitor company poached him? Is he unhappy with his wife? Does he have mental problems? Did somebody jinx him? Does he have some incurable disease? Nothing made sense.

Then, after a month and a half exactly, Ganesh Oak came back as abruptly as he had disappeared. Returned at about the same time as he usually did from work. Wearing the same pants and the same bush shirt. He came to the building and calmly went to his apartment. He didn't look embarrassed or uneasy or tense. Had a smile on his face, as always. He sat on a stool, took off his shoes, then his socks. Then turned the socks right side out and put them back in the shoes. I saw everything from our apartment. His wife came out of the kitchen. I couldn't see her well and but she seemed to have stopped in her tracks. 'So, what's for dinner?' I heard him say. In a few minutes, I heard laughter coming from that apartment. He probably did not give his wife a chance to ask questions.

I didn't go to their apartment even when I saw he had come back. That was because I didn't usually go to their apartment before. So I didn't go there now. But before he got up from the stool to go inside, he waved at me. I waved back. He usually came to our apartment in the morning before work. That was his routine.

Sure enough, the next morning he came in and sat down and said, 'Bhau, order us some tea!' Nothing in his manner betrayed an awareness that something unusual had happened recently. I, on the other hand, felt sheepish; I didn't know what to say. What do you say to someone who had disappeared for a month and a half? He had erased the memory of the past six weeks, but I couldn't. I somehow kept my balance, and in a normal tone of voice asked my wife to make us some tea. 'See, Ganesh is here.' For a while I couldn't hear what he was saying. Then he took out some money from his breast pocket.

'This is for you, Bhau. I heard you spent a lot for us in the past six weeks.' I pushed the money aside. I was angry. Not a word about how worried we were for six weeks. The ass! Offering me money!

'Forget the money. First tell me where you were. Do you remember?'

He smiled a little and said, 'Bhau, I remember every second from the time I left.'

Still angry, I said, 'So you left knowingly! What you did is your affair. But you could've at least left a note!'

He said, 'Bhau, please don't get angry. I'm not going to talk to anyone about what happened, but to you I must tell everything. The only thing I'm not able to understand, or explain, is the moment when I got off the bus. But I'll try. I got off the bus and everything started to look unreal to me. For a moment I didn't even know where I was standing. My job at the factory, my wife, my kids—everything seemed to be borrowed from someone else's life. I remember thinking, what is all this? What is going on? How long have I been doing this? Now, keep in mind that I had not forgotten anything. I was not hallucinating. Except, things that had happened, and events that had occurred, and objects around me—all seemed like a shadow. I was the only real presence in the middle of all this. It was as if I had not met myself until that moment, and finally I was meeting me. I thought if I just kept walking, how will it matter? It's difficult to describe, Bhau, that moment, but I was so calm! I was not hopeless, I was not indifferent, I was not angry either. I was just calm. Totally calm.

'For example, when the idea came to me to leave my bag with the paanwallah, I did that calmly. I'll be right back, I told him. And it was true. I did come back, didn't I? I left the bag with him, got in a rickshaw, and went to the bus depot. There, I looked at the list of names of various towns. Why I don't know, but the name Audumbar popped into my head. I got on the bus and reached Audumbar the next morning. The river there, the large trees, and the peaceful atmosphere! I was happy, as if I was coming home. I went to the river right away, took off my clothes and swam!

'That month and a half were so joyful! At first I tried to do yoga, but realized that it was not for me. Chanting was good, though. So I started to spend my day without thinking about anything in particular. All day long, I just walked along the river, or sat in the shade of those trees. My mind was empty, except for the joy. Six weeks later, some tourist recognized me and said hello, and memories from here rushed into my mind like a waterfall. Immediately I decided to go back. There is no point in struggling or being of two minds. I'll go back again when it feels natural to go back.'

As he said this, he looked so blissful that I was furious.

'So here we were scared, and you were gallivanting in Audumbar!'

He simply said, 'Bhau, sit on the banks of a river and you'll see how peaceful it is.'

I was still angry. I asked, 'Didn't you remember your wife and kids?'

'When I stepped on the bus I forgot everything.'

'Your work too?'

'Yes, Bhau.'

'Me too?'

'Yes.

'You had no feelings of love, duty, tenderness?'

'Yes, that's how it was.'

'If you only knew how many ways we searched for you....'

'Where did you search?'

'At first we thought your rival stole you. Then we felt maybe you had an accident. You know the traffic nowadays. Then we said maybe you left your wife and took up with some other woman. Or you took money from your company and absconded....'

He started to laugh, and couldn't stop laughing. I had to laugh too. 'It never occurred to me that you may have gone to Audumbar. Actually I should have thought of it right off. We have a tradition, don't we? Why we forgot about it, who knows!'

Translated by Jayant Karve

MANJULA

ARVIND GOKHALE

The train swayed and stuttered, heaved and gasped as it ran along. Every compartment crammed with humanity. Spaces between seats suffocating. Windows and doors plastered with bush coats, and sari pallus, hairy heads, and taut limbs. People hanging on the outside too. Like a serpent riddled with ants, the train snaked along its tortured track. Every time this two-headed worm halted, the filth inside disgorged and then more of it stuffed in.

People…people…people…. Emerging from chawls, occupying footpaths and platforms, then trams and local trains—they were everywhere. The crowds in the locals reached their peak at the time when one had to submit to this living hell twice a day, to get to the office in the morning and then return home in the evening. There was barely any space in the compartment. No matter how much you shrank into yourself, someone or the other shoved you. The rim of a hat brushed your head, or your shoulder got a thorough rub-down. Unfamiliar fingers pressed into your thigh, shoe soles left an imprint on your foot. Your whole body got a proper massage. Better not to look this way or that. Beads of perspiration on a smooth, bald head, prickly stubble on an unwashed chin, layers of talcum powder caked on a throat, such visions would assail your eyes. Even if you stood absolutely still, you breathed in someone's exhaled breath, the fetid smell of stale sweat flooded your nostrils, enough to make you puke. Deadened minds and sickening bodies everywhere—in your eyeballs, under your nostrils. People, people, people!

The return journey was a shade better, no doubt. In the

mornings you had to catch the train having barely swallowed your lunch. Then hang on, as the train jolted and pushed. Then make that trudge from station to office. In the course of the rough and tiresome ride, the morning bath was soon forgotten and the make-up rituals seemed in vain. Pieces of hastily chewed, half-digested chapatis would stab the stomach. And then the headaches at the office! On the return journey, though there was chaos and confusion, there was also the fond hope that you could have a thorough wash and eat and sleep in peace once you got home.

Wilted and worn, men and women emerged from the 6.15 fast and hastened towards their burrows and coops. Men with loosened ties and evening newspapers in their hands. Women wiping the last vestiges of sweat from their brows with dirty kerchiefs, managing somehow to keep the purses dangling from their shoulders. Sighs collected and yawns gathered as tired eyes impatiently waited for their station. And when the train stopped, mustering the last bit of energy, they rushed forward to alight.

As the train approached Andheri station, Manjula tried to make her way to the exit. She had been standing uncomfortably, all the way from Churchgate, beside a seat occupied by a fat Gujarati gentleman. The man was staring at her and trying to inch closer to her. He had even offered to make some place for her to sit, but she had continued to stand, holding on to the back of the seat. A bhaiyya was seated opposite, his milk cans at his feet. Leaning on her was another young working woman. People were jostling her from all sides. Though the crowd ebbed and flowed, it remained constant.

Manjula found it impossible to make her way towards the door. Walls created by the Gujarati, the bhaiyya, the working girl, and the men and women in front of her and behind her stalled her. Finally Manjula wrapped her pallu tightly around herself, held firmly on to her purse, shut her eyes, and started inching forward. Several shoves, pinches, nudges, and tugs later she found herself on the platform.

Manjula came out of the station and started walking swiftly along the road. Her hair had come loose and was flying all over her face. Her lips were dry and her eyes felt heavy. Her armpits and midriff were sticky with sweat. Hammering at the typewriter all afternoon had made her fingers ache. And now, as she walked, her feet began to pain.

'Manjula...Mrs Kharkar....'

Manjula turned around and stopped, surprised. Kashi Kulkarni was coming towards her swinging her handbag. She worked in the office next to Manjula's. Both of them took the same train in the mornings, but Manjula hardly ever saw her in the evenings. They walked along the edge of the road. Manjula asked her, 'You take this train every evening?'

'Che! Only today. It's the 7.30 usually.'

'You work so late?'

'No...we finish at six. Then I go looking for a place to stay. Whenever someone suggests something I go. But I am disappointed.... If anyone....'

Manjula warmed up as soon as she heard about the hunt for a place. She had been through this very same torture just a year ago. But she was also fed up of hearing the same stories about the shortage of accommodation and the difficulties finding something, day in and day out.

After a pause she said, 'Better get married, Kulkarni, then you....'

'My marriage is fixed. That's why I am looking for a place. It's been a year and a half...six days in the week both of us go in search of accommodation. On the seventh day, dejected, we give up, go out of Mumbai and celebrate our love.'

Suddenly Manjula's face fell. Not because of Kashi's story but because she too had fallen in love, found a place to stay, and then got married, but....

'I want to buy some vegetables, will you wait a bit?' Manjula asked as she went towards the vegetable carts on the roadside.

She tied the onions in her handkerchief, put green chillies and coriander in her purse, and held the coconut in her hand as she set off again. Kulkarni looked at her enviously and unable to help herself, she blurted out, 'So lucky you are, Mrs Kharkar!'

'You also will find a place, definitely! I will ask around for you, haan...Subrahmanyam from our office usually knows about these things.'

The two smiled wryly at each other and Kulkarni went on her way. Manjula hurried along. She still had a long way to go. Once she got home she had to cook, and collect and store water. She wanted to have a bath. She was hungry as well. If Sharad was home, then she would have to make tea for him. When she thought of Sharad, Manjula was startled. Ever since she had stepped out of the house it had been the ticket checker, the blind beggar on the train, her boss, Subrahmanyam, accountant Kavale, Mary D'souza, and Saral Sathe, Bhat of the tea stall, the old man near Churchgate who winked at her, the fat Gujarati, Kashi Kulkarni, and the bhaiyya selling vegetables who were on her mind. Sharad was nowhere among them. Suddenly, she felt a deep need for him—the man she loved above all else, with whom she had set up a home. But the very next moment her heart hardened and her feet slowed down.

A car passed her and slowed down. It was Aloo Billimoria. Stopping the car she called out, 'Lift, Manjula?'

'No, I'm almost there...' Manjula replied and walked on, thinking about Aloo. She was also a working woman, had a job with some airline. She was happy. She had ditched her husband a long time ago and now had a new boyfriend every day. It was his car, his money. Even the frocks she wore and the lipstick on her mouth were from the boyfriends. The whole world called her names, but Aloo didn't care. Once when a group of their college friends had gone on a picnic to Ghodbunder, she had unburdened herself to Manjula. 'Marriage doesn't suit me...my husband doesn't earn enough, and I can't help my extravagant tastes. The stream of relatives never ends and the pressure from his family is too great. Even if a childhood friend of mine visits, they all get suspicious....' Aloo had rebelled. She had freed herself. At least she seemed free. But she behaved in a most reckless fashion. The more Manjula thought of Aloo, the more frightened she became. Her Sharad was earning well, he did not bring his innumerable relatives home all the time. I didn't want any friends myself, nor was I given to a lavish lifestyle, she thought. Aloo had always referred to Manjula as the happy housewife, and yet....

By the time Manjula reached the chawl, it had become dark and the lights had come on. When she realized that the day had ended, she frowned. The men were all seated, bare bodied, outside their kholis, their rooms, chatting, playing with their kids. Seeing their half-naked torsos and the many children, Manjula felt nauseated. Radios and phonographs blared popular film songs, enough to give one a headache. This cacophony had destroyed her love for music forever. She felt completely alienated from it all.

She climbed the stairs to her rooms. Sharad was lolling on the easy chair. Taking off her chappals, she said, 'When did you come?'

'Just now.'

'I missed the 6.05 train....'

Throwing her purse and the vegetables on the table she went inside. There was no water in the bucket. She had filled it up in the morning before she left. Sharad must have used it all up. Manjula was annoyed. At least he could have filled it up again! The pyjama he had taken off still lay on the floor. But so did her sari. Manjula shoved the pyjama and sari into a corner with her foot.

Sharad called out, 'What are you doing? Let's go out for a bit!'

'Yes, re buwa...but I've just come home na....' She picked up the bucket and as she went out she said, 'Let me have a wash, then we can go.' With a bucket in hand she walked out onto the veranda towards the water tank. She was very upset that Sharad hadn't even offered to fetch the water for her. She stood there by the tap helplessly. Whose bucket, whose wash! What difference! She half-filled the bucket. Where was the energy to carry it full!

Once she'd had a wash and changed her clothes, Manjula felt much better. She looked at herself in the mirror, long and hard, then said to Sharad, 'Let's go.'

He was lying there as before. 'Where do you want to go now?' he said roughly. 'It's already eight o'clock. For a whole hour you were decking yourself up....'

Manjula was angry. She was about to retort when Sharad remarked, 'Do you pay attention to anyone else except yourself? You didn't even ask if I wanted some tea....'

Instantly Manjula's face fell. For a long while she did not know what to say. Finally, she managed to mumble, 'Ay, sorry, han...here, look at me, I was so tired...ay, don't be angry na....'

Sharad remained glum. Pushing her away he said, 'It's all right. I'll get it from a hotel. Don't bother to make it. Really....'

When he stood up, she asked, 'So we are going out, then?'

'No. I'm not in the mood. And barely will we have gone when you will start saying "Let's go back, I have to cook, water has to be collected"...all excuses.'

'We will eat out then! Water can be collected in the morning.'

'You've developed a taste for eating out it seems! Where's the money for it? I have just two annas left...enough for a cup of tea.'

Manjula was infuriated. She picked up the coconut from the table and banged it hard to break it. She wanted to drink the water, but she was so angry she just let it fall to the ground. Picking up the onions and the coriander and green chillies from her purse, she went into the kitchen.

Sharad went back to his easy chair, lit a cigarette, and started blowing smoke rings.

Manjula cut the onions and coriander, lit the stove, put the vessel on to prepare the bhaji, then took it off and put water for the tea to boil. Absent-mindedly, she dropped the onions into the tea water. She threw it out and put some fresh water on again.

Sharad came and stood behind her and whispered, 'Manju....'

Tears welled up in Manjula's eyes. Taking the hand he had placed on her shoulder, she said, 'Tea is ready.'

'You shouldn't have made it...I really don't want it. And, yes, let's eat out.'

'The tea is ready now,' she said, straining the tea into a cup. Seasoning the vegetables, she told him, 'No need to go out. See, I've made your favourite potato rassa.'

Pressing her shoulders affectionately, he drank the tea and then said, 'Don't make anything else.'

'I'll make chapatis, na....'

'Don't. Your hands must be aching. I will get bread.'

'Actually there is some bread and one and a half chapatis, but if you are going to get something, a new Sindhi hotel has recently opened across the road...some mithai....'

Seeing Manjula's cheerful face Sharad asked, 'Why the sudden craving? You're pregnant or what?'

Manjula's face turned pale. His remark drained the colour from it.

She began stirring the vegetables in the pot.

Without saying anything, Sharad walked out of the room. And out of the chawl.

The tears she'd held back for so long gushed forth. Manjula recalled the doctor's advice. Take care of your eyes, he'd said. But though she tried to control them, more gathered. The doctor had also advised a change of scene. Manjula's feet were aching from long hours of standing, her toes from being trampled upon. Her fingers and hands were tired from banging on the typewriter continuously for six, seven hours, and the clackety clack of the keys was reverberating in her head. The head that was firmly fixed on her shoulders so far began to throb, as if it would fall off.

She finished cooking and went out. The front door was wide open. Manjula looked around the room. At her entire household therein—the easy chair, table, cot, books...how much joy she had felt when acquiring one item at a time! Just a year and a half ago. And already the enthusiasm was seeping out. Why, she asked herself. Why am I feeling this way? We had faced hard times earlier too. But compared to so many others, we were fortunate! Kashi Kulkarni can't find a place to stay, Aloo Billimoria's husband cannot make a decent living. But look at us—a two-room flat, two jobs, and still there are arguments and quarrels. What's gone wrong? Where is the problem?

She stood in the middle of the room for a few moments, then stepped into the veranda. She was back in an instant. It was impossible to stand there. Too much coming and going, too much noise. Cooking fumes and film songs. Besides, she was in no mood to chat with the neighbours. It was the same story, they were all caught up in their own busy lives. She felt less disturbed inside. But not quite calm. It was half past nine and Sharad hadn't come home yet. She wanted him to come but she also didn't. They would have their dinner, she would clear up, and then…. The thought distressed Manjula.

She did feel lighter as soon as Sharad returned. And when she saw the sweetmeats he had brought, she was overjoyed. She quickly served the food, gave Sharad a bigger helping of the potato rassa and the sweet, then ate some off his plate. She laughed with him as she told stories about Subrahmanyam. After they'd finished eating, she sent Sharad to the outer room and washed the dishes.

By the time she went out, Sharad had spread the mattresses and was relaxing in the easy chair, smoking. The smell of the smoke and the sight of the mattresses blighted her spirits. A mixture of fear, revulsion, and anger churned her insides. She paused for a while, then said, 'Why are you smoking just before going to bed?'

'It's not sleep time yet!'

'Past ten o'clock….'

'You go to bed then.'

'I can't sleep with the light on.'

Sharad was annoyed. He took a long drag of his cigarette and stubbed it out. 'The light bothers you, the cigarette bothers you....'

Manjula said nothing. She lay down and covered her eyes with her left forearm. Still sulking, Sharad got up, shut the door, switched off the light, and spread himself out on the other mattress. Soon it was all calm and quiet.

Very softly Sharad said, 'Come....'

A thousand needles pricked Manjula's body. The quarrel she was afraid of was standing over her like a ghost in the dark. Somehow she managed to mutter, 'No....'

'You're angry?'

'Unhun....'

'What's the matter then? Why are you acting like this? Come, na....'

'No, let me sleep.'

Though it was dark, Manjula didn't take her arm off her eyes. She actually wanted to throw it around Sharad's neck, but there was no energy left in her body. The mattress felt like it was stuck to her back and her head seemed to be knocking against the wooden frame of the cot.

'Sleep is forever perched on your neck. Sleep now, forever....'

Hearing his harsh words, Manjula sat up at once. Tremulously she muttered, 'How angry you get. You, and I too. Come on, let's chat...shall we play a game of chess? Or will you come for a walk?"

'No, you sleep. Staying up is bad for your health.'

'What's wrong with my damned health?'

'That's what I don't understand!'

Manjula noticed the desperation in his voice. She understood. Sadness and helplessness congested her chest. Her eyes filled with tears. She shuddered.

'You are angry, I can see that,' she cried piteously. 'But I swear to you, I don't enjoy it...I just don't want it.'

'You used to want it all earlier. Only of late have you become cold, indifferent...it's me you don't want any more.'

What does one say to this, she thought, but still she replied, 'Don't fill your head with ash…try and understand me.'

'All the same….'

'I get tired, re…tired of cooking, tired of filling water, tired after the commuting, of the typewriter in the office….'

'What about me? Don't I get tired too? Don't I also work? Women all over the world are working now. Why are you telling me all this? Give up your job if it's too much. I can't tell you to do that, can I? It will show up my inadequacy, my inability to….'

Manjula was perplexed. How could she explain to Sharad? How could she explain to herself? She didn't know what to do. Finally, she made up her mind. She opened her eyes, bit her lip, and got up.

'Don't close the window!' Sharad shouted. 'As it is the heat is killing me.'

Manjula was startled. Moving away from the window she said, 'The neighbour's guest puts his cot by our window because there's no place in their house.'

'Let him be. You go to sleep as usual.'

Manjula was extremely annoyed. She stretched out on the easy chair. The ominous silence became too much for her. She said, 'First thing we will buy next month is a fan.'

Sharad taunted, 'Which means you can escape for a whole month.'

Manjula's temper rose. 'What are you saying, Sharad?' she snapped.

Twice as viciously he replied, 'Am I lying? Is it not true that our husband–wife relationship has ceased to exist?'

Manjula was trembling with rage. 'Sharad! Sharad…' she stuttered. But then she lost her courage and began to sob softly.

Once more there was complete silence in the room. Outside, vessels clattered, irate voices were raised, songs from movies continued their din—the background score for the turmoil within.

Sharad sat up and slowly moved towards the foot of the

easy chair. Manjula reached out and lovingly stroked his head. Sharad's voice was gentle. He said, 'Why do you behave like this, Manju? You used to be so joyful earlier. Have you forgotten it all? Remember the week we spent in your village soon after our marriage? We'd be up all night...and even when dawn broke, you were reluctant to leave the room. Even here, when you came home in the evening you would cling to me.'

Manjula couldn't control her sobs. Through her tears she stammered, 'I do remember, I remember everything...Sharad, I love you so much...I want you...my....'

Sharad moved closer to her eagerly. In a placating tone he said, 'Of course I am yours. You are being silly. Look, most people don't have any privacy...houses with ten people living together... as for the labourers.... So what is the matter with you? I agree the intensity, the urgency wears off after a while, but even so....'

Gripping both his hands, Manjula sobbed, 'Even after the newness wore off, I wanted you! But this humid weather, this rushing around, this mechanical existence. I just can't take it any more, Sharad, let's go away from here...somewhere, anywhere... just take me away....'

Her words and sobs whirled around in the air. After a long pause Sharad found his voice. 'You are fed up. Seems to me you want a child....'

'Possibly, but if we are to have a baby I will absolutely not live here. My child will not...' clicking her tongue helplessly, she said, 'Forget it...this is a pointless discussion.'

Manjula's tears dried up. Sharad's enthusiasm too had waned. Dryly he said, 'If we don't compromise with the existing situation, we will only make ourselves miserable. I don't like this stress either. But what to do? After the exhausting grind of the whole day there's only one way to cope with the strain, to relax, and even that you....'

These words cut right through Manjula. She felt a strong revulsion. A contempt. Her Sharad ought not to say these things, behave like this. She felt like getting up and walking way…far away.

Just then Sharad dragged her out of the chair and muttered angrily, 'For a whole month I have tolerated your behaviour… you have become really weird.'

His embrace held no pleasure for her. She felt suffocated by it. And the heat. His body enveloped her like the oppressive, claustrophobic rush in the local train. And his kisses were the fingers of some stranger pinching her.

Shoving her away Sharad exclaimed disgustedly, 'Die!'

And Manjula felt it would be better if she could die. She did not have the means to unite with her lover, her husband, anymore. She began to feel disgusted with herself. Which of my likes and dislikes, my thoughts and emotions have remained intact, she thought. So why am I holding out on this? Don't countless women give in, regardless? Doesn't her Sharad also behave like that?

Anguished and piteous, she cried out, 'Come, take me.'

Sharad was furious. 'I can't make love to a corpse,' he said contemptuously and stood up. 'As of today, our relationship is over. Finished. You have pushed me away yourself. You may be able to do without, but I cannot. It's impossible. I must find my happiness elsewhere. I have no time for your pride. I'm going.'

Manjula's brow was furrowed. Equally angrily she yelled, 'Go! Go wherever you want.'

'Scared of your father, am I?'

'Take it, take the money from my purse if you want and GO….'

Manjula's fury was unchecked. A spark could become a conflagration. Her head felt like it would burst. Suddenly, a strange fear gripped her. Tension and sadness made her dizzy. Caught between the two emotions, she was being torn apart. With a mighty effort she took hold of herself and crawled towards Sharad, grovelling at his feet.

'Forgive me. Take me under your wing…try to understand me…I love you, I need you, I want you….'

Fuming, Sharad went to the chair and fell into it like a stone and lit a cigarette. Abjectly, she moved closer to the chair and pleaded, 'How shall I explain my thoughts, my feelings are very different, Sharad. When the mind is calm, the body fresh and firm, the atmosphere clean and beautiful, my senses are aroused. Here we are surrounded by constant movement, noise, screaming and shouting, angry words and abuses...it really upsets me. Sweat rolls down. Fleas bite. The head aches. The body is drained, sapped of all energy and passion. The endless slices of bread, the lascivious eyes in the train, the typewriter keys...they torment me. The mind is defeated and the body benumbed. All this has become repulsive. It has acquired a veneer of revulsion. It's like animals. I don't want to become one, Sharad. I value my feelings, my sentiments, my senses, I consider them sacred. Let me preserve at least that. Don't mock me, Sharad, don't humiliate me!'

Manjula didn't know when her broken words stopped. They had dissolved in tears. Her back was about to crumble and her eyes were getting glazed. She was being pushed and shoved in the local train, stared at by a hundred lecherous eyes. The lewd remarks on the road, the circle of children from the chawl who would not leave her alone. Fleas were nibbling at her, sweat was gathering in puddles around her, and she, she was falling asleep, her head on Sharad's lap....

Translated by Keerti Ramachandra

GOLD FROM THE GRAVES
ANNA BHAU SATHE

When he heard that a rich moneylender in the next village had died, Bhima's heart leaped inside him. He could expect something good now. Excitement filled him. He looked in the direction of the village and then up at the sun.

It was setting. Rain clouds crowded the sky. They looked like land that had been furrowed and was ready for planting. Mumbai was bathed in the fading light pouring through those higgledy-piggledy clouds.

A gentle breeze rustled through the jungle in the middle of which about fifty huts huddled together. Old leaves, mats, planks, and sacks had been cobbled together to give the appearance of homes; and in these, people managed to live. The disused thus gave shelter to the useless. For inside each hut, there lived those who had worn themselves out with the constant hustle to fill their bellies. All the stoves were lit. Dark shadows from the green trees were beginning to inch into the settlement. The children were still at play.

Bhima now sat under a huge tamarind tree, lost in thought. In his heart, a huge storm raged. He began to feel the pull of the dead moneylender. His soul had already travelled several times to the cremation ground and back to the tamarind tree. Again and again, his eyes turned, of their own accord, to the village. He needed darkness, wanted it to descend. As he waited, he fidgeted. His favourite child, Narbada, was playing nearby; his wife was heating the bhakri. Bhima was a well-built man. Red turban, yellow dhotar, a pairan of thick cloth, his clothes were typical of

Satara. He looked like an all-in wrestler. The combination of his bull head, thick neck, bushy eyebrows, bristling moustache, and surly face had caused many hoodlums to quake.

Bhima's village was far away from the edge of the Varana River. Though he was as strong as an ox, he could not fill his stomach, and so he had come to Mumbai. He had crossed the whole of the city looking for work and found none. He wanted to get a job, to become a worker, to earn a salary, and buy his wife a gold chain, but he had been unable to fulfil these dreams. Disappointed, he had ended up in this suburb. Mumbai may be the city of everything but it has no work and it has no homes. Bhima was filled with rage at the city. He had managed to find work in a mine on a hill close to the suburb.

This had meant work to do and a place to stay, both of which had made Bhima happy. Every day, he would pit his bull strength against that hill. The hill retreated under the pressure of his considerable might. It turned a melancholic stone face against him. He worked with all his might and all his will.

The contractor was pleased by this and Bhima was also happy for he had been drawing a salary. But then the mine closed down after six months and, once again, Bhima found himself axed. One day, when he arrived at work, he heard that the mine was closing down. Bhima knew he was going to be unemployed again and the news rocked him. He was facing another period of hunger. Now he was in the grips of anxiety. He could only think: what of tomorrow?

He left home with a cloth tucked under his arm. He stopped at a stream. He had a bath and went back home, still despondent. Then his eye fell on a pile of ash. Human remains. Half-burned bones were scattered around. These charred remnants of a human life made Bhima even sadder. It must have been an unemployed person. He must have died of sorrow. 'He's free now,' he told himself. 'I will die like this one day. Narbada will fast for two days and will sit grieving. My wife will be miserable and I will not be able to do anything about it.'

Just then something glittered in the middle of the pile of ash. Bhima was about to walk past but now he turned back. It was a ring, one tola of gold. Bhima pounced on it. One tola of gold in a pile of ash! He was delighted. There was gold to be found in the ash of the dead. This was a new way to live.

From the next day, he began to walk around the entire area. He would scour the cremation grounds on the banks of rivers and streams. He would gather up the ashes of the corpses and sieve them. And in that ash, he would often find a little bit of gold. Sometimes it would be an earring, a ring, a nose ring, a bangle…each day, he found something or the other.

Bhima's new enterprise roared along. He sieved human remains with no fear at all. Sometimes the gold would melt in the fire and meld with the bones of the body. This did not deter him. He would crush the bones to get at the bits of gold. He would break skulls, crush wrists, he would do anything but gold he would get.

In the evening, he would go to Kurla and sell the gold. On the way home, he would buy dates for Narbada to eat.

Now he lived on the gold from corpses. And so the difference between life and death seemed to evaporate. If there was gold in the ash, it meant a rich person had died; and if not, the dead person had been poor; this was his understanding of things. The rich should die, he thought; the poor should live. He announced to his neighbours that the undistinguished poor should not die at all. His opinion was that if you could die with at least a tola of gold on you, you were a lucky person.

He had known the ravages of unemployment. He would not go back there. He would not be hungry again and so he searched for corpses, day and night. This became his way of life. His life had taken on the likeness of death.

And so it came to pass that a series of miracles began occurring in the area. The remains of corpses began to move. The corpse of the young daughter-in-law of a businessman had left the cremation grounds and ended up by the edge of the river. The people of the area were terrified. They found it strange and terrifying that a corpse should rise up and head to the river. The police were sure that someone was interfering with the dead and so they were on the alert. But it wasn't easy to keep watch over dead bodies.

Now the sun had set. Darkness spread everywhere. Bhima's wife served him his dinner and he began to eat with a serious mien. She knew he was going somewhere and so she said softly, 'You seem like you're going out tonight? I think you should stop doing this work. Find something else to do. Corpses, their ash, the gold from them, all this is ugly. People say things.'

'Shut up,' he said, though her words had hurt him. He added irritably, 'I'll do what I want. What do I care? Are these people coming to feed me?'

'That's not it,' she said softly, seeing her husband's angry face. 'There are ghosts in those cremation grounds. It's not good to wander about like a ghost or a demon. I get frightened, so I'm telling you.'

'Who said there are ghosts in the cremation grounds? Mumbai is a city of ghosts. The real ghosts live in the big fancy houses; the dead ghosts rot in the cremation grounds. Ghosts are born in villages, not in forests,' said Bhima.

She had no answer to this. Bhima began to make preparations to leave. He growled, 'I walked the whole of this city, but only when I sieved the ash of the dead did I find gold. When I broke my back in the mine, I got two rupees a day. That ash gives me ten rupees.'

With that he left. It was late in the night. There was a deep silence all around. It was dark. He had wrapped cloth around his head. He had a shawl around his shoulders and a sack over one arm. He had a crowbar tucked into his armpit and was striding along. Dense darkness surrounded him but he was afraid of nothing. He was focused only on getting a fine sari, a skirt and blouse, and dates for Narbada. Even so, today he was bewildered.

The air was sour. It grew more ominous with every passing moment. A pack of foxes went by, baying. From time to time, snakes would slither out of his way. In the distance, an owl hooted, a single, long off-key note. The uninhabited jungle looked desolate.

Taking calculated steps, he neared a village. He sat down and studied it carefully from a distance. The village was quiet. The silence was broken only by an occasional snore. A lamp or two blinked in the darkness. Bhima was glad to see that the time was right. He slipped into the cremation grounds and began to look for the moneylender's pyre. Kicking aside broken pots and biers, he leapt from pyre to pyre. He subjected each one to a careful examination, prodding at them with his stick.

The sky was thick with clouds and so the darkness grew deeper. Lightning flashed from time to time and seemed to be dancing across the cremation grounds. Rain seemed imminent; this frightened Bhima. If it did rain, he might not find the newly burnt corpses, and so he speeded up his operation. Sweat poured off him and he began to lose all sense of time and place.

By midnight, he had scanned the entire crematorium. He had checked every pyre.

Disappointed, he sat down. The wind was picking up. The broken sticks of the old biers were creaking. It sounded as if someone was grinding their teeth. A terrible growling seemed to be coming from the crematorium. Someone *was* growling, grunting, and scrabbling in the grounds. It seemed odd. He moved forward but everything went quiet as soon as he did so. Silence returned. But once again, in a few seconds, it seemed as if something was moving around, scrabbling, and he froze in place. Fear flashed through his body. For the first time in his life he was afraid.

But in the next instant, he regained his composure. For he discovered the truth of the matter and was rather ashamed of himself. Quite close to where he was crouching, there was a fresh grave and around it a pack of foxes had gathered. They had scented the smell of decaying human flesh. Stones had been placed on top of the body but this had not deterred the foxes who had started digging in the mud some distance away, trying to create an underground tunnel to get at their prey. As the smell of flesh began to filter through the mud, they began to turn on each other. They snarled and snapped at each other, establishing precedence, until a fresh whiff of decay set them scrabbling at the earth with all their energy.

Seeing this, Bhima grew angry. He took a huge leap and landed on the top of the grave. He began to take the stones from the grave and hurl them at the pack of foxes.

The foxes pulled back at this barrage. Startled, they crouched low to the earth. This gave Bhima fresh energy. He decided that he would do what the foxes had planned to do and so he began to dig up the grave.

And at that moment, the foxes saw Bhima. In a frenzy, one of the foxes leapt at Bhima. He snapped at Bhima and raced past him. Bhima was dismayed to see his sack was torn. A shiver ran through his body. The fox had turned and was ready to mount a fresh attack. Bhima braced his body and got ready to counter the animal. He got his crowbar ready. As the fox raced towards him, he hit out at it. Though his body was shivering, he was braced and ready. He dealt the fox a lethal blow. The animal fell to the ground and after writhing for a while, died. Bhima turned to the grave again to dig it up but the entire troop set upon him. A great battle began. Bhima had succeeded in uncovering half the body. But now the foxes returned to the attack in dead earnest.

They had him surrounded on all four sides and whenever one of them made a sally, he would retaliate. The foxes would retreat for a moment and then return to snap at him.

An unprecedented war had broken out near the village. Named after Kunti's most physically powerful son, this modern Bhima was now fighting an epic battle. He was fighting for tomorrow's bread, for tomorrow's corpse. Man and beast were locked in a life-and-death battle. All creation was asleep. Mumbai was at rest.

The village was also somnolent. And in the cremation ground next door, the battle was on. Bhima was attacking the foxes with his crowbar. The foxes were eluding the iron rod and getting in some vicious bites or where he made contact, they were whining and howling in pain. He tore a ligament and began to moan. He spat abuse. The abuse, the moaning, the whining, the howling, all sent shudders across the cremation grounds.

After a long time, the foxes gave up the attack. They lowered their bodies to the ground to take a break; that was when Bhima took his chance. He began to dig up the grave and free the corpse. He wiped the sweat from his face and came down from the mound. The foxes resumed their attack but they were defeated by his immense strength. Eventually, they accepted defeat and went to earth.

Immediately, Bhima dug his hands into the grave. He put his hands under the carcass' armpits and pulled it out. Then he lit a match to examine it. The body was stiff. He groped at the hands of the body. He found a ring there. There were rings in the ears, which he ripped off. Then a thought occurred to him: surely there would be gold in the corpse's mouth. He stuck a finger into its mouth but the teeth were set tight. Immediately he shoved his crowbar between the jaws and wrenched the corpse's mouth open. On one side he had his crowbar and on the other side, he inserted his finger into the mouth of the corpse and at that very moment, the foxes began to howl from the bushes. Then they fled. That woke the dogs of the village. The dogs woke up the village. 'Arre, the foxes have got to a corpse,' someone shouted. The cries from the village frightened Bhima. He had to work fast now. There was no time left.

He pulled a ring free from the mouth of the corpse and jammed it into his pocket. He thrust his fingers into the mouth and explored the cavity just to make sure he had got it all....

In a hurry now, he pulled the crowbar free, forgetting that his finger was still inside the mouth. The jaws snapped shut and the corpse bit down on his finger, the teeth sharp as a nutcracker breaking through a supari. Pain raced through his body and at the same moment, he saw people coming from the village, bearing lanterns aloft. Bhima was now terrified. He yanked his finger. He was enraged at the corpse. And the sight of the villagers approaching incensed him further. He slammed the crowbar down on the jaw of the corpse. But this only seemed to secure his finger tighter in that vice-like grip. The teeth were now buried in his finger. A cold sweat broke out all over his body. This was a ghost, this was a ghost that would give him up to the villagers. The people will come and beat me to death, or at least they'll beat me soundly and hand me over to the police, or so he thought. He was filled with terror and confusion. Gathering all his strength, he began to attack the corpse. 'Pimp, let me go,' he screamed.

The villagers were getting close but Bhima was stuck. Finally, he stopped to think and, inserting the crowbar into the jaws of the corpse, he prised the teeth apart and got his finger out. Despite the waves of pain, he began to run for his life.

He got home. A fever was raging through his body. Seeing his state, the house was filled with lamentation.

That day, the doctor cut off two of Bhima's fingers.

And that very day, they got news that the mine was reopening. Hearing this, Bhima the monolith began to weep like a child. For the fingers with which he had attacked the hill were now left behind in the crematorium grounds, sacrificed for his gold lust.

Translated by Jerry Pinto

HYMN OF THE DECEASED
GURUNATH ABAJI KULKARNI

Like the skull scalded by blazing sunlight, the sea remains still. Like a filthy and thick garment, its surface seems immobile and heavy.

The sea is simply quiet.

Charred in the fiery gusts of the sweltering heat, everything around it appears lifeless. Though the sea looks like an unevenly carved-up slice stretching out right up to the horizon, there is not even a slight ripple to wrinkle the surface of its uninvolved waters. The murky scene resembles the corpse of water lying unattended on a chilly night. One comes across dry mineral rocks on the shore. Nonetheless, even the slightest bit of shadow cannot subsist for a moment on them. The rocks look termite-eaten. Winds have inscribed several insufferable figures on them. Some of them resemble human figurines. But the figures appear like the drawings of human beings who are cursed for beholding what they should not have seen. There are reflections of the neighbouring hills in the water. The sea simply carries those reflections, unconcerned whether they look like the rangoli drawings of celebrations or the white spots of leprosy.

The sea is simply speechless.

Dry and scorching sand extends out from the other side of the water. There is no sign of undersized shrubs or a line of perishing yellow grass on its endless expanse. The winds seem like the undead soul of the shining sea wandering discontented near the warm waves. Its footsteps scatter the human-like figures on the sand and the entire territory looks stretched and tense as if in anticipation of something unparalleled about to happen.

However, there is a different kind of whiteness in one spot in the sand. Remains of prehistoric animals whose skulls were bigger than the hills lie scattered all over the place, their hardness tempered because of an uninterrupted downpour of heat. These huge shapes disintegrate from the touch of the blind wind and they begin turning to dust. The only sign of life on this dead expanse was this change of state. The mineral figurines on the rocks would change and there would be a corresponding change in the reflections on the water. But the sea cannot make out whether this is a fresh kind of delight or the sting of an old agony.

The sea is simply heartless.

But one day a spot shows up on the horizons and gradually becomes clearer at an extremely unhurried pace. After a long time and for the first time, some forms other than the footprints of wind have shown up on this landscape. After a while, that old traveller arrived at the feet of the mound of skeletons. One could still catch a gleam in his dissatisfied eyes, which is that of a person who sees one's own bright star in the ordinary pervasive sunlight, the gleam that others would term as the gleam of insanity. His body was as arid as sacrificial wood and his white beard covering it appeared like a garment made from millions of pearls. He calmly looked at the mound of skeletons. One gigantic skull in the mound was still full and complete. Its eyes, which were once like wellsprings, were now annihilated and looked like empty cavities. The rows of long teeth, which would have attacked and destroyed a terrible enemy with ferocity, now look like two meaningless lines written in the script of Death. The old man entered the skull with difficulty and its shade provided much-needed relief to his body. Profoundly contented, he kept his hands on his knees and was fully absorbed in his meditation on the mysteries of life and death.

The blazing sunlight carried on its work incessantly. In the end, the skull could take it no longer and gave in. A scrawl of a line surfaced as if proclaiming its death, it gave out one last cry as it cracked up into countless pieces and was dispersed. The scorching glare of the sunlight now descended on the old man's body. But he did not feel anything. His aged hands were still and his meditation undisturbed. However, his determination began to weaken from the tyranny of the sunlight. His fragile body crumpled into the sand. Shadowy cavities now showed up where his eyes—which once had seen the flower in the roots sustained by the earth and seen the earth sustaining the roots in the flower—had once been.

The unwieldy grey curtain of the sea is still. The rocks stand unmoved because they feel that they undeniably exist to see their reflection in the waters. The sea is simply a witness.

There was a slight movement where the waters touched the sands. The sands ruffled and a thumb-sized insect with a crust surfaced from that spot. But no sooner did the fiery blaze of sunlight touch it than it rolled its dot-like eyes and blindly ran as fast as it could in any direction its feet would take. It reached near the old man's skull. On entering the skull, the burning sensation on its crust subsided and the fear in its eyes disappeared. It folded its feet and settled in one corner.

The old man's skull now cracked and its pieces were scattered in the sands. Before its feet could move, the insect's hardened shell heated up and cracked as well. Now there was a slight movement in that place, just near a piece of bone. An ant came up to the surface. Its eyes, which though were small like a tip of thorn dipped in ink, said they were enough for its tiny life. It entered the insect and settled down in a moist spot inside.

Somewhere a creature smaller than the ant is waiting for its turn.

The endless expanse of the sea is unperturbed. On its shore, dead forms of precipitate are born on the rocks and leave the marks of their reflections on the waters. But this does not disturb the sea. As it has no high tide, it does not ebb either. There is no explosion of birth in the sea and consequently there is no implosion of death in it either. As the sea does not fear death, it is immortal.

Only, the sea does not have thoughts, as all its thoughts have ended.

Now the sea simply is.

Translated by Sachin C. Ketkar

A FACELESS EVENING
GANGADHAR GADGIL

That Mumbai evening was dreary as usual. The sun's rays had dusted her greyish hair and obliterated her face. A truly terrible sight. A faceless evening. Yet no one thought anything of it. Neither did I. Cutting a path with my feet, I strolled along on my way home. Hundreds of other feet were doing the same. Funny, isn't it? But no one was amused.

A spark flew from a horse's hoof, coppery gold. It shot diagonally upwards and vanished. Alive for one second. One moment in time and one moment of light. A chance encounter, slipping from sight.

What fills the eyes are the huge glittering Marathi letters. All standing in a row. Some on one leg, others leaning to one side. Some flaunting their semi-curved topis. And the crowds drawn towards them, trying to make sense of their shape and meaning.

A mother gave a one anna coin to her baby. The infant held it in its unsteady fingers and looked at it uncertainly. It waved its hand to make sure the shiny object was actually in its grip, then broke into a big toothless smile. Its neck lolled to one side, the eyes almost shut in the web of crinkles, a stream of saliva trailing down the side of its mouth. Startled, it glanced up at a huge colourful poster. A popular actress looked down from it, a permanent smile fixed on her face. A million-dollar smile!

The shrill sound of cars was tearing through the silence, piercing the ears. Uniformed chauffeurs, red-lipped plastic women, balding spineless bureaucrats, long-haired men flushed with youth—all screaming 'Get out of the way'. The uniformed chauffeurs and red-lipped women speak in one voice, and one language. The government officials speak brusquely and rudely. No one is surprised by this. Nor is anyone afraid of it.

A loudspeaker in one of the roadside shops blared out some song without moving its mouth. That's all it had, a perpetually open mouth. No face. And the small group around it mindlessly swallowed the music. Three minutes of devotion. Three minutes of love. Three minutes of the agony of separation.

Goods on sale. Three, three annas. Company bankrupt. Bargain sale. Three annas. Which company is this? Universal Enterprises Limited. Limited, okay?

All these sounds were drowned out by another, bigger sound. A car with a banner crawling along the road. Peace in Korea! Appeal for peace! Slogans hooting through the loudspeaker like cannons. Peace in Korea! Peace...peace...peace....

A man I knew was coming towards me; he saw me and smiled. I saw the smile but it didn't register. Peace! Peace! I also smiled. But it didn't register with him either. I saw his mouth move. I moved mine too. We did this a couple of times. But our words got lost somewhere. There was no room for them in the world of noise. Not now, not ever. With wordless smiles we parted.

From its ever-open mouth the loudspeaker was shouting 'Peace, peace!'

That barking silence receded from me and my choked ears regained their hearing. My eyes began to see again. People's legs criss-crossed the road. They were all the same. It seemed as if there was a huge foundry beyond the turn in the road from where these people were emerging. Their hair was styled after their favourite film stars, their complexions soft and smooth. And emotions? Perhaps these too were smooth and soft. Like an ill-fitting topi, a guilelessness had settled on the faces of all the women. Baby-faced filmy cherubs.

The creators of these babes, the particular actors and actresses, stood on the posters high above, smiling triumphantly. Million-dollar smiles. Smiles worth lakhs of rupees. Reflecting the smiles of lakhs of people.

Could a handful of actors have so many babies? No. But it had become possible. Science has made so many things possible. Women could get impregnated by strange men without intercourse. Men's sperm could be preserved for years. Hitler could be the father of a child born fifty years hence. Through biological intervention, the unborn baby's personality can be determined.

> New Delhi, 1991—The factory for producing children scientifically was inaugurated here this evening with great pomp and show by Prime Minister so-and-so. The first child so produced was presented to the prime minister. According to the PM, that child was programmed to have a strong streak of patriotism. In the course of his address, the PM said this was the first step towards the nation's progress. 'I feel confident that a big obstacle in the path of planning the nation's future will be removed.' Our special correspondent reports that scientists doing research on the 'choose your dreams' pill have met with positive results and it is likely that these pills will be commercially available very soon. Informed sources are reported to have said that they expect the black pills, which induce frightening dreams, will also be in great demand.

And our man Shakespeare asserts that 'Life's a tale told by an idiot…signifying nothing.' The fool!

Did the faceless evening laugh? Or was it a sob?

No. A faceless, no, a baby-faced young girl was looking at me with a smile. I returned to my senses and looked back at her.

'Aiya, where were you lost?'

Her hand, as if automated, opened her purse, took out a kerchief, wiped her face, and then opened the purse again.

'Oh, I was lost in some random thoughts,' I replied.

'Thoughts?' she said, with a wink, 'of whom, may I know?'

She straightened her sari pallu and shuffled her feet. I laughed. She smiled.

'Did you see that film?' she asked. She tried lowering her gaze. This was a gesture she was still learning.

'Are you going to watch the match tomorrow?' I asked.

We took leave of each other. Having played a three-minute record of her existence, she had moved on. The same record would be replayed further up. She would open her purse. Take out her kerchief, close the purse....

A three-minute record that played in every home.

Buy a trumpet for me, will you,

Buy a trumpet for me....*

And then? And then what? The record was stuck. The same words repeated over and over again.

Car brakes squealed. A blood-chilling scream was heard. Groups of people ran. A ring was formed. A man was dead. Everyone was looking on curiously. Every eye reflected curiosity, anticipated fear. They wanted to see the broken leg. They wanted to know who he was from his face, from the papers in his pocket.

It's not that these people had no feeling. They would have held a glass of water to his lips, had he been alive. They would have called an ambulance. But the curiosity in them was cruel. They were full of contradictions. If a georgette-clad actress was jilted in a film, they would have shed tears. A patriot's speech would have inflamed them into fighting for their country. They would have also fled from a policeman's lathi charge. And laughed loudly at their lucky escape. On seeing a romantic scene on-screen they would have whistled. And re-enacted that scene faithfully at home. All these traits were present in them and there was no telling when and how they would act. But on that occasion, they should have been afraid, the scene was that frightening.

---

*Refers to a poem by Keshavsut a leading poet; pre-Independence, the poem was used to raise self-esteem.

The stream of blood had stopped for a while. Their eyes were waiting to see where it would flow. Finally it found a direction. It began to flow towards those people's feet. With an alarmed yell, they hastily jumped back. Everyone burst out laughing. I heard the laughter and at that moment I was more scared of the men alive than the man dead. Afraid of that which could not be named, could not be rationally explained—that laughter. The dead man's slippers that they had picked up and carefully placed beside the body, I was afraid even of that. And then the science that could explore the secret of their lives and the power that shaped the course of their lives terrified me even more.

I felt that some scientist would come, apply some chemical to the man's leg and stick it back to his body. He would give him an injection and bring him back to life. Then the man would put on the slippers the people had so kindly kept near him, and with a smile, shake hands with the driver who had run over him, saying, 'Dost, that was such a fantastically scary experience! Dying has its own charm, I tell you. Thanks!'

Many people will start killing themselves for the fun of it. Businesses to kill and revive people will proliferate. People will rush to buy their shares. Laws, ideas, attitudes, and human responses to death will undergo a transformation. One stroke of science will cause an upheaval in the course of human existence. By the time it comes to terms with this, another blow will break its back, until, finally, it will succumb to these unbearable blows. And then on this uninhabited earth, the cultural community of bees will flourish. Terrible! The possibility of something like this happening is truly terrible. And those living men? They too were very, very frightening.

An exhibition of human existence. The chief attraction...the merry-go-round of revolving fear. A visit to a temple costs one paisa. To sit in this cradle also costs the same. In a temple, the eyes close with devotion. In the cradle, they snap shut with fear. What remains is groping in the dark. We come to this fair with one paisa of common sense and this is how we use it.

Why not eat sticky sweet revadis instead?

But even revadi eaters are gently lifted up into the cradle of fear and spun around.

Fear! Fear of the bold headlines of newspapers. Big black letters. Fears standing in a line, nameless, faceless. Fear of beauty, fear of ugliness too. Of knowledge and of ignorance. Of bonds and of liberty. Fear of others and fear of oneself.

Enormous coils of fear. Life is a game of snakes and ladders. Climb up the ladder, slide down when the snake swallows you. Big snakes next to big ladders. High up and low down. Rattling in the hands, an unknown fate. The revolving cradle of fear.

That Mumbai evening was dreary. And making scissors of my feet, I was cutting the road to my way home.

A gust of breeze blew in from somewhere. A paper kite up in the sky shivered. The tiny leaves of a tree trembled. A child raised its little hand crying 'Oh!' and began to run. The peanut vendor's son quickly popped a lump of jaggery into his mouth. After tossing the dust from the road hither and thither, the breeze disappeared.

My thoughts were stirred. Shuffled like cards. Someone handed me just five cards and asked, 'What's the trump?'

I thought for a while, then said, 'Open card.'

No matter how many were dealt, the pack of cards did not finish. And my trump card was undecided. Just then one card accidentally overturned, nudged by someone. The Queen of Hearts!

Who could have nudged it? She! Who's she? I didn't know. I had seen her only a couple of times. She was standing right there with her back towards me. Short and stout with plump arms, she was looking up and talking to someone. Her ears appeared reddish. Waves of light washed over her hair. Because she was looking up, her hair was lifted slightly off her fair delicate neck. As I watched her, someone cupped my heart in both hands and gently held it up. As she was talking, her tightly-wrapped sari pallu came loose and hung from her shoulder. The fair and attractive triangle peeped out of the V-neck of her blouse. And my gaze descended from the point of the V and rested briefly on her round breasts, then fell to her pink feet.

They were firmly rooted. I couldn't take my eyes off her. My head began to throb. Self-control shattered. I wanted her.

I couldn't tell why it happened. Because she was like all the other young baby-faced girls. There were indications that the record of her would play for only three minutes. I did not speak to her. It wasn't possible. And yet I was obsessed with her.

'Love? What love, saheb! First love? Flush-pink love? Mischievous, rebellious, forbidden love? All for three rupees, saheb!' Books are too expensive as gifts...' someone whispered in my ear. I ignored it.

'The scientific reason for this is ...' a scientist from the child-producing factory began to speak. But I paid no heed to his words.

I cast my heart at her feet and moved on. She trampled on it and moved away. It lay there, crushed, in the mud. And the boys were delighted. Blood did not flow out of its wounds, it flowed in their delight.

Leaving my wounded heart behind, I quietly clipped the road with my feet and made my way home. What had happened was truly unbelievable and horrendous. But I felt nothing. Lighting up a cigarette was the only thing on my mind....

That Mumbai evening was dreary. Her hair was grey. And she had no face.

Translated by Keerti Ramachandra

MORNING GLORY

SHANKAR PATIL

The afternoon was burning like an open-flame stove. It caused the air to blow in hot blasts. The sky was so bright, so white, you couldn't bear to look at it.

Shiva was in his hut, trying to take a nap. But the heat was fierce, it made napping impossible. He turned from one side to the other, wiped himself with the end of his dhoti, and changed sides again. But you can't fall asleep on an afternoon like that. You can't even think straight.

When the sun went down, Shiva got up. He yawned, saying ai-ai-aiai, then stretched his arms and cracked his back. But his whole body was stiff no matter what he did. For the past two or three weeks, he had worked on road construction, and now he ached all over. Every single bone was sore. Even the soles of his feet looked like tired old shoes. Working all day long in that sun had made his eyes bloodshot, and they itched as if there was sand stuck in them. He didn't know what to do. Now that the road job had ended, the problem was how to feed four mouths. He locked his fingers and cracked the knuckles one by one, as if savouring each mouthful of a spicy dish. Then he reached for his patka and unwound it. It was threadbare, but smelled of food. That smell calmed his hunger somewhat. He wound the patka around his head and stepped out to stand near the path to his hut and looked around.

The field looked pitiful. The black topsoil had stretched all over the field and large cracks had appeared in it. The black fields were waiting for rain, saying, 'Come down, Father Rain,' but the Father refused to budge. The trees at the boundary had no leaves left, just dried branches. Like people, the trees, too, had withered in the drought and perished. The field used to be green, but now it had no life left.

Shiva's gaze turned to the mango trees he had planted on the boundary, and he wanted to cry, his stomach churned. Keeping these trees alive had been such an effort! The water from the well did not reach them, so he had watered them himself, one bucket at a time. He had constructed a fence around them so grazing cattle wouldn't get to them. He had made a gate in the fence with a heavy stone as a doorstop. He had cared for the mango trees as if they were his children. Now they had grown taller than him. This year they could have flowered perhaps, could've given him some mangoes. But that was not to be. Now it was doubtful if they would survive.

Shiva couldn't bear to look at the trees. He moved away and stood by the well, looking down. The well had dried up, there was nothing there. The mud on the bottom had cracks in it, like the lines on his palm, criss-crossing each other.

Suddenly, there was a loud crash behind him, like an old mud wall collapsing late in the rainy season. Shiva ran away from the well taking long strides, then turned around and saw a column of dust from one side of the well. Clouds upon clouds of dust. He couldn't see much, couldn't make sense of what had happened. What had fallen? There was nothing that could crash this way. There was just the old tamarind tree, but that was still standing.

So what crashed?

When the dust settled, Shiva went closer to the well, dumbfounded. A huge dry section of the morning glory vine that had all but surrounded the tamarind tree had come crashing down. It had clung to the tree for so many years, but today it had collapsed. Shiva had known this vine since his childhood. Even then, the big, strong tamarind was all but covered by the vine. The vine didn't care if the tree was covered, it grew any which way it wanted. Year after year, the morning glory went on with its embroidery of green leaves and blue flowers. Rainy seasons and dry seasons—the vine had seen them all. Tornadoes and downpours, they came and went, but the vine had fought them all and survived. Such a strong plant, but this three-year drought had exhausted it; all its dignity lost. No leaves, no flowers, just a filigree of dry twigs was all that was left. Still, the plant had endured. Once this drought was over, it would have no fear of perishing. But today the drought had conquered the old vine. There was no tornado, no storm, it fell all of a sudden. Its days were over. The tamarind was overwhelmed by this. It bent over to see what had happened to the vine.

Shiva went to the tree and stared at it with unfocused eyes, as if he was watching a dead man, as if a relative of his had died. Wordless, and with a quaking heart, he returned to his hut and sat down. He saw the empty harness posts. The oxen had been sold off last month, now just the posts remained. Now the animal feed was gone, the animals were gone, what money he had was gone. Soon the people will go, too, he thought. Why wouldn't they? They are only here now so that they can go away later.

Shiva got up and left, leaving behind him the hut, the harness posts, the well, and the vine; he left them and came to the narrow footpath at the edge of his field. He sat on the slope on the side of the path, hoping to run into someone. That was a good way of passing time, he thought. And, sure enough, he saw a group of people coming up the path. People from his village. Who could they be, Shiva wondered. Who are they, walking like in a caravan? But he didn't see any horses, so it couldn't be a caravan. And they couldn't be the Lonars, because there were no donkeys with them. There were a few goats there, though. Were these people leaving town?

The people came closer. He was devastated: these were his people, leaving town. That was Dattu Manjre, Shiva knew his entire family. The one next to him was Patekari, and the one behind was the old man of Jambhale, the one with cataracts. Now where would they go to fill their bellies? And the kids, the little ones, the babies! Some were being carried, others were on foot—oh God! What a disaster! Babu Patekari was carrying his old mother on his back, her skinny legs dangling with each step he took. Now where will they go? What will they do? Where will they live? One of them carried a bundle of clothes, another had something under his arms, and pots and pans, and earthenware pots...so much to carry! Taking all this and going to some other place.

When they saw Shiva, the walkers stopped. What to say! There was nothing to say, really.

Dattu Manjre came closer.

'You're leaving town?' Shiva asked.

'What else?'

'To where?'

'Someplace where we can eat,' Dattu said. 'Going to Ankali, for now. There is a job. Cutting sugarcane. I'll do the job, and sleep on the grass. I'll live as long as I can. Please keep an eye on our house.'

Shiva sighed, and said, 'What's there to keep an eye on!'

'That's true. At least there's the house.'

Dattu's wife said, 'We've locked it. And I put some cow dung on it.'

'On the lock?'

'Yes. To seal the lock. We'll come back when the rain comes,' she said. 'Until then please keep an eye out.'

Jambhale's old father looked up at the sky with his opaque eyes and said, 'What rain are you talking about, girl! There's no water to cry with! Look at this sky, bright and white. Like God has washed all his dhotis and hung them out to dry. Spotless white.'

Babu Patekari, who was carrying his mother on his back, came closer and said, 'Shiva, come here, see what my mother is saying.'

Shiva stood up, went to the old lady, and said, 'How are you, Grandma?'

The old lady didn't have the energy to say anything. She raised her eyebrows and made a gesture as if she was gulping something down. With an effort, she said, 'Haven't seen Tara for a while...'

'We were on the road construction job. By the time we came home, it was late. The same thing the next day. How can one meet anyone?'

'The kids, are they doing all right?'

'They're not dead, so they're doing all right, I guess.'

'God will give them a long life,' she said, as if blessing them. Jambhale came to them and said, 'All right. Now let's go. We have to be in the next village by sundown. Let's not stop here.'

The old lady spread the fingers of her wrinkled hand and said, 'Now who knows if we will come back or live somewhere in some strange town...please tell Tara that I went. I had borrowed some flour from her a few times. Tell her I'll return it if I come back in one piece.'

'Grandma, who's asking you for that flour? You come back in good shape and that'll cover everything. Come back, come back soon.'

The group of people moved on. Dattu hesitated a little. They had been wrestlers from the same club. They had made a name for themselves in local wrestling competitions. Every Saturday, they used to give each other massages. Now Dattu was at this crossroad. He didn't know what to say, and couldn't bring himself to leave.

Finally, Shiva said, 'One thing's for sure—you have courage.'

Dattu sighed and said, 'What's courageous about it? Instead of dying of hunger here, we're going to some other place where there's food. But the village doesn't let you go easily. Your heart can break all it wants. But what can you do? Nothing else will work.'

Jambhale called again, so Dattu moved. Shiva waved to everyone, and said, 'All right. Come back. Come back soon. Write us a letter or something. Let us know you're alright.'

Dattu took a few steps, but turned around and asked, 'Shiva da, the vine....'

'It had seen its days. It fell down today.'

The people in the group looked at the tamarind. Someone said something, someone else said something else, and the group moved on. Shiva didn't move.

The group left, leaving behind the village, the houses, the relatives. It went away and was seen no more.

Shiva suddenly remembered his house. His wife had reminded him over and over.

'There's nothing to eat this evening. Last week I cooked split peas, but now those are gone too. Do whatever you need to do, but bring home some food. We can drink water and go to sleep, but what about the kids? Don't they need something?'

He couldn't think of any place he could go. There were a couple of houses, but he couldn't show his face there. How to ask them again and again? And why should they give? And to how many people? He suddenly remembered Mithari anna. He could at least ask him. The most he will do is to say no. But it wouldn't hurt to try. Suddenly he felt a burst of energy. He got up and started for the village.

He won't say no, Shiva thought. When I tell him that we don't have anything to eat, he won't say no. I've worked for him plenty. Done all kinds of jobs for him.

He left the dirt road and came to the village. Then past the gate of the village, down an alley by the temple. Mithari anna's house was nearby, and Shiva slowed down. How many times was he going to ask Mithari anna for food? It's one thing if Anna is in a good mood. Otherwise he'll get rid of me, like I was a dog. But what to do? There's no food in the house. Well, you just summon up the courage and go.

Cautiously, with stealthy footsteps, Shiva went into Anna's house. There were quite a few people inside. Mithari anna was sitting on the porch, leaning on a cushion, with many children surrounding him. They must be his grandkids, here on vacation. His daughter must have brought them with her, from Hukkeri. Their toys were spread all over—wooden things, plastic things, toys of all colours. Nothing was lacking. Two fair-skinned girls with bright red lips and three plump boys had surrounded Anna, who was making paan for them. Shiva approached them soundlessly, but sat on the steps instead of going on to the porch. He waited for Anna to notice him. Anna did notice Shiva, but acted as if he had not, and busied himself with the kids. He gave a cardamom to one kid, some mace to another…Shiva sat and watched. All of a sudden, Anna wrinkled his brows and said, 'Shivya, why are you here? You're not here begging for food, are you?'

Since Anna was being so upfront, Shiva had no reason to be subtle. All he had to do was to say yes, but Shiva couldn't bring himself to say that one short word. He scratched behind his ear, and somehow said, 'Yes, Anna.'

'Oh really?' Anna said. 'How many times are you going to beg like this?'

Shiva looked down and said softly, 'Anna, help me out this time. We haven't had anything to eat for the past four days.'

He had said this to soften Anna, but Anna raised his voice. 'Arre, instead of dying here hungry and badgering people like us, why don't you go someplace to fill your belly? Arre, there are mills of all kinds, and factories. Just work as a porter at the station and you'll fill your belly! It's not like there's no work! How come you don't have food?'

Shiva felt as if he was being scolded. He rubbed the instep of a foot and said, 'Yes, in the end, that is there, if nothing else….'

'Why do you say "in the end"? Why say "nothing else"?'

Shiva looked up, and said, 'Anna, how can one just up and go, leaving behind home and field?'

Anna was furious. 'What's there to leave behind? Where's your big estate you keep fussing about? Just a house and that piddly little field, right? That's not going to run away if you leave, is it?'

Shiva was forlorn. He said, 'You're right about that....'

'So what's holding you back?'

'My mind's not in it.'

'Mind!' Anna said sarcastically. 'Who are you—some kind of lord, or a prince? What do you need that mind for? Why don't you want to go someplace that gives you a job? His mind's not in it, he says! Now, let me tell you what's on my mind! I gave you a recommendation for the road construction job, why did you leave it? Are you too good for it?'

Shiva pulled at a bit of dead skin on his foot and said, 'It's distasteful to talk about.'

'What is distasteful?'

Shiva exploded. 'This drought has made me poor. Otherwise who'd tolerate this kind of treatment and why would they?'

'Get up first. Get up now. Get out of here.'

'I'm talking about the supervisor there.'

'You get up first. Don't tell me a thing.'

'Please listen, Anna. When he was paying us our wages, he'd grab my hand. All right, so I'm poor. But don't I have shame? Don't I have self-respect?' Shiva put a hand on his heart and plaintively said, 'Anna, it felt like I had a hole in my chest. But I didn't say anything because I'm related to you.'

'Oh really? Get up. Now. What I've heard is plenty. And if you've got holes in your heart, go home and plug them with something. I've got guests from Hukkeri. My daughter and her kids. Now, do I talk to them or bargain with you?'

'Yes, I'm getting up.'

'So why are you still sitting? Get going. And don't show up at my door again.'

Shiva was rattled. The permanent and painful break made him recoil.

Looking at Anna's face, he said, 'Never come back?'

'That's right. Nevvver come back.'

'Do you think I'm lying?'

'Just keep walking.'

'Sounds like your guests have told you something.'

'First you go. No talk. Out!' Anna snapped his fingers and pointed to the door, and Shiva, sighing, left Anna's house. Putting one foot after the other, he crossed the front yard and came to the gate, and the children, who had been quiet till now, laughed. But Shiva didn't look around. He came out and stood on the street. He remembered the morning glory vine that had so abruptly collapsed that afternoon. All its attachments, all bonds were gone, as they did for him now. He had worked on so many celebrations in this house! He had helped set up awnings for all of them. He had brought buckets of water, one at a time, and filled the water tanks, then helped serve the food, then cleared the plates too. And then he had to climb the mango tree to get some mango leaves for the ceremony. That was a lot of work! I did a lot of work, he thought, my wife did, too…grinding grain and grinding chutneys till she got blisters on her hands…I even cleaned up his kids' shit and piss, what more does he want? And on top of this, he asks me to never come back! Nevvvver come back, he says! All right, man. Who wants to work for you anyway? Everything has collapsed, everything is gone. Gone.

Shiva walked down the lane and came to the village square. Where to go now? His mind was too chaotic to go to anybody's house. Going home was not going to be pleasant either. His wife would ask him if he brought anything to cook. His hungry, hopeful kids would gather around him.

Shiva sat on the steps of the school. The shops in the square didn't seem to have any customers. He sat there, swinging his feet, when he saw the tailor shop. Vishnu sat at his sewing machine, busy with his work, his foot moving up and down. I made a mistake, he thought. Two years ago, the government man came to the village and taught sewing for free. On top of that, he gave a stipend, twenty rupees each. I didn't learn. I kept working my farm. Now look at Vishnu. He doesn't have a drought. Just sit and stitch. Does he have to sweat in the sun, or get up early, even when it's cold, and get his hands dirty with muck? He just sits at his machine, twelve months of the year, and collects fresh money. Oh yes, he's doing well. It was me who lost out.

He was tired of sitting, but where to go? There's no factory around here, no work. You could go someplace and ask for work. But where to go? Where do you go asking for a job?

He thought of going to the bus terminal. Spend some time watching the buses come and go. He got up and went to the bus stand, somewhat hesitant. There were people sitting on the retaining wall like crows on a tree. Some were waiting for their bus, others were just sitting. Shiva, too, sat under the tree.

The sun went down. Shiva's stomach growled. If I'm this hungry, how hungry the kids must be, he thought. They're not accustomed to being hungry. Maybe I could go to Desai anna. I have asked him twice already. How can I ask him again?

A bus came, and Desai anna himself stepped out. He said, 'Shiva! How come you're sitting here? Are you leaving town?'

'No, no reason, just sitting.'

'Oh, just sitting. Well, take this heavy bag and come with me.'

Shiva didn't have to go asking for work; work came to him, thank God. Desai put a massive trunk on Shiva's head and a heavy bag in his other hand. The bag was stuffed too; Shiva's fingers could feel the weight as soon as he picked it up. Desai's hands were empty. 'Good thing I saw you,' he said.

'You had gone out of town?'

'Arre, I was on the Bharat darshan tour, don't you remember?'

Shiva didn't know what Desai was talking about. He said, 'To some temple?'

'Arre, I told you: Bharat darshan.'

'Where exactly is that?'

'You dimwit!' Desai said and laughed. 'It won't penetrate your thick skull. You just keep walking.'

Keep walking! The handles of the heavy bag were biting into Shiva's fingers. He stopped, then changed hands, took a deep breath, and resumed walking. He was impatient to go home. Should he ask for four kilos of grain? But that won't be enough, he thought. He has to ask, in any case. Then why not ask for a sackful, up front?

'What happened? Are you tired?'

'No, just changed hands.'

'Arre, we're almost there. Doesn't matter which hand, does it?'

They reached Desai's home. Instead of leaving the luggage outside, Shiva, wanting to be extra helpful, took it all the way in, came out to the entryway, and stood. Anna did not show up for a while. His daughter-in-law came out and said to Shiva, 'Don't go. Wait a little while. He will be right out, he is washing his face.'

'Yes, yes,' he said and sat down massaging his sore neck, wondering how he should broach the subject. Anna came out, looking relaxed and rested. Someone brought two cups of tea. He offered him a cup. 'Have some tea.'

Shiva took the proffered tea, but kept looking at the cup and saucer.

'Please, take it. You carried all that luggage, you should at least have some tea. They would've made me some tea anyway.'

Anna finished his tea, but Shiva had not taken a sip. 'What's the matter? How come you're just sitting there?'

He didn't want to say anything, but said, 'To tell you the truth, Anna, looking at this cup and saucer like this, with pictures of flowers on it, and the tea with lots of milk, makes me think of my kids. They don't get to drink tea like this. They don't get to see anything like this, let alone drink it. My stomach is churning. I don't want this tea. How can I drink it by myself?' He put the cup and saucer down.

Desai anna got angry for some reason. He said, 'Arre, you carried the luggage, that's why the tea. Stop complaining and drink up. Otherwise get out of here. It's not going to go to waste. Plenty of people here would want it.'

Shiva didn't raise his eyes. 'Do this instead, Anna....'

'You're teaching me what to do? All right, tell me. What should I do?'

'Please don't be angry. Instead of the tea, give me some grain to eat. My kids are starving.'

Desai anna said, 'Get up. It doesn't matter to me if you drink the tea or not. Get up and go home.'

Shiva joined his hands in prayer. 'We don't have anything to eat.'

'You silly man, I've come home after such a long time away, travelled the whole country, and here you're snivelling. Do you have any brains? Whenever you see me you start grabbing. So you carried the luggage. Is that such a big favour? Wait. Don't go. Here's a quarter. Take it and leave.'

He went inside. Shiva got up silently and left without taking the money.

It was late at night when he came home. The door was open, Tara was sitting in the entryway, waiting for him. The light was off, the slant of moonlight was the only light in the house. As soon as he stepped in, she said, 'Where have you been?'

'Yes, it's late. Why are you waiting?'

'You'll bring something and then I'll cook. That's why I'm waiting.' He did not say anything. He took a swig of water, spread a quilt on the floor, and lay on it.

Tara did not say anything. After a while, she said, 'Are you sleeping or what?'

He changed sides. 'What else can I do?'

She said, 'You have such a hard heart. Oh, at least you could've asked me.'

'Asked you what?'

'Did you ask me if the kids ate anything, or went without food? Did you ask me about anything at all?'

He didn't say anything.

Finally she said, 'You may be hard-hearted, but I'm not like that. If you didn't hustle and get something, I have to, don't I? I managed to find something, and I've made some soup. Have some of that first, then sleep. But first, get up.'

Saying this, she took a brass pot, poured some soup in it, and sat. She nudged him. 'Get up.'

'Did you have some?'

'How could I eat without you?'

'Then you have it.'

'I ate a little, here and there. My stomach is churning.'

'Churning?'

'Yes. I'm not hungry.'

'Then you don't want any?'

'I want nothing at all. You go ahead and finish it all. I'll sit here and give you company.'

Shiva sat up. He folded his legs and rested his head on the wall behind him. 'Tara, our morning glory fell today.'

Tara lifted the brass pot to her lips. 'Morning glory? The one on the tamarind?'

'Yes.'

She took a big gulp from the brass pot and said, 'Oh that's a good thing! It'll make a couple of carts of firewood.'

'Firewood?'

'Yes, we'll chop it down with an axe, make bundles, and take them to town to sell.'

Now his stomach really churned. He sat there as if all words had left him. He stared at her without blinking. He didn't see her. In front of his mind's eye was the intricate green design of the leaves, the embroidery of flowers...which he would never see again.

Translated by Jayant Karve

THE HUSBAND
BHAU PADHYE

The first time I saw Kaku, it was at her wedding. A mundavlya covered her head; her dark hair flowed freely down her back, a gajra glowing in it; green bangles ran right up to her elbows, two glittering necklaces around her neck. She was glowing with the anointing of turmeric. Her eyes were huge and dark; her mouth a small moue.

Who knows what I felt on seeing this vision? I simply clung to her. I felt—she is mine, mine! Such a beautiful woman and she is now mine. I will never let go of her, never, never. I was going to spend every moment with her. I would stick to her, even when I was eating or sleeping. That night, I was going to sleep with Kaku but Aai got angry. I paid her no heed—I'm going to sleep with Kaku.

Everyone said I couldn't. I was not willing to let her go for even a moment. They said: he's acting up. I don't know why people were saying these things. I wasn't acting up. Hadn't they said, 'Deepu, this is your Kaku'? And if she was my Kaku, then how could I be acting up if I said I was going to sleep with her? Baba took out his stick. I got a whack and a thwack. I began to bawl. I grabbed hold of Kaku and refused to let go. No one was going to part me from her. Aai grabbed my arm and began to pull me away but I had a death grip on Kaku's arm. And then Dada turned up. My big brother is a toughie. He picked me up, lock, stock and barrel, and carried me into the next room.

The welts from the stick were aching. I was shrieking my rage and pain. They locked me up in the dark in the store room. I hate the darkness. I was terrified but they had locked the door from outside. I closed my eyes tight and curled up to my old cradle. Slowly my legs unwound themselves and I fell asleep. At some point, Kaku came in. She picked me up and took me with her. Kaku is a good person. She kissed me quickly on both cheeks. 'Poor little mite. He loves me. Or else, I might have to wait for him for the rest of my life.' She cuddled me to her. I opened my eyes just a little bit. She had tears in her eyes. Why was Kaku crying? Someone shouted at her? Someone beat her? Kaka was sleeping like the dead. His torn banian gave off a sweaty smell.

Aaji–Aajoba and Baba began to call out. Frightened, I got up and started to slip under the bed. But Kaku said, 'Nothing to worry about. No one will beat you.' Kaku opened the door. Aaji–Aajoba, Baba–Aai, all came in. Kaka got up and rushed out. Everyone came up to the bed and looked at it and then looked at me.

Aai said, 'Was he here all night long?'

'Yes,' said Kaku.

Aai said, 'Come now, Deepu.'

I got frightened. I thought I was in for it again because I had spent all night with Kaku. I grabbed Kaku again, but this time Aai did not pull at my arm. And Baba didn't take out his cane either. I was allowed to stay with Kaku. No one got mad at me. Only Kaku would get angry after that. If I had a runny nose or if I peed in the bed, she would get angry. If I stammered, Kaku would get angry. She would even beat me. But I still loved Kaku. One day, something funny happened. One of Kaku's friends came over. Kaka had gone out somewhere. 'Hey, where's your husband, woman?' they were asking her.

I had come from school. I dropped my school bag and ran up to Kaku. Kaku hugged me. She put her hand on my shoulder and said, 'This is my husband.'

What? I was startled. Me, a husband? I didn't like the idea of husbands. If you were a husband, you had to have a wife. I didn't like the idea of a wife. I didn't want to be Kaku's husband. I twisted out of her grasp and ran away. Our house had a terrace. I went and crouched behind the water tank. This was the question: was Kaku going to marry me? I had already decided that I was never going to get married. I decided I was not going to break my vow, not even for Kaku. I broke with Kaku after that. I started sleeping next to my mother. I would not even say a word to her. If she called me, I would run away. I still loved her but the thought of her being my wife gave me a twinge in my tummy. Kaku would say, 'What's going on, Deepu? You don't come near me at all? You don't even come to sleep with me? A husband shouldn't sleep apart from his wife!'

I was very embarrassed and Kaka got very angry with Kaku. I thought he was going to give me a good beating so I ran off to Aai. One day, I left my red ball pen in Kaku's room by mistake. It was lunchtime so I thought Kaka and Kaku would be in the kitchen. I thought I could slip in, find the pen, and slip out to Aai again. But everything went wrong. Kaka and Kaku were in their room. Kaku was sitting cross-legged and furious on the bed and Kaka was slapping her across the face. She was not making a sound. 'Narendra should not come to this house again. I won't stand it. If you want to stay in this house, you'll have to end your relationship with Narendra.'

How much he beat her! Kaku's cheeks were swollen. Then he saw me and he walked out of the room. Kaku looked at me, and I looked at her, not moving, not saying a word. Kaku said, 'Come here.' I thought she would cuddle me and cry. That was how she behaved when she had just arrived in the house. But Kaku was not crying.

'What do you want?' she asked. I said nothing. I had forgotten all about the ball pen. I wanted to cry, looking at her. She was so sweet. How cruelly he had beaten her. Suddenly Kaku began to laugh. That scared me and I said, 'Kaku, Kaka beat you, no?'

'What of it? The more he beats me, the more I will laugh.'

I slipped out of the room. Why does Kaka get angry with Kaku? Why does he beat her? Why does Kaku go to meet Narendra? Can't she not go? Then the beating will stop, no? I would think a lot about this. I had a friend, Subbya, full name Subhash. I asked him what he thought. 'What does it matter if Kaku meets Narendra?'

One day, Subhash said that he had heard the elders in his family talking. 'Narendra is chasing your Kaku. Kaku has lost all sense of shame, they were saying.'

What does that mean, 'lost all sense of shame'? Narendra is chasing Kaku? How? I began to think Kaku must have done something wrong. She must have sinned, sinned before God. That was why Subbya's parents were angry with her. I should tell Kaku, 'Stop all this with Narendra. Have some shame.' But I was not talking to her. That was because she would tease me, calling me, 'My husband, my husband.'

One day I was bathing when she came into the washing area. She pulled off my shorts and left me naked. I began to cry. And then Aai came there. I told her, 'See Kaku pulled off my shorts and left me like this.'

Aai got angry and said, 'What do you expect of someone like this whore? Don't go anywhere near her.'

I did not go anywhere near her. But I wanted to tell her, 'Don't be lost to shame.' So I thought I should write her a letter. I wrote a letter, 'Kaku, stop all this with Narendra. People say you are lost to shame.' I wrote this in my handwriting and when she was sitting on her bed, reading a book called something like *Kadambari*, I ran in and threw it down and ran out again. My heart was thumping loudly. I was shy around Kaku. But how shy could I be? After all, at some point, I had to go near her.

One day Baba sent me to Kaka. I was in front of Kaka. Kaku was in the inner room. She saw me and immediately came out. I shot out of there like a bullet. She said: 'Idiot.' Baba and Kaka would fight about Kaku. Aai would also muck in. She too would bad-mouth Kaku.

'You should find another place to live…you may have no shame but we do. We can't show our face in public as long as this prostitute is in the house.'

Kaka would say, 'You brought her into this house. Why blame me? You tied her around my neck.'

Kaku would not say anything. Let these people fight as much as they want, she seemed to be thinking. One day, there was a terrible fight. Kaka dragged Kaku and threw her at Aai–Baba's feet. I thought they were going to beat her the way I had been beaten on the day of her wedding. I was shocked. I wanted to cry. There was a tight coil in my tummy. I pulled out my school books and sat down with them. But my attention was on the fight. They were all shouting loudly. How could I pay attention to my studies? I began to chant the name of Rama.

'Rama…Rama…Rama….'

'We want nothing to do with this tramp. You take care of her,' said Baba to Kaka. 'Who's going to keep a woman of this stamp at home? There will be a line of clients tomorrow, waiting for her services.'

Suddenly Kaku flared up. 'Who are you calling a tramp? What am I supposed to do in this house, with this man? You got me married to this spineless nonentity and I'm supposed to sit here, untouched all my life? Would you have stayed with him? You would have gone tramping the streets, looking for some clients yourself. You're at fault and you're blaming me? Who needs this? I'm leaving this house myself. I don't want to see your faces in my life again.'

She went into the room. Kaku was going to leave? My world would be turned upside down. Kaka and Baba and Aai were left staring at each other.

Then Kaka exploded. 'Whatever she is, she's my wife, whether she's a whore or a tramp. I will look after her. For the rest of my life. I'd prefer to live with her a thousand times over living with renowned thieves like you lot.'

Kaka took a single room close by; he and Kaku began to live there. There was a road in front of the room. We would play cricket on that road. Our shouting troubled lots of people. The old folks of the area—Old Man Babu, Saawatle bai—were dead against us. Saawatle bai got hold of six of our cricket balls and hid them. We would argue with her—'What do you mean, hiding them?'

I would see Kaka–Kaku coming and going but I never spoke to them. Aai had warned me. We were not on speaking terms. So I couldn't speak to them. These people are bad. I began to believe that Kaku was also a bad person because she and my mother were not on talking terms. Kaku would call out to me but I would run off. Slowly, she began to stop calling out to me. Kaka never spoke a word to me. I was afraid of him. If he came near me, I would hide my face. The other person I feared was Ramakant dada. He was a burly wrestler. He had long hair. He wore coloured banians and smoked cigarettes and generally behaved like a goon. Meaning, if someone else was behaving badly, he would step out and slap it out of him. But my mother called him a goon. A goon is not a good man. Do good men beat people? Do they smoke cigarettes? Kaka was now a friend of this Ramakant dada. He too began smoking cigarettes and behaving like a goon. Only, he didn't beat people up. No one was frightened of him. But Kaka and Ramakant dada were buddies now. They were always together. Subbya said, 'You know what? Ramakant dada and Kaku are having an affair.'

'An affair?'

I didn't know what he meant but Subhash explained what it meant. A horrible scene appeared in front of my eyes. This cruel monster Ramakant dada crushing my beautiful and delicate flower of a Kaku. My head began to throb. I began to be terrified for Kaku. I could not sleep. I didn't want to eat. But that was nothing compared to what I was fated to see soon.

One afternoon, I saw Ramakant dada going to Kaka's house

alone. I could not control myself. I wanted to see how he was harassing my aunt. As soon as he entered the room, the door closed. For a moment, I didn't know what to do. But then I realized I could get on to the window and look into the room from the transom. I peeked in through the transom and there Ramakant was kissing Kaku; and she was kissing him back. And he....

I was disgusted. There was a drumming at my temples. My chest was pounding. I was terribly sickened. My beautiful Kaku, my flower-like Kaku and that demon, Ramakant dada.... I shuddered with disgust. But I couldn't stop seeing it inside my head. I saw everything. I was stunned. I ran to Subbya.

'Subbya, Subbya, do you know what happened?'

I told him everything, all that I had seen.

'I saw it too,' he said. He had seen many people doing it.

'But why do they do this?'

'They like it. Women like it. Men like it too!'

My hair stood on end. I kept thinking about this. My entire body was throbbing. I didn't know what to think. I felt I was going mad. The next day I did not see Ramakant dada going to Kaku's house. So I went there. She said, 'Come in, Deepu.' She was reading a novel. She was lost in it.

Thinking of what Ramakant dada had done to her, I went and sat on the bed. But she wouldn't look at me. I thought: maybe she was so busy reading, she hadn't understood why I had come. So I went and sat next to her.

'Your parents are well, no?'

'Yes.'

'I'll just finish this page and make some tea, okay?'

'Yes.'

I was looking at her fair cheeks. Ramakant dada had kissed those cheeks. I got up on my knees and kissed her cheek.

'What are you doing, idiot?' She wiped away my kiss and went back to reading.

I put my hands on her breasts. She slapped my hands away.

'Stop it. Don't annoy me. I said I'd give you tea, didn't I?'

She was not paying attention to me. She liked this kind of thing, right? So why wasn't she paying attention to me? I slapped the book out of her hands and kissed her. I tickled her body and pulled at her sari.

'What are you up to?' she said angrily and pushed me away but I held on to her tightly. I would not let go. I pulled at her clothes. I pushed my hand into her blouse. Now she realized what was in my head. She threw me off her and took out a stick and began to beat me.

'Disgusting little brat, is this what you learn in school?'

She began to rain blows down on me. I didn't shout, I didn't cry. With each blow, I felt as if I had got my Kaku back.

'Go on then, go home.'

'No.'

'Will you go or shall I...?'

She threw me out of the room and bolted the door. From outside, I said: 'I'm not going anywhere, Kaku. I'm going to stay right here. Remember you were the one who told your friends: I am your husband.'

'Go away,' she screamed from inside the room.

Screamed through tears.

I could hear her sobs clearly through the door.

Translated by Jerry Pinto

KING MARUTI
VYANKATESH MADGULKAR

On a wet morning in June, a huge langur turned up in the village. He came alone, without friends or family. A langur is a rare sight in our parts. That is what makes him an object of wonder and respect. The last time we saw one was at least ten years ago. Who knows where this one had appeared from and why. But he came in style, waving his tufted tail as he walked through the village and went straight into the Maruti temple. He entered the sanctum sanctorum, emerged after a few minutes, and settled on the dome. His long tail waved as he soaked in the sun.

The priest Pandu Gurav's wife saw this wondrous sight, picked up her daughter, and made straight for the jungle where her husband had gone to graze his horse. He had to know what had happened. Maruti had come to the village. He had paid a visit to the temple.

The village brats who came swinging their slates and satchels to the school across from the temple sat on its steps. The school had still not opened. The teacher had still not come. He had still not had his tea. They sat in a tight row on the steps like sparrows on a wire. Their drowsy eyes were taking in the lustrous glow of the early morning sun when they spotted a creature they had never seen before sitting atop the Maruti temple. Their hearts trembled with joy, amazement, and fear. Then a bold boy rose, took a step forward and, scratching his snub nose, shouted, 'Monkey monkey chee chee, on your tail a pound of ghee.'

The others joined in the chant. The monkey turned its black face towards them and bared its teeth to scare them off. Then it got up and danced. The bold brat picked up a stone and aimed it straight at the monkey. The stone got him in the back. He jumped high in pain and fled screeching chee chee. He climbed to the topmost branches of a peepal tree and hid behind the foliage. The kids gathered under the tree. He looked down and scolded them roundly. This excited them even more. They began to throw a regular stream of stones at him. But the monkey was too high for the stones to reach him. The animal was clever enough to see this. He relaxed among the leaves, munching on the tender ones.

Meanwhile Pandu Gurav had heard the news. He rushed home, picked up the basket in which lay a quarter bhakri, and carried it to the peepal tree. He gave the kids a few whacks and drove them away. 'Where will you pay for this sin?' he shouted. 'Twelve devils from twelve homes get together and fling stones at our Marutraya! What harm did he do you?'

Driven away by Gurav, the wicked imps ran off screaming abuses at him and informing the world of his affairs with loose women.

Holding the piece of bhakri up high, Gurav began pleading with the langur. 'Come down please and have this, Hanumanta.' But the monkey did not as much as glance at Gurav and continued eating leaves.

Old Abbanana, who had halted on his way to the jungle to watch the show, thought Gurav had gone mad. Swinging his chin left and right he called out, 'Pandya you idiot, what day is it today, haan?'

'Saturday, Nana.'

'So how will Marutraya accept bhakri today, eh?'

'Then?'

'Then get him some snack, you donkey.'

Nana was a Varkari, a follower of Vitthal. Very pious. He would collect a handful of villagers together and sing bhajans. He had all the required paraphernalia at home—cymbals, mridang, this and that. He never failed to celebrate Ram's birth, Maruti's birth, and other such sacred days. The old man's word was highly respected in the village.

Gurav saw sense in what Nana said. He returned home in great haste and came back with a handful of peanuts. Once again he pleaded, 'Dear Lord, please accept these. Come down, dear Lord.'

But all the monkey did was peer down, blink his strange white eyelashes, scratch his underarms with his slender black fingers, and continue grabbing and eating leaves.

Seeing that the monkey did not heed him, Gurav called out to Nana, 'Nana, he doesn't want to eat from this sinner's hand. See if you fare better.'

Nana stepped forward, took the peanuts, and began pleading, 'Dear Lord, I have been the slave of your slaves. Please accept my offering. Don't test this old man.'

As Nana continued to plead in a variety of ways, calling the monkey by names from the scriptures, the monkey deigned to begin climbing down. By now a crowd of villagers had collected. When they saw the monkey climbing down, they became impatient.

The monkey had now reached the lowest branch of the tree and was sitting in its fork. Nana went closer and raised his hand. The monkey leaned over, reached out, and grabbed Nana's hand in his black paw. He looked around, enjoying himself. Nana said, 'Please take this. Don't be offended now.'

All of a sudden, the monkey thrust his face forward and scratched Nana's hand as one scrapes corn kernels off a corn cob. Then, hoisting his tail high, he leapt up to the top of the tree again.

Nana winced with pain and flopped to the ground. The villagers ran to him, picked him up gently, and helped him home to bed. They applied homegrown medications to his hand. When the old man's son saw his father's lacerated hand, he blenched. The old man would be of no use now with the sowing. He would have to hire help on daily wages. The thought distressed him.

The villagers began to whisper. It was probably true that the old man had a thing going with his daughter-in-law. Why else would the monkey have attacked him! After this, nobody was willing to offer peanuts to the monkey. They didn't dare. Why test poison? At the same time how could they keep God, who was visiting their village, unfed? This was unacceptable to Gurav. He handed the peanuts over to his eight-year-old daughter and pleaded with the monkey, 'My Lord, this little one is innocent of sin. Please accept her offering.'

That poor innocent soul stood under the tree with peanuts in her hand. The monkey came down again and slashed at her calf. He then parked himself on the lemon tree outside the goldsmith's house. Gurav's wife beat her chest and cursed the monkey. Gurav put the child on his back and went off to the medical centre in the taluka town. The villagers whispered, 'The Gurav may be a womanizer. But his wife's no better. What's happened is their fault.'

The monkey would not accept food from anybody's hand. The village fell into deep anxiety. They abandoned their betel leaves and nuts and stood around in groups discussing the problem. In the meantime the monkey had left the goldsmith's lemon tree for the ironsmith's jambhul tree. The ironsmith, who was quietly beating the dents from a bucket, spat out a mouthful of betel leaf juice, rose, and said to his wife who sat nursing the baby, 'Get me a handful of peanuts will you. The monkey has come to our door.'

'You mad or something? To hell with that monkey. Look after your work.'

'Woman, he's at our door, of his own will. Shouldn't we feed him?'

Without waiting for his wife, he picked up a fistful of peanut pods from the lot that had come to him by barter and walked out. Showing the handful to the monkey, he urged him to come down. Seeing that there was nobody else around, the monkey leapt down, took a large bite of the ironsmith's thigh, and ran up the tree again. With the village's only ironsmith laid low, who would make their farming tools now?

The monkey ran wild all day like a rabid dog, testing his teeth on whoever came by. It was evening. Nana's eldest son could no longer contain his rage. He picked up a handful of stones, stood under the tree, and said to the monkey, 'Raya, you've gone done enough harm', took aim and flung a stone. The monkey sidestepped it nimbly, bared his teeth, and ran down to charge at Nana's son. The boy, no less alert, picked up another stone and stood at the ready. The monkey leapt away lightly on all four feet into Anna Jarga's orchard.

Nana's son raced after him like Nemesis, stone in hand. Infected by his ferocity, other lusty young fellows of the village ran alongside him carrying sticks and stones. A few miles of furious chasing and the monkey was fagged out. He was too slow now to dodge the stones. A dozen or so stones hit him and he fell. Instantly, the boys surrounded him. Realizing the game was up, the shrewd monkey made pleading signs, held out his hands, turned around himself. The grocer's son Sada held back his hand and said to Nana's son, 'Look he's folding his hands, touching our feet, begging us not to hit him.'

But Nana's son could not control his rage. He stepped forward and brought a stick down on the monkey with immense force. The others stoned him mercilessly. With blood bubbling from his nose and mouth, the monkey thrashed around and died. He lay still with his paws linked together, the thatch of hair on his head matted with dirt.

Nana's son was filled with pity at the sight. He said thoughtfully, 'Listen, chaps, one of you stay here. We'll go get cymbals and drums and give Maruti a right royal funeral.'

His voice had grown incredibly tender. Sada cast a compassionate look at the dead monkey and said, 'Poor chap died at our hands. Bad thing.'

Following the general view, he stayed back to keep the vultures off while the rest of the boys returned to the village. When news of the monkey's death reached the village, they joined their hands together and asked Maruti for forgiveness for the crime that had been committed in the village.

The lads returned to the jungle with the village bhajan singers. They bore the monkey respectfully to the stream, chanting Lord Rama's name, and cremated him like a human being.

Nana's heart grieved at what had happened in the village. When he recovered from his illness, he built a square stone slab on the spot where the monkey had died.

Now pious folk bow worshipfully to it as they pass by.

Translated by Shanta Gokhale

SORROW

KAMAL DESAI

A shower comes like a crazed thing. Then goes. The veranda is drenched. The swing too. A small spray hits Saraswati bai's face as she sits on the edge of the swing. A copy of the *Times* flutters in her hands. Her body trembles at the sudden freshness. Then she recalls: her grandson's bride is coming today.

She sets the *Times* aside and wipes her glasses with her sari pallu. These days even glasses do not make things any clearer.

She should come now, at a time like this, she thinks. Half drenched, she will step in on soft, wet feet. She will bend to touch my feet. Her glass bangles will tinkle, their green sound moistened with the rain. She imagines her as a small, dainty figure. Perhaps she is really like that. Perhaps she will come exactly like that. But perhaps not. It does not have to be the way she imagines it. She could be different. How strange.

Somebody has told Saraswati bai she is dark. Mature and serious. She has been working as a clerk in a private office for the last five or six years. She once went to morning college. Nobody knows why she suddenly threw that up one day.

My grand daughter-in-law should have been highly educated. To match me. If they had to find a match in the marriage market, could they not have chosen another?

She finds it difficult to get a measure of things in this age.

She hears a sound in the yard. The girl comes just as she had imagined. Like the figure in her mind. She is petite and dark but attractive. Today's girls are not gauche as we were. She recalls a snapshot of herself wearing a jacket. She smiles.

The girl comes. She bends and touches her feet. Saraswati bai is a little confused. This is not what she expected. Not quite this. Something else. Something's wrong. But her hand touches the girl's head instinctively. Her hair is thick and soft. The girl moves a few steps back. Now Saraswati bai can see her full figure.

Her bright coloured Kashmir silk sari troubles Saraswati bai's eyes. Her short blouse makes her skin tingle. She does not approve at all of the way she has draped her pallu. The large pendant in her necklace suits her. It is nice. But should it be there or not? She cannot decide.

She is being drawn in. But she cannot stomach being drawn in. A long time elapses before she realizes she has not said a word.

'Are you wet?'

'Not very.'

'I hope Shridhar is here with you.'

'Yes, he is. He'll come in a while. He must have met friends on the way.'

'Shall we go in?'

'No please. I love swings. Let's sit here till he comes.'

The girl murmurs in a very low voice. She sits down gently beside her. Saraswati bai senses every tiny vibration of her body. The swing moves faster. Its rise and fall makes the pleats of her sari flutter and fall tenderly across her feet, tickling them. Her perfume hidden within the pleats swirls around the veranda. She now notices the colour on the girl's lips. It disturbs her. This is what she must be. Shallow. Loud. But perhaps she is not. And yet these are the signs by which the contours of her existence are to be read.

Her eyes rest on the girl's exposed midriff. They alight on the colour on her lips. The girl senses this. She feels suffocated. She wraps her pallu hastily around both shoulders. She rubs her lips with a tiny handkerchief.

Shridhar once told her Granny doesn't like all this stuff. His voice suggested that he was rather unhappy with it too but did not want to hurt her. If I don't do these things, I don't feel I'm me. I feel I am being erased out of existence.

'I couldn't attend your wedding. Shridhar's grandfather was very ill. And I find journeys difficult these days.'

'I know.'

Saraswati bai did not expect this response at all. She is stunned. The girl too realizes it. Something has gone wrong. She did not mean to say what she did. She has surprised herself. She must pick up the pieces now. How difficult that is. How exhausting.

'We missed you so very much.' Suddenly, out of the blue, she is overwhelmed by emotion. She says almost without thinking, 'But I am so proud to be your daughter-in-law.'

It makes Saraswati bai smile. Those empty words fall at her feet. She lets them lie there.

The girl feels suddenly ashamed. Words have deceived her again. Exposed her. Saraswati bai has caught her. But where did those words come from? She has never felt what they said. From the day she got engaged she has been hearing about Saraswati bai. She knows it all by heart.

'Let me tell you. She went to university back in those days. Her father was an active reformist. He had a name. The family had status. Yes...the family was well known. And let me tell you. You may not believe me, but the story of this woman's marriage is pretty romantic. What happened was that this young man was a neighbour. He was a quick, sharp thinker. He would wear his cap and sit below the framed pictures of Tilak and Agarkar, studying for his law degree. He had watched Saru, lost in her own world, fetching water, her nine-yard sari tucked neatly out of the way. He had also watched her, her hair pulled back in a tight bun, sitting by her window reading her law books. Suddenly one day he got up, went straight to his father and told him...get it? And let me tell you, this is how the whole story....'

This is what her father's friend, who had proposed Shridhar as a match for her, had said. It had meant nothing much to her.

A woman said, 'She taught in our school. We used to fear her although she was very affectionate. But a strict disciplinarian. The girls were being rowdy once during her Sanskrit class. That was enough. She marched out of the class. We were terrified....' The woman could not remember what happened then. Perhaps nothing of the sort had happened. The woman had deep respect for her. That is about it.

'Nalini, you are so lucky!' a friend had said.

Perhaps she is. But it makes her uncomfortable. Why does everybody talk about her constantly? She's got the point. Saraswati bai was a formidable woman. But so what? Are there no other people besides her? I want to see them. Get to know them.

Shridhar too kept talking about his grandmother. She once said to him, 'You never talk about your mother.'

How true. They had never talked about Mother. She had slipped out of his mind altogether. That was not so nice. But that was not how it really was. He talked a lot about his grandmother. As for his mother, he was simply a part of her. 'Our mother made the most delicious puran polis. She managed to give them such a delicate yellow colour. The taste was like nothing else. It was like itself. Her touch pervaded every nook and corner of the house without your ever being aware of it. And in her spare time she dug the earth in the backyard and planted beds of blossoming mogra bushes. She also planted lots of tulsi bearing leaves shaded in black and red. She nurtured her plants with great care. The slightly acrid smell of the tulsi would blend with the heady scent of mogra....' Shridhar laughed.

She has been listening to him in breathless silence. She sees a woman gliding silently around the house without a word. Involuntarily, she feels the embrace of the woman whose being blossoms in the midst of mogra beds. Surely this is what contentment means. She struggles to catch the strength of Shridhar's mother's ability to immerse herself.

'Shridhar told me you are fond of embroidery. You could

attend an embroidery class if you wanted to.'

The girl feels as though a needle has pricked her finger. It is a much desired pain. But the blue fabric rips apart. All she hears is a cacophony. Pain is totally meaningless. Every cell in her body is tense. Saraswati bai is looking at her curiously. Her silence taunts her. 'Shallow and irresponsible,' she mutters.

She does not like this at all. But she gathers the words calmly and casts them out. She does not even raise her eyes. Saraswati bai is deeply hurt.

'I am not insisting on it. But one should do something. It's good.'

How naive and childish. All so simple. But that is not how it is. Not how it is. Yet it is difficult to say how it is.

'So?'

'I haven't thought about it. And I don't think I'm interested in that sort of thing.' Then she is silent.

She gets off at the kindergarten school on her way home from work. Her five-year-old is having fun among a crowd of kids. He says something and bursts out laughing.

She wants to pick him up. Pinch his cheek. But her tired body rejects the idea.

He walks home holding her hand. He is chattering away. She only goes 'hunh' as she walks. Sudhir fought with Mukund today and broke his slate. There's a new girl in his class. She has a funny nose. So what if she does. He likes her very much. His teacher can't sing like his mother. He imitates how she sings....

Why walk upside down,
with your feet touching the sky.
How can anybody's feet touch the sky?

She wishes the child would not talk so much. Her feet ache. Her back is stiff with sitting in a chair all day. I have committed so many things to memory without questioning them.

'Tell me.'

'What?'

'How can feet touch the sky?'
'They can't. It's not possible.'
'The sky isn't our home.'

His mother does not seem to have understood that. He is a little scared of her. He becomes suddenly solemn. Then recites the poem again. Then falls asleep. But what is the sky? The question is not answered even in his sleep.

Shridhar comes home. He is very tired. But he enters briskly. However quickly he tries to move, he cannot escape feeling the usual sadness. Things are really perfectly fine. Why does he feel this dead weight then? Perhaps things are a little beyond him.

'You're late today, aren't you?'
'Not at all. You're imagining it. Perhaps you came home early.'

She has grown used to his habit of dropping his clothes wherever he happens to be. She picks them up without a word.

'We're meeting at Keshav's place today. We're going, aren't we?'
'Not me. You go. It bores me.'
'You're always bored.'
'You think you go because you enjoy it?'

He is startled. She has changed a lot in the last ten years. She has never felt she owns her life. She has always been a stranger here. His grandmother used to say, your wife is like a riddle. She puzzles one. She is like someone from another world. I find her difficult.

He wanders all over the house. And comes in to have his tea.

'It's years since Granny died. We've almost forgotten her.'
'You were madly fond of her.'
'Whereas you never liked her. But neither you nor I have managed to understand what she understood.'

But had she really understood? Understood what? Who knows. Maybe. Or maybe not. All one can say is that Grandmother belonged to her time. That is the truth. That is the only truth. She had achieved a lot. She had made herself useful. She was contented. If she had lived in our times, would she have felt the same way?

'Say something.'
'Say what?'
'You are very bitter. Very. Very.'
'This is how I am. I know nothing beyond this.'

Shridhar climbs up the steps. He bends down and touches his Granny's feet. Saraswati bai feels she has found the child Shridhar again. Really this is how he always came. Always smiling like this. She is happy. She knows Shridhar. He will understand her.

But it does not last. Shridhar's smile fades away. None of them knows what they want to say. What they want to tell one another. Shridhar is surprised. He had wanted to tell Granny about this and about that. About so many things. She would even have said to him, 'How you jabber. You still haven't grown up.' He would have felt deeply contented then.

But they stand facing each other in silence now, as though they have forgotten how to speak.

Saraswati bai glances once at Shridhar and then at the girl. I will never be able to read these two now. They are indecipherable.

Translated by Shanta Gokhale

REVOLT

BABURAO BAGUL

Two years later, the reply came. Parbhu had asked that his son be given a job. And although he was now at death's door, here it was. His son, Jai, was studying for his matriculation. When he refused to take the job as a Bhangi, a wave of anger erupted against him. But he was adamant; even if the entire community rose up to oppose him, he would not take it. He was in full revolt against his parents who were insisting he give up his studies and become a Bhangi. He stood now, waiting for his father to say something so that he might attack him using his powerful vocabulary. In the school and in the settlement, he had been able to defeat the great and the good in debate and even now, when his father was on his deathbed, he was intent on demolishing the old man's decision to make his son a Bhangi.

Lying wearily on his cot, Parbhu was trying to assess the mental state of his angry son who was standing by the foot of his cot. He was trying to find the words to dispel the white-collar dreams his son had been nurturing. His sixteen- or seventeen-year-old daughter-in-law, Shanti, was sitting on the bed, pressing his feet. She had drawn the edge of her pallu from across her head to her chest. And as always, she was beating her husband in the secret spaces of her head. She wanted to tell him to take her, to abandon his education, to get a job, to settle down, and begin a physical relationship with her. Her mental pain communicated itself to her father-in-law almost as soon as she touched his feet. Taking courage from her touch, he began, 'Jai....'

Without giving his father an opportunity to say a word more,

Jai shouted, his interior revolt now in full fight:

'Pitaji, whatever happens, I will not give up my education. I will not take up this job of a Bhangi that is being thrust upon me. In fact, when I finish my education and I am as wise as Socrates, I am going to destroy this inhuman practice of untouchability.'

This answer was a sharp sword slicing through all their hopes.

For here was a man who could snarl at his father like an animal when the latter lay on his deathbed; a man who could ignore the poverty and deprivation in his own home; a man, who though he was physically male, would not so much as look at his own wife. And for her part, his wife began to see him as stupid, unfeeling, and intensely selfish. She began to look at him from behind the veil of her ghoonghat; and his physical beauty excited her. That she should be thinking such thoughts—and in the presence of her father-in-law—made her feel ashamed of herself. She bowed her head again and applied herself to pressing his feet.

This gentle service from his daughter-in-law stirred the old man's heart. He feared that after his death the girl might suffer even more; he feared that his son's complete refusal to look at his wife even by mistake would drive her to search for the comfort of another man's arms. These fears made him speak with no little bitterness and no less determination. 'Jai, can't you see the state we live in, the condition your mother is in? Don't you hear your wife's sighs?'

'Just for this I should become a Bhangi? Give up my education to clear up the dirt of the village? Carry filth on my head? If you wanted me to do that kind of work, why did you have me educated? Why did you let them light these lamps of independence, knowledge, and humanity inside my mind?

The yearning in his voice caused the old man's eyes to moisten in sympathy. He began to see his son's sorrow. But Shanti's mind filled with hatred for him. She saw her husband as a useless fellow. She cursed her own fate and began to weep, and Jaichand, full of the anger of rebellion, let out a roar of revolt.

'I am not going to do that job. I will never become a Bhangi.'

It was as if the revulsion he felt for the work he was being asked to do had turned into electricity and was coursing through this refusal. Shanti was reduced to ashes and the old man was scorched by the radiant heat of this sun. However, Parbhu persisted in trying to explain their situation.

'...But you are the son of a Bhangi. What problem can you have with doing this job? People pay to get these jobs, hundred, even a hundred-and-fifty rupees. And here you're getting one free. We need you to take this job. If you had a job, I might not be so near death. Your mother would not be reduced to a skeleton. This girl would not live in this state....'

'Where is it written that a Bhangi's son must become a Bhangi?'

'In our poverty. In our dharma. In our country.'

'What dharma? If it breaks a person and turns him into an animal, is that dharma? In this country that invests greater significance in a stone than in a human being? I will not heed such a dharma. If it has given us only this poverty, this deprivation, then it behoves us to reject it. But we are not going to do that. I will. Just let me pass my examinations....

'Until that time, let me go where I can beg for food...or sin for it...for the sake of my stomach.

'Those who do not have patience may feel free to commit such sins for their stomachs.'

Hearing this, the river of tears running inside Shanti's head turned to acid. Her hands stilled on her father-in-law's legs.

Fearing that the force of his hatred for the job might overheat his son's brain thus driving him to madness or to suicide, Parbhu tried for a more conciliatory tone to quell those terrifying visions.

'Do this job until you find another. You can go to night school. When you pass, and you find another job, you can give this one up.'

'I will not. If you want, I'll leave school. I'll rob or become a dacoit. But not this job....'

'It's not a Bhangi's job. The muqaddam has requested the boss. Your mother has fallen at everyone's feet. Go and see at least....'

'No one will listen. Even if one boss is Christian and the other one is Muslim, they will all only see me as a Bhangi. They will never see me as an educated person. No one at school sees me as a student, Pitaji, only as a Bhangi. Nowhere in the world is there a country like this one, which persecutes you every step of the way. How much must we bear? How much must we swallow? Is this a country or a prison, a jail? And why must I, an innocent man, live the contempt-ridden, insult-filled life of a prisoner? Why endure this hell? Why? Why?'

Hearing his son's ear-splitting cry, the old man trembled. He looked at his son with compassionate eyes; seeing his father's tears and his shivering, Jaichand sat down. He began to stroke his father's chest with his clean, delicate fingers. He wiped his eyes. And feeling the love in those fingers, the old man drew his son's head down to his chest. He began to caress his son's head. Over the past few years, Jai, though he had lived in the same house, had grown aloof and had isolated himself; so now he simply let his head rest on his father's chest and allowed himself to enjoy the feeling of being loved. He felt like he was in a field now, a field that had been burning in the sun and was now drinking in the rain, releasing a fragrance, and beginning to blossom. He felt himself opening up, and he began to tell his father of the uncountable dreams he had for his life.

'Pitaji, when I pass my exams, I am going to become a clerk. I'll go to college. I'll get my PhD. I'll make sure you all live happy, rich lives. And when the two of you go to your heavenly homes, the journalists will write stories about you. They'll say you were the parents of Dr Jaichand Rathod.'

The old man could not find the courage in his beleaguered heart to listen to his son's ramblings about his beautiful dreamworld of the future. He closed his tear-filled eyes and continued to stroke his son's head.

For years the love that had been suppressed under the boulders of their disagreements began to squeeze its way out. His son was no parasite. He loved his family but his heart was filled with zeal, with good intentions. That he should have wanted to deny such a jewel his education, that he should have shouted at him for refusing the job of a Bhangi caused him such terrible sorrow that he began to murmur to himself:

'You should not have been born my son, not in this country. Your soul has suffered too much. I married you off young and tied you down. But now don't ruin this poor girl's life; she's as good as gold...even if you're keeping her at a distance now because you want to finish your education, don't let it always be so.... And don't behave badly with your mother.... You never call her Mother in public.... You don't want to go anywhere with her. She longs to show off her well-built and well-educated son to all her worker-friends. But you avoid her as if she were a wild animal seeking your blood. How much she weeps about this. She keeps all her sorrows to herself. When she can't bear it any longer, she tells me or this poor child to ask you to change your ways.... Jai, let her be a mother to you.'

Jai's eyes filled up at his father's words. He put a hand on his wife's shoulder and asked in a choked voice:

'Is this true, Shanti?'

Shanti ducked her head in embarrassment. This was the first time he had spoken to her or touched her after he became a man. That made her very happy. The hatred she had begun to feel for him lessened. However, her mind had gone through a series of reversals. In a profoundly despairing voice, Jaichand began to say:

'What kind of culture is this? Where a man can treat the mother who gave him life with contempt simply because she does the work of a Bhangi? Where he can insult her and refuse to eat the food she cooks? If this culture had not created untouchability, I would not be the chief tormentor of my poor, aged mother....'

He fell at her feet. She had turned to give him a piece of her mind but he was weeping and pressing her feet to his face. 'Forgive me, Ma, forgive me.'

This boy who would not eat what she had cooked even after she had washed her hands with soap was now kissing her dust-laden feet? What was this? Had he run mad? Her heart skipped a beat. She began to tremble. She wanted to speak to him but her tongue seemed to have cleaved to her palate.

'She'll fall over,' Shanti said, frightened and then startled by her own audacity, she ducked her head and sat down.

'Come, Aai,' he said and brought her outside.

'No, son, you don't have to go. Let's send Shanti. Let's ask about her,' said the old lady.

'Then who will cook for me? Who will serve me with her own hands?' and, putting his hand on his mother's back, he urged her to walk with him. The happy awareness that her son did not hate her, that he loved her, was somewhat dispelled by his words, 'Who will cook for me? Who will serve me?' She dragged her feet a little as she walked.

But he was urging her forward. And watching his son make a bonfire of his dreams as he went forward with the resolution of a martyr, the old man began to burn with regret.

Bhani had collapsed completely. She was being dragged along like a log, impelled forward by her son's velocity. This was how they came to be standing in the courtyard of the office. The Christian boss looked at Jai and Bhani.

Seeing the beautiful powerful youth who looked like something out of the Classical Roman era, he called to the muqaddam:

'Muqaddam!'

'Yes, sir?'

The muqaddam, who was assigning work, stopped to offer a namaste.

'Give him a cart.'

'A cart?'

'Yes, a cart. They asked for a Mehtar's* job.'

'A cart?' Bhani was shocked.

'A cart it is. When someone joins as a Mehtar, they start with a cart, said the boss, a cigarette clamped between his lips.'

'He's studying for his matric....'

'Let him. But he's a Mehtar. And he's here to be a Mehtar. Go.'

The boss had nothing more to say to Bhani. The educated children of Bhangis often came for jobs, impelled by their destitution. When they were faced with the terrible, demeaning work of the cart, they ran away, leaving the vacancy his to sell again. There were two vacancies like that. He would take a hundred rupees and give the job to someone for four months; and after that, he would get another hundred from someone else. This was the third such post from which the boss had earned a lot.

Jai walked quietly with the muqaddam. Behind them, carrying the burden of her pain, walked Bhani. Her fever had increased. Her face was pale. Her mouth was dry. She was sweating profusely. Her feet moved with effort and the belief that they were doing something criminal to her son was lacerating her heart, so full of maternal love.

The muqaddam and Jai arrived at an area in Ghatkopar. It was a crowded, tense area. There were a number of small and large buffalo stables there. These were surrounded by a throng of chawls and huts. This enormous population was served by thirty-two toilets. It was in front of this block of toilets that the muqaddam stopped and said:

'This is your job. Bring the cart here and go in and bring out the boxes and pour them into the cart. Then you have to clean the boxes. You will have to clean the toilets as well as the staircases and the area around. If you don't do the job well, out you go and the job goes back into the boss's pocket. Today it

---

*Mehtar is both a caste descriptor and an occupation. The two are used interchangeably.

will seem horrible; tomorrow you'll be glad of the job. I'm off.'

And he walked off proudly.

Jai remained standing there. The little children had already fouled the place. Looking at those turds made gooseflesh break out all over his body and inside it, revolt brewed. He stood stock still, looking around him.

Looking at her son standing there like a statue, his proud eyes beginning to fill with tears, Bhani, tormented by shame, anger, and self-hatred, said in a guilty tone:

'Son, you don't have to do this job. Go home. Go.'

'Why?'

'It's not work meant for you. It's for unlettered folk like us. It's for those who are already broken in mind, body, nose, forehead, broken everywhere, broken and dead.'

'So it's for you? That's....'

'Never mind, my son. Don't say it. Don't use these slippers to hurt your mother. Go. Go. We don't want such a job. We will not eat and drink and make merry over your body. I beg of you, go.'

He was looking at her. Controlling the wail that was rising inside her was making her lips and cheeks tremble. Tears were streaming from her eyes. Seeing this, he felt like crying too. But the fire of resolution running through him dried the tears. They simply would not get past his eyes. His revolutionary mind was now fighting the dharma and the nation. He had debated these issues with the nation and with the dharma. When the yellow flames merge with the red ones in a furnace, a series of muted explosions results; and this was what was happening inside him. Just then the shit cart arrived and stopped and the driver called out, 'Bhani, what are you doing here?'

She turned around to look. So that she would not come down the narrow passage between the blocks of sixteen back-to-back toilets, Jai went clattering down the stairs.

'Jai,' she called and her voice froze the blood of the listener, for it came from a shattered heart.

It was the sound of a mother forced to bear witness to the death of a child.

The stench emanating from the thirty-two toilets filled his throat. His breath was plucked from him. Darkness swam before his eyes. He closed them. Then he began to understand why his eyes had grown heavy, where his pain had come from. His brain was thrashing about like a fish thrown on burning sand, his veins seemed ready to burst open and were beating against his forehead and the back of his head, and it seemed as if someone had shoved a churn into his stomach and was rolling it about again and again and the nerves of his stomach seemed ready to rip their way out of his mouth. He closed his lips firmly. The strength went out of his legs, which had begun to tremble, so he stood still. He began to look around him with eyes peeled.

He turned his eyes to look at each tin under each toilet. Each glimpse brought fresh rigors to his body. His blood was boiling. There were thirty-two of them, each filled with filth, some surrounded by accumulated and rotting waste which was alive with maggots and flies; in one or two places there were blood-stained cloths, balls of used cotton wool, bandages, and gauze strips...all this filled him with revulsion. His body trembled; his face was covered with sweat. He felt he was going to slip and fall. He felt he had to do something terrible, something destructive. He was Abhimanyu in the chakravyuha, surrounded by armed enemies. Were these the common enemies of all mankind or was it only the crime of having been born in this country that meant one had to be thrust into this hell? And what kind of evil nation was this that any man should ask another to do such hateful work for money? And what kind of people would accept that it was their lot in life to do such work? How could they be willing to do this to make ends meet? Mankind, who has named everything in the world, who has created the Gods and the dharma, who has conjured up creation out of nothingness. Mankind...greater than all the five elements and more powerful. Man does this work...why? What demon does he fear? What terrible draught must he drink?

As blood gushes from a wound, the thoughts rushed from his head while the carter, tired of waiting for the load of filth, shouted:

'Arre, have you fallen asleep in there? Sonny, I have the whole village to clean up. Get on with it....Hurry up....'

He turned to look at the man calling out to him from above. Seeing his paan-stained lips parted in a smile, a violent flame was lit in Jai's light eyes. And the man above stepped back involuntarily: 'Deewaana!' (Mad man!)

Knowing that her son was standing there thinking, Bhani was herself a stone doll, petrified by shame and pain.

She slowly raised her feet and limped up to her son and with more strength than she had in her body, she loosened her tongue, and shouted, 'Ja...a...i!'

And then she slipped and fell, turning as white as a corpse, and so that she might not rise and come down herself, he jumped to it, grabbing a full tin and pulling it, but just then he found his fingers covered in shit. And again the hair rose all over his body. And though his mind was filled with revulsion, he hurriedly hoisted the pot to his shoulder. This blind hurry meant the tin shook and spilled. The contents spilled over, glug, glug, on to him. And just as a man who finds that a snake has coiled itself around him and has bitten him lets loose a scream of agony, Jai screamed, 'Aai!'

Hearing his cry, the carter who had been helping Bhani sit up, looked down to see Jai standing in the pit of hell, and in a voice full of disgust, said, 'Idiot.'

Jai, filled with the destructive desires of revolt, began to run up the stairs. His anger and disgust at all that had happened made him almost unaware of the filth that was all over him. When he got to the top, he dropped the tin and was about to pounce on the carter when he saw his mother, sweat-soaked, corpse-pale, and said, 'Grab that.'

'Go on, throw it in. Don't dirty her up as well,' said the carter, disgusted at the boy, even as he looked affectionately at his mother. This disgust caused the revolt, the hatred, the horror that was running through Jai's nerves to rise up within him. And so he took the tin he had brought up with him and threw it wherever it went, and then he grabbed the carter with both hands.

'Animal, are you going to teach me? Are you trying to rub salt in my wounds? Do you want to mock me?' And so saying, Jai began to beat him, his hands flying and falling with the intensity and fury of a monsoon storm.

As the sea in a storm whips the fishing boats again and again until it destroys them, he lashed out at the carter. The latter was shouting in an attempt to save his life, 'Help, help!'

The bhaiyyas who were tending the buffaloes came out with sticks in their hands. The folks from the chawl gathered. But none of them tried to stop the dangerous fight that had broken out between the two Mehtars. Unwilling to be polluted by touching either one, the north Indians stood with their sticks, unmoving. And the rest did not intervene for fear that they would come in contact with the village's accumulated shit. They simply watched as the two were locked in a death struggle.

Bhani, wailing like a cat, was wandering around them, screaming and crying, begging people to stop them.

When the carter fell at last, lifeless, a corpse, the rage began to recede from Jai's body. He hugged his mother to his chest and shouted: 'Maa, break my fingers...cut off my hands...slash open my body, throw away my corpse.'

As a man who has soaked himself with petrol begins to scream a cry that tears through the heart, so Jai screamed.

And Bhani could only wonder if her son had gone mad; this shock made her teeth chatter.

The people stood and watched. But no one could make

sense of the flame of revolt that was burning inside Jai. There was no way for them to understand it. For their minds had been murdered long ago by Manu.*

Translated by Jerry Pinto

---

*Several attempts have been made to ban dry toilets such as the one described here. However, the law has not been enforced.

THE GOD OF BRAHMINS
HAMID DALWAI

Once some Muslim boys from our village picked up an idol of the god worshipped by Brahmins from Brahmin waadi* and threw it in the nearby stream.

I was very young at that time. These boys were at least ten years older than us. Their act of throwing the Brahmins' god was not one of religious fanaticism. At least at that time they didn't have any idea about what they were doing. As usual, this also was a part of merely causing mischief.

These boys were very strong. We never dared to cross their path. Our parents strictly warned us to stay away from them. The teachers ignored the boys even if they did not study in school because the teachers thought that the boys had already crossed the age of studying in school. It was nearly impossible for any primary school teacher to dump these boys of eighteen to twenty years in classes for the third and fourth grade for the whole day.

At that time, our school was new. We had a primary teacher named Ambarao Ghadashi. When these boys were admitted to school for the first time, Ghadashi sir asked one of them, 'So, Rakhnuddin? What were you doing for so many years?'

Rakhnuddin gave Ghadashi sir the evil eye. Then he looked at all the students in the class and said, 'I was filling water with a colander.'

'Who has taught you to answer back this way?' Ghadashi sir asked angrily.

---

*Farmyards where Brahmin families lived.

'Your father,' Rakhnuddin said.

The class laughed and Ghadashi sir thrashed Rakhnuddin with the stick he had in his hand. He tolerated all the beating without a word and as soon as Ghadashi sir moved aside he walked out of the classroom with his bag.

Ghadashi sir thought that he had gotten rid of this headache, but it was a misunderstanding. Rakhnuddin not only came to the school the next day, but also spread stinging nettles on the chair before sir came to class. As Ghadashi sir sat on the chair, the nettles stung him like a scorpion. His body was itching and burning. Dying in pain he left the class halfway and went home.

Ghadashi sir immediately took a transfer and Kazi sir replaced him. But Rakhnuddin had left the school by that time. Along with Rakhnuddin, all those older boys also dropped out of school and began wandering aimlessly in the village.

Some of their deeds really annoyed the villagers. During the evening, they robbed the sticks that are kept for oiling the wheels of the bullock cart. Sometimes they escaped with the fish that they stole from the fishing nets laid by other people. They removed every single stalk of stored harvested rice. They picked all the mangoes from someone's farm during mango season.

These boys sometimes stood on the road early in the morning to trouble the villagers travelling on their bullock carts. The half-asleep bullock cart drivers would drive their carts towards the bazaar. These boys, standing at the top of a lane, would slowly lead the bullocks towards the lane that led to the Brahman waadi. The bullocks would stand there once they reached. Some bullock cart drivers would become alert as soon as the sounds of the bells on the bullocks' necks stopped. They would divert their bullock carts back to the bazaar road. Some drivers would remain asleep till morning. These boys would go to such people and say, 'So? Is this the way you ride your cart? Instead of Chiplun you will reach Guhaghar some day in this manner!' The shamefaced villager would hurriedly get up and begin hitting his bullocks, wondering how this happened.

A girl named Zainab from our village was recently married off in the neighbouring village. This village was on the other side of the river. One day, she was returning from her in-laws' home. The walking path was covered due to the rising tide. She stood on the riverbank and began calling out to the boatman.

The boatman was not at his place. Rakhnuddin and his gang were at the riverbank fishing. They heard Zainab calling the boatman, and so, they took the boat to the other side. Zainab sat in the boat. They rowed the boat and halted it after reaching the centre of the river. They said to her, 'Zainab, you have to kiss us.'

Initially, Zainab thought that they were joking. Irritated, she said, 'Don't be mischievous! Row the boat to the other side immediately. I have to return by the evening.'

'We won't take you to the other side until you kiss us,' Rakhnuddin shouted. He placed his legs on the sides of the boat and began to swing his body from side to side. Along with him, the boat swayed and river water began to fill the boat.

The boys looked at her desirously and shouted, 'Will you kiss us or not? Or should we drown the boat?'

Zainab was entirely confused and before she could say something the boys hurriedly kissed her one by one.

The newly married girl hid her face in her palms, sobbed, and swore at the boys, 'You rascals! You scoundrels! You have no shame at all. How dare you touch me?'

By then, the boat had moved to the other side of the river. Some of the boys began to throw out the water which had filled the boat. No one said anything to her and they kept laughing amongst themselves. When the boat reached the bank, they said to her, 'What's there to cry so much? We just kissed you. That's it!'

She did not wait to listen to this and ran away crying. As soon as she reached home she immediately shared everything with her mother.

This was not something the villagers could ignore like the

usual incidents. That night, Rakhnuddin and his friends were called to Zainab's home. All the elderly people from the village were present there.

'Boys,' my father asked, 'what did you say to Zainab?'

No one answered. They just stood there hanging their heads.

'Kissing, hun? You feel you are all grown up!' Kader Khan said, moving around in the passage. 'How uncouth can one be! Haan?'

'Bend down...hold your toes,' Bale Khan shouted.

Immediately they all bent down and held their toes.

They were made to stand this way for almost an hour and sent home later.

They did not step out from their own home for the next two to three days. 'Now why have you become sheepish like the women?' the people at home said to them. 'Aren't you ashamed of your behaviour?' They simply ignored what was said and after some days they resumed their behaviour.

Then the incident of stealing the idol took place.

Before this incident, no one had consciously noticed the god of the Brahmins. It had been placed under the banyan tree at the entrance of the village. He was probably not even worshipped every day. One day, some women from Brahmin waadi visited this place and noticed that their god was missing. They hurriedly returned home and shared this news with the men.

Subsequently, one by one, everyone from the Brahmin waadi gathered near the banyan tree. They began to solve the puzzle of their missing god. One of them stepped forward, observed the place, and announced, 'Someone has pulled up the god from the ground!'

'Pulled up?' asked Govindrao. He seemed sceptical. 'Who would pull up our god...and for what?'

'It is clearly evident that the god was pulled out of the ground. Look at that stone. It was uprooted and has fallen on the wayside,' someone explained deeply.

Govindrao stepped ahead and observed the place. After that, he was convinced that someone had really heaved the god from the ground. He was unable to understand who had done this.

This incident remained unclear to all that day. Gradually things began to fall into place. Two days ago, Rakhnuddin and his two friends had gone to this place when a Brahmin lady saw them waiting below the banyan tree.

Govindrao came to my father the next morning.

My father was getting ready to go to Chiplun. He was tying his turban looking in the mirror. On seeing Govindrao he said, 'Govindrao! How come you are here in the morning?'

'I am here to invite you to see our god,' Govindrao shared without sitting.

'Why? What happened to your god?'

'He is not in his place!'

'Not in his place? Where did he go?' Father asked, surprised.

'I am convinced that somebody has done this on purpose, therefore I came to you.'

At that time Father said, 'Those boys must have done this! They stalked Zainab last time. You remember, right? Did you meet Kader Khan?'

'No, I came to you first.'

'No problem. I will meet Kader Khan and Bale Khan to understand what has happened. I will find your god. You don't worry.'

With this he allowed Govindrao to leave. But he was shaking from within. He had never thought that the boys from our village would reach the level of stealing the Brahmins' gods. He had never imagined that one day Brahmins will have to complain about our behaviour. He went to Kader Khan before going to the market. He shared with Kader Khan and Bale Khan what had happened.

That night, Rakhnuddin and his gang were made to stand in front of us. Cane sticks were bought from the bazaar in the morning. After whipping the boys on their palms, Bale Khan asked them in a stern voice, 'Where have you put the Brahmins' god?'

Initially nobody said anything. They just stood there with

their heads down.

'Pinch their balls so that they open their mouths! Rascals!' Kader Khan thundered.

Father said angrily, 'What were you thinking? It's almost a situation where we would lose our respect forever...do you understand? Just tell us the truth!'

Then Rakhnuddin opened his mouth. He said, 'Yes, we picked up the god.'

'Why?'

'Just for fun!'

'For fun? We are put to shame forever! What about that? Where have you put the god?'

'In the nearby stream....'

'Don't you have any shame?'

'They have lost all sense of shame,' Bale Khan said.

And then all three began to thrash the boys with cane sticks. The boys tolerated the beating without a word. In the end, the hitting hands were tired. They returned to the bench behind and sat there.

'Rascals! Is it a body or a wooden log?' Kader Khan asked. 'Do they even feel the beating?'

'Bastards! All this would have led to severe disturbances in the village.... Do you even understand?'

'Leave it now. Tomorrow, show us where you have put the god.'

The boys felt relieved when Father said this and left shortly after.

The next day the boys were taken to Govindrao's place. As soon as Govindrao saw them, he understood that the god had been found.

'These boys have put the god into the stream near our village. Let's go. We shall help you to take it out,' Father said.

Govindrao collected all the Brahmins from the Brahman waadi. They all gathered near the banyan tree. Father asked the boys, 'Where is the god?'

'Wait, I will get it,' Rakhnuddin said.

'But where have you put it?' Govindrao asked irritably.

'See, it's there in the stream,' he pointed out.

The god's idol was resting amongst a clutter of stones in the water. As soon as Rakhnuddin folded his lungi and began to get into the water, a Brahmin said, 'Wait. We will bring our god and place it by ourselves. You don't go!'

Rakhnuddin stepped behind in sadness. Four Brahmins entered the water. They brought the idol out and installed it below the banyan tree.

Feeling anxious, Father said to Govindrao, 'Last night, we beat the boys up. They will remember it for the rest of their lives. They will not commit such an offence again....'

'Thank god we found the idol,' Govindrao said, 'I had become truly restless.'

'...and what do you think? We could concentrate on our work? It was almost time for us to hide our faces in shame from you....'

Govindrao said, 'They are children. How much could they understand? They have no knowledge of what they do!'

During this talk, Rakhnuddin and his group were standing there with their heads down. Someone from the crowd said, 'You rascals! What are you waiting for? Get out from here....'

Later, the boys did not step out of their homes for the next two to three days. They regretted not being able to place back the god which they themselves had put away. They began to feel that by putting away the Brahmins' god in the water they had crossed the limits of their mischievousness. From that incident onwards, they somehow stopped annoying the villagers.

On the other hand, my father and some other people from the village began to say, 'The boys had gone completely out of hand but the god of Brahmins taught them some wisdom. The god of Brahmins blessed them!'

Translated by Deepali Awkale

VACANCY
RATNAKAR MATKARI

'I've been sent here by your head office...' the young man who stood in front of Kedare's desk said.

He had curly dark hair, dark complexion, bright eyes, and a crafty, cunning smile that seemed to belong to a trickster. Seeing that smile, Kedare's own face grew sombre.

He thought: this young man means to steal something from me, but I will not give it to him, no matter what happens.

'Do you have a letter from the head office?' he asked the man.

The young man held out an envelope.

Kedare opened it and read that this man was sent to work as a stenotypist. He was to start work immediately.

Kedare was surprised. There was a typist in the office already. Her name was Sarita Shahade. She was not being transferred. There were no complaints about her work. Kedare didn't have a personal problem with her; nobody else did, either. Theirs was a tiny little branch office with no more than a couple of dozen employees. So then why did the main office send him another typist?

Something was out of kilter. 'There is no vacancy for you here,' Kedare said to the man.

'Then you tell the head office,' said the young man. Was there a tinge of insubordination in what he said?

'All right, I will let the head office know,' Kedare said, unperturbed by the tone of the man's voice. He jotted down the man's name, address, and the reference number of the letter from the head office.

The young man took the envelope and stepped out of Kedare's tiny office. Kedare felt relieved. He took a deep breath.

But the next day, when Kedare came to the office, the young man, who was sitting on the bench, stood up and said 'Good morning'. Kedare returned the greeting by habit, but when he saw the man, he was puzzled.

'What are you doing here?'

'I'm waiting to take charge of the job.'

'That will take some time,' Kedare frowned. 'I've dictated the letter. Now it'll have to be typed up, then signed, and it will go in today's dispatch. It can easily take a week to get an answer from the head office.'

'But the head office has already instructed me...' the man said. Kedare couldn't decide if the man was insubordinate or stupid. 'But there's no place for you to sit,' he said, irritated.

'Okay, I'll wait,' the man said calmly. 'I'll wait until space becomes available.' Kedare didn't quite understand what the man meant, but he felt uncomfortable.

The man sat on the bench all day long, as if he was waiting for something. In front of him, but at a distance, Sarita Shahade sat, busy with her typing. The man sat and stared at her.

The next morning, when Kedare came in to work, the man greeted him again. Kedare did not appreciate it, but he could not think of what to say. He walked past the man and went to his office.

The same day, in the afternoon, Sarita Shahade started having powerful spasms in her abdomen. All the office staff gathered around her. Kedare immediately called for the doctor. The doctor was confused by her symptoms. He advised that she be taken to the hospital. In the hospital she was diagnosed with food poisoning. All night long she convulsed with pain. All night long the doctors tried to save her, but towards the morning she died.

Some of her co-workers went for her funeral. Others paid her their respects and went back to work. Without a word from anyone, the young man sat at Sarita Shahade's desk, now empty, and started typing. When Kedare saw him typing, he started having heart palpitations. He could not ask the man to leave, because he had the letter from the head office with him. There was a vacancy, and now the man had filled it. But who had authorized it? And how did he know beforehand that there would be a vacancy? How could he wait calmly for a vacancy to occur? He must have wanted to fill Sarita's seat. But she…the whole thing was scary.

'I've been sent here by your head office.'

A new man stood in front of Kedare's desk. He showed Kedare the envelope. Kedare opened it. This man had been sent to work as an accountant. Kedare was astonished.

He was to start work immediately? But accountant Kundaikar has not been transferred!

'It's all right, I will wait,' the man said.

Kedare stared at the man. He had eyebrows that met above the nose, which made him look cruel, and he had a habit of tapping the desk, which Kedare thought was rude.

He said in his best official voice, 'I cannot tell you anything till I hear from the head office.'

'So what should I do until then?' the man said. 'The head office has given clear instructions.'

'All right, you'll start tomorrow,' Kedare said, and a chill passed through his body. 'I'll find you some other job.'

'No, we cannot do that. You have to hire me as an accountant. The head office states so quite clearly.'

'All right,' Kedare said, reluctantly. 'Pull up a chair and sit with Kundaikar. Learn the job.'

Kedare took out a pack of cigarettes, lit one, and breathed the smoke in. But that did not help him. A terror crawled up his whole body. He started to write a memo to the head office. He did not dictate many memos nowadays. But he was afraid that the new stenographer would make fun of him. Last week he had sent just such a memo to the head office. He had not received any reply to it. If he were to send another...he was scared.

For the next couple of days, Kedare saw the new man sitting with Kundaikar, who did not seem to be aware of his transfer.

On the third day, Kedare heard a sudden hubbub outside the office. All the employees ran out. There was a group of people gathered near the corner. The security guard came out. More people came out. A stone from the old building on the corner had come loose and fallen down on the head of a pedestrian. The man had died instantly.

Though the man's skull was crushed and his face was covered with blood, the employees from the office recognized him easily: it was Kundaikar, the accountant!

The work in the office didn't slow down because, although Kundaikar was gone, the new man had taken over; he was now the new accountant.

Kedare, however, was terrified. He couldn't understand how the same thing could happen again. He felt as though something beyond his understanding was developing around him, a dark cloud of something obstinate and violent, and it was spreading. It was taking over.

He decided to do something that was rarely done: he would make a call to the head office. The head office was far, and getting a long-distance phone line was difficult, but it was necessary. Perhaps by coincidence or by some unknown machination of events, two employees were dead after the two letters from the head office. He wanted to alert the head office not to send new employees to replace the old ones.

Chances of the call connecting were slim, but somehow he got through to the head office.

'I am the branch manager,' Kedare said, as if under duress.
'Yes?'
'Sir, two new employees were sent to fill vacancies *before* the

vacancies occurred. Why is this happening?'

'Are you questioning the decisions of the head office?'

'No, no, no, sir. Please don't misunderstand me. Why is this happening? I don't understand.'

'We are not obligated to explain our decisions....'

'Yes, sir.'

'Are the new employees working out well?'

'Yes, sir. But I am scared...please send someone to come and take a look. Sometimes I wonder if these new employees are human.'

'Mr Kedare, don't talk rot. Your fear is affecting your head. All right. I'll send someone to come and take a look.'

'Thank you, sir. I feel relieved now.'

∽

Indeed, as was promised, a man from the head office came to Kedare's office. Kedare welcomed him eagerly. This serious looking middle-aged man had silvery hair and a smile on his face. He showed Kedare an envelope.

'I've been sent by your head office,' he said.

'But...but...' Kedare's words were swept away by a tide of pain in his chest, and his dead body slid to the floor.

The man with the silver hair walked toward Kedare's chair, now empty.

Translated by Jayant Karve

A BLACK HOLE

JAYANT VISHNU NARLIKAR

'This crazy computer is really harassing me!' said Prakash as he stirred his coffee vigorously. 'I must have queried it at least fifty times in the last week, but it responds with the same reply!'

'What is the computer saying?' Sanjay asked him, feigning innocence. Sanjay, being a student of pure mathematics, looked down on the computer, like an artist looking down on a house painter.

'The computer is telling me that my postulations are all wrong. I thought that I'd hand over all the data received from the Prof to the computer, be done with it by the end of the day, and then proceed to the hike as planned. But the fact is—man proposes and computer disposes.'

Prakash had received some new data from the Yerkes Observatory regarding the planet Jupiter and he was expected to validate it.

'Maybe you got the calculations wrong.'

Sanjay expressed a regular mathematician's belief that physicists are weak in mathematics.

'You see, if at all there is any mistake in it, it is not mine, but that of Newton and Einstein. Even with your limited knowledge, you know that the planetary motion is decided as per their laws. Yet, the computer says that the new data does not fit into its laws. The Prof is sure that the data is accurate. So where is the hitch?'

'I think you should keep chanting the names of the dashavataras—the ten big incarnations—in astronomy for inspiration,' Sanjay mocked him. 'Say hail Newton, hail Halley, hail Herschel, hail Adams, hail Eddington....'

'Adams...Adams...you just said something marvellous! Wise words should always be welcomed even when uttered by a kid!' Prakash slapped him hard on the back and simply took off, leaving behind the half-finished coffee in the room.

Sanjay stood gaping after him. In this institute, the mathematicians had the monopoly on eccentricity, so he probably did not approve of Prakash's.

'Prof' meant Professor Ramesh Agrawal, a professor of astronomy who worked in the same institute. He had earned a worldwide reputation in celestial mechanics—a branch of theoretical astronomy that deals with the calculation of the motions of celestial objects such as planets. In the beginning of the twenty-first century there were very few scientists who were conducting research in this field, and whenever any incomprehensible problem arose, the scientist working in that area unfailingly sought his advice. That's why the new data regarding Jupiter had been sent to him.

Prakash Pawate was his favourite student. He had scanned the recent data and sent it to Prakash for a detailed examination. He did not need to tell him 'Do not meet me till you have reached a definite conclusion.'

A week had passed and there had been no reply from Prakash and the Prof began to wonder about it. Just as he was thinking of contacting Prakash, Prakash himself came rushing into his room.

'Calm down! Calm down! And speak only one sentence a minute so I can follow what you are saying,' he said rather mildly.

'Sir! Around 1846, Adams observed some irregularity in the trajectory of Uranus and with the help of logical speculation and maths discovered the new planet Neptune. I am sure that a new celestial body has arrived in the vicinity of Jupiter. The replies given by the computer definitely indicate that.'

The professor had firmly embedded in the minds of his students the principle—never make a statement without a proof. Yet, this statement of Prakash was so unexpected that he decided to enter the fray himself. And over the next ten days, after employing several astronomical methods to test the hypothesis, the two of them came to the conclusion that this statement was correct.

When the renowned scientific weekly *Nature* from London published the paper written by Agrawal and Pawate, it caused a sensation in the world of astronomy. The irregularity observed in the speed and trajectory of Jupiter was caused by a new celestial body that has arrived in its vicinity was what the paper said in essence.

They had temporarily named this body X and had published the details of its weight, velocity, and trajectory in relation to Jupiter. All kinds of speculation began about the nature of X. According to some, it was a new planet that may have been formed by the fusion of stray asteroids that were in orbit around Mars and Jupiter; while others thought it could be a comet that had entered the solar system from outside. Soon there began a competition amongst the astronomy observatories of the world to physically sight X.

But no one could observe anything!

Three years passed. Although X was not sighted, scientists were convinced of its presence, hence it was decided to send a spacecraft towards X. For this was a very important issue. The future of the age-old law of gravity depended upon it. Since Indian scientists had discovered X, the launch of the spacecraft would happen from Sriharikota base in India. Prakash Pawate had the honour of being the scientist-traveller in it and he had only one co-traveller, a Captain John Falkner from the USA. Falkner was a very skilled engineer. This was the tenth spacecraft of the World Space Organization launched towards Jupiter from India. It was named WIJ 10. After deciding a suitable date to launch the spacecraft, preparations began.

During these three years, Prakash Pawate and Sanjay Joshi had obtained their doctoral degrees and had continued in the institute as fellows. It had been a year since Sanjay had been married, but Prakash was still single. Their friendship had continued as before. Their chats and verbal duels continued as before. A week prior to the launch of the spacecraft, Prakash visited Sanjay's home on the occasion of the naming ceremony of Sanjay's newborn daughter. He had carried a teddy bear for her as a present.

'Vahini, what have you named your daughter?' he asked, advancing the teddy bear towards her.

'Anupama. Would you like to hold her?'

'Oh no! I'm fine at a distance. I am quite scared of holding a baby in my arms.'

'Okay, then tell us from a distance, whom does our daughter resemble?'

'She resembles both of you,' Prakash answered diplomatically. 'She is really cute. You'll see how boys will want to woo her in about eighteen, twenty years.'

'In that case, why don't you wait for another eighteen, twenty years? We will happily accept you as our son-in-law.' Anupama's mother was already on a mission to find her son-in-law. Prakash became awkward when the topic of his marriage—be it after eighteen days or be it eighteen years—was discussed. He hurriedly took his leave and almost escaped from there.

'You unnecessarily frightened that poor bachelor!' Sanjay reprimanded her.

WIJ 10 was launched as per plan. During its journey, it continued to communicate with many stations on earth. Communication remained normal and regular till WIJ 10 reached the atmosphere of Jupiter. Prakash sent the following message to the mission control room:

'I think we are now close to X, but we have not sighted anything yet. But we do see many bodies like the meteorites and asteroids accelerating rapidly towards X. Had X been a luminous body, I would have said that it reminds me of the description of the moth flying into the flame in the Bhagavad Gita....'

'Okay. Enough of your poetic ideas. What are you planning to do next?' the mission control room cut him short.

'Listen, when Oppenheimer witnessed the atomic explosion,

he thought of the Bhagavad Gita. What I see or don't see here is far more abnormal than the atomic explosion. If permission is granted, I wish to see it at a closer distance.'

'You have permission, but if you sense any danger, retract immediately.'

'Certainly, I'll take full care of WIJ 10.'

These were the last clear words from Prakash that were received by the mission control room.

John turned the spacecraft in the direction of X. Gradually it began to gain speed. 'Take it easy, John. We should not go too close,' Prakash warned John.

'I shut off the engine some time ago. Can't understand why the velocity is still increasing!' John said with a worried look at the speed counter; the needle inside was surging ahead.

Then it hit Prakash like lightning. He rushed to the computer inside the spacecraft, took out a programme from a drawer, and loaded it into the computer. This was a programme that had not been used till now. It was called Black Hole. He punched in the information regarding the rapid acceleration of the spacecraft and the computer answered within a few seconds. He read it and hurried towards John.

'John, John, the mystery of X is solved, but it is too late for us. X is a black hole and we are hurtling towards it.'

A black hole is a dense body formed by the extreme contraction of matter. It has such strong gravitation that even light does not pass through it. That was the reason why X could not be sighted from Earth or from WIJ 10, which was much closer to it. According to Einstein's theory of gravity, black holes can exist in the universe, but till now no black hole has been found by scientists. Very few scientists have put forth this idea and the majority has not supported it.

'So what next?' asked John, even though he almost certainly knew the answer.

'We are most probably heading straight into the mouth of X.

But there is a ray of hope. Our original trajectory is not towards its centre but around it. The computer cannot tell us accurately yet. It'll need more data on our orbit. I'll get it reactivated. Until then, you try and contact the mission control room.'

John tried to send a message, but it was futile. The mission control room was sending some messages, but they sounded garbled, as if they were spoken with extreme rapidity and were incomprehensible. Just then Prakash came back, his face was ashen.

'John, the computer has virtually predicted our death. It says we will approach X, complete a million rounds around it, and then perish by falling into it. What does the mission control room say?'

John explained the situation to him. Prakash realized that the contact with the mission control room was lost for good and they had to take their own decisions.

'There is still hope for us. We will be passing the unstable circular orbit that rings the black hole. I am going to exploit the indefinite nature of the path. If we can fire a rocket at the opportune moment, the unstable conditions created around it could possibly deviate our spacecraft away from X. If that happens, then well and good. Otherwise we say goodbye to the world. We must wear our space suits right away.'

'What is the need for the space suits?' John asked.

'As we approach X, the tidal power of its gravitational force will be increasingly felt by us, just as the Earth feels the tidal power of the gravitational force of the Moon, resulting in a high tide in the sea. Now imagine that as you are approaching X, your head is closer to X and the feet are distant. In that condition, your head will face a greater gravitational force compared to your feet. Can you imagine what could happen then?'

'My body will be stretched from head to toe?' John was beginning to think now.

'Right! And this pull will be so great that we will not be able to bear it. However, if we are in a space suit then our organs may not be affected as much,' Prakash explained.

'You keep the spacecraft in auto-pilot mode so that the computer can guide it back to Earth. If our luck holds, the people on the base will wake us up.'

After making all the preparations and before getting into the space suits, their eyes hovered over the galactic space around them. The constellations seemed brighter to them. Was that going to be their last view of the universe?

When WIJ 10 landed at the Sriharikota base, the technicians there were taken aback. Nobody remembered a spacecraft by that name. There was no announcement or notice regarding its arrival. They checked this uninvited, unknown spacecraft thoroughly, then brought out the two Kumbhakarnas sleeping inside, and straightaway sent them to the Maximum Security Medical Section (MSMS). These two people's names and faces were completely unknown to all.

'Sir, please take it easy. The doctor hasn't allowed you to move or think,' Sister Anupama from MSMS said to Prakash. 'Very soon, the chief scientist will be with you. Please tell him everything.'

'Let me at least call up a couple of my friends, just to let them know that I am back and well. This automatic watch of mine tells me that it has been three years since I left this place. They all must be worried about my whereabouts....'

'Three years?' exclaimed chief scientist Dr Ramaswamy, who was just entering the room. 'No spacecraft has left this base in the last three years. For the last five years we have been sending only unmanned space crafts.'

'That's impossible! Do check your records,' Prakash exclaimed in great surprise. 'As per my watch, John Falkner and I took off towards Jupiter three years and fifteen days ago. Ask John. Or contact Professor Ramesh Agrawal so that you can confirm this.'

'John is still not conscious, but Dr Agrawal, whom you mentioned, retired recently. Let me see if I can get his address,' Dr Ramaswamy told him.

Prakash felt dizzy. When he had begun the journey with WIJ 10, Prof had just turned forty. He asked quite apprehensively,

'What year is it now?'

In response, Dr Ramaswamy handed him the newspaper. Prakash almost fainted when he saw the date on the newspaper.

He had returned to Earth twenty years later.

Prakash took two weeks to regain his senses fully. Sister Anupama played a crucial role in his recovery. And it began to look like the confirmed bachelor was going to be bowled neck and crop. The doctors had warned Anupama not to refer to his space journey in any manner during their romantic conversations. She observed this to the letter.

After his recovery, Dr Ramaswamy brought Prakash and Dr Agrawal together. Dr Agrawal congratulated him on his safe return and also on having found a suitable girl for himself. After that he proceeded to explain to him the passage of time. This was the alchemic effect of the fierce gravitational force of the black hole. Prakash and John were asleep while they were in orbit around the black hole but only for a second as per the time scale of the black hole, for the gravitational force had frozen the lapse of time for them. During that time Earth had moved ahead by seventeen years. John and Prakash, still in their twenties, were living proof of Einstein's concept of relativity.

'Okay. Now, tell me, where is Sanjay? He will really be shocked to see me,' said Prakash smiling.

'Sanjay who?' asked Anupama.

'Sanjay Joshi. He is a close buddy of mine. We were both researchers at the same institute. We would often argue about.... Oh! What happened? Why are you crying?'

'He was my father. He and my mother...they both died in an aeroplane accident, leaving me an orphan...' Anupama explained amidst sobs.

Thus, Anupama's mother's matchmaking efforts did succeed. Thanks to the black hole.

Translated by Anil Zankar

RELATIONSHIPS

ASHA BAGE

It was 2.30 p.m. on a scorching summer afternoon when Bhaskar came home for lunch.

The shadows of the trees on the street seemed to have shrunk into themselves and the long strip of sunlight stretched unbroken.

Neena went out, closed the gate Bhaskar had left open, and came back into the house.

'You've left the scooter outside?'

'I've locked it.'

'I know. Are you going back immediately?'

'I'm thinking whether to go or not.'

Saying this, Bhaskar handed Neena the postcard he was holding in his hand. 'Darshan's wife died. Of burns,' he said.

The card slipped out of Neena's limp fingers before she could even look at it. 'Veena died? Of burns? How? Suddenly?'

'It doesn't say anything more. Just conveys the news,' Bhaskar snapped. Then he added contritely, 'It must not have occurred to them to give details. You need someone to advise, to offer support at a time like this, a family member or someone close...poor Mama, he's bedridden and helpless, good thing Mami isn't around.'

'I know. Is their Deepti even a year old yet? We should go and meet them, na?'

'Let's see.'

'I need to be here for the children, it's exam time and all... why don't you go?'

'How will I get leave?' Bhaskar sounded peeved. 'It's better that I take care of the children for a couple of days and you go.'

Neena didn't say anything. But while heating the food she thought, Darshan is his first cousin, his own mama's son. I am related only by marriage. Really speaking, he should go. Besides, in this searing heat, the crowded bus, the sweat, the stickiness... why go through all that!

Just as she placed the food on the table, Bhaskar turned to the phone.

'You're calling?'

'Let me speak to Darshan and see what he says. The postcard was dated the day before yesterday. No point rushing now. They must have finished everything that day only. I'll talk to him on the phone. We'll see about going later.'

Neena felt disturbed. Darshan's wife, there till yesterday, not there today. Bhaskar says they must have finished all the rites by now. Her pallu must have caught fire first. That's the beginning of the end...and then the hospital rounds, the treatment, the saline drips, the medication, the tension, and finally death.... All a ritual, a mere formality. We are here today, gone tomorrow. And yet we get so caught up with life in the interim! Such a big loss, Darshan's wife dying, and here we are, looking for escape routes.

As he started mixing the rice on his plate, Bhaskar grumbled, 'Why do you heat everything up even when it's so hot?' Neena said nothing. Feeling a little embarrassed, Bhaskar tried to make conversation. 'The worst thing is their daughter is so little, just over a year old.'

'I know it was almost exactly a year ago that we had gone for her naming ceremony. Our gift for the baby was the prettiest. Everyone was full of praise. Veena and Darshan had together chosen the turquoise blue sari for me. I haven't even opened its folds yet.'

Neena was startled by this train of thought. Poor Veena, died so horribly, of burns, and here we are only talking of Darshan, or the child. And of course ourselves. Why aren't we even slightly concerned for Veena? Not even a thought for her. What must have gone through her mind when she was on fire? Why are we not thinking about that?

When giving me the news, Bhaskar had said: Darshan's wife died. Was that all she was to everyone? Die one must, but when alive, is one so insignificant? Does one's existence mean so little? What does one leave behind of oneself?

Bhaskar finished his lunch. Neena was still squishing the rice in front of her. Bhaskar couldn't figure out if she was offhand because of his impatience or because of the news. As he walked towards the washbasin he stopped by her chair. 'Sorry I was so harsh. Are you angry? Somehow this news has really upset me, ga.'

Neena's eyes filled with tears. Was it because of Bhaskar's remorse or the emotions that had been held back, left unexpressed earlier? Bhaskar became more conciliatory. 'I think we should both go. The children can be left for a couple of days. We can ask Gita bai to stay with them. What do you say?'

Neena nodded.

As Bhaskar was leaving for office, Neena said, 'You were going to call, na?'

'I'll do it from there,' he replied. 'In the meantime, if Darshan calls, you speak to him.'

'Oh no, no, I won't have the courage to speak to him!'

'Well, then give him my number,' Bhaskar said and left.

Neena went into the house to wait for the maid who came to clean the dishes, and the children who had gone for their class.

Bhaskar, who never came home before 7.30 or 8 p.m., was back in an hour and a half.

'What's this?' Neena asked him in surprise.

'You were alone at home, I too was restless in the office, so I came back.' After a long pause, he said, 'Neena, will you come for a movie?'

'Movie?' Neena was astonished.

'Yes, I want to get over this. Need a change…staying home will not do it.'

'How will it look?' she wanted to ask. But refrained. Bhaskar was getting ready to go out.

As he was washing his face, he casually remarked, 'I got through.'

'Oh you did? Who did you speak to?'

'Darshan himself.'

'Poor man. What did he say?'

'What can he say!'

'Have they all got a hold of themselves somewhat?'

'Yes, they have. Life doesn't ever come to a standstill, ga. And you know what, Neena...Darshan had just got a promotion! He was to leave for Bangalore. His friends were hosting a farewell party for him. She was wearing a nylon sari. She lit the stove, since the gas had finished. By the time Darshan reached her she had 90 per cent burns.' Bhaskar was saying all this matter-of-factly, as if it was just an impersonal narration.

Neena could not enjoy the film. It was a useless movie anyway.

When they came home, Babu kaka's son Sanjeev was waiting for them with pedhas.

'Where had you gone, ga? I've been waiting for so long to tell you...a qualified doctor now, with a gold medal in surgery...I came to see you...and you people had just disappeared.'

Sanjeev offered them the sweets, then bowed down to touch Neena and Bhaskar's feet. Neena suddenly felt lighter, freer. The tension caused by the news of Veena's death seemed to have eased a little. Wholeheartedly she congratulated Sanjeev. 'You are the first doctor in our family, Sanjeev! Babu kaka should have been here today. What all he went through to educate you....'

Again Neena's eyes brimmed over. Just like a little while ago. But these tears had nothing to do with the earlier emotion.

She carried on an animated conversation with Sanjeev—his future plans, travel abroad for specialization...advice...don't take on the yoke of a job so soon, private practice is much better, but not immediately...as long as you can study, do it...but come back to practice in your own town. That was Babu kaka's wish. The place where you were born, where you grew up, that place must benefit from your knowledge, he would say... These and many other similar topics Bhaskar, Sanjeev, and Neena talked about.

Neena spoke from her heart and it made her feel so much better. She was assured that at that moment, one end of this chain of events was firmly in her hands. She had full control over it. The knowledge lifted her spirit. Thoughts of Veena's unexpected and unfortunate death had blown away like dry dead leaves once their fresh greenness fades away.

When she switched off the light and got into bed, Bhaskar was waiting for her. Taking her hand, he said hoarsely, 'Why so late, Neena?'

The next morning when Gita bai came in to cook as usual, Neena said to her casually, 'His mama's son's wife got burnt and died. We need to go. You will keep an eye on the children?'

'Of course I will.'

'You will have to sleep the night here, too.'

'Not a problem. I have to lay my tired bones somewhere... ekat jeev sadashiv...a solitary soul, God's soul.... When are you going?'

'Haven't decided yet.' Neena told her the whole story. Actually she had been wanting to unburden herself to someone all this while.

'Just see this, Bai,' Gita bai remarked disapprovingly. 'You women work by the fire wearing those nylon-phylon saris...and see what happened. Accidents don't come with warnings, do they?'

Once she finished the cooking in Neena's house, Gita bai went to make chapatis in a couple of other homes.

Neena tidied up the house and went into the bathroom. She was going to wash her hair. She had barely rubbed the shikakai powder into her scalp when the phone rang. The children were at school, Bhaskar at work. Who would pick up the phone? Neena allowed it to ring. After several rings it stopped. Then it started ringing again. Neena decided to ignore it. She concentrated on her bath. She had started to wash the shikakai off when the doorbell rang. It was followed by a rattling of the door latch.

Neena threw a sari around herself and walked to the door. Opening it slightly, she asked, 'Who is it?'

'Me, Aruna, Pathak.'

'What's it, ga?'

'Open the door na.'

'Aga, I am having a bath. Tell me what it is.'

'Your Gita bai got severe chest pain while making chapatis in our house.'

'Okay, come in and sit. I'll be back in a minute.'

Neena poured the entire bucket of water on herself, somehow wrapped her sari around her, and came into the outer room.

'What happened, ga?' she asked.

'Severe chest pain. While making chapatis.'

'Aga, but then the doctor....'

'We took her in a rickshaw to Dr Khandeshwar...he suspected a heart attack...admit her in the government hospital, he advised.'

'So did you?'

'That's the problem, na! Gita bai refuses to budge without you. Take me to the bangala, she kept saying. Mumbling incoherently about dying only in your house. To make her see sense is beyond us now. That's why I called you from the doctor's clinic. No one answered. So I came myself. You'll come na?'

Neena's hair was still dripping. Her hastily wrapped sari too was wet. 'I'll get ready, you wait,' she said to Aruna and went inside.

As they were leaving the house, Neena remembered that the children would be home soon. Where could she leave the house key? But there was no time to worry about it.

'Where is Gita bai now?' she asked Aruna.

'Must still be at Dr Khandeshwar's clinic. Couldn't have gone to the hospital. She was so adamant. Let's go to the clinic itself. Your cooking's done?'

'Gita bai finished doing it before going to your place, na.'

'The lump of chapati dough is lying as it is in our house. Now my mother will have to make them. Why do these people take on so many jobs if they cannot cope?'

'Gita bai has become old now, tired too....'

'That's what I'm saying. She keeps falling ill. So much inconvenience it causes us! We are having a function in our house day after tomorrow. We planned our list because we were depending on her, and now....'

Neena immediately felt a sense of relief. The cooking in her house, at least, was done!

'Actually we too were to go out. My husband's cousin lost his wife...got burnt...we were depending on Gita bai to be with the children...and this happens. How to go now? If we don't it will look bad...such a mess....'

'How did she get burned?'

Neena told her the whole story, in great detail, right from the promotion, the farewell party, the relocation to Bangalore. As she spoke she felt much of the tension drain out.

They reached Dr Khandeshwar's clinic. On seeing Neena, the doctor came forward and said, 'I forcibly sent that woman to the government hospital. She kept insisting that she only wanted to go to your house. Finally, I lost my temper. These stupid people will die of their foolishness eventually.'

'What exactly is the problem?'

'We'll need an ECG to say for sure. May have to take her to Nagpur even.'

'She has no one, who will take her to Nagpur?'

'That is not our problem. If she has to go, she has to. You mean she has absolutely no one of her own?'

'No one except me. She has been working in our place for many years now. One of our family....'

'Then can't one of you....'

'Oh no, that's not possible. Just can't get away at this time.'

Neena paused and then said, cautiously, 'It's not a question of money. If it comes to that, can you arrange to send her to Nagpur from the government hospital in an ambulance? What do they do with destitutes like her? Will you please speak to Dr Gyanchandani, Doctor?'

'Don't worry, I understand your difficulties,' said Dr Khandeshwar in English.

When Neena reached the government hospital she found Gita bai still short of breath and suffering from spasms of chest pain. Yet as soon as she saw Neena, she smiled.

With tears in her eyes, she gripped Neena's hand and said, 'Bai, I am going to die. I will not survive this.'

There was no sadness in her words. Only resignation, acceptance. Of death.

'I have done all the cooking. Only the snacks had to be made. Thought I would do them after finishing work at the Pathak's house.' Another wave of pain came over her.

'Gita bai, just lie there quietly, don't worry about the house,' Neena told her.

At that moment, Gita bai remembered that it was Monday, Neena's day of fasting.

'Baisaheb, the children will come home for lunch...it will be late....'

'Let it be. They'll serve themselves. It's not a big thing if they do. Don't talk anymore, Gita bai....'

After a moment Gita bai spoke again, 'Bai, I don't remember if I switched off the gas....'

'Gita bai....'

'I haven't even boiled the potatoes...the pain had started that time itself....'

Neena was utterly baffled. Here was this woman whose journey was coming to an end, but she hadn't a thought about herself. She'd spent her entire life in this town; marriage, husband, the eleven children who did not survive...all that would end here. At one time her husband was a diwanji, a manager. They had a comfortable life. Her own brother cheated them of their savings, leaving her with a rolling pin in her hand, to roll out chapatis. She talked about it to Neena sometimes. What in the course of her life had been lost? What retrieved, what saved? Did she remember any of it? Think about it? Shouldn't memories of the ups and downs in her life's journey hold her back at this moment? How has she become so detached from her own life? And totally involved in ours?

When she had asked the doctor what they do with destitutes like her, he had said, 'I understand your difficulties'. What did he mean?

Just then Dr Gyanchandani arrived and Neena came back to the present.

'Who is with this woman?'

'Me, tell me whatever it is,' Neena stammered.

'You are Mrs Dighe?'

'Um, yes.'

'I've had a word with Dr Khandeshwar. The ECG report is favourable. You need not worry. We can treat her here. But complete rest is essential,' the doctor said, interspersing his Marathi with English words.

Neena sighed in relief. The responsibility of taking her to Nagpur was avoided.

'Right now we have no beds in the general ward. Besides she will not get any rest there, so a special ward....'

'That's all right, I will pay,' Neena said spontaneously. Then she asked, 'For how long will she have to be there?'

'That depends....'

Immediately Neena's calculating mind replied, 'In that case as soon as the general ward....'

'Okay.'

'But whatever medicines she may need, please arrange for them. Don't go short on that.' As she was uttering these words a thought crept into Neena's head...Gita bai certainly has the right to expect this much from us.

When Neena got home, it was 2.30 p.m. and she was exhausted. Bhaskar was having lunch. He was furious that she had not bothered to inform him. 'You could have made a call to the office...or left a word with the watchman...only when the children came to the office sweating and tired I got to know.... What is this Gita bai to you anyway?'

Neena wondered whether she should tell him it hadn't occurred to her. Circumstances were such. But then why bother to tell him about the path she had travelled at that moment? Would he understand? Every emotion a person feels is separate from another. Unrelated. Unattached. Like destitutes.

She had her lunch in silence after Bhaskar finished eating. She didn't have the energy to make the fasting food for herself. The day was half gone anyway.

After a while, she went into her room and untied the hastily knotted wet hair and looked into the mirror. Bits of the shikakai still clung to it, hadn't been washed off completely. To think I went out in this messy state, Neena thought to herself.

And suddenly she burst out laughing. She felt light.

No one belongs to anyone. No one has ownership of anything. Even the joys and sorrows we believe are exclusively ours are not. Life goes on and without our being aware of it, someone binds us to themselves. In a bond we cannot deny. Nor break. Just resign ourselves and accept it. How strange life is!

The comb was stuck in her hair as Neena sat still in front of the mirror. Just then Bhaskar came in and said to her, 'If Gita bai is not there, how can we go to see Darshan?'

Neena was quick to retort, 'Look here. If we have decided to go, we will. With the children or without them. They are not kids anymore. Why depend on this or that for every little thing? First make up your mind if you want to go at all.'

Bhaskar stared at Neena, puzzled by her firm, impatient tone.

He couldn't understand her.

Unaware that she had said something beyond Bhaskar's comprehension, Neena calmly ran the comb through her hair.

Translated by Keerti Ramachandra

CONTINUITY

SHYAM MANOHAR

ONE:

A cold, cold breeze. I couldn't see a thing. Neither on the road, nor in the air between the road and the sky. No matter how hard I stared. If I poked my head out of the window, craned my neck, and looked up, I would see the shining stars. I could see the sky in their dim light, but I couldn't make out its colour. One would say 'blue', remembering the afternoon sky. But poking my head out of the window and twisting my neck was quite a task! Those sitting by me wouldn't let me do it. The driver would momentarily forget the situation and shout at me. On top of that, outside the window there was a cold, cold breeze. Moral of the story—I could either see the darkness that filled the air between the road and the sky, or nothing at all. The vehicle was racing ahead. Further ahead were its headlights. Like glaring, wide open eyes, they spewed straight beams of light that ran on the road ahead. The black tar road glistened like dark skin. It felt like when the lights are suddenly switched on when one is sleeping without clothes, naked. I would feel embarrassed looking at it. That is why I was looking down and sat with my shoulders hunched. My uncle had wrapped his arm around my shoulders—from this one to that. It felt heavy but assuring.

I tried sniffing hard to smell the odour of my mother's corpse from beyond the partition. If I did manage to catch a whiff, I tried to recollect what it was.

They built the funeral pyre as if they were building a sculpture.

When the pyre was lit, light and warmth filled the air as if the sun had risen.

I couldn't decide which thought to latch on to—whether I was free from being watched, or I would be watched by everybody all the time and I would have nobody to hide behind. But I grew petrified in that sunrise. My mouth dried up.

TWO:

I came to live with my uncle. Uncle's wife, my aunt, despised my mother after my father died. Uncle would drop by our place a couple of times a month. He would unfailingly visit at Diwali and give mother a gift of fifty rupees. I used to visit Uncle and Auntie at festivals. My mother never came. She used to say to Uncle, 'Come here whenever you feel like seeing me. She doesn't like it when I come there. Finds it burdensome. Whenever you come here, this house will become my maternal home.' Uncle would listen quietly. And do as he was told. This formulaic behaviour that he had adopted angered me. I felt that he and Auntie were in cahoots and were cheating my mother.

After I finished school and got a job in the postal services, I vented my anger at Uncle. 'You don't like it when my mother goes out to work. Then what are we supposed to do? Should she work for you for free and silently eat her heart out? What does society provide for widows?' I recklessly lambasted him.

My enthusiasm didn't last long. Uncle turned out to be prudent and tactful. He didn't say a word then. Stayed quiet. Till the heat of my anger subsided.

I can't fathom their manner of expressing love. Their love, anger, hatred never boils over like mine does. But he rushed to me when mother died. In fact, they took me to live with them. Auntie serves me hot rice. As if I were her own child. Is this prudence or compassion?

THREE:

I left a little early from the post office. Damle was with me. He and I ate hot vada and had tea at the restaurant opposite. He asked, 'Pande, want to catch a movie?'

'Yes,' I said and went with him. It was an English film set in a jungle. Handsome, muscular men and delicate women. Lions and cheetahs charging, their deafening roars almost tearing the screen. Humungous, frothy waterfalls and hundreds of kisses on their banks. Invisible waves of odours emanating from the audience.

'Did you enjoy it?, Damle asked me as our tongues began to turn red with the betel leaves we had eaten after the film.

'I forgot everything for a while. I liked the change.'

'It was a change for me too. My wife is visiting her parents. I saw these scantily dressed women on screen. This much is permitted in my brand of morality. I too liked the change.'

I ate at his place from his tiffin. 'Mangala isn't there. The house seems empty without her. I feel like eating since you're giving me company. Otherwise, I wouldn't have touched the food,' he said as he ate. I just nodded. Why unnecessarily point out the contradictions in his behaviour?

I wanted to ask him, 'Can a wife be a substitute for a mother?', but I couldn't.

It was eleven o'clock when I reached home. My plate was set on the table. Uncle and Auntie were waiting for me.

'Had you been to watch a movie?'

'Yes'

'Which one?'

I told the name.

'Great! A jungle film. It's fun. Dense jungles. Tigers and lions. Their roars. To live there. There's a thrill in it. A tiger charges at you, but when you escape you realize the true happiness in living.' Uncle spoke as if he had experienced that life. Auntie was fiddling with the rice on her plate. He looked at her and asked, 'Should we watch it this Sunday? Bhau will come with us again.' Bhau meant me.

I didn't tell them that I had already eaten. I kept eating at an unhurried pace till they finished dinner.

Love thus seeped through the skin. Deep into the flesh and blood!

I felt like mumbling, 'I misunderstood you, Uncle.'

Or, blessed be that skin that let this love seep deep into the flesh and blood!

FOUR:

Damle's wife must have returned from her parents' place, and he might no longer need to watch the barely blossomed scantily dressed women on screen. Or, perhaps, he and his wife will watch the jungle film like Uncle and Auntie did one Sunday.

The lion roared and attacked the hero. The hero fought off the lion for barely a few seconds in the two-and-a-half-hour film. But it felt like a long battle. Uncle was so engrossed. 'Look, the hero's neck is more muscular than the lion's neck.' He was explaining the film to Auntie. Once in a while he would explain a scene to me.

We returned home at one o'clock that night. Uncle was still under the spell of the film. He kept recounting scenes. The hero is feeding grapes to the heroine. He holds the purple-black grapes slightly above her face. Naturally, she looks up. She opens her mouth a little. Her blue eyes are parallel to the purple-black grapes. Uncle enacted this scene. Instead of grapes, he held his hand slightly above Auntie's face and Auntie stared unflinchingly at that hand.

Auntie, where did you learn to look like that? In how many different ways can the both of you behave? Do I possess those buttons too? Will these shades emerge from me as well?

In that post-midnight hour, I couldn't fall asleep. Uncle and Auntie must have been fast asleep in the downstairs room.

I, however, was wide awake, staring out of the open square that was the window! I don't know how long after, but I saw the sky fill up with dark clouds. Pitch black. Sudden bursts of lightning like a knock on a closed door at midnight! I stood still! Supported by the light in the room. Looking out into the darkness. Suddenly the electricity went out. The darkness that was outside entered my room. I eased up, opened my arms. In a very hoarse, base voice I said, 'I wholeheartedly welcome you, O Darkness.'

Then rain came crashing down like intense pain.

In the morning, the eastern sky lit up like a funeral pyre. In it I probably understood—Auntie's ill-will towards mother, how she looked at Uncle; and children, Damle with his wife, and Damle pressing down on his thighs and whistling while watching the film—and since that moment I kept feeling as if I were unravelling!

Or that everybody had turned approver!

FIVE:

After that, I once had a desire to behave irresponsibly, but I didn't know how. Actually, I couldn't do it. I couldn't figure out where to begin. That is the nature of a job in postal services. In our society a job is considered to be terribly important. Also, if you have finished school and worked in the postal services or the revenue department or the bank for a couple of years, it's not easy to leave your job. If you submit your resignation, your boss says, 'Mr Pande, you know how difficult it is to get a job these days! Decisions taken unthinkingly in a moment of weakness come back to haunt you later in life. I think you need to calm your mind. I will not accept your resignation today. Are you not feeling well?' He saw me standing and offered me a chair. There was a huge glass-topped table between him and me. He rested his elbows on it and started speaking to me. 'Take a week off, Mr Pande, if you aren't feeling well.'

I thought the huge table would protect me! That's how it is.

Somebody feels affection for you, somebody feels love, somebody feels anger, somebody feels hatred, somebody feels pity, somebody feels compassion, somebody feels concern. Whether they know you or not, somebody is always feeling something. Then what you believe in the beginning gets tainted. Honestly, while reliving an old memory, I've even felt like taking revenge on Auntie. But recently, when I heard the schoolteacher next door speak ill of Auntie, I argued with her quite aggressively.

All in all, I've never been able to act either irresponsibly or responsibly. After that, I would constantly check what others felt about me or one another. Thus, my time would pass well.

SIX:

In such impersonal times, I became acutely aware that Uncle and Auntie were childless. Very rarely have I had that kind of awareness and one that was so true!

My life fell into a standard routine. I started spending all my spare time after my work hours with Uncle and Auntie. At the pristine twilight hour, I would read out the Ramayana and Mahabharata to Auntie, and on a dark night I would discuss news items from the papers with Uncle. We were able to easily resolve the issues of capitalists, communists, Hindus, and Pakistanis.

SEVEN:

Sometimes I would be at the window, selling stamps in the post office. One by one people would move forward in a long queue. They would buy postcards, envelopes, stamps, whatever they liked. I never said a word to them. The power to take simple pleasure in being able to conduct a slow, straightforward transaction—well, should I call it creditable to me?

'Well, Mr Pande, meet my friend Dr Shankaran,' Natu introduced me to a tall, lanky, dusky man. At that time, the queue in front of the window had emptied as if it had been poured away.

Natu is a clerk in my office.

'Glad to meet you,' I shook hands with Dr Shankaran. (One ought to be able to interact with anybody easily.) Natu said, 'This is my childhood friend. He has returned from the USA after becoming a doctor. As a child he used to be called Shankrya. He can help anybody with a vagina bear a child with the help of medicines alone. He has done research on it and received a doctorate in medicine.' And Natu laughed uproariously.

I just couldn't understand what I had done to deserve this. Why do people speak like that?

I was very upset for two days. I couldn't read out the Ramayana properly that evening. And I kept feeling as if I were snubbing Uncle.

The next week I happened to meet Dr Shankaran in the street. If I have to speak to him, I must start the interaction afresh. I must discard the previous incident like one tears off and throws away an erroneously written paper from a notebook.

'Hello, Mr Pande, I am very sorry,' Dr Shakanaran said. 'We were introduced the other day, but you seemed to have been hurt by it. I am Maharashtrian. My name is Shankar Walunjkar. And even I don't call myself Shankaran. It is not as if I am a great upholder of the truth. It is just that I am no longer interested in the idea that changing names or adding letters to a name brings prestige. Everything else that Natu said is the truth. He used extremely indecent language, though. In short, I am a gynaecologist....'

'I respect my aunt. I also respect sex,' I warned him.

EIGHT:

One week sped by. It was my mother's death anniversary. I saw the date on the calendar.

NINE:

Natu met me in the street. I was ambling along. He came up from behind me and put his hand on my shoulder. I looked at him and flung his hand off my shoulder. He said, 'I met Dr Shankaran after ages. You and he don't like it when I call him Shankaran. I know, but I am still going to call him that. He looks like a south Indian. I like to address every person as he appears.' I didn't say anything. I just listened. He carried on. 'So, he told me a lot about you. He knows psychoanalysis. Why don't you do this? What is your auntie's age? I think it is still possible. Take her to Dr Shankaran. He'll get a client and your auntie will.... And you too must think of getting married now...it'll be good fun....' I didn't let him finish. Taking advantage of the darkness on the road, I boxed him hard. He groaned. 'I respect sex...' I warned him, even in that condition, and returned home like a blameless person.

Auntie's hair was greying. Uncle was still strong. Uncle and Auntie truly ought to have a child. My father died. Then, last year, my mother died. I am their son, the one that works in the postal services as well as the one that boxes Natu, all of it. Uncle and Auntie ought to have their own son or their own daughter. Fair and chubby. Or dark and lean. Or too fair and too thin. He may or may not get an education. He may become a big man when he grows up or he may work in the postal services or the revenue department or as a clerk in a bank. Or he may become a general manager. Or a collector. Or a governor. He will become something. And he will love, fight, get angry, become furious, feel ashamed, surrender, become vain, be happy, give respect, show disdain, feel depressed, feel exhilarated, have expectations. He will want something. He will receive something. Satisfaction or disappointment.

When we are alone together, I will whisper in his or her ears—be sadness when you feel sad, be fury when you feel furious, be happiness when you feel happy, be envy when you feel envious, be love when you feel loving. Be.

Translated by Rupali Bhave

AND THEN IT POURED[*]
GAURI DESHPANDE

Ammi is my mother, not by birth, my stepmother. But you shouldn't conclude that this is a typical story of a stepmother abusing her stepdaughter. Forget about raising her voice at me, Ammi rarely even lifted her gaze to meet anyone's eyes. As for her raising her hand to spank me, even those who knew her couldn't have imagined anything like it in their wildest dreams, let alone she herself. If anyone was abused at all, it was her by me. She was so meek that she almost invited such exploitation. But if you think I will follow in the footsteps of many revered gurus and teachers and hang the story of a virtuous mother around your neck, then you are certainly wrong. This is Ammi's story, and in my view, remarkable enough as is. But since it is I who will tell the story, of course, I will bend it to my own will here. And since I am not at all virtuous or exemplary, if there is even the slightest moral to this tale, then attribute it to your own love of literary writing.

Anyway, when Appa married Ammi, I must have been thirteen or fourteen years old. I never felt the need for a mother as a kid. In fact, in my class, another girl and I were the 'poor girls without mothers'. The other girl would start crying uncontrollably

---

[*]The Marathi title 'Paus Ala Motha' is a line from the popular children's rhyme, 'Ye re ye re pausa/ Tula deto paisa/ Paisa jhala khota/ Paus ala motha (rain, rain please do come/ I will give you a paisa/ the paisa turned out fake/ and then it poured).'

whenever anyone started singing 'Aai Mhanoni Koni'* (and since that poem was in the school textbooks, such occasions arose frequently). I would always be amazed at that. Not wanting to be mocked by the other girls, I also pretended to cry at those times. But later, when such dramatic situations started happening three or four times a year, I gave up the pretence of weeping. But people pitied me despite that. Appa had a travelling job and he earned a lot of money from it. At home we always had a throng of servants and maids, secretaries, cooks, and chauffeurs. I didn't have the time to feel lonely or neglected. Why Appa should get married thirteen or fourteen years after his first wife passed away, at the age of forty, that I can understand very easily. But I never figured out why the twenty-year-old good-looking woman married him, not until she died. One day Appa returned from his trip to Mangalore with Ammi in tow. A simple everyday saree, nothing else on her except the mangalsutra around her neck, smudged kunku on her forehead the size of a ten paisa coin, scrawny and pale presence, and wisdom beyond her years on her face.

In his usual manner, Appa said, 'This is Amala, my wife. And this is Savitri, my daughter. This, the house. Savi will explain all. It's your house.' And with noisy shoes, he started walking towards the office room. I didn't really mind any of this. Children are generally self-absorbed. I said to myself, *So she is Appa's wife, what's it to me? There are so many people in the house, what's one more.* I said, 'I want to go to my friend's house,' and escaped from there. I don't know what Ammi did after that.

She did not join us when the two of us sat down to have dinner. As usual, Appa was reading some documents, and I, a comic book. As I turned a page, I asked, 'How should I address her?'

---

*'Aai Mhanoni Koni' is a famous Marathi poem by the poet Yashwant. This was also featured in an equally famous film, *Shyamchi Aai* (1953). It is seen as a tear-jerking, sentimental poem about the loss of a mother.

Appa said, 'Hmmm.'
I asked again, upon which, he frowned and asked, 'Who?'
'Your wife?'
'Her relatives called her Ammi.'
I said, 'Um-hmm.'

After dinner, each one of us retired to our own room. The next day at chai time during breakfast, I saw Ammi again. She occupied herself with my schoolbooks and asked me some superficial questions about school. I told her, 'Feel free to take any book to read if you like.'

She looked down and said haltingly, 'I cannot read or write.'

I found this extremely strange. Until then, I hadn't met anyone who could not read or write. I think that was the first time I expressed some interest in someone else. I asked, 'What will you do the entire day?'

'I will manage,' she said and changed the subject. But what exactly she would do the whole day, I never found out. After all, she had entered a well-established home as the mother of an adolescent girl. She had hardly any work to do. Now when I think back, I don't remember her spending time talking to the servants nor do I remember seeing her walking in the garden. If I returned home unexpectedly, I would find her lying on the divan in the balcony upstairs, watching the world go back and forth on the street. The house was run impeccably as always, and within it, we behaved as before, trying as much as possible not to get entangled in each other's life. These were the last years of my school life. Visiting girlfriends, movies, theatre…it went on endlessly. I had to return home by six, other than that Appa had not imposed any other rule on me. Once he had laid down the rule, he assumed that I returned home on time. And at least until then it had not occurred to me that I needed to break this rule either. But sometimes because I was lost in chatting with friends, or because there were play rehearsals and one could not just get up and walk away in the middle of it, if it turned out six o'clock became six-thirty or seven, there was no reason for him to know about it. So, one day, as I returned carefree at six-thirty and climbed the stairwell outside and stepped into the living room, I unexpectedly faced the early arrival of Appa.

'You are late.'

'Yes, but....'

'Starting tomorrow, every day I want a phone call to my office informing me that you have returned home straight after school.'

'But Appa, the drama rehearsal....'

'No excuses.'

'Am I a child to be treated like....'

'Savitri, you cannot speak to me in that tone!'

'Then you shouldn't in that tone either....'

'Shut your mouth! Get out!'

'You say get out? I refuse to listen to you. If you yell at me like this, I will yell back ten times louder. To be utterly stifled in this manner, and then handed such an overbearing judgement, have I committed burglary or murder? Do I tell you what to do when....'

A sharply delivered slap to the face cut out the rest of the statement. Before Appa's other hand could slap my other cheek, someone dragged me to my room and locked the door on the other side. Outside, Appa's voice was shaking in anger.

'Amala, you should not interfere here. She is a rude and feckless brat and she must be disciplined and brought into line.'

Ammi's tone was subdued and fearful.

'You slap your daughter, a fifteen-year-old girl who has been raised by you, in front of the servants! Really? Even if she has abandoned all shame, surely you aren't juvenile like her.'

Ammi was actually talking back to him and in that tone! My anger had long since melted in the surprise of it all. I silently put my ear to the door. But there was some murmuring outside and then both of them went away. The next day, the door was unlocked, and at breakfast Appa tried to pretend as if nothing had happened. While leaving, he shoved his chair back and said to me, 'Don't you forget the rule—come home straight after school.'

I bit my tongue.

I was home at four-thirty every day. Time to chit-chat with Ammi. There was an age difference of a mere six or seven years between us. She must have felt much closer to me than to Appa. But in that forced friendship of some six months to a year, she never said a word about herself, something I realized only many years later. Mostly she sat on my bed mending clothes, and I used to read out things to her, while reading something myself, or doing schoolwork, or browsing through a magazine as I lay on my back on the carpet. If he returned home early, Appa used to go straight to his room, and she wouldn't bother to go to his room to serve him tea or snacks either. Wasn't there the butler or the servant-boy? Once the heat of the sun had clearly diminished, we used to take walks in the garden around the house. Ammi used to make long garlands of rubber plant flowers and gulbakshi flowers and wrap them around the trees. Her first reaction would be to laugh at anything I told her. She was amazed by everything. Once I told her that a girl in my class was named 'Maharukh'. That was the first time, I think, that she could not control her peals of laughter even in front of Appa. After that, for many days, I just had to say the word 'Maharukh' and Ammi would start laughing helplessly. In my case, she would praise every little thing I did, that even though I was no longer a child I wore frocks, that I had a boyish haircut, that I spoke English fluently, that I acted in plays, that I swam, that I played, nothing was left unappreciated. Frequently, I would ask her in frustration, 'You didn't live on the moon or some other planet before this, did you? How are you so rustic?' Then she would shut right up. Just as he did with others, Appa was as distant and curt with her as well. He never called out to her, never told her anything, at least not in my presence, except for that one incident outside my closed door. In fact, given the minimal talk happening in our home, she would have felt as if she were in a school for the deaf-mute if I hadn't been there. Also, Appa had gathered around him servants who spoke as little as he did, and my friends never visited me at home. Before Ammi joined us, even if someone did come over, because of the deathly silence pervading the home, there was little possibility that they would ever return. I did not mind this because I was used to it from the beginning. On the contrary, upon listening to the commotion in others' houses I used to prefer my own home.

That year in June I applied to go to college and the frail relations between Ammi and I descended into less than nothing. New friends, new issues, conferences, and meetings, debating and drama societies, picnics, play, all of this meant that I was hardly at home anymore. That I came home to eat lunch was itself a feat. Because of this and many other reasons, it was a constant battle between Appa and I. It was he who had brought me up so I was equally reckless, scornful, and brash. I did not let a single accusation from anyone pass me by, nor did I hesitate to say anything for fear of how it would be taken. Ammi was at her wits' end. Appa never again raised his hand to hit me, but that was more than compensated for by his words. Appa yelled more at me in those four years of college than he had ever spoken to me at all in his entire life. I used to bring my friends home when he was not around. And very pointedly I would introduce Ammi to them, 'This is my stepmother.' How strange and provincial she was, that was the topic of our conversation. This easily lasted all of four years. I found the 'weird' relationship between Ammi-Appa very useful to show how I had led a different life from that of others. Later, when I studied Psychology, I would discuss seriously with my gang of friends how Appa must have had a complex because he married such an extremely young girl when he was so much older himself, or how Ammi must have had a father-fixation. Now, I regard a man in his fifties as mature, in his prime, etc., but as a twenty-year-old, I saw a man of forty-five as being almost in the jaws of death. Unless he suffered from some kind of a complex, why would he enter the world of married life that is rightfully the space only for the young? That was the logic. And that he should constantly quarrel with me, or behave churlishly, that seemed quite significant.

I had applied to all kinds of educational institutions in my last year of college. I was successful and got admission in an institution in Mumbai to continue to study further. Of course, that meant facing another quarrel. 'I am not saying you shouldn't study further, but why must you leave home and go to Mumbai for that?'

My intention in studying further, at that time at least, was precisely in order to leave home, hence there was no sense to this argument. I decided I would go for the win in this battle and I reached for the heart of the matter.

'But, Appa, you are not going to provide for me my entire life. Once I become a specialist in this topic, high-paying jobs will be aplenty. Then you need not worry about me at all.'

'But, Savitri, it isn't like they are piling the wood on my funeral pyre just yet.'

'But don't they say nowadays that the years between forty-five and fifty-five are the most dangerous?'

Ammi said under her breath, 'Savitri!'

Appa was a little uneasy. But he persisted and asked, 'Don't you want to get married at all? You have so many friends who are boys, anyone special among them?'

I was slack-jawed and stared in disbelief. He too must have felt awkward, but still he waited for a response. I laughed with derision and tossed the standard reply at him, 'I don't want to get married at all.'

'It is good to get such things done in time, Savi.'

His sweet tone only enraged me.

'What did you do in time for me? John-butler was with

me when I got braces for my teeth. Information about periods and so on I got from the family doctor, your steno went to buy bras for me. I got the "facts of life" from the stealthily-read *Samajswasthya*, while hiding it inside my desk, and *Time* magazine informed me about the pill. Where was there any connection between your life and mine?'

Performing the typical father's role, Appa jumped into my trap:

'Savitri!' he thundered. 'Why do you need information about the pill? Do you dare to tell me....'

'Don't be medieval, Appa!'

Of course our quarrel took the predictable route:

'Go to hell, do whatever you like, do not come back to show me your face.' Saying this, Appa walked away fuming.

At night, as I was packing to go, Ammi came to inquire what had happened. 'The quarrel about "the pill" etc. had taken place in English so she hadn't understood anything. Appa had left his dinner uneaten and was walking up and down angrily, muttering to himself, she said.

I laughed out loud. 'Serves him right!'

'But, Savi, why won't you get married? You have such lovely men friends!'

'Yeah, right! Your very happy conjugal life should absolutely inspire me to get married, yes?'

Ammi had been holding a pile of clothes in her hand. She set it down slowly. Weighing each and every word of hers, she retorted angrily, for the first and last time in her life, I think:

'Savitri, what faults you find in your father, what you say to him, I have not interfered in that until now, and will not in the future. But how he should behave with me, whether it is appropriate or not, that is our issue—you do not have the right to speak about that! Do not talk about this with me again ever.'

She was about to turn and leave. I was mortified. As soon as I had uttered it, my churlish tongue itself had minded it. But a leopard and its spots. Gathering some nerve, I said:

'Then you don't have any right to meddle in my affairs either! Don't come to me asking any more questions.'

I had thought she would be hurt. But turning, she smiled and said, 'It's true, my mistake' and walked away.

I left for Mumbai in the morning. Of course in those two years I never returned home nor did I write any letters to them. On his work travels, if Appa was ever in Mumbai, he would call me. How are you, I am fine, was the type of conversations we had. As I had predicted, I got a well-paying job in Mumbai itself after finishing my studies, and I settled down there. This topic of my study, my knowledge of it, its use, all of this became really interesting to me now, so the days, full and busy, passed by quickly.

It must have been the second or third year of my job when Ammi suddenly appeared in my doorway, bag in hand. It had been four or five years since I had last seen her. I didn't even recognize her initially. I was getting ready to go out to eat somewhere.

'What is this? How come you are here?'

'I have come to stay with you. At your place.'

She had come in by then. Then I noticed the absence of the ten-paise coin size kunku on her forehead.

'Ammi....'

'Yes. Your father passed away a fortnight ago. Heart attack.'

I felt like an idiot, I could find no way to respond. I said, 'Didn't I always say that it's a dangerous age?'

Ammi said, 'Yes.'

I sat down. And what came to my mind first and foremost? That now there's no point in going out to eat. Then I thought, many years ago I would have had to pretend to cry when they played the song 'Aai Mhanoni Koni'...it's a similar situation now. I lifted the phone and stated, 'Sorry. I will not be able to come. I just heard that my father has passed away.' But then I stopped. How do I tell them he died a fortnight ago but that I only came to know just now? Putting the phone down, I screamed at Ammi, 'Why didn't you call me? A phone call, a telegram—'

She actually smiled a little and said, 'He forbade me.'

I smote my forehead with my palm.

I called some people in the office, told them I wouldn't be coming for two or three days. Listening to their shocked condolences, I kept staring at Ammi. Watching me and listening to my sad voice, she continued to smile. I slammed the phone down and said, 'Ammi, this is the limit! How am I supposed to face people now? My own father died and I didn't even know of it for an entire fortnight! So, okay, Appa forbade you to contact me while alive. But you could have contacted me as soon as he died. Some acknowledgement of custom, of tradition....'

My voice died down in the face of her silent laughter. She responded in a quiet, calm voice:

'The will leaves the entire estate to you, the only condition is that you take care of me in your home as if I was your own mother, with love. A few shares or some such have been placed in my name and their interest comes to me. Before I die, I will turn them over to you.'

I didn't understand. 'So you will stay here with me? Forever?'

'Yes,' she smiled again.

I kept staring at her face. Slowly, I realized that Ammi has no one else now. Her husband has died. I might have felt bad about losing a father, but for her....

I got up shamefacedly and rubbed her back to console her. She spoke in a nonchalant manner and asked, 'It won't be a problem for you, will it? I will take care of your home.'

We didn't talk much after that.

Ammi settled down. So much so that one could wonder how I managed before she arrived. But our behaviour with each other was the same as before. She must have gotten used to the eccentric nature of our 'family'. She never spoke unless specifically called or addressed. It was I who used to think how strange she is. Two people live in the same house and yet not more than four sentences are exchanged between them, and she feels nothing about it. If at times I felt embarrassed about always spending time outside, I would ask, 'Want to join me at the cinema? Want to go out shopping?' She would say, 'No, I don't understand those things.' Only when friends visited home did we talk with each other a little more in front of them. With hesitation, I would introduce her: 'This is Ammi, my mother.' Then turning towards those who were listening, she would add with a smile, 'Her stepmother.' To which, embarrassed, I would add, 'Yeah, she has harassed me no end!' and at this standard joke everyone would laugh dutifully.

Ammi fell ill six months after she came to my home. Something quite simple, a cold or cough, or something. But she insisted, 'Take me to the hospital.'

Though I was a little irritated, there we were at the hospital. When it was time to go inside to consult the doctor, and I got up to accompany her, she said, 'You wait here.' Frowning, I sat there for half an hour when the nurse came out and said!

'The doctor wants to see you.'

I stepped inside and he said, 'Do sit.' Ammi was nowhere to be seen. I sat down. He said nothing. I pointedly looked at my watch. He cleared his throat and fumbling with his stethoscope, said:

'Miss Raghavan, your...your....'

I added, 'Mother?'

'Mother. Well, your mother has...' he inhaled sharply and blurted out, 'Your mother has leukaemia. She doesn't have too long to live.'

My eyes turned as wide as saucers and seeing the extreme shock on my face he got up hurriedly and came towards me and, patting me on the back, said 'There, there' or 'Now, now' or something like that. The nurse came there and said, 'Come this way please.' Stumbling, feeling as if I were dead, I went where she took me. To Ammi's room. She was sleeping on the bed. There was a bottle of blood attached to a drip in her arm. She saw me and said, 'Sit down.'

I sat down and the two of us stared at each other. Finally, I stood up abruptly and in a cutting tone and asked, 'So you knew about this all along?'

'Yes.'

'And Appa?'

'Yes.'

'How long have you been ill?'

'Since I was nineteen or twenty. The doctor had said then, even if you get four or five years more, that would be a reach. Now the time has come.'

I stayed silent for a long time. Then again, I blurted out, 'But why not tell me? Either you or Appa? How is one supposed to know that....'

'What difference would it have made? Would you have changed anything just because I was going to die at any moment?'

Again we were silent. Then I thought of something else.

'Did Appa know this before the wedding?'

'Yes.'

'Then....'

'My father was his classmate. On his travels, Appa used to visit us from time to time. Once when he visited us, it was when my father had just passed away from typhoid. I had no one else. Like you, my mother also died when I was very young. Thinking that you and I could be company and support for each other, he brought me home.'

She started panting a little. I was silent again. The nurse came in and said, 'You should go. She tires easily. Come back again in the evening.'

I got up and mumbled 'Ammi, Ammi....'

She smiled a little. Then said, 'Sometimes we don't realize the story we are in, Savitri. You still have a lot of your life ahead of you. You go now.'

That was the last thing Ammi said to me. She died sometime that night. I was sitting in the waiting room outside when the nurse came and told me.

The death of the mother never-seen forced me to face again the old quandary of crying at 'Aai Mhanoni Koni'.

When my own father died, all that my mind had mustered up was, 'Today's dinner date is cancelled.'

But now with a lifelong sorrow that could never be assuaged, I wept bitterly.

*Translated by Anjali Nerlekar**

---

*The translator would like to thank the first readers of this translation for their valuable suggestions: Prachi Deshpande, Arnab Chakladar, Shashank Nerlekar, and Aseem Nerlekar.

KALLURI'S RADIO

VILAS SARANG

Jattu did not know what to do with himself after Kalluri left. He would slip away from home, making sure his mother did not see him, and loaf around the village. He would fling stones at trees to knock down fruits or birds. The other boys in the village would do chores for their mothers. Occasionally Jattu's mother Illha would ask him, too, to do something and shout at him. But he paid her no heed. Jattu's father had died four years earlier. People said with no father, there was nobody to control Jattu.

Jattu often walked to the end of the village. There was a huge rock out there. He would sit on it for hours, his back to the village, looking out into the distance. The slope below him was bare, then came a hill and trees and bushes. There was nothing anywhere that could be called a path. Hardly anybody came to the village or went out. So who would make a path? Once a year an itinerant trader would come, walking beside a donkey laden with goods. He would exchange oil, salt, sugar, cloth, and stuff like that for grain. Nobody else came or went. So all you did was point and say that is the way out of the village. Jattu would sit looking at the hill that stood in that direction. Beyond the hill lay the world. Nobody knew how far away it was, or how many days it would take to get there. Behind the village, in the opposite direction, stood a tall hill covered with dense vegetation. Nobody had ever gone that way.

Jattu often wondered whether Kalluri would ever come back. When he was in the village, Jattu would be around him all the time. Kalluri knew things that nobody else in the village knew.

He knew of things that grew underground. He knew about birds' eggs. He could tell stories about gods and ghosts. Jattu found them particularly mesmerizing.

The villagers said Kalluri would never return. To reach the world from the village was a difficult thing. Once out there, to get back was even more difficult. But one day when Jattu was on his way to the stream to fetch water, he heard that Kalluri was back. Abandoning his water pot, Jattu raced towards Kalluri's hut.

Kalluri smiled at him. Jattu was his favourite. Kalluri had always been thin. He looked even thinner now. His dark skin had grown darker and drier. But his movements were as brisk as ever. And his eyes still shone. Jattu began bombarding him with questions one after the other. He asked if Kalluri had seen vehicles that moved automatically. He asked if he had seen that thing of many linked compartments that ran over iron rails belching smoke. Soon Jattu realized that Kalluri was not giving clear answers to his questions. He was fobbing off questions about where he had been, how he had got there, what he had seen. Kalluri had always been secretive. He was even more so now.

Soon people from the village began to gather around. Many were disappointed to see how little Kalluri had brought back. The general opinion in the village was that Kalluri lacked common sense. Just then Illha came shouting, carrying the water pot Jattu had left behind. Jattu got up with a grimace. As he left, Kalluri whispered in his ear, 'Come in the morning. I'll show you something.'

Jattu could not sleep that night. He was tormented by the thought of what Kalluri was going to show him. As soon as day broke, he ran to Kalluri's hut.

Kalluri pulled a thing out from the bottom of his bundle. He held the thing before Jattu. His teeth shone bright.

Jattu took the thing. It was a black box nestled in a black leather case. Jattu held it up to his eyes. It was a small box, about a span long and half a span tall. He ran his hand over the case.

This is not leather, he said to himself. It looks like leather but it is something else. The false leather case did not cover the front of the box. If you flicked your nail on the uncovered part, it made a hollow tiktik sound. It was clearly not metal. Perhaps it was some metal that he had not seen. A transparent band ran across the face of the box. A nail flicked on it produced an unfamiliar sound. It was not glass. Jattu thought the whole thing was strange. Something that looked like leather but was not leather. Something that looked like metal but was not metal. Something that looked like glass but was not glass. Behind the false glass band there were a whole lot of marks crowded together. The box was punctured on one side and fitted with two discs. Jattu decided they were there to help open the box. He dug his fingers behind them and tried to open the box. It would not open.

'How do you open this thing?' he asked.

Kalluri took the box from his hands and said, 'It's not meant to be opened.' Then he twirled one disc. Jattu noticed that twirling the disc made a vertical white line behind the transparent band move. Instantly the box was filled with a crackling sound, and soon after by what sounded like speech. Kalluri stopped twirling the disc. The white line stopped travelling, but the speaking did not. Jattu listened in wonder.

To begin with, Jattu thought the speech was in some unknown language. But then he began to recognize some words. As he continued to listen attentively, he heard more words that were familiar. It occurred to him then that the speaker was speaking in Jattu's language but with a different accent and pronunciation, using several unfamiliar words. It was impossible to make out what he was saying. Jattu asked Kalluri. Kalluri could understand the speech a little better than Jattu. But that did not help him understand what the speaker was talking about. And so the two sat listening to something they could not understand.

A long time passed. Then the voice in the box changed. The first voice stopped and a woman's voice took its place. Jattu found it sweet. No woman in the village had a voice like that. The woman spoke briefly and then a song began to play. Jattu leaned forward to hear better. He thought he understood more words in the song than he had in the speech. The song was beautiful, enchanting. It was so different from any song he had heard in the village even during festivals. The instrumental accompaniment was equally wondrous. Jattu could make out the familiar sound of the big drum. But the other sounds were quite unrecognizable.

After that Jattu began to spend practically the whole day in Kalluri's hut. News of the talking box had spread through the village. Villagers came in ones and twos, listened for a while, and went away. A handful would come after work in the evening and sit listening. Initially, like Jattu, they understood little of what was said. But gradually they began to understand more.

Two places in the talking box produced speech. When the white line travelled left, it hit one spot. When it travelled right, it hit the other. Kalluri discussed this with a few visitors. They realized that the voices spoke in a distant place and entered the box by magic. What flummoxed them was whether the two voices at the two ends of the box came from the same place or from different places. Voices from both sides spoke the same language, but the villagers found that they felt closer to the voices that came from the left. They were clearer and easier to understand than the ones that came from the right. Generally, people preferred listening to the voices talking and singing on the left.

One day old Itanna came to listen. Many years ago, Itanna had gone away from the village and returned after a long time. He revealed that the two voices came from two different places. The voice from the right belonged to Astipur, the capital of our country. The voice from the left belonged to Hakimabad, the capital of neighbouring Shufristan. Others present instantly objected, saying that the voice from the left was clearer and sounded closer to how we spoke. How could it come from another country? Surely the voice from our capital city would be clearer? To this Itanna said our village was on the very border of Khaurdesh, our country, and was nearer to Shufristan. Their territory started just beyond the hill at the back of our village. Shufristan was a small country. That's why its capital was closer to us than our own capital. Naturally, the language we spoke was nearer to theirs and we could hear the voice from there more clearly.

People had nothing to say to Itanna's clarification because nobody knew enough about these things to challenge him. Indeed nobody knew the names of either Shufristan's capital or their own.

A young man named Komva said, 'I always thought different countries spoke different languages. They are two different countries because their languages are different. That sounds right. If our Khaurdesh and Shufristan speak the same language, why should they be two separate countries? Wouldn't it be more convenient to make one country of places where the same language is spoken?'

Old Itanna laughed and said, 'In a way you're right. But these things are not so simple. It is difficult for backward people like us to understand how educated, developed people think.' After a pause he said, 'I'll tell you something stranger than that. The languages spoken in our Khaurdesh and Shufristan are the same, isn't it? But we call our language Khaur and they call theirs Rufidi. Now, tell me, would you believe that?'

At this the gathering laughed as though to say, 'What a strange world this is.'

Gradually the village got used to the talking box. Jattu now knew at what time of day the box played songs. He would arrive at exactly that time. Like him, others in the village also found the talking boring. Only a couple of them would drop in once in a while and listen to it with thoughtful expressions.

One day Kalluri showed Jattu a little secret about the talking box. He removed a plate at the back. Out came two red cylindrical objects. Jattu felt them in the palm of his hand. They were small but heavy. Kalluri demonstrated that when they were out, the box stopped talking. You could move the white line inside the transparent band as much as you liked, there would be no sound. But the minute you popped the cylinders in, the box began to talk. Jattu was surprised and curious. Kalluri said, 'The magic of the box is in these cylinders.' Feeling the cylinders, he said, 'A man's manhood is in his marbles. That's how it is with the box. Take them out and the box is neutered. It's like what we do. We pick smooth stones from the river bank, smear them with paint, and turn them into gods. So someone who knows mantras has painted these cylinders and put a powerful spell on them. Nobody in our village has so much knowledge of spells as to be able to make a box like this. This mantra scholar from the big world must be a powerful man indeed.'

Kalluri stared at the box with wide-open eyes. He had some knowledge of spells and charms. He had occasionally been able to heal some villagers of their illness. Jattu was watching him, wondering whether Kalluri was asking himself how he could acquire this powerful knowledge of spells.

Although the sound from the left side of the box was clearer, Jattu preferred the right side. The left produced mostly talk, and little song. The right played a lot of songs. Meanwhile Kalluri had found something else that was even more engrossing. If you brought the white line just a little this side or that side of the point where you could hear talk clearly, the box made peculiar sounds—whistling sounds and gibberish. Jattu found those sounds amusing to begin with, but then they bored him. With Kalluri the opposite happened. He got more and more drawn towards those sounds. When he was alone, he listened to those sounds, not songs, and was overwhelmed by them.

Kalluri wondered now where those sounds came from. They did not come from this or that city. They were not human sounds. They sounded more like the sounds that the villager Turakkal made when he was possessed. A thought struck Kalluri. There was a burial ground between two hills at the back of the village.

Generations of villagers had been buried there. Kalluri would occasionally visit this place of earth mounds with large and small stones placed on them, aiming to explore the world of charms and spells. He recalled that the sounds from the box were quite like the sounds he heard there, whistling and gibberish. Those were the sounds that the dead and supernatural creatures made. It was clear to him that there was a connection between the sounds that came from the box and from the dead souls and supernatural spirits of the burial ground.

To sit listening to these sounds became a daily practice with Kalluri. These sounds did not come regularly as did the voices from the right and left in the box. There were times when you could hear them, times when you could not. Times when they came loud and clear, times when they came faintly in little bursts. After all, they were made by ghouls and spirits who were not bound to a fixed timetable. They began their gibberish when the mood took them. Kalluri discovered something else. Whereas the voices from right and left in the box would fall silent after a certain time at night, these sounds continued through the night. In fact their volume increased at night. There was nothing surprising about that. Nights were their very own time for spirits. When human beings quit the box and went home to sleep, ghouls took charge of it. The more he listened to their gibberish the more Kalluri was convinced that it was a proper language. He recognized certain recurrent sounds. Kalluri was certain that if he could only connect the sounds in their syntax and structures, he would begin to understand the language. Kalluri's blood ran fast to think of the enormous treasure he would be the master of if that happened. He began to listen to the sounds with even greater concentration now and grew restless when he could not hear them.

Then the rains came. One day the sky was densely overcast. Lightning flashed along the horizon. The ghoulish voices in the box grew in volume, speed, and frequency. Kalluri thought the spirits must have descended to the lower clouds because the upper sky had become stormy. And now they were chattering frenziedly. Kalluri listened to them with his heart and mind in his ears. After days of listening, he had begun to feel he stood on the very threshold of understanding the language. He had become familiar with the stresses and cadences of the language. One of these days, without warning, the riddle would be solved. *Right now the spirits that have gathered below the stormy sky are chattering at the tops of their voices trying to tell me something; and here I am, a miserable wretch, unable to understand what it is.*

As he sat listening, his despair grew. Tears gathered in his eyes. Holding the talking box in both his hands, he stared through the door of his hut at the world outside. A clap of thunder burst through the sky and the first showers came. The constant clatter of the pouring rain blocked all other sounds. Kalluri could barely hear the chattering in the box. He twirled the disc and shut them off. He put the box aside. He rose and stepped out of the hut. Standing in the rain, he spread his empty hands wide, getting drenched.

All through the season of rains the voices of the spirits continued to chatter in the box. It was the other voices, both from the right and left, that made listening difficult. The voices of the spirits appeared to have dominated and defeated human voices. Jattu could not hear the songs clearly and lost interest in the box. To make matters worse, Kalluri was so engrossed in the chattering sounds that he had become oblivious to everything else. He had withdrawn into his own world. He hardly ate or drank. His face had begun to look drawn. His eyes had changed. Forget talking to others, he barely talked to Jattu. Jattu stopped going to his hut.

The rains came to an end. The weather grew cooler. As was his practice during this season, the old trader arrived in the village with his donkey laden with goods. Along with salt and sugar, he would also bring colourful beads. The village women were very keen on them. But he did not bring them this year. The reason he gave was this: 'I used to buy the beads from a town in Shufristan called Tasariya. Earlier you could cross these mountains and enter the town whenever you pleased. We were free to cross the border as and when we liked. But this year I found soldiers posted at the border. They stop you from crossing the border. They even patrol the mountains.'

The story of Kalluri's talking box reached the trader's ears. He went over to see it. After the rains the voices of the spirits had grown faint. Kalluri was busy twirling the disc back and forth to see if he could locate them anywhere at all. But the white line produced no sounds till it reached the place on the left from where human voices came. The trader looked at the box and said, 'This is called a radio. So you are listening to speeches from Hakimabad I see. These days people from our towns and cities don't listen to programmes from Hakimabad. Our government doesn't like it. But that shouldn't affect you in this remote place.'

One day after the trader had left, Jattu went over to see Kalluri. He saw him looking very worried. He started the box; but however frantically he twirled the disc, all they heard were faint voices. Kalluri said the force of the spell was wearing out. The box was dying.

As days passed, the force of the spell became weaker and the voices progressively fainter. Kalluri grieved. The box was losing its life before his eyes. He saw clearly that those otherworld voices too would soon fall silent forever. He felt completely helpless and took to sitting around the hut despondently.

These days Jattu, rather than go to Kalluri's, would loaf around and sometimes sit on the rock at the edge of the village. One of those days, when he was sitting on the rock, he saw men in the distance approaching the village. He was thunderstruck. Men coming to the village was nothing less than a miracle. He narrowed his eyes and looked. The men were coming on horseback. They were all dressed in khaki and each one carried something on his shoulder that looked like a metal pipe. Jattu watched them till they were halfway up. Then he leapt off the rock and raced to the village.

The villagers were surprised to see the men, policemen or soldiers whatever they were. Very seldom would they come, once every five or six years. Now their leader asked a question. Nobody understood it. Then a man from the back stepped forward and asked the question another way. They were looking for the man who owned the talking box. The villagers took them to Kalluri's hut.

The soldiers dismounted. Kalluri was led out of the hut. The soldiers' leader looked boyish and had the face of a rich man. He took the talking box from Kalluri's hands and turned it around this way and that. 'This radio has been made in a communist country,' he said to one of his companions. 'Naturally we don't import this make. He obviously bought it in Shufristan.'

Then he began to question Kalluri. Where had he gone last year. What had he done there. Kalluri decided that they suspected him of listening to otherworldly voices in the talking box. They must expect him to have amassed an enormous amount of spell power. It would therefore be prudent to hide the fact that he had been listening to those voices. 'Oh no. I wasn't listening to the spirits' voices at all. I would listen to the voices coming from here,' he said, pointing to the white line which was standing on the left side.

The soldiers' leader proceeded to ask him questions about what he had heard from there. Turning to some of his men in the back he directed them to ask around the village what they had heard over the radio. Three or four soldiers began to question the men in the village. They returned half an hour later to report that the villagers did not appear to have heard any propaganda from Shufristan. 'The people are quite stupid. They don't seem to have understood a thing of what they heard.'

'They could well be ignorant and stupid. But we have to act with caution. Shufristan is infiltrating these parts.'

He then ordered all able-bodied men in the village to be rounded up. They were brought to an open space. The soldiers mounted their horses and the leader began to address the villagers.

'People of the Urufikal Valley. Do not forget that you are citizens of Khaurdesh.' Waving Kalluri's radio before them he said, 'If you hear anything on this radio or on any other brought here by anyone else, do not believe what you hear. Shufristan has been carrying out a vitriolic propaganda against our nation. Oil has been discovered in these mountains.' He swept his arm over the range behind the village. 'This is a great treasure bestowed on our nation. This place which has been neglected till now, will soon be developed. Shufristan had never said a thing about this territory until now. But suddenly, since oil was discovered here, they have raised their voice claiming that this entire territory that belongs to our native tribals, actually belongs to them. They say they want to reclaim it. They have been carrying out this propaganda consistently over the Hakimabad radio station. They are trying to incite you. They promise to liberate you. It is nothing but a sham. They call themselves socialists, champions of the poor. But in fact they are a ruthless dictatorship. Your radiant future lies in Khaurdesh and nowhere else. Jai Khaurdesh!'

'Jai Khaurdesh,' the soldiers chorused after him. Some villagers tried to join the chorus. Nobody had followed much of what the soldiers' leader had said. But none of them said anything about it. Women and children sat in a circle around the group of men in the centre. Jattu was standing among them looking first at the mounted leader and then at Kalluri.

The soldiers now got ready to leave. Kalluri was hoisted onto one of the horses. The village children ran behind the horsemen for a while, shouting. Jattu was among them. Then the others fell behind and Jattu continued to run behind the horsemen alone. He stared at Kalluri as he ran, but not once did Kalluri turn round to look at him. He sat erect on the horse, staring into space.

The soldiers were almost at the village border. The leader

dipped into his pocket and pulled out the radio. Holding it out to one of his men he said, 'Keep this with you.'

The soldier took the radio, looked at it carefully, twirled the disc, held it up to his ear, and said, 'The battery is practically down.'

Then he opened the lid at the back and removed both its battery cells. He glanced at them once and threw them away. He shut the lid and put the radio away in his knapsack.

Jattu stopped in his tracks. He stared after the horsemen as they trotted further and further away. Soon they had gone past the rock at the village border and left the village. He saw their figures as they descended the hill and their smaller figures as they came up the hill on the other side. Then the hill rose between them and him. Their heads had dipped below the hilltop. Jattu moved quickly then. He stepped forward and picked up the two cells that lay gleaming in the grass. Grasping them tight in his hands, he raced home.

Translated by Shanta Gokhale

CROWS

YOGIRAJ WAGHMARE

He spots the funeral procession making its way to the cremation ground. Immediately, he asks Mrs Crow, 'Whose body?'

Mrs Crow thinks about it for a minute. His keen vision makes it possible for him to identify the kind of body that is on its way. He lets out a 'Caw caw' so that the folks in the procession should know that there are crows on the banyan tree at the cremation ground. He flies to the top of the tree. He conceals himself in the crowd of green branches. The relatives arrive at the bottom of the tree and look around hopefully, seeking the crows.

Meanwhile, Crow is talking to Mrs Crow, telling her everything that comes into his head.

'So, my love, have you managed to guess who is dead?' he asks again.

'Why do you always ask me? Once in a while, why not just tell me who it is?'

Crow laughs raucously. He teases her: '*Because* you can't tell who it is, I have to ask you, no?'

'Never mind. Do you think I'm a fool?' Mrs Crow says, feigning anger.

'Silly, how many years have we spent on this cremation tree? We've had children. Our children have had children. And all this time, how many souls have come through his cremation ground and been turned into ash? And you still can't tell whose body it is.' As he says this, he snuggles up to her and brings his beak close to her left cheek.

She grows shy and says, 'Get away with you. The procession is almost here.'

He comes to his senses. He springs up and perches on one of the highest branches of the tree.

He swivels an eye around to look at the corpse. It has been beautifully adorned with garlands of flowers. But the flowers are beginning to droop. Not too many people either. Four or five women at the rear, one supported by the others. She has wept herself into a state, sobs still breaking out, tears still pouring forth. The corpse is now being set down on a platform. The rest get down to the business of cremating the body. Two of the men begin a discussion about the direction in which the head of the corpse should be placed. Crow bursts into laughter. Mrs Crow covers his beak with a wing.

'Is this the time to laugh? Someone has just died.'

'That is what makes me laugh! Human beings seem to know everything about the rites and rituals of birth but those surrounding death always leave them confused,' says Crow in a show of wit.

'Enough. Will you say whatever comes to your head?'

'My dear, I see this every day. The head must be placed pointing to the east. Then you need forty maunds of wood. If you can't manage, then cow dung will do. And if you can't manage that...?'

'What then?' she interrupts.

'Then throw the body in an abyss as if it is unclaimed and have done with it,' Crow says, without expression.

'What rot you talk! These poor people have just been bereaved and you're saying such things about them?'

Crow could answer Mrs Crow but he does not say a word. He decides to remain silent.

The preparations are finished. One of the men says, 'Come on...get on with it....'

A commotion ensues. The women begin to wail and weep.

'Tell them to stop it....'

'Listen, Kusum, stop crying and look upon his face...you won't see it again,' someone says crisply.

Kusum wails: 'Dada....'

For a moment, the world is silent. Everyone freezes. No one can move. For a moment, their hearts stop. There are tears in every eye, a general feeling of helplessness. But all this lasts only an instant. In the very next moment, someone moves. A mouth opens.

'Enough of that now...we have to get on with it....'

That voice electrifies everyone. The corpse is hoisted on to the pyre. The rest of the wood is placed on top of it. Someone pours kerosene over it and a young man, standing by with a torch, ignites it. In a moment, the pyre is wreathed in flames.

Mrs Crow watches. A teardrop steals from her eye and falls on a banyan leaf. Crow stares into the distance, his face unreadable.

She asks, 'That's done with, then?'

'What?' Crow asks.

'All this...the poor man...' she says with a sigh.

'What is there to sigh about?' he asks.

'How you talk! Those people haven't left yet....'

'They won't go until the skull bursts.'

'It will in a little while.'

'Not a chance,' he says confidently.

'What do you mean?' she is startled by his vicious prediction.

'They should have put more wood near the head,' he says, with the air of an expert doctor suggesting a cure.

'Rubbish! Why would anyone know so much about corpses and how they burn?' Mrs Crow taunts him.

'Didn't you just ask about unclaimed corpses ending up in abysses?'

'I think you have a thing about corpses,' she says irritably.

'It's not a liking.'

'Then what is it?' she cocks an eye in his direction.

'Rage.'

'What?'

'Rage.'

'Oh dear, rage about what? Are they kith and kin?'

Mrs Crow is now completely confused. She wonders whether her husband has really run mad. 'Is this the effect of living at a crematorium?' she wonders. 'He speaks in riddles. Has he been possessed by a spirit? Which is why I keep saying: "Why must you inspect these human corpses with such care? Let's go perch on a distant tree. We can come back when it's all done." But no, he pays me no heed. I say, "Why can't we build a nest somewhere else?" He won't listen to that either, this idiot husband of mine. And then he talks rubbish.'

She began to feel a prickle of fear. Why was he so angry at human beings? Shouldn't he share his feelings with his wife? Why was their relationship so different from everyone else's? He never wants to bill or coo; he never explains what he means. And then this rage against mankind that he carries around, like coals of fire on his head.

Close to tears, she flew up to perch by his side.

'So tell me, what is this rage about?'

'Listen,' he began. 'Before I came here, I lived in a village, a small one, surrounded by lime and banyan trees. I built my nest in an acacia. Right in front of my nest was a mansion. There were flowering trees, plumeria, and pomegranate around it. In the afternoon, I would fly to the mansion and perch in the pomegranate tree and watch the goings-on. There were a lot of people in there. I would sometimes fly from the tree to the veranda. At first, I was a little scared. The sparrows would fly in after me but they would go straight into the house. They would peck at the rice, the bajri, the wheat. I was too scared. I would hover outside, keeping a safe distance. From time to time, I would caw, just to be on the safe side. If I heard footsteps, I would immediately hightail it for the plumeria and settle there. Once things settled down, I'd venture near the courtyard again.

And so I got familiar with the mansion. I began to lose my fear. I thought the mansion folks were good people.

'Another reason I began to care about the mansion was the little child of the mistress of the house. It was about one-and-a-half years old, a sweet little thing. It would crawl all over the house with a bowl of milk. Sometimes it would try to stand up. With one hand clutching the bowl, it would use the other hand to try and stuff its cheeks with bread and milk. Sometimes, the milk would spill and splash all over the courtyard. That made me very happy. The baby would spot me and sometimes it would fall asleep, or laugh, or try to hide the bowl from me. And I would hop around, following the babe. Sometimes, the baby's mother would take her in her arms and pointing to the tree say, "Caw, caw". The baby would laugh happily. I would love this and I would reply: "Caw, caw."

'But then everything changed one day. In my opinion, I did nothing wrong. But the child's mother saw things differently. Seeing her behave this way had a deep impact on me. I grew angry with the whole human tribe, one that could change so radically.'

Mrs Crow interrupts to ask: 'What actually happened?'

'That day the child was sitting with its milk bowl in the courtyard. It had spilt rice all over the ground. I hopped and skipped and flew into the courtyard. I nipped at the rice that was closest to me. Nothing happened. There was no one else around so I grew brave. I began to get quite close to the baby who seemed to be smiling and enjoying it. I thought I might get at the rice right near the child so I went quite close to it. Just as my beak was getting at the rice, the child got frightened and began to cry. Startled, I turned around to fly off and in so doing my left wing brushed against the child. The mother saw this happen and the fat was in the fire. It was an inauspicious thing, according to her. She began to cry. Seeing its mother crying, the child began to wail all the more. It began to crawl towards the mother who refused to pick it up. This was completely unexpected and shocked the child. It began to scream in panic. I did not understand any of this. What was going on? How could a touch of my wing turn this mother into an unfeeling block?

'I flew back to the acacia to watch, feeling like a criminal. Hearing the commotion, the neighbours gathered. The mother told them between sobs, "A crow touched my baby." This shocked them too. They all moved away from the child. Until that moment, all of them had always been willing to play with the kid and cuddle it but now no one would go near the poor, terrified thing. It was locked in this labyrinth, alone and afraid. Then a servant came forward, picked up the child, took it out to the field, touched its head to the hedge two or three times and then brought it back. The child was bathed. And handed back to its mother. I was watching all this. My touch had separated them. Why was I so inauspicious? These human beings had always been conscious of caste, but we birds, never. If that poor child had to bear so much just because of the touch of my wing, it would be better not to stay there. A storm blew up in my head, a storm that blew me here.'

Crow stops for a moment after telling his story. He is looking somewhere far into the distance. Then he sighs. 'Got it?'

Mrs Crow sighs and says: 'Hmm.' Her face shows her anger but his is lined with a deep rage. She feels his rage is justified. She is about to say something when she sees people coming from the city again. A group has come to perform the thirteenth-day ceremonies. The person leading the procession carries a basket containing naivedya. This is a common occurrence—every hour or half an hour, a group of people arrives. There are groups who come with a corpse, there are those who come for the third-day or the tenth-day ceremonies. The road to the cremation grounds is never empty.

Meanwhile, a group has arrived with a body. They begin to look for a suitable place to cremate the body. They gather four stones and make a circle with them. After sprinkling gomutra all over them, they smear them with haldi-kunku. Then they light a candle. They set out the food items that the dead person had enjoyed. They put down the naivedya as well. They touch the feet of the corpse respectfully and then some of them scan the sky while others turn their searching gaze on the banyan tree, all hoping to spot a crow. The rest sit on the platform and begin to talk.

'If the crow touches it, it means he has been freed of the cycle of birth and death....'

'Generally, you see hundreds of crows but today? Not a single one!'

'What if a crow touches the body....'

Mr and Mrs Crow hear such conversations every day. Mrs Crow keeps looking at him now. With her eyes, she indicates that he should go and touch the corpse.

'Uh-huh, not me.'

'Why?'

'It's a woman's corpse. How can I touch it? You go!'

Mrs Crow says: 'Why are you talking like this? We need to make a decision.'

Mrs Crow gives up. She falls silent but then she can take it no longer and says, 'Aaho, go now!'

Crow winks and caws softly. The people sit up and pay attention. They have heard the sound of a crow and begin to look for it.

'Hey, did you hear that? It was a crow...'

'Yes, I heard it too!'

All of them begin to look around. Crow laughs to himself. Mrs Crow doesn't like this kind of tomfoolery. She says again, 'Go!'

Crow caws again, caws softly. Again, the people look around, startled. But they cannot see a crow.

Crow is now toying with them. They grow fed up of this. Crow is simply acting up. He has been doing this for a while now, for there had been a time when he had been alone. He had had a great big banyan to himself to live in. A stream flowed close by. The city could be seen at a distance. The land around was barren. Even during the day, it was a bleak sight. Not even a bird would come near the place but on that day of rage, on the day when he had touched the baby, Crow had just wanted to get away. After a long flight, he had stopped at this tree. His head was a maelstrom of thought and emotion. He had no idea where he was. Night came and he could not remember when he had fallen asleep. But when he awoke, he found himself enjoying the shade of the tree. He hopped from branch to branch. He flew around the tree a couple of times, hovering here and there, looking at it carefully. He cleared his throat and cawed but he was answered by the sounds of silence. But still, he liked the place. He decided that he would make his home there.

One day, sitting in the cool shade of the tree and cawing, he spotted some people coming from the city. It was not a large group. They were in no hurry. But somehow they made him uncomfortable. He felt he should swoop over them and attack each one, pecking at them with his beak. But as the people came close, he realized that it was a funeral procession. But still he sought to hide among the leaves of the tree.

They arrived at the banyan, built a pyre and lit it. When they heard the skull crack, they left. Crow watched all this from above. He wanted to remain concealed from their sight. When the people left, he waited a while and then examined the surroundings.

People came every day. 'Oh, this is a cremation ground,' he realized. 'That's not a bad thing. Corpses are better than live human beings....'

For the mourners would bring rice and roti on the third or the eleventh or the thirteenth day. They would pray for a crow to touch the corpse. That would mean the soul's liberation. If not....

Crow was quite pleased with himself but sometimes, memories of the old place would come back to haunt him. And then he would find himself sad again. This was the kaleidoscope of emotions with which he lived.

One day, a group arrived to commemorate the thirteenth day. They were carrying naivedya with them and waited for a crow to appear. Crow flew from the twig on which he was perched and swooped down to a long low branch. Now he could see rice, roti, and bits of jaggery spread out. He checked whether this was a trap, a trick. But there seemed to be no sign of that. The humans had positioned themselves some distance away. They were clearly waiting for him. He flew up and around the tree to make sure all was well. Then he approached the offerings and began to eat. He took a piece of roti and flew back to the tree. But the men simply got up and left for the city.

In the safety of the tree, Crow began to eat his roti and began to give voice: 'Caw, caw'. And suddenly, he heard an echo from the other side of the tree. That startled him.

He tried again: 'Caw, caw.'

The reply came, 'Caw...caw...'

The voice was sweet. It was of course a female crow. Crow stopped thinking about his roti. He began to look around frantically. He began to call, randomly, loudly, wildly. And each time, there was an answer. Now he was sure. In this tree, in his tree, there was another crow. It was this sound that was drawing him close. The female crow had lost her way. When he finally met her eyes, he was filled with happiness and she began to look coy. Delighted, he showed her around his entire kingdom.

They began to live together on the same tree. As a pair, they spent hours talking to each other. Or they would play hide-and-seek in the tree. When the spirit took him, he would sing to her. And she to him. Each enjoyed the other's singing. And each day, a funeral procession would arrive. They had a game going. Whose turn was it to make that final journey? Was it a male or a female? Was it a child or a youth? She always lost. He always won. She enjoyed losing to him....

They had no need to leave their tree. Every day, there was food, rice, or rotis, brought by the mourners. He loved rice. But because she loved roti, he began to enjoy it too and she took to eating rice because he enjoyed it.

The decision whether to touch a corpse or not was his. But in one case, she insisted on having her way: when it was a child's body, she felt he should not delay too long.

'Agreed,' he said without demur.

But he had a condition too: 'We will never touch a buried body or an abandoned one.'

'Agreed,' she said.

Days passed peacefully. One day, she gave him some good news. The eggs had hatched and they had children. They celebrated with a meal of rice. The fledglings grew and the tree was no longer large enough for them. They flew to the top of it and raised a ruckus. As the days went by, their noise grew louder. They began to fly; the sky was indeed their limit.

One evening, another pair of crows comes and perches on the tree. Crow thinks the couple will rest for the night and leave in the morning and so he says nothing. But Mrs Crow hears the new pair talking. One says to the other, 'This is a nice big tree. It's a good place to raise a family.'

She tells Crow what she heard; he gives his assent with silence. This is the first of many other couples, all of whom raise their infants there. Now the lonely tree is alive with their croaking and cawing.

Crow cannot quite fathom what is going on.

One day, he flies to the top of the tree and sees how much the city has grown. The houses are growing faster and farther. No shortage of corpses either. The numbers keep increasing. Now the crows do not wait; they fight to be the first to touch the dead body.

Crow cannot believe his eyes: 'What is going on? Crows must behave like crows. They should restrain this bestial eagerness and make the relatives wait for liberation.'

But even more than this, what worries him is a sight he has witnessed. One day, he sees crows falling upon an unclaimed body. He is filled with rage and roars at them, 'Idiots, what do you think you're doing?'

The crows are taken aback; they don't understand.

'What's your problem?' they ask.

'What are you lot up to?'

'We're eating, what else?'

'Shame on you. Feasting on an unclaimed body. Do you have no shame? It would be better to die than....'

For a moment, the crows stop but then they simply forget about his objections and go back to the corpse. In a towering rage, Crow flies to his nest and says to his wife, 'Come on, we cannot live here any longer. There is no difference between a dead and a living crow on this tree.'

'Where we will go?' Mrs Crow asks in shock.

'Wherever. But we must be able to live as crows do.'

And they fly away from the banyan tree.

⁓

The city expands and surrounds the cemetery. Huts crop up around the cremation ground's walls and swarm right up to the banyan tree. When the crows wake up in the morning they find concrete houses all around the cemetery. The living have taken over the space for the dead. They get together for a meeting.

'What do we do now?' one asks.

'What do we do about what?' asks another.

'We should live here like that old couple....'

But there is no one to hear him. For, at that very moment, a woman comes out of her hut with scraps of food and throws them into the gutter.

The crows swoop down and fall upon it....

Translated by Jerry Pinto

RED MUCK
BHASKAR CHANDANSHIV

The bell rang. School was out. The doors burst open and the boys poured out like water breaching a dam. The playground was soon covered with children, bubbling and burbling. They formed little groups and blocked every path. The kids from the peth rushed back. Those who lived close by scuttled off home. The kids from big families mounted their cycles, tinkled their bells, and edged through the crowd. The girls, a flock of chattering mynahs, made way for them. The teachers and the principal inched through the crowd, watching their step, chatting away to glory. Us boys from the fields were also in a rush and so we stuck our bags on our backs and made tracks. Some were off to the produce brokers and some were already hurrying to the village. Some sat down to eat their bhakri by the handpump. But I was in a great big hurry. Monday is bazaar day, see? So half-day school. Hefting their burdens, the village folk were running along. Goats, hens, buffaloes, and pulses were being brought in to sell; the animals were milling about and more were coming, oh yes. The whole road was a mess of donkeys, horses, carts, and cycles. Men and women were hurtling about with their bits and bobs and bags and loads. Others walked down the familiar streets chatting about this and that. The bazaar was picking up and everyone was running to the taluka....

I was also hurrying in the same direction, ducking in and out of the crowd of people and watching them too. The heat was tiring. I was late, which worried me. The wheels in my head were speeding faster than my feet. Aaba and Mai had both warned me, again and again, about being late. When I was leaving, Mai had warned me.

'Bapu....'

'Yeah, what?' I was almost out of the door with my new bag on my back.

'Now don't do like last time's bazaar, okay? Find a good spot, near the market entry, close to the tap, got it? Take your time but get a good spot.'

'Okay,' I said and got out of there.

When I got to the bit of the road near the river, I took out my English textbook and began to study the words. I couldn't do this if the other boys were with me. But sometimes when I was alone I would take out my Marathi textbook or my history textbook and walk and read, walk and read. All the way to Kalamb, studies, studies, studies. Coming to the village, more studies...it was fun too. I would play and study, study and play. I stand first in class. But this is the matric year so I want to study harder. I explained this to Aaba and Mai. I read them the letter the teacher gave me. But Aaba has a different way of looking at things. He might want many things but how can he get them done? But I wasn't giving in so easily; I was going to dig in my heels and finish this examination.

But first, the Monday market to get through.

Someone touched my bag. Startled, I looked back. 'You're deaf or what? How much I yelled!' Kaalya's Jina shouted angrily.

'Why? What happened?' I turned around and asked him gently.

Jina took out some bhakri from the corner of his dhotar and gave it to me. He said irritably, 'Your old lady sent this. And she said to get hold of a good spot...' Jina bit off and was gone, mumbling to himself. I lost him in the crowd.

I shoved the bhakri into my bag. Bending down, I slipped under the wire fence, crossed the compound, and entered the bazaar. I wandered about looking for a good place for us to sell our stuff, a free space. Not easy. The market was crawling with people. They had spread pieces of cloth, baskets, or stones to mark their places. Some had made chalk rangolis or used stones to let others know that the place was taken. I wandered about, aimless as a bat. All around, shops were doing brisk business. Carts and handcarts were being wheeled about. The chaiwallah's dirty kettle was doing the rounds. Carts and handcarts were shoving and pushing. Cobblers were setting up shop. The sour smell of hide and meat had spread everywhere. Stalls selling brooms, dusters, and ropes were being set up. On the other side of the market the potters had set up their stalls. All the sellers were waiting for customers. I walked and walked and at last I found a place. I pulled the cloth out of my bag and spread it across the space. Three or four stones now to hold it down. There. Aaba and Mai would sit there. Now, how about me? I began to look again. I took another round. Spotting an empty space, I dropped my bag down. There was a man thumping pegs into the ground, so I asked him: 'Uncle, is this spot free?'

'What're you selling?' he growled without looking at me. He was concentrating on what he was doing.

'Vegetables, some stuff like that,' I said, still standing.

'Which village?' He went on thumping away. I thought: not a good sign. Should have just sat down and behaved like a stone. But to end the whole conversation, I said loudly: 'Hasyagaon.'

'Okay, but keep your distance,' he said. I put down some stones and sat down with a sigh, cross-legged, my bag on my lap. I took out my bhakri and broke off bits. I dabbed the chutney and began to chew. Now I was eating so I didn't have to be speaking.

He had finished with the thumping and was now tying his ropes. Looking at my bag, he said, 'Go to school?'

'Yes.'

'Which year?' He put fruit out on the tins.

'Matric.' I was making stabs at the chutney with the bread.

'Matric? Tough time,' he said, wiping his face with a cloth.

I kept on eating and paid him no mind. But the words 'tough time' began to dance and prance in my head. I thought about what Joshi master had said in class.... In the Mahatma Phule story about the farm labourer, I saw something of my father....No, it was almost the same...I was restless...I had to stop thinking about all this, so I pulled a book out of my bag. As I was eating, I began to flip through the pages; the words passed in front of my eyes and began to enter my heart. I began to read.... 'When the farmers bring their produce to the city, they are taxed heavily by the municipal corporation. They bring cartloads of goods to sell in the city, they have to pay for the hire of the cart, and then, when they return home they have to fight with their wives in front of their children. As long as the farmers have leaders like these, how will the lot of the farmers improve?'

These words were now making sense. I could look at the market and verify them. Every Monday, we bring our veggies and stuff to the market. Shouting ourselves hoarse, we manage to sell them. We shout and we wave them about. But in the end? Like pissing in the sand and hoping to save the foam.... I thought about the British and our history. Dadabhai's speeches and Joshi sir's voice began to echo in my ears. The white British left and the black British took over...our Aaba-Mai and my elder brother and our four bullocks work through the night and day like slaves...our shoulders have been ruined. Somehow, by making sacrifices, we managed to get the land ready for the crop and then sat with our heads in our hands—but what do we get in the end? Two years ago, the bathroom wall collapsed, but where's the money to repair it? In my head, all of history comes flashing back. The Mughal wars, the looting of the farmers, the British trade, the government institutions, atrocities on Dalits...Joshi sir gave us many examples of these atrocities. An image of the lower castes appeared in front of my eyes, enduring all, bearing all, and never getting anywhere.

I was lost in my own world.... The English improved our

lot? Chhya! They only looted us. And what about the current government?'

'Hey, boy!' It was Satva Teli, oilman to the village.

'What?' I tied up my bhakri, picked up the books, and pushed them into the bag and looked around. 'Have you seen my parents?'

'Duffer, sitting pretty. There your Pa's wandering about with a death load on his head…didn't he tell you to find a good place?'

And Satva dissolved into the crowd again. I looked at the spot I had caught and the cloth I had spread out. Leaving my bag there, I went off to find my parents. I picked up my heels and slipped through the crowd. Then I saw my old lady carrying two huge bundles of mirchis. And so I went forward and helped her take the load off her head.

She was exhausted. She gasped, 'Take it easy, son, or you might strain yourself.' She took a sack of onions to the place I'd reserved with the dhoti. I opened a bag of green beans, rich and luscious. I arranged them in a way that might attract the attention of the buyers. The old lady began to help as well.

I got my shop in order and went to help Aaba. Mai had poured out a small heap of red onions. She was moving them around, trying to bring some order to them. I looked at the two huge sacks of tomatoes in awe. They must weigh a tonne. Aaba had brought them in a basket. He had carried them on his shoulders to save them from getting squished. My mother helped him unload. There were bunches of castor leaves, carefully wrapped in a rag. Aaba and I began to open the sacks. Inside, deep red tomatoes, fresh and firm. Sizers, these were. Three or four would make a kilo, right enough. We opened only one of the sacks; the other we stored away under some leaves. We took out the weighing scales and the weights. Aaba explained the pricing. He gave the market a once-over, and said, 'Consarn it, there's tomatoes everywhere, every blessed where…' His face fell as he sighed.

'Come and get 'em, *cheap* tomatoes, fine tomatoes, red tomatoes…' he called out, putting a special emphasis on cheap.

Mai joined the chorus. And I slowly went back to my spot. My heart wasn't in it but I tended my shop. I piled up the green beans so that they might catch the eyes of the passers-by. I wanted to know how much to ask for them so I started chatting to the chap next to me. I talked up a storm about this and that, to get to know him better. Then I asked him what I really wanted to know. 'Can one make a profit selling at these prices?' He looked at me as if thinking: The boy has a point. Massaging a small hill of green chillies into shape, he said, 'You can't just sit there and make a profit, can you?' I got what he wanted to say. But when I talked about the seller making a living, about the labour of carrying things, he looked at me curiously and smiled. Then he said, 'How will the brokers earn anything then? They get by on this too. We can't hit them where it hurts.' And he began to laugh. I got what he was saying but I also thought it odd, because it was the farmers who did all the work, right? So why should the broker get anything? Take the case of my parents. They had brought four sacks from the village, carrying them all the way to Kalamb. If one of the labourers had picked up just one of these sacks and carried them to a truck standing right there, he would have charged one rupee. But my mother, my father, my brother, all of them, each with sacks, all the way from the fields to the village to Kalamb.... What was the truth of it? All these calculations were spinning about in my head, I felt like I was going down a slippery slope inside my head.

'Got a kilo weight?' my neighbour asked. He settled for a half-kilo. I sat there watching his customer. It was his first customer. He took the money, touched it to his forehead, thanking Bhavani Ma. So I started up again: 'Who decides the prices for these vegetables and all?'

'Who knows? Accept your fate and clean your plate....'

Then he broke off to call out, 'Line up, line up. Green chillies, hot as fire. Red chillies at rock-bottom prices....'

His first sale had pumped him up. He began to wave his hands about, wanting to attract attention to his wares. He was talking to them too. Then he said to me, 'You sit silent like that, you'll have to take it all back with you and feed it to the cows. He who yells, sells. The mute get the boot even if they have wheat to sell.' On his feet, one hand behind his ear, he went back to his hollering: 'Come and get 'em. Red hot and happening...red chillies.... green chillies...green....'

The market was full now. Well-heeled customers were now roaming around, dangling their bags. Some of the women were huddling under colourful umbrellas, their little girls carrying net bags and watching the spectacle.

They were all bargaining hard. I felt sick at the way they haggled over five or ten paise. But also some pity. These customers would hunt in packs. They'd sit around in groups. They'd inspect the goods, poking and prodding at everything. Then they'd ask the price of a kilo of this and then say they wanted a quarter kilo. And when they had got their goods and were getting up to go, they would say they didn't have change and give five or ten paise less. For ten paise of coriander, they would wander around the whole market looking for the best buy. Men were not so bad but women! They were the real deal. There were those who were looking to pay half now and half next week. There were others who were importuning the agents for their money. Others had brought bullocks and goats to sell. And the smells of all these, of eggs, of hens, of Bombay duck, of fish, all came together and floated over it all. There were piles of grain everywhere. There was a lot of pushing and shoving at the shops, at the chaat stall. The vessel sellers were bargaining. People were also meeting each other. The agents were talking to their chief. Ice lollies and batashas were being sold. Wives were in search of their men who had gone in search of alcohol. They were cursing at them and at the very gods too. And when the children began to cry, they would give them a good one too.

Then suddenly a familiar voice boomed in my ear. When I turned, it was my father, bawling his lungs out. Not just that, he was also waving his arms about. He seemed to be intent on tearing his throat open. My mother's voice followed in his thunderous wake. I was squirming inside. I thought I should stand up and caterwaul too. But just then some classmates appeared...a bunch of girls too. They would look at me and laugh...then they would come to the vendor next to me and bargain with him, pointlessly, and go away again. Tomorrow, class would be difficult. My life was looking yuck.

And the teacher would deliberately look at me and say, 'One should not be ashamed of one's profession'. Now my life was not worth a heap of beans. Suman Joshi, Anagha Deshmukh, and Vimal Raut, all three wandered by my corner. I wiped my sweaty face. And even as I was looking at them, my father's voice erupted again.

'Come and get them, great tomatoes, fine tomatoes...not a seed in them...fine tomatoes....'

The customers would stroll up, stick their hands into the baskets, squeeze the tomatoes as if they were cricket balls, and then ask him to halve the price. Aaba would wave them off. If the man had dark glasses on, Aaba looked like he would bite him. But swallowing his rage, he would say gently, 'Uncle, come next week. You're not getting them at that price today.' The customer would mumble something and depart and Aaba would go back to shouting. And then he'd give it to Mai, 'Oy, trouble and strife, lost your voice? Come on, shout. Put some energy into it,' he'd say in between his announcements. Then, balling up his fist, he'd give me a look and send off a volley of abuses, 'You fat lump, don't just sit there, get on your pins and shout. Get up, now.'

That meant I had to get up and shout. If I saw someone I knew, I would get up and scream. I'd shut my eyes and scream my throat out. 'Come and get them. Green beans. Fresh green beans. The best beans at the best price....' Then I'd open my eyes just a fraction and check if they were still around. An hour passed and another started off.

In class, we were studying about Dadabhai Naoroji and how he exposed the financial exploitation of the British. He appealed to the people to fight this ruin visited upon them, to start a movement. He told the white British administration with no hesitation, 'Your empire is built on the sweat and blood of India. You export our raw material to Britain and then bring the finished product here to sell at a profit. Your country became rich while India remained poor.'

Today we are independent but Dadabhai's analysis still holds. The white British have left but we have a new class of black Britons who behave the same way. The labourer has not got his due. The Dalit is still the slave of these interests. I was listening to all this, absorbing it all. And I was making notes. This explained our poverty, our helplessness. The British may have left but they had left their influence behind. Macalo* said he wanted to develop men who were black of skin but white in their thinking. That's what Macalo may have said but what is happening now? They may have gone home but we have held on to their way of thinking. What do I know of all this? Do I understand it fully? Either way I have to get past this examination. Everything the books say, and what Joshi sir and Jadhav sir say, remains in my head. Then when I get home, I light the kerosene lamp and study all night. All this on half a bhakri. I talk to the characters in the books, and I feel they are talking to me as well. I analyse everything they say. I compare what the kings of the past and our present rulers. Dissatisfaction, anger, rage rise in me but I keep on reading, keep on making notes. If Aaba has some free

---

*This is Macaulay, of course, but our young narrator has some problems with a name he has probably heard in class and not quite got the hang of.

time, I tell him some things. Aaba and Mai were in a good mood once, so I said softly,
'Aaba....'
'What?'
'Can I ask something?'
'Go on then.'
'No, you'll get angry.'
'First tell me what you want to know....'
For the first time ever, he drew me to him and stroked my back.
'Are you going to keep me in Kalamb until my matric?'
Aaba drew his knees up to his body and said in a voice full of sorrow, 'Boy, don't you think I understand? Don't I want you to study? Become a big man? A mamlatdar, a district officer? But what can I say? And even if I tell you, what would be the use?'
Aaba's face seemed to be full of tears. I am sorry I mentioned it. He is silent and then after a while, he calls Mai to him and makes her sit down near him.
'What do you think?'
'About what?' she leans back and ask.
'Should we sell the buffalo?'
Mai was shocked. Her eyes widened.
'We can get another buffalo but will his matric year come back again?'
Aaba's voice was full of sorrow. He seemed to be on the verge of tears. But then in a moment, his tone changed. He himself changed the topic.
'What does education mean now anyway? Where are the jobs? Instead, we should get another buffalo. And start delivering milk to some families. Or maybe sell it to the dairy. Who knows what will happen tomorrow?'
This time, there was a decisiveness about his voice, as if he had made up his mind. So I just shut up and listened. Then who knows what happened but Aaba sat up and asked me to

come to him. 'What does she know about all this? Education can never be wasted. But there are problems, too. Because you're in school, we have your masters as customers, and the hostel too.... If all goes well, we can set up another stall in the market.' Aaba couldn't think beyond these things. Because I was a poor but promising student, the other students and the hostelites would make sure they bought their vegetables from me. He valued this business. But I didn't like the way the rector talked about me. I was ashamed of their pity. It stuck in my throat. But there was no help for it. Aaba's calculations were simple. What would happen if I lost a year? I could sit for the exam the next year and in the meantime I could help the family. It didn't quite work that way, I knew, but how was I going to change his mind? Once he'd got an idea, he didn't budge. And I knew all this. But I was also determined to get through. Day and night, I hit the books. Monday always went badly. I'd think: I must have sinned in some past life to end up in a Kunbi family.

Now it was near closing time. Carrying their bits and bobs, people were heading home to their villages. The sellers wanted to get rid of their goods; the buyers wanted the best possible price. The vendors had it tough: they would have to sell at a loss but if they didn't, then the produce would end on the rubbish heap. Damu, the Mang, had slashed the price of rope from four rupees to three. A quarter kilo of vegetables, which was two rupees, was now a rupee. And the buyers were moving quicker now. They were eager to get home. No one had looked at Aaba's tomatoes from the morning. He had refused to lower the price and so only half of a basket out of two full baskets had been sold.

The second one hadn't even been opened. This month, the price of tomatoes had taken a beating. The crop had been very good. Tomatoes had painted the market red. But this bargaining cut us to the heart. While we weighed them out, the soul protested. But the customers wanted the best deal. Aaba was now willing to give a two-rupee kilo for a rupee, but still they wanted a couple extra in the bargain. I had a couple of kilos of green beans left. Mai's onions had all been sold so she was sitting and watching Aaba struggling. She did not have the guts to say anything to him so she simply watched, one hand to her chin.

The market was thinning; some shops had closed. The people were now few and far between. But Aaba was still at it, shouting.

'Come on, come on, take them for seventy-five paise, fine red tomatoes.'

But the people would not stop as they walked past. They would look at him and laugh and walk on. This enraged Aaba and he deliberately shouted louder. 'Let's go, let's go, take them, they're now fifty paise...fifty paise...fifty paise....' Even then they did not stop to buy. No one even came close to look and the day began to fade—darkness fell and the bazaar began to empty. Not that Aaba even noticed. He kept at it, still shouting. And then at last a customer approached.

'What price were you saying?' he asked, prodding at the tomatoes in the full basket.

'Fifty paise a kilo,' said Aaba. He was still shouting. The customer picked up some tomatoes.

'Should I?' he asked himself.

'What does that mean?'

'You said fifty paise but what's your last price?'

Aaba could take no more. He was on the point of exploding. His ears began to flame. His lips began to flutter, but he made an effort and got control of himself.

'How much do you want?'

'If you had spoken nicely, I might have taken a quarter kilo,' he said calmly. He chose a few of the juiciest and best tomatoes and put them into the weighing scales.

'Let's say twenty-five paise a kilo....' he said.

'What?' Aaba roared. He was out of control now, his body was shaking. He roared at the man: 'Madman, monster, don't you have any shame? Get out of here and never come back.'

The man got up immediately. He backed away, mumbling something under his breath. Aaba was standing there, as if made of sawdust, his face inflamed. Wherever he looked, he saw tomatoes and still more tomatoes.

'Fifty paise a kilo is too much? Twenty-five paise, is it? Or maybe ten paise, even, or five.'

'Why not take them for free?'

Then he overturned the baskets, scattering the tomatoes. Now he was knee-deep in a mound of fresh and juicy tomatoes, crisp tomatoes, tangy tomatoes. And he began to dance on them, crushing them, smashing the tomatoes....

Aaba, dancing in the red muck of his own creation.

Translated by Jerry Pinto

THE ECLIPSE SHALL PASS....
URMILA PAWAR

The loud voices of the girls' laughter and their joyful chatter from the terrace penetrated three floors right down to the ground floor. The lunar eclipse was about to start. All the girls staying as paying guests in Auntie's third floor apartment had gathered to watch it and had set themselves up on the terrace as if they were celebrating the harvest festival of Kojagiri Purnima, the full moon night of the month of Ashwin, when everyone is supposed to be awake and making merry for the better part of the night. Some of them were working women, a few were college students, and one or two were enjoying their stay at the expense of their parents or boyfriends. Some were trying to identify the eclipsed spot on the edges of the pale white moon. Others were searching the sky for constellations. And all the while, the girls were climbing up and down the stairs, fetching this and returning that. The scene was reminiscent of the hustle and bustle at a marriage ceremony just before the wedding takes place.

Only one of the girls was absent, Sumati Sabnis, Sumi for short. Even at other times, when she would be amongst them, she would behave as if she was never quite there. Lonely and detached like a drop of water on a leaf. Today, after leaving the bank and returning to Auntie's apartment, she had been lying on her two and a half by six foot berth just below the roof. It was hardly a berth, more like a plank for storing luggage. She lay on the narrow berth with her four-foot body drawn into a foetal position. She was badly hurt by the words of Suresh, the regional manager at her bank. His words had pierced her heart.

Suresh himself had a forearm missing from birth. Yet, in spite of his own incompleteness, he had insulted her for being a midget, and the insult had set her very being on fire.

Hurt by this rejection, she stared blankly at the round window near her feet. Sometime in the past it had been a ventilator window with glass panes. Now it was nothing but an empty hole. Sumi had never bothered to find out what there was beyond that emptiness. Nor had she concerned herself with whether or not it provided ventilation. Beyond that hole there was supposed to be a loft in the next room that belonged to Auntie. In the murky light of the cobweb-ridden loft, one could barely make out the dust-laden stacks of papers and some scattered paintings it contained. Once she felt she could hear someone crawling and rummaging through the papers in that dark cavernous space. She was scared then. But then she came to know that the crawling presence was just Auntie's son. He was an artist and lived with his friend. Once in a while he would appear, suddenly, like a comet, take away some of his paintings and papers from the loft and disappear. But Sumi had no desire to know more or see what lay beyond that empty space. She would often feel as if the round empty space was trying to pacify her and soothe her, sometimes as a friend, sometimes as a sister, sometimes like a mother. The wall of her village house had a similar circular recess where an oil lamp would be lit in the evenings. That place was her refuge. Whenever she was scolded, or whenever her will was ignored or violated, she would come and sit beside it in complete silence.

No one noticed it when she was born, but sometime later everyone began to notice that she remained much shorter in comparison to others of her age who kept getting taller. And that was the beginning of the bastardly questions and comments—Why was she not growing? How come she was so short?—the creeping eclipse of her dwarfishness which had cast a long shadow over her vigorous growing mind and her emotional world.

Everyone was free to comment on her shortness—on how she could not reach things kept on the upper shelves, on the size of the clothes she wore, the smallness of space she occupied when she sat, or on her short stumpy legs dangling as she sat on a stool or a chair. She would be pulled out and forced to stand beside her siblings while comments were passed: wrinkling their noses, people would say—Why is she growing downwards into the ground? She may be short, but she is bright. But it'd have been better had she been taller than brighter; hold her across a window during an eclipse, stretch her, and she will become taller than a coconut tree! And invariably these words were followed by titters. And at the time of an eclipse, it would be open season for comments like the last one.

Every laugh would sting; every look would pierce her heart. Nevertheless, even after she began having her periods and until the age of eighteen, Sumi secretly clung to her dream of eventually growing taller. But slowly the dream wilted. She realized that she was not going to grow any taller than she was. She would remain 'one and a half foot', she would tell herself and laugh at herself for saying it. Slowly she became inured to people's comments, or perhaps she could now feign indifference to them. She decided to concentrate on her studies. She joined the college in her tehsil town, endured being constantly made fun of by her college mates, endured the withering looks, and like a wavering lamp protected by the fold of a sari, managed not to lose self-esteem and secured a first-class with high grades in her B. Com finals. She scoured the classified ads and applied for every job that she could—and one day a reputed bank called her for a job interview.

The call letter gave her goosebumps as usual. A woman is judged first by her geography. IQ and other abilities come second. The watchful eyes would cover all possible angles. As if she existed only from shoulders downwards. And questions would be so tough that no one could answer them. Better to fire away an answer and walk out rejected like a piece of paper scrunched up into a ball and thrown away in the dustbin. She was restless and was in two minds as to whether to attend the interview or not....

She sat thinking in the dark in her favourite place beside the oil lamp recess. Her mother came into the room, placed the lighted lamp in the recess, and asked her, 'Why are you sitting in the dark? Aren't you supposed to be leaving tomorrow? Why have you not packed your bags yet? Come on, get up. I am making some gram flour laddoos for Kunda. Come and help me make them.'

Her mother's words passed her by, unheard. She remained motionless. Her mother prodded her and said, 'Are you worried about where to stay? Do I have to tell you that your sister Kunda lives there? Her place is small but how much space do you need anyway? Go stay with her. After all, is she not your younger sister? She is the one with whom you can now share all your joys and sorrows.'

At that instant her mother smelt something burning and rushed to the kitchen. Sumi felt like laughing out loud. The man who had come to see her at her so-called 'looking ceremony', where the groom's family inspected the bride and decided her fate, had rejected her outright; had thrown in her face the fact of her four-foot height and had brazenly asked instead for her younger sister Kunda's hand—as if it was a cattle market. Select an animal, if not this, then the other one, hold its horns, and complete the deal.

A date was fixed, issues of give and take settled, and in no time Kunda's marriage had taken place. All the while Kunda's husband behaved and later continued to behave as if he had done the family a big favour. To top it all, her father declared, 'Henceforth if we call someone to consider Sumi's marriage proposal, we should tell them that Sumi is Kunda's younger sister.'

Her lack of height had been so convenient for everyone, especially for her sister who did not cast even a single backward glance and happily and eagerly went away with her husband.

And this was the sister who was to share her joys and sorrows?

Sumi left her bags at a friend's place and entered the maze of the interview. How high did her head reach when she entered the interview room through the flap door, up to the middle or the bottom of the flap door? And the table, did it come up to her chest or her waist? And what about the chair? Everyone's gaze measured her height, freely ran all over her body, and settled on her chest behind her dupatta.

Across the table she could see a row of brawny male hands resting on the table and spoiling for a fistfight. Her unsettled gaze finally settled on a shiny reddish pink, obviously plastic, hand protruding from an arm tightly buttoned up to the wrist. It belonged to a middle-aged man of medium height who was sitting behind a name plate that declared his name to be Suresh Murugkar. A strand of his broom-like stiff hair dangled on his forehead which made him look younger and a bit cute and romantic. She fixed her gaze on that innocent looking plastic hand of Suresh Murugkar and successfully answered all the questions she was bombarded with. And then, even though her biodata was in front of them, came the inevitable question:

'What is your height?'

She felt like asking them, can't you see? Are you blind? But she managed to swallow her bitterness and answered them firmly. Now the hands in front of her moved restlessly.

'Everything else is fine, but what about her height? Bank counters are quite high,' someone whispered softly. And all of sudden, that plastic hand was banged on the table, and in the manner of an expert on the constitutional clauses of both the nation and bank, Suresh spoke in a clear and authoritative voice, 'We are a free country and all our citizens have the freedom to work and choose their work with the exception of old people, children, criminals, and patients suffering from incurable diseases etc. Ms Sumati Sabnis does not belong to any of these categories. And it is not as if the carpenters needed to fit her a chair are on strike. So....'

He once again banged his plastic hand on the table and gave her a brief but sweet smile. Sumi felt the taste of a honey drop on her lips and felt so comforted and secure that she felt it would not matter to her now whether she was accepted or rejected. Still euphoric with what had happened, she walked out of the room and whispered into the ears of one of the girls waiting for the interview, 'Is there a hostel nearby where I can stay?'

The girl gave her a contemptuous look and gave her Auntie's address.

Auntie accepted her as a paying guest by virtue of her willingness to pay and her small body. She was allotted space on a narrow plank that went by the name of a berth. It was the topmost berth just below the roof and by the side of the ventilator. Even the neediest girl would not accept it because it was too small and sometimes lizards and cockroaches would enter through the open ventilator. But Sumi had no choice. She just wanted a place to rest her head.

Auntie accepted her with an unwarranted remark, 'You have such a small build that you will have more than enough space, and it will be easy for you to climb up and down with your small frame.' As she said this, Auntie managed to play with her sari in a manner that emphasized what she was saying, and all the girls broke into a laugh that sounded like slop being slapped into a drain.

Sumi knew that there was a lack of residential places in the cities and people are desperate for accommodation. But this was the first time that she saw how perversely it was exploited. In two bedrooms out of her four-room self-contained block, Auntie had fixed planks on the walls right up to the ceiling in the manner of two- or three-tier railway compartments, and fifteen to twenty girls crawled on to and off them like four-legged animals. On the floor, in the spaces between the berths, were the beds of girls who paid extra money for the privilege. Climbing up and down without disturbing them was an art that was nothing short of acrobatics.

'I have provided adequate comfort to all the girls staying here. They are all very happy here,' was Auntie's refrain and all the girls had to listen to it every day as they went about their business. The comforts she provided were a gas range on a kitchen platform to make tea or coffee or at best an omelette, a small locker to hide your most important things, two clotheslines in the balcony at the back on which you were allowed to dry only your underclothes, and a shared phone on which one could receive, but not make calls. Girls who were in love and had boyfriends were quite happy with the arrangements. Moreover, the eating joints, bus stop, and market were all nearby. So the girls never complained even though Auntie raised the rent every six months.

The girls' main complaint was about Uncle. He was Auntie's second husband. He was at home all the time. He moved around the house in his underwear. And he had a habit of listening in on the girls' phone conversations. He wanted the girls to look at him, talk to him, and would drool at the girls all the time. Auntie used to take him along whenever and wherever she went. In their absence, the girls used to mimic them and make fun of them. At some point of time, Uncle used to run some business. It collapsed and now Uncle was totally and permanently dependent on Auntie. In fact, the flat belonged to her first husband. He had willed it to his wife and son. No one knew why her son did not stay in the flat. Some said he had objected to the inhuman treatment of the girls. Some said he hated Uncle because he had misbehaved with his girlfriend. Whatever it may be, Sumi had not failed to notice that this ageing man, who lusted after the girls, ignored her the way someone would ignore a small shrivelled grape from a bunch of fulsome grapes. For her it underlined the everyday negation of her very existence and she could feel her otherwise strong sense of self-confidence being shaken. Sumi, however, had never seen Auntie's son. But according to the little information she had, he was slim with a wheatish complexion, like Auntie, but there seemed no doubt that unlike Auntie, he had a very sensitive nature. If only he were here.... Sumi used to smile at this thought, because, in that case, none of the girls would have been here. Auntie disliked being asked about her son. But she did not mind it if the girls asked anything about Uncle or made fun of him. Indeed, she often joined them in making fun of him.

Even now, seeing Auntie alone on the terrace, someone asked her, 'Where is Uncle? Has he broken the cord of his underwear? Or is one of us girls on the phone?'

'Nothing. He is not feeling well. He is sleeping.'

'Wake him up; it is not good to sleep during an eclipse. He may end up sleeping all the time.'

Someone pinched the girl who had spoken and whispered, 'Why do you want him to get up? Are you missing his underwear?'

'He will be the only one who will miss the eclipse, isn't it?'

'No, there is that one and a half footer who is still downstairs.'

'Oh, yes! Now I wonder why she has not come.'

'When has she ever mingled with us? She goes about silently with a sad face as if she is carrying the burden of all the world's miseries on her back.'

'That is what must have reduced her to one and a half foot!'

The entire terrace rocked with laughter at this remark. A while ago, when she left the bank, the smile that Suresh Murugkar wore on his face under the garb of consoling her suggested the same thing, one and a half foot....

'Look, watch that cloud. It looks like the face of a toothless old woman.'

Sumi remembered how in her childhood she would see her grandmother in the sky. She had been very short, and Sumi had supposedly turned out like her. And silently, inside her head, Sumi would cry out to her, 'Aaji, why did you not grow taller?' Then as she grew older she realized that stature was not bodily stature alone.

Look at bright Wyadh (the star Sirius) and the three-star arrow he has shot into the Mriga Nakshatra (the Orion constellation).

The deer and the arrow piercing its heart...do you see it?'

Hmm, dear women, the arrow that pierces the heart is not just to be seen...you have to suffer it. The way I am suffering from the words that Suresh threw at me a while ago. Sumi, whose gaze was fixed on the ventilator, wavered a little. Does that conversation I hear refer to me or is it just that I am interpreting it that way?

Today, in the afternoon shift, there had been very few customers at the bank. Hardly five or six may have come in.

Someone also remarked, 'Not just the moon, but even the customers seem to be affected by the eclipse.'

'Actually, what is the time of the eclipse?'

'When is it going to start?'

'It will start. It is supposed to start at seven past five. It's in the papers. See page three.'

'That news is that of the rape of a minor girl.'

'Yech! News about rape and all that is a routine affair. Below that is a box item about the eclipse.'

'Come on, let us go home early today. Suresh, can we go?'

'Can you watch an eclipse only from your home or what?'

'No, but today's eclipse is a rare one and a comet is also supposed to appear.'

'That is very inauspicious. Even the panchang says that today's moonlight will have bad effects.'

Without looking up from his work, Suresh said, 'If that is so, I better go home. My right hand also may get affected!' And he laughed.

On hearing this, Mrs Mirkar whispered in Mrs Tawade's ear, 'Once the eclipse begins, we should stretch his left-hand through the window. Who knows, it may become longer by one or two inches!'

'Yes, yes!' Mrs Tawade laughed discreetly without showing her rotten teeth, and her kohl-like dark pupils swivelled towards Sumi.

Sumi realized that now it would be her turn and she resolutely immersed herself in her computer screen. Her mind lingered on that news item about a minor girl's rape. She began to wonder, how old would the child be? Would she be as short as her? Would she be as slightly built as her? What might she be feeling? How would she have endured the pain while her body was ripped apart like cloth? That kind of attack is not just an attack on one's body but on one's mind, indeed, on one's very existence.

Once Suresh had casually invited her to have coffee with him in his room. And the experience of what happened next...the experience of a body crumpled and the throbbing pain...and yet something that left behind a longing to taste it again. In fact, it was the same day their friendship began to wane. Suresh, whose words in the beginning seemed to come from deep within, soaked with emotion...Suresh who said that the humanness of human beings was beyond age, religion, caste, height, skin colour.... Suresh who was well aware that she was revelling not only in his words but in the very air that emanated from him and which she drew inside her...the same Suresh suddenly went cold on her, cut her off. Recently he had started avoiding her altogether. Even now who knows why he is the only one who has so much work.

Slowly the rest of the staff left. The pale white light of the tube light looked to her like a patch of leucoderma against the desolate dark wilderness of the empty hall behind the tall counters. And within that wilderness, she could see Suresh's outline through the glazed glass like a satiated tiger now lazily slumbering in his lair. The iron door opening into the garden had already been locked and bolted by the watchman who was now yawning, barely able to hold on to his gun, and blindly waiting for Suresh and her to leave.

Sumi was also trying to get a hold on herself. This was the time to go and stand in front of Suresh, to gather together all her emotional unrest into one single sentence, and ask him that one question.

The way you were there for me on the day of my interview, will you be there for me the same way all my life? This question that had blossomed forth in all the cells of her body, which had so frequently come to her lips only to stop there, and which was now almost shrivelling, it better be asked before it loses all meaning.

She collected the printouts of the account opening papers to hand over to him and got down from her chair. She had to get down from the high chair with the help of a small step fixed onto its legs. Once again, she felt a barren sadness at what she already knew, that her feet did not reach the ground. She also remembered the whispers exchanged during her interview. She pushed the cabin door open and though he was aware of it he asked her, 'You have not gone to watch the eclipse?' Earlier he used to address her with the respectful 'you'. She liked it because it seemed to increase her stature, her height. Later he used the intimate 'you' and that too was nice. Now he was back to a distant, respectful 'you'. As if he had drawn her near and then thrown her away.

'I want to speak to you,' she said, trying to keep her voice open and even.

Though he did not raise his head from the file before him, she felt him stiffen. But feigning carelessness he said, 'So, tell me, what is it.'

'Um...not here, outside...the way we used to.'

'No, not now. I have some work that needs to be completed.'

And then he raised his face and gave her a direct, dry look and said, 'Sit.'

With his right hand he lifted his plastic hand from his lap and placed it on the table. Whenever he needed to support himself he had to do that, even when he wanted to get up. Sumi had noticed that.

'I am tired of staying as a paying guest. I am tired of being alone.' Sumi stopped herself. Why am I dodging what I want to say? She asked him straight away, 'What do you feel about me? About us getting married?'

There was complete silence for a while. Then he brought his left hand down on the table the way he had at the time of her interview and started talking in a soft tone.

'I am aware of the incompleteness of life. Is it worth living because it is incomplete? But there has to be a limit to the incompleteness. How do I explain it to you?'

Then he looked at the guard at the door and looked at her, and as if to protect himself from the strong expectations her eyes held, and said in an even softer voice,

'I do not want any more incompleteness in my life. Please do not be upset. But you are not sexually attractive, and oh yes, neither am I!' he laughed out aloud and banged his left hand on the table as if to console her.

She felt shattered by this unexpected and humiliating rejection. She felt dizzy and her head was in a whirl. She got up and, in the barren light, managed somehow to find her way through the abandoned tables and chairs. The guard slid away the chain on the door and she kept walking, digesting the halahal poison she had just consumed, crushed and buffeted by the crowd as she walked. 'You are not sexually attractive.' She kept hearing Suresh's words amidst the constant cacophony of road traffic…but then… but then, when you called me for coffee at your place…wasn't it this same body of mine, Suresh? Her mind kept screaming this question loudly inside her head.

With unseeing eyes but practised legs, she somehow made it to her room. Two or three girls, about to go to the terrace, stopped at the entrance of the staircase. One of them, cross for no reason, wrinkled her forehead and said, 'Hope you have not had dinner because today there is dinner arranged for everyone upstairs on the terrace. We forgot to tell you in the morning.'

With the devastation showing on her face, Sumi dragged herself forward and entered her room.

'What happened to her? Why is she walking like that? Here I am telling her out of concern for her and look, she doesn't even listen. Silly one and a half foot!' They felt slighted because Sumi, this nobody, had crossed them without even looking at them.

'Once the eclipse starts, let us pull her through the window and hold her by the ears and stretch her. She may not gain height but at least her ears will become long enough to hear us.'

'Let her be, something seems to have gone wrong with her. She will join us after some time. Come along.'

'Look, look. Up on the right side of the moon you can now see a black spot.'

'Yes, yes. On the right side, near the ear of the rabbit. The eclipse has begun.'

'Oh, the eclipse has begun. Look, look. Let us watch it through the binoculars. Look how Rahu is swallowing the moon.'

Outside, she could hear the beggars chanting, 'De daan...sute giraan...de daan'—give alms...the eclipse shall pass...give alms.

Inside, the girls were screaming their heads off and laughing wildly. Downstairs, Sumi was lying silent on her berth. Her gaze was fixed on the circular void near her feet. She suddenly remembered how their cow had given birth to the calf and the shape of her widened vaginal opening. Not only the cow, she thought, her mother's vaginal opening must have looked similar when she had popped out of it. But was there an eclipse then? No, because then the midwife would have pulled her out and she would have been taller. And then, she would have been sexually attractive to Suresh. And she would have given birth to his child in the same way.

But first, into this circular void...is she growing bigger inside this void? Is my body being stretched in the void? Was she being stretched like a rubber band? Yes, yes, she was being stretched. Certainly, but why were her hands and head thrust into the dust and papers from the loft. And what are these paintings flying in her face? What is happening to her waist? Her legs were still stretched on her berth.

And oh, Mummy, what was this deadly pain that resembled

birth pangs? It pains so much! Oh, her waist was stuck. How was she to get out from here? Everything went dark. There was darkness everywhere. Her throat was parched. Oh Mamma, come, someone come and free me, free me.

'Oh my! Look at this. You can see someone's legs coming out of the wall up there!'

'Whose legs?'

'Oh my, that is Sumi! It is her berth, isn't it? Oh. Hey, Sumi. Hey, Sumati Sabnis.'

Auntie heard the noise the girls were making and came running. She looked up, and let out a big shout, amazed.

'Hey, Sumi, what do you think you're doing there? Where are you going? Come out of there right away!'

'But why would she go through that ventilator?'

'What do you mean why? Obviously, to eat shit.'

'Oh, do you mean Uncle, that old man, is sleeping over there?'

'Yech! So cheap and dirty. So that is why she was trying to get to that side!'

The girls started babbling, saying whatever came to their minds. Auntie got angrier and angrier. 'She is hardly one and a half foot; isn't she ashamed of her actions? Just because she did not get any one, now she is seducing him. What? How long has this been going on?'

Uncle had been woken up by all the commotion the girls were making and stood there confused in his underwear as usual while Auntie glared at him. The girls started giggling at him and he broke out into a sweat.

Sumi was in distress, the dirt in the loft was choking her. Her waist and ribs were hurting badly. She started throwing her hands and legs about like an animal caught in a trap. Paintings and papers flew about around her torso and onto the floor of the adjacent room.

And then, Auntie's son entered the house. He had a small, broom-like beard, and he had tied his long hair into a ponytail.

He wore cotton pants and a kurta and a shabnam bag was slung on his shoulder. He shouted, 'Who is rummaging through my stuff up there?'

Auntie pointed her finger at Sumi, 'See, she is the evil woman rummaging in there.'

Auntie's son didn't understand what was happening. Thoroughly confused, he asked, 'Why would she want my paintings? And if she wants them, why is she trying to take them from there?'

Then he realized that she was stuck in the vent. This realization spurred him into action; he went to the other room, pulled out a stool and with its help climbed onto the loft.

'What are you doing here? What were you trying to do? Oh, I see, is that what you were trying to do? Only someone like me can do that! Anyway, don't be scared...trust me and just keep still....'

He was smiling and he put both his hands under Sumi's armpits and slowly pulled her out of the ventilator the way a baby is pulled out of the womb during a difficult delivery. Sumi was devastated. If it was true that the Earth had opened up and taken Sita back into her womb, she wished that likewise the Earth would open up take her back into her womb.

Auntie's son climbed down with Sumi, and as they reached the floor, Sumi's legs gave way and she slumped onto the floor and Auntie pounced on her with a volley of questions.

'Come on, tell me the truth. What were you trying to steal from our room? Or was it some other kind of stealing that you had in mind?

'Why were you trying to enter our room? Was it because he was sleeping there and you were going to climb down and go to him?'

Auntie was fuming and the doubts in her mind pursued her like ghosts. Auntie's son got a glass of water and offered it to Sumi.

'Come on, Mummy. What are you talking about? Look at her scratches and bruises. She is bleeding. She has been hurt badly. Here, drink this water.'

Auntie knocked away the glass of water from her son's hand. 'No, I must know what she was up to. Tell me the truth and then just get out of my house. I don't want to see you again, ever.'

What could Sumi say? She no longer remembered when and how she had entered the ventilator. And now here was Auntie ranting like a mad woman...the girls surrounding her and giving her disgusted looks, poisonous words...somehow Sumi gathered her frail body together and got up. Each and every part of her body was paining. She had scratches all over her body. Her tongue had retracted into her dry mouth and she was unable to say a word. And yet, she wanted to stand straight and tell them all what she felt.

'None of you will understand my pain. This pain that has accumulated inside me from my childhood. The pain that grows every time you make fun of me. The perverted pleasure you derive from it. I sit on a chair and my feet do not reach the ground. My hands cannot reach the upper shelves. You laugh at me for that. You say because I have a stunted body, I must also have a stunted mind. You avoid me. You consider it beneath you to talk to me, relate to me. You conveniently forget that inside me, just like you, is a mind, and a heart that gets hurt, and can die.

'No one can control what body one receives at birth. Not so with the mind. You can make it beautiful. Have I troubled anyone? Been angry with anyone? Ever teased anyone? Or hated anyone? No. Even then no one found me attractive. No one ever accepted that I am a normal person. A woman's body may not necessarily be beautiful, but there should be plenty of it to make it sexually attractive. For rape, even a minor girl's scant body is fine for you. But for marriage, even though I am a complete woman, I will not do because I am not plentiful in body. That is the requirement. But as a foetus I grew only this much in my mother's womb. You were asking me to stretch myself and make myself taller? I have grown up with this burden on my mind. I do not know, but perhaps all that was in my subconscious burst out when I heard that the eclipse had begun. And I must have reached that empty space up there....'

Sumi felt her tongue go numb. She felt her words rising inside her like a fountain from deep within her but all she could do was keep sobbing.

She did not realize that all the while she had actually been speaking out loud. The fire accumulating within her had burst out and she felt herself being scorched by it, again and again. She was racked by deep sobs. That 12-by-12 room had frozen into silence.

And just then someone shouted, 'Look, the comet has arrived.'

Those words broke the spell and all the girls shied away from Sumi as if they had found a slithering snake beneath their feet and ran screaming onto the terrace. Behind them, Auntie too ran up the stairs. So did Uncle. But they had no effect on Sumi. She stood where she was, torn and frozen. Auntie's son emerged from somewhere and said to her,

'Are you not going to watch the comet? Come, let's go. It's such a rare event. Come.'

Yet Sumi stood still and rooted to the spot.

The son approached her, and as he removed some cobwebs from her hair, said to her, 'Did you see my paintings? Did you like them? We will arrange them nicely later.' And he smiled.

Sumi thought his smile was very different from the one that Suresh had given her on the day of the interview. It was like a cloudless, unblemished blue sky....

Translated by Swatija Manorama and Suhas Paranjape

THE DUST OF VAIKUNTHA
RANGANATH PATHARE

Like she did every day, Jijai started her tongue-lashing without pausing for breath as soon as Tukaram picked up his castanets and started for the mountain.

'Keep banging your cymbals, smear yourself with ashes. But God doesn't reach your mountain with a bale of grains to feed us. How do you expect me to feed our brats? Knowingly and shamelessly you wrap the cloak of ignorance around you! Why the hell did you marry me, if clicking your castanets is all you wanted to do? Have you no shame? The jaggery in your shop has turned to mud with flies buzzing all over it. Nor do the kids' noses stop running....'

Tukaram, that great soul and straightforward person, always followed the same straight path to the mountain every day. He rolled Pandurang's name on his tongue each day, wondering if it would stop that voice from reaching his ears or whether he could ignore the corrosive emotion behind those familiar phrases. And daily he was assailed with doubt, was it of any use at all. Sometimes Tukaram also wondered if God is somewhere beyond this material life, children, worldly pursuits, daily expenses, household, all of it, if He too, is pestered by His wife.

But today his mind, a bubbling cauldron of confusion, was preoccupied by something else. Jijai was the same as always. So as Tukaram walked farther away, her hoarse voice got louder so as to reach him. On top of that, the children were fighting, screaming, and weeping. From time to time, Jijai socked one of them and then raised her voice to drown the child's loud crying.

The more there was of this cacophony, the faster Tukaram walked, and Jijai's voice would climb to an even higher pitch. Such was the battle every morning. Those who witnessed this regularly had developed the art of turning a deaf ear to it.

One thing about Jijai though. She never quit her post in the courtyard. The poor woman never ran after Tukaram, never corralled him, or dragged him back. She was not educated enough to say that she had drawn a boundary line for herself like the one drawn by Lakshman for Sita in the Ramayana. Some worthless God sitting above in heaven had joined her fate with that of Tukaram, this Valhoba Ambile's son. She had had no control over it. The bunch of brats she had brought into the world, the cattle in the shed, the calves, the jeering neighbours, and those worthless freeloaders of the neighbourhood would have been the end of any other woman. But Appaji Gulve's girl, Jijai, was no weakling. She had more strength and more patience than the cattle she raised. And a lot of innate wisdom she had. She knew no limiting line drawn by Lakshmana. Every evening, many jobless followers of Tukaram would come home with him, chanting 'Pandurang! Pandurang!' loudly. The clamour of the boisterous kids was ever present. Jijai would pat down jowar rotis to the rhythm of this din and feed all the wastrels. Once they got what they wanted, those poor souls too, chanting 'Shrihari! Shrihari!', bending and bowing, would depart from there as if not wanting to trouble the poor woman any more. And tired from sounding the castanets the entire day, Tukaram would also lie down quietly. It was as if this put the renewed strength of an elephant in her. She would coax and cajole and feed the kids, close shop, do the cleaning and the washing, clean the cattle shed, water the cattle, even kiss the calf despite being in a hurry, milk the cow, coop the hens for the night, make the kids' beds and put them to sleep, sometimes with love, and other times with shouts and threats. She never had a moment to spare. Too much talking makes you weak was not an adage that could be applied to Jijai. Her angry chatter, or if calling it chatter is unfair, let's say the stream of wisdom escaping her lips, must have actually been a respite for her. Or so one would have thought upon hearing that incessant flow of words. Whether anybody was listening or not, the stream continued to gush. Those present could choose to heed it or not. She herself never felt the need for any reaction.

What was important was that despite all this, the task at hand would continue to get done flawlessly. For example, though she was unable to read or write, her account keeping was faultless. Her father, Appaji Gulve, was a renowned moneylender. Account keeping and interest calculations were a part of his daily routine. Of course, back then she was not required to do it, but as they say, 'A singer's offspring never cries off key', that same instinct helped her learn it well. And later, when the great Tuka abandoned all worldly concerns, it was enough for her tongue to start the blather.

Thus Tukaram started for the mountain and the usual bunch of cymbal-clutching admirers followed him one by one. Mahadaji Kulkarni, Gangaram Bandal, Santuba the barber, Kondiba the milkman, Narba the carpenter, and Bhilaji Patil, they all followed chanting the God's name, 'Jai Jai Ramakrishna Hari!' A babaji from Otur had initiated Tukaram, and ever since then all these believers began following him as if in a trance. The drought had receded a little and most people returned to their household matters. Who had time to spare for these cymbal-clutching believers? And familiarity breeds contempt. So this daily march continued, mostly unhindered, undisputed.

Mahadaji, Gangaram, Santuba, Kondiba, all had sons who looked after their households and their families well. Only Tukaram's household rested on the unyielding cattle-strong shoulders of the acid-tongued Jijai. She shouldered everyone's responsibility, and took care of Tukaram. Having taken care of everyone, the cymbalists, the kids, the cattle, it was then her daily unfailing job to massage Tukaram's feet as he lay down to sleep for the night. Tukaram could have easily massaged her feet instead or run a loving hand on her head and that would have made her immensely happy. But why would Tukaram, consumed by the longing for Pandurang, even think about such petty things? In fact, things invariably were quite the opposite. Tukaram, clicking castanets and chanting 'Pandurang! Pandurang!' the whole day as if possessed, would eagerly start entering the world of flesh at the touch of Jijai's calloused palms. And finally with alacrity he would celebrate the night in the same fashion as any married couple. 'I go beyond body when I see You, oh Vitthal!' No truth in that! The sensory body was very much there and was uncontrollable. What to say? Of course this was not always the case. Many a time as befitted his age, Tukaram would fall asleep, but whenever he did succumb to the demands of the flesh, Tukoba would spend the rest of the night wide awake while Jijai's tired body, having dutifully completed the last chore, would turn into stone and become one with the earth.

This was Jijai's life. She was like Ahalya, whom the lord heeded occasionally. But that was enough for her. And she never spoke about it. But on such occasions, while perennially oscillating between the material world and asceticism, Tukaram would visit her, he seemed to be anchored to the real world and she would fall asleep in hope. Such was the state of things.

But something was amiss today. It was not as if Tukaram's voice rang the loudest with the daily chants of 'Jai Jai Ramakrishna Hari!', but his castanets would indeed keep clicking rhythmically and the string of his ektara twanged sharply. Sometimes he would even swing and dance to the beats. His headdress, his moustache, the bag of finger cymbals hanging from his shoulder, all would swing rhythmically.

But today Tukaram walked with heavy feet, in complete silence. His castanets were silent. His accessories were immobile. The cymbalists set up a loud chorus of 'Jai Jai Ramakrishna Hari!', but Tuka stayed silent.

The village was behind them. The open road beneath their feet. Apparently, Tukaram had forgotten the custom of starting an abhang—poem of devotion—while crossing the village boundary. People found this strange. Mahadaji tried to put things in order and started to sing Tukaram's abhang, '*Oh Lord, the worldly concerns are killing me....*' Everybody joined in a loud chorus, repeating the lines over and over.

Tukaram walked on but gradually he started comprehending some of the worldly concerns troubling him.

Tuka had always been soft-hearted, even as a child. He led a carefree life under the protective support of his family. They were doing well in business as well. His first wife Rakhmai bai kept falling ill, so the second marriage to Jijai. No sense in saying that the cart of a householder's life runs smoothly when both the wheels run in unison. As the first wheel, Tukaram was weak; he was like a self-centred child! It was fortunate that Jijai was strong. His parents passed away. Rakhmai died. Elder brother Savji left. There was a terrible drought. The world turned upside down. He was bankrupt. Tukoba felt freed from all worldly concerns. The mouths to feed, the household, the sharp-tongued Jijai....

'Oh Lord, the worldly concerns are killing me....' Like a soldier deserting the battlefield, Tukaram turned to asceticism. Thus began his many charades, spending hours in the temple reading scriptures, plastering the walls of the temple with mud. Whenever any ascetic passed through the village, Tuka would follow him like a shadow, beating the finger cymbals like crazy, chanting 'Hari! Hari!'.... It was madness! He never had been good at running the household. Now it was all crumbling. But like clockwork, twice a day, he felt hungry. Eventually even that feeling stopped. The awareness of the body itself started waning. Then Jijai took over. A single wheel started pulling the weight meant for two. Running the household, feeding Tukaram, and last but not the least, keeping him tied to the material world. When you are fed twice a day without fail, you return to your bed at night. And if one doesn't remember—sometimes people who have lost their mind don't, but so what?—then remind him and keep the reins of the marital life firmly in your hands, that was Jijai's fail-proof strategy. Now it is true that Tukaram was like a bow pulled taut. When the bowstring is pulled tight, the arrow gets released and travels fast to its destination. Tukaram was unable to implement even this simple thing in his life. The reason was Jijai, the tower of strength! Tukaram's mind was set free of all worldly concerns, he wanted to go beyond the material world. But how could she let him? Like a heartless moneylender—after all, she was a moneylender's daughter herself—she kept dragging him back into the material world. And Tukaram's mind stayed a taut bow that could not find release. Even that worthless God up there should not be made to face such torture! What a situation to be in! The bow string stretched to full, the arrow pointed at its mark, but no release! Such a cruel state, this state of arousal and no release!

But how can one say that Jijai alone was responsible for it? Why should she alone be blamed? She might have dragged him back, but then why would he come home in the evening like a fly trapped in molasses? And once desire arises, it is uncontrollable!

His son Waghoji had been a baby then. At night when Tukaram was busy in the act, the baby sleeping nearby woke up. It's true that the baby was wailing loudly, flailing arms and legs, but was least interested in what was happening beside him. He was probably hungry or thirsty and wailing as a means of announcing it. There was no aspect of censure in it. But Tukaram wouldn't have it. Right in the middle of the act and without stopping for a moment, he placed his palm on the baby's mouth. The baby choked and started to flail its arms and legs even more. Jijai snatched Tukoba's palm away and started comforting the baby. Jijai's body was busy fulfilling the demands of her husband but her heart was with her baby. What a tug of war! Only Jijai could manage to resolve this. The touch of her calloused palms soothed Waghoji and he fell asleep but Tukaram went on, undeterred....

With the act over, Jijai would turn to stone like Ahalya and start snoring and Tukaram would keep tossing and turning, his thoughts tormenting him. This uncontrollable desire of the flesh bothered Tukaram tremendously. 'I go beyond body, when I see You, oh Vitthal!' Yes, I go beyond the body. The mind transcends, goes beyond everything. 'Beyond pain or pleasure, I don't sense hunger or thirst.' True, absolutely true, that! There is no falsehood in it. That is the ultimate Truth.

But then why does Vitthal punish me again and again like this? Why can I not transcend this barrier? Why does desire awaken in me? There was a drought. Cattle died. The Devil's armies raided the living. There was chaos everywhere. 'Highborn beauties stood rejected, but faces of common maids kissed, promiscuous women flourished, and pious women woeful.' This became the norm. He might criticize and say this to others but wasn't he himself doing the same thing? A flowering shrub, when deprived of water, bursts into blooms in desperation and tries to create new life; similarly desire grew stronger in the drought.

Mahadaji finished the abhang and Santuba the barber started next, '*Roof of the sky, the earth is my seat, my mind is lost in contemplation....*'

It was not as if Tuka had fallen silent like this for the first time. This had happened many times in the past as well. But usually his silence would give way after a while and he would say something new, full of devotion, something very interesting. This had happened several times. So the followers were not unduly disturbed. Everybody had a fair idea about the travails a great being like Tukaram had to undergo every day. They had heard the corrosive, acid-filled words of Jijai ringing in the ears like redhot bullets, and what they didn't hear—not because Jijai heeded their presence, nobody thought she ever did that, but supposing she did heed their presence, then that which was uttered in their absence—they could very well imagine and guess the extent of pain caused to the saint by those words. Even in their imagination, they did not dare face Jijai alone. They did not have the smallest doubt that Tukaram endured it all because he was Tukaram. It was all for the sake of Tukaram, for the sake of the love they had for him, otherwise do you think they would choose to eat the bhakri that Jijai made? A lot of people called them cheapskates, freeloaders. Jijai would often insult them. But they learnt patience from their saint. And, upon returning home, if they did not need to ask for food from their hearth, the wives and daughters of the house were happier and let them sleep undisturbed, which was an added bonus.

'Roof of the sky, the earth my seat, my mind is lost in contemplation...' the follower's chanted louder. Tukaram stood staring at the mountain.

The barren mountain. No trees, no creepers. Only the seat of the earth and the dry, burning blue sky.

> Barren mountain, barren Vitthal,
> Your unyielding household, dear God!

Sitting alone on this mountain, what a massive universe Tukaram had created with his words! And at the bottom of it all was an unyielding classic obstinacy. The world saw the greatness of Tukaram, they saw his devotion to the Lord. People were impressed by his immense knowledge. Drawn by his eloquence, singing his bhajans, people from villages afar came in droves, attracted by his words. Just for a vision of him, to hear his words, they came thirsting from afar, and invariably ended up hearing the hard sermon by Jijai, who would climb up the mountain with a basket of food on her head. This wild dance of words! What should one call it? It was like the roasting grains on the festival of Nag Panchami, bursting and spraying mindlessly in every direction. The newcomers would be embarrassed, scared. The regulars would pretend to be dumb and deaf. Their devotion and respect for the saint would increase manifold. With his eyes closed, Tukaram would sit unmoved, like the mountain. It seemed as if the words were bumping off his bald head, from under the headdress, and popping and bursting like popcorn. Tukaram would stay divinely silent. Only he could understand the point of Jijai's words and it would make him increasingly angry. But his face would not betray any emotion. The closed eyes, and silence draped around the whole body like Karna's armour. Then the basket of food would be flung down. Aamti in a pot and with a seasoning of sharp, angry words. The great saint Tukoba would endure everything with equanimity borne of unyielding stubbornness. The respect and devotion of the devotees would only deepen. No one valued Jijai's words. Only the aghast newcomers, completely dumbfounded, would try and listen. Their dread of the material world would grow. But when the saint was fed and sated, Jijai would slam the pots back in the basket and leave, and Tukoba would open his eyes and start singing happily, '*Today is the day of bliss! Divine bliss!*'

They reached the mountain and then approached the usual seat in the shade. But Tukaram walked on. The followers were singing the abhang that Gangaram had started off, '*I have lost my mind with longing for you, I look for you everywhere, O Pandurang*', but what Tukaram was looking for, nobody could guess.

In the morning, as Tukaram was about to leave the house, the youngest child played nearby. The older kids kept their distance. They weren't that attached to him. They had realized quite early on that it was not fruitful to be attached to a crazy person like this, it won't help you later in life. But what of this mattered to the youngest child? From time to time he would clamber onto Tukaram's back or sit on his lap to pull his moustache. It was Tukaram who did not care for this gift of the child's happy company, so willingly and freely given. 'I have lost my mind longing for you....' But this child's babbling, running around, and stumbling, hanging on to Tukaram like a limpet, this was also enough to drive one out of one's mind. And it was enough to make Tukaram lose his focus. But Tukaram was selfish to the extreme. He knew how to take all of it without giving anything back in return. So the youngest son said to him in the morning, 'Baba! Shall I come with you?' Why would Tukaram say no? And if he didn't say anything, it wouldn't have been the child's fault to have interpreted the silence any way he wanted. The child clambered onto Tukaram's back. Tukaram stood up, but still he still wouldn't let go. With his child's arms and legs, he clung to Tukaram's back like a baby monkey. Tukaram leaned forward slightly, so as not to drop him, his one hand holding the castanets, the other hand holding the ektara and a bag hanging from the shoulder. Jijai moved forward, she smiled but did not start her usual diatribe, 'You fool, don't tell me you want to join this gang of cymbal beaters too?' Her words might have been rough but they were full of love. Even the child could sense the tenderness behind them.

'We are going to the mountain! I am going with Baba,' the child babbled. Tukoba stood still. No movement. Silent. No joy. No resistance.

> The tug of the household, pulls at the heartstrings
> This blind love for you, O child

Jijai pulled the child off Tukaram and, whacking the child on the back, she held him tightly in her arms. Then she ran her mouth as usual, 'Do you want to be a wastrel? He has no sense and you want to emulate him?' That set Tukaram free and he set out undeterred. Or so he thought for a moment. Because the next moment Jijai appeared in the courtyard and started her long sermon. As usual, the kids gathered around her and with rapt attention started drinking in her words that extolled this worldly life. The poor kids always provided accompaniment to her sermon, crying, screaming, or shouting. As if on cue, even now, they picked up the task with great enthusiasm. The one in her arms set up a loud howl. The usual cacophony followed.

At last Tukaram stopped. He stood under the open sky with the glaring sun and turned to the followers. He looked at everybody once. But that was it. Nothing more. Tukaram just stood like a mute pillar.

Everybody bowed. All the usual followers were there. No outsiders today. The householders are people who devoutly follow the tradition of engaging with the other world only when the concerns of this world are completely fulfilled. Leaving the jowar that needs to be harvested for the sake of other worldly concerns was ridiculous. But for Tukaram this was not important. He had given up on the material world himself and these followers had children who looked after their worldly concerns. And in the evening they ate food cooked by Jijai! In the afternoon, when their guru broke bread, they chewed tobacco. They fasted in the name of God. The teacher would have fasted too. But Jijai wouldn't let him. What could he do? He was helpless. There were no 'Jijais' who would bring a lunch basket for the followers. And they knew that Jijai fed them in the evening only to get rid of them. These matters were never expressed in so many words, but they were widely known.

> For the company of pious people, the saints endure pain
> Quenching hunger, that's just a bodily chore.

Such was the nature of the cymbalists. This was exactly it! They truly believed in Tukaram. The glory of their belief was true! So be it. Anyway, Tukaram stood under the sun like a pillar. He did not take his cymbals out of the bag, there were no castanets clicking and the ektara was hanging by his neck. Tukaram's moustaches were drooping. His head was bowed. The headdress was covering his bald pate. The mountain of Bhandara and the burning blue sky. Nobody knew why the saint was silent today. Nothing out of the way had occurred. There was no unusual news of any kind. Jijai's words were harsh, of course, but that was the daily routine.

So what was wrong with Tukaram that day?

Why was Tukaram silent?

Mahadaji leaned forward and inquired, 'What is our fault? Did we do something?' Everybody started asking him the same question one by one. But Tukaram remained silent. His face was impassive.

Something like this had happened before. Tuka had gone silent then as well.

Dhanaji Tikune had a crazy daughter. A total lunatic. Her name was Rahi. Old Dhanaji died and the mad Rahi was orphaned and without any support. The young kids harassed her. They pelted her with stones and she would howl and yelp, trying to hold together the rags on her body. She had lost all awareness of hunger and thirst. Often she would sit in the barn near the village gate, cackling from time to time like one possessed. Strangers would be scared witless. And Rahi's mad laughter would chase them as they quickly took off. Sometimes Jijai would coax her home. She would wash her like a cow being washed in the river, and feed her. The mad girl would just laugh maniacally. She would cackle even with her head under water or when glancing at food. If she ate, she just didn't stop. Whenever she saw Tukaram, this mad girl would mock him, laughing and jumping and clapping all at once, chanting 'Pandurang! Pandurang!'

One day Tukaram was walking at the lower end of the village. This end of the village had a dense cover of trees like mango, lime, acacia, tamarind, and silver date palms. It was a place of ancient temples, bats, bird droppings, beehives, and donkey manure—there was a stench. Tukaram heard the sharp staccato of horses' hooves. He saw a swirling cloud of dust in the distance. He quickly sought refuge in the shrubbery. This was common. The marauding armies came like a swarm of locusts. They would rout the village, beat up everybody, rob and steal, and rape the women. It was worse than an attack by hungry wolves. So it was customary for everybody to look for a place to hide and stay there.

Tukaram entered the temple and went straight inside the dark sanctum. He sat there, almost clinging to the black idol.

He was reassured by the darkness, the bushes outside, and the stinking lonely place. Also, God was at hand, to be invoked as a last resort. Thus there is definitely security here.

Tukaram was not worried now.

But if things start falling in place as per our expectations like this, the unfathomable, incomprehensible acts of God would have no place in this world.

Something similar happened and soon Tukaram heard drunken voices and laughter. Tukaram clung tightly to the idol. 'If you are benevolent, I'll give the last scrap of cloth I possess, but my stick will break your head, if you are not.' One utters these common sayings, but when does one do it in practice? Tukaram's heart beat faster. His ear caught phrases from various dialects: Dakhni, the southern dialect, Yavani, used predominantly by Muslims, and Kannada. Soon, the speakers came closer. Tukaram peeped out. The men were armed and drunk. They were glancing in the opposite direction. The sound of laughter followed them but it was quickly suppressed. Tukaram's heart thudded against his ribs. He recognized that laughter. That was Dhanaji's Rahi! They brought the girl into the temple and knocked her down on her back. They tore the rags off her body. In the course of the scuffle, she found herself ungagged and she laughed again. That terrible laugh echoed and fluttered inside the dome and the dark sanctum like a bird trying to break free. Tukaram's heart fluttered like a captive dove. One of them gagged her immediately and another one launched himself hurriedly between her thighs. Tukaram was clinging tightly to the idol now. Since she was gagged, no laughter escaped from the girl but she was moaning and whining from time to time. The first one got off then the second one came and then the next. The moaning was now becoming weaker and weaker. But the dark silence in the sanctum did not break. It was difficult to see who was clinging to whom, Tukaram to the idol or the idol to Tukaram.

All of them left after what seemed like ages and Tukaram stepped out. His heart was heavy in the chest. Dhanaji's daughter was lying there stark naked. Her eyes were wide open. Her mad face reflected her uncomprehending shock. Her lips bitten and torn, mouth wide open, eyes open, breasts, thighs, everything bare and ravaged. The hapless orphan was lying like a rag. Tukaram picked up her tattered clothes and covered her limp, ravaged body with them.

After this incident Tukaram stayed silent. He never ever breathed a word about this to anybody. But afterwards for a very long time, he was angry with God. At the very least, he could not deny this.

> Why this body? Who owns it?
> A mad life, O God, with what aim?
> Clinging to life so shamelessly
> Aren't you a coward, larger than the sky?

If you are a coward, you have no right to call others a coward. We can add that this moral precept was not applicable to Tukaram and his relationship with God.

Finally Tukaram moved his hand. He raised his right hand and then lowered it. With that gesture, everybody sat down. The chanting of God's name began, 'Jai Jai Ramakrishna Hari!' A wave of enthusiasm passed over the followers. Better to sit down rather than stand in such scorching heat! Of course, such a selfish thought would never cross their minds. Expecting Tukaram to say something about bhaktiyog, and the path to devotion, they were all ears. This was the chance of a lifetime. The saint who usually avoided preaching asked the disciples to sit down and was himself standing. Was there any distinction between Pandurang of Pandharpur and the saint? The two were almost one. Now it would be Pandurang speaking to them through him.

Everyone joined their palms and waited with bowed heads.

Doing kirtan was one thing, but preaching was something else. Tukaram gave kirtan many times but he could never get into the pretence of preaching. But a time came when he was compelled to preach. Of course he did it without pretence. But nothing he said was acceptable to the followers. He was being absolutely sincere and still they did not believe him. It happened thus: Tukaram was on the mountain, the very same mountain. It was high noon. Jijai came with the usual basket of food. That day the followers were present in large numbers. They insisted that Tukaram preach. Or initiate them. They repeatedly insisted but Tukaram was unyielding. Finally, Jijai thundered.

'People come to you abandoning their duties, leaving their cattle to fend for themselves. What is the use of banging cymbals if you cannot counsel them? Why do you lure these people? You should counsel them and accept the offerings they bring. At least it will help with running the household. And they also will benefit from it. All this banging the cymbals and chanting "Hari! Hari!" That doesn't feed anyone....'

Jijai's words had the desired effect. Tukoba stood up. He folded his palms and said, 'Friends! I am a scoundrel. All of you have gone mad. Why do you come here? I have not crossed over to the other world, nor have I found release from this mortal nature. I tell you this sincerely. I don't lie. I have not reached attainment. I have not achieved salvation. I was fed up with worldly problems. I went bankrupt due to the drought. I sold groceries, bred cattle, and did everything I could. Whatever I earned, I consumed. I never gave anything to anybody, neither to a Brahmin, nor to a beggar, not even to a dog. I gave up everything at last and ran away from the household; but even in this pursuit I failed. I never succeeded in anything. My ancestors were pious people who worshipped God, I just follow them. That's it. It is not as if I have some great devotion for God or anything....'

When Tukaram started talking in this vein, the followers were scared out of their wits! How to digest this unconventional advice from Tukaram? It wasn't as if somebody else was laying down these details. It was Tukaram himself! Jijai was extremely happy though. She was satisfied at last. She said, 'If you know so much, why run away? I'll take care of everything. I'll look after the cattle, the children. You sit at home. Why go on with this charade?' She then turned to the followers and said, 'Go home. Look after your own household. What he just said is absolutely true.'

But the people were not so easily duped. They were disciples after all! They said Tukaram is a great soul, so it's natural that he would say such things about himself. Their respect for Tukaram increased a hundredfold. They refused to quit. So Jijai got up and left in a huff. Poor thing, she had a household to look after. So everybody stood with their heads bowed, with Tukaram immobile like the stone idol of Pandharpur.

A minute passed. Then two. Then three and four. The followers with their heads bowed and Tukaram like Vitthal of Pandharpur. The sun was so hot that even the dog's tongue was hanging out. The followers sat with heads bent. Almost an hour passed.

Somebody raised his head. Somebody else followed suit. Then the third one raised his head and then one by one everybody looked up. Tukaram stood unmoving as a rock.

'What happened? What's wrong? Please forgive us our faults,' Mahadajipant started meekly.

Everybody else waited with folded hands.

But Tuka did not move. The hot sun was scorching, biting. The followers were drenched in sweat. Their brains were also melting in the shimmering waves of heat. Add Tukaram's silence to that. It was getting unbearable.

'Are you here or are you there at the back? Which one is really you?' Bhilaji Patil pointed to the upper slopes of the mountain and asked. It seemed like his head had started spinning. He just couldn't understand whether what he saw was real or an illusion.

'Where? At the back?'

'Just look, he is going back there.'

'Really?'

'Yes, check for yourself?'

'But can't you see him right in front of you?'

'He is back there and he is also in front of you, what is this mystery? Buwa,* why don't you speak?'

'Are there two or three of him? I can see three!'

The followers created a commotion. Tukaram was standing where he stood earlier. But why didn't he say anything? Why didn't he tell them, I am here, what you see behind me is an illusion.

Mutely he stood there.

'Come on, let's go. This is beyond our comprehension,' Kondiba the milkman said and stood up.

'Buwa is not part of us anymore?' asked Narba the carpenter.

One by one they all got up. The scorching heat was unbearable.

'We must inform mother Jijai,' said Mahadajipant. Everyone believed beyond doubt that she alone could bring him out of his trance.

'We'll be back, Buwa,' said Mahadajipant and touched Tukaram's feet. Turn by turn everybody bowed at his feet. Any other person in his senses would have moved to bless them! But Tukaram stood still like a dried stump of a tree.

The followers swiftly descended the mountain. The sun was merciless. Add to that, the miracle that Bhilaji Patil saw! Which Tukoba was real? Many people had had doubts earlier. Maybe their brains were not as overheated as Bhilaji's. But Bhilaji was so certain about what he saw that people reined in their doubt. They thought that Bhilaji could see the vision because of the pious influence of the saint. Then, so as to not appear lacking in piousness, they too started to affirm the vision, vying to outdo each other. One of them vouched that he saw Tukaram bursting and fragmenting into many Tukarams, who roamed everywhere. The other spoke about his aura. The third one saw his eyes dripping with piety.

---

*The term Buwa (which literally means a man) is sometimes used to address a preacher, singer, or wise man.

It was getting late, time was passing. The scorching sun was beating overhead. So they convinced themselves beyond doubt that what they said was true.

Anything is possible in the case of Tukaram, such a great saint. Casting doubts about him is blasphemous. Or so they thought.

In short, something was not quite right with Tukaram. First he had gone dumb. Then multiple Tukarams burst out of him and they were all going higher up the mountain path. And there was a single Tukaram standing at the bottom. Who could that be? That surely must be his earthly remains!

> Trapped in the earth, for a few moments
> The form infinite, I saw with my eyes
> All the forms collapsed, merged together
> The God and the saint, both are one

What remained on the ground was the earthly body. But what about all those Tukarams going up? Weren't they bodies too?

Where was Tuka headed? Was this the coming of the end? Was Tuka going to Vaikuntha? In his mortal body?

Many such questions were bandied about and by the time they reached the village gates everybody was convinced that Tuka was going to Vaikuntha in his mortal body!

Strangely enough, Jijai, to whom they rushed with these tidings, was leaving for the mountain with her usual basket of food. And today she had all the children accompanying her. Did some instinct tell her that today was the moment of nirvana? Why was she taking the entire bunch of kids with her? That in itself should make one believe in the mysterious and infinite wisdom of God's merciful acts.

Upon hearing the news from the followers, Jijai rushed to the mountain bellowing like a cow. She never believed the bilge about bodily ascension to Vaikuntha or any such thing. But she knew something was amiss, something was about to happen. She couldn't have put it in so many words—that the bow string had been stretched and the arrow was about to be shot. But she was out of her mind with worry and went up the mountain path like one possessed. She and her little ones. The progeny of Tukaram and her.

In the meanwhile, the pious followers started spreading the word about the miracle they had just witnessed to all and sundry, the old men sitting idle in the village, the kids, the women going to the fields, the menfolk with their creaking footwear, to anybody they came across. Tukaram was ascending bodily to Vaikuntha. The news spread like wildfire. The entire village now ran to the mountain.

Tukaram stood still under the sun. He watched the village swarming like a beehive pelted with a stone. People were emerging from everywhere and running towards the mountain.

At last Tukaram saw Jijai. She had almost reached him. Jijai, with the basket on her head. The children running around her and getting under her feet. The steep mountain and the scorching sun. Jijai was panting. Her swollen, protruding belly leading, and she behind it!

The previous night, after everybody had fallen asleep, Jijai had come to Tukaram and started massaging his feet. It was the usual touch of her calloused palms. Jijai's work-roughened hands and the soft feet of Tukaram. Naturally the bowstring came unstuck and Tukaram was dragged back into the material world. What more can one say about what happened next? It was the usual household ritual. Jijai, like a battered ship and Tukoba desperately trying to hold on. This was something that had happened many times.

But what followed was something out of the ordinary.

At the end of this regular ritual, Tukaram's hand accidentally touched the woman's belly. The touch told him of the firmness of the belly. The firm, protruding womb. Tukaram looked at his wife's face. She had turned to stone. Fast asleep! Regret and shame engulfed Tukaram. He remembered the incident in the temple.

The stark naked daughter of Dhanaji Tikune....
Tukaram was moved to tears.

> My mind desires You, I embrace and cling to Your feet,
> The problems of this world dissolve to nothingness

If I experience this kind of oneness with God, then why do I disgrace myself, Oh Pandurang?

Why? Why do you force me into it again and again? What was my karma in the last life that I cannot control this hunger? Why can I not be freed from this, even as old age assaults my body? Why this torture? Why does Jijai put up with this? Tuka lay sleepless the whole night, tormented by these thoughts. He dared not touch Jijai again but he couldn't put the touch of the firm belly out of his mind. The image of Dhanaji's devastated daughter kept dancing before his eyes.

Jijai came closer. She flung the basket down. She could see only one Tukaram, his earthly body. Tuka was as silent as a pillar.

'There is no Vaikuntha, no nothing. Let's go home. When you fill your stomach with food, Vaikuntha comes home. If you have to go, let's all of us go. Let's go to hell. No need to go to Vaikuntha....'

Jijai was thundering.

But Tuka was silent.

The children started crying. The villagers were approaching. The cymbalists were singing devotional songs. They were certain beyond doubt that Tuka was going to ascend to Vaikuntha in his earthly body. One of them saw a heavenly chariot, the second one saw petals being showered. Somebody else saw the heavenly apsaras waving fans. There was even someone who saw the God with his chakra descending on the carpet of showered petals. Each one of them started seeing something or the other. They were blessed. Jijai alone was fighting with Tukaram, the mute pillar, from within her own lakshmana rekha. She could neither see the heavenly chariot, nor the floral carpet. She didn't see any God leading Tukaram with great respect. She didn't see the apsaras either. When she saw that her sharp words are having no effect whatsoever on the silent Tukaram, she lost her temper and crossed the line. Breaching the lakshmana rekha she moved forward.

And then something unheard of happened.

Tuka, who was standing still all this while moved. He bowed. With folded palms he saluted Jijai.

The surroundings filled with good, the time auspicious.... The forms coalesced, darkness banished....

In a fraction of a second that lasted an eternity, Tukaram lived his whole life again and then he fell down. His heart stopped beating and his body turned stiff as wood.

Shouts hailing him rose from all sides. The heavenly chariot took off. Tukaram sat on a high pedestal and the God was sitting at his feet. The apsaras were waving fans. The gandharvas were singing. The other gods were showering petals with great gusto. What a glorious exit! What a glorious end! Such a great experience! People almost ran out of words as they described to each other what they saw. 'Hail Lord Tukaram!' The chant echoed on all sides.

But Jijai fell on the bow-like dead body of Tukaram.

Singing paeans of the saint, the crowd started moving towards the village. The sun was unrelenting and the blessed eyes which witnessed this divine scene absolutely needed the respite of the cool shade. It was but natural that they would seek the coolness of the old Hemadpanti* temple, if not their homes, where they closed their eyes in order to capture the vision forever.

At last only Jijai remained on the mountain, with her kids scorched by the sun, and Tuka, stiff as a log.

But Jijai was not silent. She was arguing, quarrelling loudly. Tukaram's head was on her lap and she was screaming, her screams ear-splitting. Like a drum beating incessantly, without

---

*Hemadpanti: a style of architecture in medieval India where the structure is erected by putting stones on top of each other without masonry.

keeping any rhythm she talked, she cried, she moaned, venting her uncontrollable grief in erratic bursts. She was cursing God in heaven.

Tukaram had gone to Vaikuntha. The villagers, the cymbalists had reached their humble homes. But the mountain was steadfastly there till the very end.

> The sky fallen, the mountain shattered
> Such was the grief of Jijai

Near the living shrine on the mountain of Bhandara at a particular time of the day on the second day of new moon in the month of Falgun, one gets to hear the beating of the drum. Or so a lot of devotees would have you believe.

Translated by Anagha Bhat Behere

THE BOSS AND HIS DOG
BHARAT SASNE

Makarand has extraordinary questions. He doesn't always express them. He doesn't speak of them always, but he does have them. He sees dreams. He has thoughts. His friend tells him that these things—questions, dreams, thoughts—are unnecessary.

For example, what's the need for sensitivity? Makarand does have answers to these counter-questions. He says, 'Sensitivity is the true mark of being human.' That's why one must be sensitive and capable of sensitivity. As for capability, you cannot create it, but you can sustain it, augment it. Secondly, is an aesthetic sense necessary while doing a job? Should a clerk write poetry? Should one walk tall with an erect spine or not? Is life only about filling up the columns of official documents? Should one remain stuck in a petty web like an insignificant insect? Such questions plague Makarand. He means 'an ordinary government job' when he says 'petty web'. His friend contends, 'Why should one think, in the first place? Somebody does the thinking for us. We only ought to implement those thoughts. Beauty is an abstract concept. There is nothing more beautiful in the world than the boss's face. As usual Makarand disagrees. He tells a story. He doesn't claim that it is a new story. He is only telling it as an allegory. This is how the story goes—

2: MAKARAND'S STORY—AKA THE DOG'S TALE!

Here's what happened—Makarand is narrating the tale—there was once a poor servant. He had a boss. Since he was the boss, it follows that he would be rich. He was also in a position of authority. That means he had authority. He had a dog. The boss would take the dog out for a walk every day. Every day he would put a collar on the dog. Sometimes the dog would bark at the other servants. Sometimes the servants would feel envious of the dog. So, once this boss told one servant, 'I'm going out of town. I can't take the dog along. I'm going to leave him with you. Take care of him.' The servant was afraid. 'What a nuisance!' he thought. But how could he refuse the boss? Also, he felt it was an honour that the boss had chosen him. He neither agreed nor refused. He kept quiet. Silence is assent. That is the code of behaviour between a boss and a servant. The boss sent the dog to the servant's home and went out of town. The servant was in a spot. He couldn't manage to feed his family. How would he feed the dog? The dog must be accustomed to rich food. The servant was distraught. He would give the dog whatever food he had. It didn't matter if his children starved. He started taking care of the dog. He would tell the dog, 'Tell boss that I sacrificed all I had to feed you, to care of you.' But how could a dog speak? The servant became terrified. The dog shouldn't fall ill. He oughtn't appear gaunt. He must look chubby. Clean. He should have enough food to eat. After all, it was the boss's dog! What if boss questions him on returning? The neighbours are watching. The fellow clerks are watching. They will report to the boss. I must take care of boss's dog. The servant starved himself and fed the dog the best of foods. He became poorer.

The boss returned. For the first few days, he didn't even think of his dog. The servant couldn't return the dog right away, could he? What if the boss thought that the dog was a burden on him? 'Boss might be occupied. He'll summon me soon,' he thought, and stayed mum. But the dog did become burdensome. Finally, the boss remembered. 'Bring back the dog,' he said. The servant heaved a sigh of relief. His children would be able to eat to their heart's content the next day onwards. He brought back the dog and said, 'See, doesn't he look well?'

The boss smiled and said, 'Wonderful! He looks so much better! You have taken such good care of the dog. I want to give the dog to you.' The servant was petrified. He kept saying 'No'. The boss thought he was feeling awkward. Or he might be in disbelief. He said, 'I'm really giving him to you. It's a reward. Take the dog. Take good care of him, though!'

The servant returned home with the dog. His family was devastated. It was quite natural that his boss would smile each time the dog went to the boss's mansion by force of habit. Everybody would see it. This reward! How and what to feed him—the boss's dog?

3: THE MEANING OF THE STORY

The dog represents the responsibility entrusted by the boss. The boss's pretence of trust. False prestige. To win his confidence. To get into the boss's 'good books'. Carrying out the responsibility is untenable and not carrying it out, unacceptable. After all, it's a matter of the boss's prestige. The dog belongs to him. Makarand explained this meaning to his friend. The friend questioned. 'So what? Just as "beauty" is an abstract word, so are "prestige" and "responsibility"!'

Then the friend asked why an aesthetic sense was needed while doing a job. Not a single government document is beautiful. It's always dull, thick, and gloomy. The handwriting on it is never beautiful. In fact, it oughtn't be. Its content is never beautiful. It oughtn't be. It needs to be full of negativity, unhurried, cynical, indifferent, and suspect. A chair is never beautiful. The chair is like the spirit of a clerk—broken. Darkness is necessary. The walls have to be painted the dull grey colour of life. One is compelled to feel grateful in maintaining the boss's dignity or carrying out the menial task that he has assigned or in living up to the fake confidence he has shown in you. So, this story need not end with the servant starving to death.

'Then how should the story end?'

'Listen to this!'

The friend started narrating the story of the boss's dog.

4: THE SERVANT AND THE DOG!

The beginning is the same. The boss summoned the servant and said, 'I'm going out of town!... Can't take the dog along!.... Take care of him!.... Take him home!'

The servant took the dog home. He started acting high and mighty. He told his colleagues that such a responsibility wouldn't be given to an ordinary person. The boss's dog! Since he has entrusted me with this responsibility, it's evident that he has big plans for me. Soon he will promote me. This is just the beginning. His colleagues remarked, 'This is truly special!' Then the servant took the dog to a restaurant. Tied the dog's leash to a pole outside while he sat inside eating fritters. Every passer-by would see the dog and enquire with admiration, 'The boss's dog?' Since the dog barked, he got fed too. His colleagues requested him, 'Bring the dog to our place too! We'd love to show the boss's dog to the wife and children!' He pretended to be reluctant and then took the dog to the colleagues' homes as if he were doing them a favour. One colleague each day. With a show of displeasure. With a great swagger. They would tell him, 'Do tell the boss of our hospitality' and he would say, 'Alright'. The dog kept getting fed. The boss was very happy. On his return, he said, 'Wonderful! You have taken such good care of the dog. Take him. It is a reward.' The servant got his department changed. He became the manager of the restaurant. The dog is being fed. So is the servant. The colleagues continue to be in awe.

5: THE OTHER MEANING OF THE STORY

The friend's detailed explanation of the tale: 'The dog represents an opportunity. Offered by the boss. The one who can take it becomes successful. An opportunity is like a whore. Use and throw. The boss never asked again about the dog. Do you want to know what happened to the dog afterwards?'

'No!' said Makarand.

'Why not?'

'It's a pretence of trust by the boss. But I want to ask you one thing.'

'Yes...what?'

'What does success mean?'

'To threaten colleagues with paper cuts from a crumpled paper to get them to approve a complex note and thus securing the selfish boss's benevolence.'

'But does being successful mean being content?'

'Contentment?'

Here, the friend's eyes moisten. He covers his face. He hides his tears. He avoids Makarand's gaze. He becomes quiet. Then he laughs dryly. Gathers himself. Laughs cunningly. Says:

'Will the tune of contentment be heard over the boss's dog's bark?'

The friend is in a senior position now. In the same department. He looked after many of the boss's dogs. He didn't keep his spine straight. His spine remained flexible from running after the dogs on a leash. His spine didn't break. Seshan too would run alongside the prime minister's car, it is said. The friend knows this. Now he is in search of an opportunity. He takes care of the boss's dog on and off. He never questions himself about what contentment is. If at all anybody asks, he cannot hear it over the boss's dog's barking.

Makarand is still a clerk. His handwriting is beautiful. He has thoughts. He sees dreams. He has not been able to figure out the system.

Translated by Rupali Bhave

WAR

SANIYA

For a long time after she woke up, Vasu lay in bed, looking out of the window. The cool blue of the unfolding morning crept into her being, soothing her. She closed her eyes momentarily when it occurred to her that today ought to be different. Not ought to be. It had to be. But would it?

She sat up in bed and looked around. The room was as it had been before. As before? Yes, as it had always been. That wasn't possible.... Ranjit's clothes lying around, his toiletries on the dressing table, and Ranjit himself.

Ranjit had come back. After many days. Days? Vasu calculated yet again. Two years and ten months.

That long? Once more her gaze travelled around the room. Ranjit's presence was unmistakable. Had it been absent all this while? Did he not hover around here in spirit even when he was physically far away? Vasu didn't want to think about it. She just wanted to lie there, in silence, with her eyes closed.

The day, which normally began to bustle as soon as she woke up, was standing still today. Why?

Ranjit had slept in the balcony saying it was cooler there. Was he awake? The door was closed. The sun must have crept into the balcony by now. Hadn't he got up yet? Vasu remained sitting on the bed. He used to want his tea boiling hot. Does he still?

Vasu felt guilty. Why am I thinking like this? Because I have started comparing? Comparing the old Ranjit with this one?

She walked up to the balcony door, then turned back. After a wash, Vasu went into the kitchen, put water on for the tea to boil, placed the cups on the table, then, leaning against the window ledge, began to read the morning newspaper. The black and white print made no sense to her. The tea was ready, but Ranjit hadn't woken up yet. Vasu went and knocked on the balcony door. Once…twice.

Ranjit reached out from his bed and opened the door.

'Getting up? Tea's ready,' she said from the doorway. He was still lolling in bed. He looked at her, smiled, and asked, 'What's the time?'

'Must be around seven thirty.'

'Baap-re! I overslept!' he said, sitting up.

Vasu kept looking at him. Where's that old swagger gone? Why do his shoulders seem to sag?

She turned towards the kitchen. Ranjit followed her and picked up his cup. 'Is Sanju awake?' he asked.

'No, he sleeps till nine. Has the afternoon shift in school na.'

Is this what couples say to each other after living away from each other for nearly three years? Isn't there anything else to talk about, wondered Vasu. What can they talk about? The war?

Ranjit was sitting there with the cup in front of him, the tea untouched.

'Have it. It will get cold,' Vasu said.

'Cold? Ah, I've got used to drinking cold tea now. Hot or cold, it didn't matter, just getting a cup of tea was enough,' Ranjit replied.

Again Vasu was lost in thought. He's right. No fuss about tea from him anymore. I am the one who got used to drinking it steaming hot while listening to news of the war on the radio.

Were things always so simple and uncomplicated? Of course not. When the thought of a husband fighting a war far away was uppermost in one's mind, who cared about hot tea? Over time, didn't it become a matter of routine, a habit?

'What are you thinking so deeply about?' Ranjit asked her.

'Um, nothing, nothing much,' Vasu replied. Then, gathering

the tea cups, she stood up.

Ranjit spread the paper out on the table, quickly glanced at the headlines on the front page but didn't really get into the details. It was all pleasant sounding idle chatter. News for full stomachs.

He looked at Vasu's back as she stood at the kitchen sink washing up. Three years. How much had she changed during this time? He was not sure yet. There was very little he was sure of, actually. Was it a kind of weariness induced by his return from the front?

War! One that would go on for months. His posting to a remote area for two years had come just before that—to a non-family station, with no housing, no schools, no facilities.

Left without an alternative, Vasu had come to this place with Sanju. And before they'd even settled down, war had broken out. He couldn't come home to meet them. He had written to Vasu, 'I am off to war, a real, actual war. Now we will meet only when it ends, when I return.'

Vasu turned around suddenly. 'I'm making gulab jamuns today. It must be a long time since you ate them, na?'

'Definitely, especially those made by you…. Boxes of mithai used to be sent to us regularly, but it wasn't the same. So often during mealtimes, the jawans would talk about the flavour of home cooked food!'

Vasu smiled, heart-warmed Ranjit went out into the balcony, deep in thought. This is my home, he thought. She's taken care of it for three years…nurtured it. She used to write about it in her letters. Is it as she had described it?

He looked down at the street below. The traffic had picked up—cars, buses, pedestrians. Where are all these people going? In such large numbers? Have I gotten out of the habit of seeing crowds?

Barracks, camps, uniforms…that's all I've been seeing. Everyone was in the same situation, everyone belonged together. Does anyone here have any idea of my life there?

To think like this is foolish, Ranjit told himself. Each one has his own path to follow. If your path is tough, well, it's a choice you made. With full knowledge.

He came back into the room. It was so serene, so tasteful. Soon it will be bustling....Aai, Dada, Ravi, Vahini, and the children were due here any time now. They must have left as soon as they received the telegrams. Their son, brother, brother-in-law, uncle was home from the war. They simply had to come and meet him.

Ranjit was confused. Why isn't anything making sense to me? Why aren't waves of happiness washing over me? Why do I feel as if my spirit has been drained out? Why am I so emotionless and unmoved? He sat down, dejected. I know I ought to get up and get ready, he thought to himself. My friends must have heard that I have returned. They will definitely come over. I must greet them warmly. They will be eager to hear stories from the front, to know what I have done in the last three years. I must show my happiness at seeing them....

Ranjit continued to sit. He felt strangely hemmed in by so much emotion. He couldn't extricate himself from it. Had he got accustomed to being away from sentimentality, accustomed to the tough life? Tough? It had seemed so at first. But it had a charm of its own. A newness. Once accepted, it became quite pleasurable. Knotty problems, day-long tension, dire responsibilities, and, in the evening hours, the comfort of intoxication. One learns to value those precious moments of leisure and freedom and friendships.

Suddenly, unexpectedly, every pore of Ranjit's being yearned for that life, that atmosphere. The intense moments of bonding, the closeness arising from a shared glass.... Where was it? Was it within these four walls? In the well-furnished room? With his wife? Their son? The thought made Ranjit uneasy.

In our years of being apart, Vasu and Sanju had settled here, much against my wishes, he thought. But they had no choice. Getting leave was out of the question. Even if I'd wanted to,

I couldn't have come down to see them. All contact was through letters. Only letters.

Ranjit's mind was overwhelmed. Memories of three years ago flooded it. It had been very difficult at first. But one had to adjust. The bitter cold, incessant rain, inadequate amenities, and long hours of confinement in the barracks. Gradually one realized it was not too bad, fun, even. The comfort of alcohol. Friends and friendships. New bonds. After a long hard day, the warmth of the small wood fire at night....

Vasu had read about it all in my letters. From her side came news of their lives—Sanju's and hers. Gradually the initial anxiety waned. Then, without warning, war had erupted. On our doorstep, before our very eyes, grazing past us. Blasts of gunfire, shrill ringing in the ears, exploding bombs, searing heat on skin. Ominous darkness split by intermittent shards of light piercing closed eyes. War! War! It still haunts me.

'Ranjit, are you still drowsy?' Vasu was asking.

'Uh?' he said with a start. 'No, I was lost in a trance!'

'Will you bathe first or eat something first?'

'No. I don't want anything to eat. They'll all be here soon, won't they? I will go....'

As Vasu began to chop the vegetables, she was assailed by a strange discomfort. She hoped the arrival of the guests would dispel the air of despondency around her. Her mind flew back.

Three years! How had I managed?

Ranjit, hundreds of miles away. At first, choking on the food at the thought of what he might be going through. Then gradually getting used to the idea of living alone. Occasionally there were visitors. Why would anyone want to give up their own lives to come and be with me? After a while it had ceased to matter.

Letters and photos. That was all. Little Sanju's antics, stories, and narrations, carefully written as remembered. With time, those too became hazy, faltering. How long could the anguish of separation last?

When the news of war came, Vasu was shaken. Her desire to meet Ranjit had been intense. But meeting him wasn't possible. Letters now came straight from the front. Then she began counting the days....

But that's all over now. The days of fear, anxiety, uncertainty. War has ended. Ranjit is home. Safe and sound.

What next?

His return was unexpected. Vasu was unprepared. Meeting after three years...Sanju, too, was surprised. The Baba from the photos was here now in real life. Those things were figments of one's mind. This was real, this was Ranjit, and he was home. That was the reality.

Vasu was bewildered. She had not known what to say. Like when someone turns up unexpectedly. It wasn't wrong to think this way, was it? Wasn't Ranjit a stranger in his own home? Wasn't this experience of home, wife, child new for him too?

Conflicting emotions continued to trouble Vasu. Although they had kept in touch through their letters, she just couldn't bring herself to accept this Ranjit as the one of three years ago. How could she convince herself that he was the same man?

Lots of insignificant things change in everyday life. Habits, tastes, preferences, yet, when Vasu noticed these differences she was perturbed. She tried to reason with herself that Ranjit's life had been in an entirely different world for the last three years. Naturally he would change. What's so surprising about that?

Vasu shook herself out of these thoughts and began to hurry through her chores. Just then, Sanju came out. She turned to give him his milk and get him ready for school.

'Where's Baba, Aai?' he asked, his glass of milk in hand.

'Bathing. What do you want?'

'Nothing...but Aai...we will all live together now, na?'

'Yes, together.'

'Here only?'

'Who knows! A transfer is possible....'

'Aai,' Sanju asked, hesitatingly, 'Baba really, actually fought in a war, na, Aai?'

'Really and truly. What did you think?'

'Then he will have such interesting stories to tell. My friends will want to hear them.'

'Yes, yes, but who has school to go to before that? Go get ready!'

Sanju left for school full of excitement. Vasu rushed around the house finishing her work. Better get everything ready before the guests arrive. Once they come, there will be complete chaos, she thought.

Suddenly she stopped. What is happening to me? Why is this strangeness, this feeling of unfamiliarity, becoming so oppressive? What is this hollowness, this sense of desolation? Had Ranjit's arrival brought it on? She couldn't tell. The unexpected, yet much longed for.... Was it on account of the long separation? Or was it more basic, the realization that something was missing? Or lost?

Vasu tried hard to put all such thoughts out of her mind, but found it increasingly difficult. Ranjit was far removed from these mundane matters. He had come home unexpectedly and brought with him real and perhaps imagined uncertainties.

Just as Ranjit finished getting ready, Aai, Baba, and the rest arrived. One of Ranjit's friends also came along. By the time he had greeted them all, Ranjit started to feel suffocated. The joy of seeing him after three years, the relief that he had returned from war, safe and well, overwhelmed them. Tears flowed unembarrassed. Ranjit endured it all. He kept telling himself he should be happy to see his loving family.

They crowded around him. Vasu joined them.

'What is war really like? Did you kill anyone yourself? Is it true that the weather is terrible? You must have got fed up of being alone for so long, so far away, na re? You missed home a lot? You are going to be at home, eating home food after so long! What exactly are you feeling now?'

Ranjit was buried under their questions. Why are they doing this to me? Why is their affection so stifling? What kind of questions are they asking? Doesn't their curiosity, their interest, go beyond home and food?

Ranjit was reminded of his sudden awareness of death. The terrifying atmosphere that pervaded the war front. When jawans put on their uniforms, pick up their weapons, and run, what do they think of? Home? Precious, carefully preserved moments? Sentiments are too delicate to survive in the harsh environment of war. Strength is all that is relevant. It comes from somewhere. There are surging waters ahead, ready to drown you. An inferno surrounds you like a huge burning pyre. War, destruction, sacrifice—something is brewing—the enemy advances, hostility rules, fury rages, where's the time to fear in all this? Where's the time to look, to ask, to find out what is going on. Nothing comes to mind, no significant events, no precious moments, not even the thought of one's own death, as if one bears the writ of immortality. Whatever bad must befall, it will. But not to me, I will remain unscathed and defiant, with hatred seething in the heart—assault is the only option. We'll see what happens.

It takes but a minute, a deafening sound rents the air and companions fall—one alone remains, like a machine, automatically, and only one survives.

And the war ends. One returns. Home. To one's people....

Ranjit raised his tired eyes and looked around. He was connected to these people. But he had seen some real people who had become cherished friends before he knew it. People who had left all other ties behind to walk the rough path with each other.

My vision has expanded much, Ranjit thought, my horizon widened. And, in the process, trivial, inconsequential moments were lost and erased. The threads I was holding on to have frayed.

This house, this street, this town, those living behind these walls, these ties are slackening. I don't want to live with them. I cannot identify with them anymore.

True, the first year was exacting. Memories of home and family tripped one up at every step. By the time one got used to it, war broke out. In the heat of battle, finer feelings melted away.

Why? Was it inevitable, or could it have been prevented?

Ranjit felt emasculated for the first time; not like a soldier who has just returned from fighting a war.

The terrifying nightmares...the fearsome days continue to haunt him. The endless expanse of the sky, rent by one cry—war! Emotions, sentiments, thoughts all surrendered to it. In total submission. Everything forgotten.

The terrible war, meaningless and purposeless. Who won? Who lost? Who was victorious? I? Or Vasu?

Vasu stood there listening to the chatter, the excited questions, Ranjit's short, terse replies. She thought—Ranjit has moved far, very far away. He hasn't got used to this home yet. He's come as an outsider, he cannot integrate.

Where had the feeling of urgency gone? Had it evaporated even as it intensified? Once more, Vasu was overcome with guilt. Was she not able to understand him?

After such a long separation, shouldn't everything have blossomed anew? Why didn't it happen?

Had the springs within run dry?

There was no reason for that to happen. Vasu had written regularly—long, affectionate letters—as if she was speaking to him. Where was that rhythm now?

Her shoulders drooped, as she sat down. Go, she wanted to tell the gathering. Go...enough...leave before your talk becomes tiresome.

But they were so animated, so affectionate. Even Sanju had come back from school and joined in the excitement, moving closer to Ranjit as if he'd finally acknowledged his father.

Why, in the midst of all this, am I so troubled? Why does this feeling of isolation envelop me, Vasu wondered. She made a sincere effort to shake it off.

Just then Ranjit looked up at her.

'Shall we have lunch? It's late....'

'Sure. Come on, everybody....' she called out.

They got up, twittering. Ranjit stood up too, suddenly feeling free. The bonds/ties/shackles will still be there, in a more subtle way, perhaps, but they will definitely remain, he thought. For how long? Until one gets used to them. Till these little moments make a home in one's life, to settle and grow.

The prodigality of war, the limitless firmament, the boundless earth, the one overpowering emotion—it had truly affected every aspect of his being. The experience had brought home to him a deep understanding, had indeed changed his perspective. What was left to say? He suddenly felt a surge of emotions for Vasu. The awkwardness between them had to end. Will she understand?

Why won't she, Ranjit thought, smiling to himself. He had noticed, hadn't he, that she was deeply uneasy, too, and it was churning her insides? Of course he had.

Translated by Keerti Ramachandra

ONCE THERE WAS A CROW
RAJAN GAVAS

Kashappa Madkari is a straightforward, practical person from the town where I work. Before anyone else had an idea, this person got an inkling that the city would be making inroads into the town. Means, it so happened that news broke of the new cooperative sugar factory and the opening of a revenue office near our town, and the process of the city encroaching into the town was accelerated. Kashappa Madkari assessed this process very practically. After several visits to the government offices, he converted an acre of land near the town into non-agricultural land. In reality, the land was too infertile to produce even a few kilos of grain. No crop was possible. Also, as the land was very near the town, people who lived around there caused Kashappa headaches by defecating there. Hence, he chose this practical alternative. The encroached town picked up this news immediately. Potentional buyers started hovering around Madkari's house. It was then that he got the honorary suffix anna, and became Kashappanna. Slowly, he plotted the whole land and sold half of it...that news shocked me. I wondered: who is going to stay in this town permanently? I cannot imagine living here, so why should I think of buying a plot or whatever? I absolutely don't like this place and, to be frank, I have decided not to stay in this town for more than two–four years.

To tell the truth, I had no interest in moving to this town. But destiny dragged me here. I didn't get a job anywhere and one post for the job of a teacher became available in the high school here. I got it by paying nearly fifty thousand in cash and appeasing a number of people. Eventually, I got married and even today I plan to leave this place within two–four years. One fine day, the wife of one of my colleagues brought news to my wife of Kashappa selling plots of land. My better half's lecture would start every mealtime! 'Will our children care about our property in the village? And even if they do, they will make money by selling the house that we build here. What is the point of spending our entire life in this rented house? Even if we have to take a loan, we will have our own plot of land...blah, blah, blah.' She would rave and rant all through the meal. It became so unbearable that I went to Kashappa's house to ask for the land. I applied for a loan of sixty thousand rupees from Masters' Bank. Loan for a job, loan for a plot...it was awful. But there was no way out. At last, I became the owner of a plot in a place where I didn't want to live. I was terribly disappointed that day. I am telling you all this in detail because it is directly related to the crows.

Woke up. Something was tossing around on the terrace. I wondered, 'What could it be? It must be an illusion.' I tried to ignore it and go back to sleep. Once again, there was a noise and now I could hear fluttering. And what's more, I heard the sound of water. I mused, 'Something must have fallen into the water tank. Damn it! The water will have to be discarded.' I was angry with myself, but I tried to go back to sleep. There was a sudden cawing of crows, such shrill cawing too, that I got up. Bloody, it must be a crow! Means, merely emptying the tank won't work. I will have to clean it too...waste of a few hours. Meanwhile, the cawing woke up my wife and she asked. 'Where did these crows come from?' I kept mum and she cranked up her voice. When I tried to give her an idea of what must have happened on the terrace, she started: 'First cover the tank'. I was already stressed. The day before, I had been busy shifting the house. Initially, there was sheer enthusiasm as we were moving in to our own house. But soon I was fatigued with the petty stuff collected by my wife. The cupboards were such a headache. They were just impossible to get through the new door frames. But, I tried and got them through somehow. While doing this, the mirror of one of the cupboards cracked and my wife gave me a stern lecture in front of outsiders. I don't know how I got into bed and slept that night. I had planned to take full rest... but this headache.

Once again, I heard a big splash and wings flapping about on the terrace. It tickled my body. That very minute, I woke up and got out of bed. There was no need to switch on the light as it was already daylight. The room was still littered with petty items. No space to step down from the bed. Somehow, I found my way, treading through the mess, and reached the entrance to the terrace. I opened the door, positioned a ladder, and climbed up. The cawing became intense. As I reached near the tank, a few crows started hovering around me. One crow had become weary of his efforts to get out of the water. He was wet and couldn't fly because his wings were drenched. When he noticed me, he rolled his eyes. Well, he was alive. He has to be pulled out. But how? Slowly, I put my hand in the water and tried to reach the crow, but it fluttered away. Bloody bird, it was not letting me pick it up. I turned to get the iron bar from the balcony downstairs and the cawing crows again began hovering close to the tank. I hurried down. While climbing down, I stumbled on the middle step and tumbled down. Calmly, I took the iron bar and returned upstairs. But the whirling crows wouldn't allow me to get any further. As I moved forward, they rushed over the tank. I had to step back. Finally, I moved the bar to whisk them away, but the same thing happened again. I guessed they didn't want me to pull the crow out and so I lowered the bar into the tank. I thought the poor creature would at least take support because it couldn't stand on the wet tank. But all he did was make a sound and fall down again. The crow in the tank turned his dying eyes around and strongly held the bar with his feet. Then, I slowly moved another bar towards him. He struggled but couldn't climb up. So, I bent over the tank, but a few crows flew over me. Cawing loudly. I sweated, and numbly returned to the balcony and shut the door. How to handle these crows?

They were cawing inside my head. There were a few other crows on the nearby tree. My wife asked as she yawned, 'What is in the tank?'

I had to answer. She saw crows from the balcony and came inside and told me, 'Take that basket and pull the crow out from the tank.'

Her idea of a basket appealed to me. As I climbed up with the basket, the crows rushed towards me. I whirled the basket in the water and slowly took in the tired crow and flicked him onto the nearby field. Hush! Other cawing crows rushed towards that crow in the field. Let them die. I don't care now.

I stepped down from the ladder and my wife started, 'Why were you wasting your time there? You should have taken the basket to catch that crow. Why didn't you do that?' I said nothing and came to bed, once again walking through the mess. I couldn't stop thinking about the crow and I kept tossing in bed.

I was exhausted. Just a few minutes later, my wife screamed, 'Hello, get up and come here. See that crow.' I got up in a flash and reached the back door and saw hundreds of crows attacking that crow; they were pecking him to death. The wretched crow was struggling for life. I picked up a piece of brick and hurled it towards the crows and they flew away. But soon they resumed the attack. I took a stone and hurled it at them once again. But they were back again. This went on for some time. At last, I dropped that loathsome activity and the crows continued to peck him. He dodged for a while and then dropped dead after some time. The hovering crows turned away and kept cawing. They all moved away, assured of his death. I watched in shock.

I searched for the tobacco pouch in the room and put tobacco in my mouth. My wife started, 'How sad! Bloody crows pecked him to death. It's good that you pulled him out of the tank otherwise they would have spoiled the tank!'

I said, 'My dear, they killed him because I pulled him out. Otherwise, they wouldn't have. The touch of human being is impure to crows.'

Saying 'I spit on my bad luck,' my wife carried on with her chores.

I took out my bicycle to go to school. Hurriedly, I got on. I was already late. I had to reach at least before the morning prayer. I left the house and within a few minutes, a flock of crows began following me. I increased my speed and the crows did too. I pushed and pedalled with all the force and the crows, in turn, raised their cawing.

As I rode into the market, the cawing stopped. I stopped outside an eatery and parked my bicycle. I was sweating like a pig. I rushed inside and quickly emptied two-three glasses of water, wiped my sweating face, coolly sat down, and relaxed. I turned my bicycle towards the school. There were no crows. I reached the school. The classes had already started. I sat in the staffroom as I had no interest in teaching right away. The supervisor came searching for me and asked, 'How was the first night in the new house? You are late.'

I replied, 'It was very nice, but...' and suddenly stopped. I shouldn't tell him anything. He continued, 'But, mister, you should have performed Satyanarayan puja. How could you dare enter the new house without puja?'

Meanwhile, the colleague who teaches math came and began, 'Pandya, you are already in debt, but even so, you should spend a few thousands and receive god's blessings.'

I just smiled awkwardly and put my head down on the table. I was depressed. When all of them pecked the crow and killed it, till then it was ok. But why did they hold a grudge against me? I should not have thrown bricks at them. Are they holding a grudge against me for some other reason? I must talk to someone about this. I shouldn't let this occupy my mind. I couldn't teach a single class. I decided to meet Bombilakar during the afternoon recess. He is the most senior and experienced person in our staff. I called him, 'Let's go for tea. I wish to talk to you. While walking to the tea shop, I asked 'Sir, do crows nurse a grudge?'

He raised his eyebrows, and his face, with the small pox marks, looked scary. Then, he said, 'Crows are a very strange community. It's surprising that people call crows our ancestors. It is the only perturbing bird. I tell you...' and he stopped. After a pause, he started again, 'There is no problem if a crow touches us, but it is not permitted for us to touch a crow. If someone does, all crows will in unison peck that person.'

'That's what happened this morning...' I almost said, but stopped myself. He continued, 'All our relatives received the message that my elder brother had died. Everyone rushed to our house. When I reached home, I came to know that my family had sent the message because he had been touched by a crow. Just a waste of two thousand rupees! Such are the stories of crows!' and he smiled. My main question remained unaddressed, so I asked it again: do crows nurse a grudge? He said, 'Crows do not nurse a grudge and all. But why are you asking this again and again?'

Then I finally told him everything and he went on, 'Pandit, I have been telling you right from the start that people must follow some customs. Before laying the foundation of the house I told you to find an auspicious time to start, propitiate the new vaastu, and to do the puja for doorframes. But every time you said, "Am I going to stay here permanently?" Forget permanently, but aren't you staying here at least till retirement? How much will it cost now?'

'You mean these crows will always chase me?' I asked.

He said, 'Not that, but difficulties will follow, one after the other.' I was scared. The tea tasted bitter.

Usually, I would return home directly from school but now

I wasn't willing to go home. I rode my bicycle to the market, and hopped from shop to shop till evening. At last, I got tired and went home. I parked my bicycle against the wall and peeped in. My wife had called all kinds of relatives—in-laws and a few women neighbours from their lane. The room was neatly arranged. As my wife sensed me coming, she dropped her work and came out. 'Did crows chase you again?' Oh! She saw me panicked in the morning. I just sighed. In a moment, the mother-in-law said, 'The crows must have forgotten by now. They chased you in the morning because the memory was fresh at that time.'

The father-in-law declared, 'Crows are bastards. They did so because they must be living here on the tree.'

I didn't want to discuss the crows again. I wanted to clean the tank and fill it with water from the tank below. I also wanted to take a bath; I couldn't bathe because of the hubbub in the morning. Also, I had to move the grain sacks to the loft. As I started to undress, my wife began again, 'Don't know how long crows will keep on chasing....'

The mother-in-law said, 'We should ask someone who is knowledgeable in these matters.'

The father-in-law retorted, 'What's to there to ask! They will chase for another two-three days and forget afterwards.'

'And if they don't stop?' my wife had an anxious doubt.

The father-in-law said, 'That won't happen, my dear. Every year crows trouble us in the jowar farm and one of us kills one of them and hangs him in the farm. But...this is a different case.'

The mother-in-law said, 'Who said that they don't chase? When your elder brother hustled out a crow's nest from the tree, didn't that crow chase him up to the house?'

The wife recalled something, 'Ma, do you remember that day we installed the door frame? One crow sat on the door frame. He was there around the house most of the time. I don't know, but the same crow might have died this morning.'

The mother-in-law said, 'If it's the same crow, it will be very then we can build one there.' The elder one said, 'If he wants to, let him build there first.'

Long discussions followed. Later on, I stopped talking about it after sensing the overall opposition. There was no use telling my wife anything about it. But I hadn't changed my mind. Quickly, I took out a loan of two lakhs from the bank. For that, I had to bribe the officer with liquor worth a thousand rupees. I laid the foundation without considering the auspicious time to start. People drove me crazy. I have made a mistake. It was an ass's business that I constructed the house, I thought, and rolled over to the other side of the bed. Once again, I saw in my mind's eye my home in the village and the crow in the tank. I got up. The lizard on the wall clucked loudly. I rubbed tobacco and lay down, my eyes wide open.

The news that crows had chased me spread all over town. Everyone looked at me strangely. Whenever I escaped skilfully from the crows, they would stare at me curiously. Women felt sorry for whatever happened to me. It went on for eight days. I lost my appetite. The discussion in school was as irritating as the chasing crows. The headmaster called me to his cabin and said, 'Pandit, I heard about you. I am sorry for that. You are strong enough to endure it. But a few of our colleagues met me in the morning,' he paused and I pricked up my ears. He went on, 'They were complaining.' He lowered his voice, 'They were saying crows might follow you even to the school. This will be a problem for the students. Then the parents will complain. They shouldn't have talked like this but such is human nature.'

Then he raised his voice, 'Why don't you do this? Why don't you take fifteen days' leave? You will be mentally refreshed and the crow problem will be resolved.' I couldn't say anything. I kept staring at him like a crow. I came out of his office. I was surprised: who could have complained to him about me?

bad. He must be one of our ancestors. He must have come just to protect our family.' My head reeled, but there was no scope to say anything. Silently, I took the torch and went upstairs. The dead crow was still lying in the field.

I couldn't close my eyes even one hour after I got into bed. I blamed myself, 'I am an ass to have built the house.' I was happy in the rented house. And, it was not as if I built this house easily. I shifted twelve houses in this town after marriage. Either there was a water problem or I had difficult landlords. Finally, I went to Babu wani's bungalow. It was quite a big house with good supply of water. Babu wani did not stay there. He had rented out his bungalow and was living in a small house mid-town. That's why there was no problem. But it so happened that my wife planted two creepers of jasmine near the house in the rainy season. They grew fast, within two–three months. One day Babu wani came there for a walk and plucked the jasmine flowers from the creepers. My wife abused him terribly. He left silently. Next day, when I was in the market, he told me plainly, 'Master, leave my house. My daughter is coming to stay there.'

What could I say? It was at that moment that I decided to build my own house, even if one of just two rooms. I am not a man who accumulates properties for sale. I have a few acres of land in my village. My two brothers, their families, and my parents live on that land. My family has very limited income from our farm. Only thing is that, even today, I never have to buy grain from the market. We took care of one another. I was the only person with a government job; my parents always believed that only I could improve the family fortune. I felt obliged to go home to the village once a week so as not to break their trust in me. One day, I told my mother about my plans for the house. There was no reason to oppose me. She said, 'You three brothers, sit together, talk about it, and decide.' I discussed the issue with my brothers and proposed a plan for the house. The younger one said, 'Let's build a house here in the village first,

Everyone was supporting me and suggesting remedies. Then who are these people? I kept thinking. I had no answer. Then I gave up thinking. Feeling perplexed, I entered the staffroom and started talking loudly. I don't know how it happened. Someone poured water on my head. Suddenly, I came to myself. I felt ashamed. I scribbled down the application for leave, took the bicycle, and returned home. As usual, the crows were there on my way. I abused myself loudly.

The news that crows had been chasing me on my way home and that now I am on leave due to the crows spread through the village. My mother and both my brothers came home immediately after getting the news. My mother asked many questions. Two neighbours and other people gathered as my mother reached. I didn't want them in my house but I was helpless. In addition, they told my mother about my panicked state on the road. Mother was stunned and blamed me, 'You failed to do your duties to God. You should have tied a cotton thread around the house. I had warned you to keep your head at the time of construction and you did this! You shouldn't have behaved like this. How much would it have cost? Just a few thousands!'

My elder brother said, 'Crows are treacherous. Last Sunday, we offered naivedya for Markalya's twelfth day after his death at the farm. We waited there for the entire day. But not a single crow turned up. They were on the tree but didn't touch the naivedya. Finally, we brought a cow to the offering. She ate it and then the crows came down immediately.' The younger brother said, 'You shouldn't have built this house. Waste of time and energy.' My wife thought that such discussions should not take place in front of the neighbours. She called all of us into the room inside. The neighbours left reluctantly.

Neighbours eyeing us with suspicion, discussions in school, the ire of family members, my wife's nagging—all this tormented me. Above all, everyone kept telling me new myths about crows. It was sickening. I didn't go out for a few days. My mother's and wife's frantic business of visiting different mystics, and constant discussions with astrologers was in progress. I wondered, 'In spite of this, why is this happening only to me?' I was completely baffled. At last, I decided to go out and watch those crows again to see if they had forgotten everything. I took my bicycle and left for school. With tobacco in my mouth, I pedalled bravely. I cycled for a few minutes and the cawing started! Suddenly, crows began hovering over my head. My head tingled. I stood still with my bicycle, bent down, picked up a stone, and hurled it at the flock. Smart crows! They dodged the stone and continued cawing with greater intensity. Their usual gang gathered in a minute. I remained firm as I wanted to see what happens. They began hovering and screeching and fluttering their wings, which almost touched my head. I decided to merely stand there, but with a stone in hand. I moved slightly away from the bicycle to get some stones and the crows attacked my bicycle. The bicycle turned into a black heap! What a stunning scene! Meanwhile, our neighbour, who was watching this unusual scene, ran towards me and said, 'Wait, sir, wait.' As he approached, the crows flew away. I was stupefied and kept staring at the sky. In no time, the sky turned blue and empty. No one would have believed that just a few moments ago it had been full of crows. Perhaps they felt relaxed, giving me their inherited property. My neighbour almost threatened me, 'Sir, do something. It is getting out of control. They have kept vigil on you. I haven't heard of such an incident ever before.'

I asked anxiously, 'How is it possible? This is new to my generation.'

He said, 'Don't talk like this. Think sensibly.' After that, he told me a number of things. I heard the words, but I couldn't understand a single thing he said. He must have realized that. He shook me and said, 'Why are you perturbed? Let's go home.' I went home with him. I still couldn't drive away the spectre of crows.

I was burning with fever and felt terribly restless, the entire house became restless as well. I was delirious and kept mumbling about crows. I was wondering: why is this happening to me? This is not the fever of some illness. I was talking nonsense about crows in a delirium. It was all very annoying. My brothers were already stationed here. Not that they were really worried about me but it was necessary for them to show concern, at least in front of our mother. People visited me and commiserated. My wife was increasingly burdened with work. No wonder her irritation was shooting up higher than my fever. Neighbours would always poke their nose into our personal matters. Someone from my school would punch in to vomit whatever they knew about the crows in exchange for glucose biscuits. My fever shot up again. Meanwhile, my wife's distant relative arrived. His name was Rammanna. After introductions, he announced, 'As there is Kakyog* in his kundli, this problem is obvious.' He recalled, 'Hariappa from our place had this yog in his kundli. Crows pecked him to death. Thousands of crows had gathered at that time. All of a sudden, they surrounded him and he was totally gheraoed. People couldn't figure out where he was. They hurled stones at the crows but they wouldn't budge. They started cawing fiercely and competing with one another. Finally, someone brought Shivanna Inamdar's gun and dispersed them by firing. Hariappa collapsed, soaked in blood, and was shifted to the hospital, but in vain.'

While telling this story, Rammanna seemed certain that the same thing would happen to me. But my wife didn't understand. She served tea and asked him for remedies. My mother didn't like this. She stared at Rammanna with red eyes.

When Rammanna left, she woke me up and announced, 'We better go to our village.' My wife asked nervously, 'How will you take him with such high fever? And what if something goes wrong there?'

Mother suddenly screamed, 'You whores, you are up in arms against my son. Lakshmi will wipe it out.' For a long time she

---

*Time of the crow (kak). It is believed to be an impure time.

kept abusing my wife. I couldn't calm her down. My wife started crying. I was exhausted from the raging fever.

Mother dragged me to the village. Only she stayed with me. Even my wife was not allowed to be with me. If anyone came around, Mother would yell, 'You pimps, you will peck my son to death. Get away from here.'

When I recovered fully, she brought me back to the town so I could go back to work. She escorted me to the door of my house and said, 'My dear, go to school. Let me see who dares to come here.'

I was scared; but there were no crows around.

Translated by Ashutosh Potdar

THE FORT
MILIND BOKIL

Every year, Dada would start constructing a fort a day before Vasu Baras, the first day of Diwali. The wall of the landlord's house extended a little outside and formed a corner by the side of the wall. There was no free space in front of any resident's house in our chawl. So, the fort construction took place at this corner. Besides, the fort would get support from walls on both sides.

The construction of a mound for the hill was easy once the space between the two walls had been filled with stone and soil. Dada would come up with a different design every year. Throughout the year, he would look at photographs of different forts and discuss them with us so as to decide which fort he should take up next. His chief adviser in the fort-making activity was our grandmother, Aaji, and I was his assistant. Ramesh Gumle was of my dada's age. But we were at loggerheads with the Gumles. In fact, Ramesh was mean and we had to keep an eye on him so that he didn't create any problems. We had seen how mean he could be the year we had quarrelled for the first time. Ramesh had built his own fort. But once he realized our fort was better, he demolished ours. No one had seen his vandalism but our aaji. Dada would not break Ramesh's fort even though he smashed ours. When we were discussing Ramesh's act at home, our mother told us not to touch his fort because we hadn't actually seen him breaking our fort. But Aaji was uncompromising. She stormed off and kicked Ramesh's fort and demolished it. She also chided the Gumles loudly.

'Don't you dare touch my grandson's fort ever again! I am not a coward like you to break the fort in the darkness of the night. Remember, you will have to face me if you do such a thing again.'

Gumle uncle stared at Aaji. She said to him, 'Mr Gumle, discipline him well. I'll break his leg if he is caught again, and you will find that this will cost him dearly for his behaviour.'

As Aaji's outraged tones pierced the chawl, the neighbours peered through their windows and doors. Ramesh didn't dare touch our fort again. Eventually, we all grew up. There were no other kids in the chawl. Pintya in Mokashi's house was very young. Dashputre kaka's Raju was in college. Raju would respond 'all good' to anything we said. I was the only company for Dada.

Dada got into the habit of building a fort because of our grandmother. She was from Pune district, and it was tradition there to build a fort in the courtyard. Our mother never discouraged us from building a fort. But she didn't encourage us either. She was self-contained and happy with herself. Aaji enjoyed all such activities. When she was in excellent health and Dada was very young, she would collect stones and soil herself. Her fort used to look rough. Later, as Dada grew older, she took to instructing him while sitting on the steps of the house. We would tease her and say that she wanted to build the fort, but an old woman like her could never do it. At this, she would dust off her palms and say, 'Believe what you want! But just build a fort.'

Building a fort meant collecting bricks and stones to feed into the fort's stomach. We would start the work with the previous year's stones. Our landlord Shevade was very grumpy. He would ask us to remove all the bricks and stones immediately after Diwali and the Tulsi marriage. Usually, the bricks would slowly disappear as children would remove them so they could play cricket there. Later, we reduced the use of bricks and stones as Dada got the idea of using sackcloth. But still, stones were required to fill in the main portion of the fort. Dada would collect the stones throughout the year. The big stones were not useful. We would collect the stones in a basket or a box and bring them to the fort construction site on a cycle carrier. Dada got his first cycle when he was in the eighth standard. He would walk with the cycle and I would follow him while holding the box of stones on the carrier.

It was easy to get bricks and stones. The main challenge was to get soil. We had an open courtyard in front of our chawl but digging there for the soil was not possible. The road in front of our house was tarred and it was always full of potholes. There were always stones lying by the roadside. Once Dada saw heaps of soil left there by the municipal corporation. We collected that soil and brought it home on our cycle carrier. In later years, we started approaching soil vendors. We would get half a sack of soil from them and carry it on a cycle.

Dada would start building the fort by looking at a picture. But the real forts looked different. He had Rajgad, Pratapgad, Sinhgad, or Panhala-like real forts in front of his eyes. These forts are long, broad, and extend across the land. How could we build such forts on our tiny piece of land in front of our house? Also, it would be difficult to build a small-sized fort as we had to carefully work on the mound. So, though the photo would be of some big fort, we would come up with something that would be possible to make. Once Dada wanted to build the Sindhudurg Fort of Malvan surrounded by water. But the challenge was to have a moat around the fort. He had seen that type of fort at Adarsh Tarun Mandal. The mandal had built it by constructing walls with cement and bricks. Besides, they used blue tiles on the floor. Dada collected such tiles but he dropped the idea later, as he realized that such construction was not possible. But Aaji saw no problem there. She would say that Shivaji had built a number of forts, and we were constructing only one.

A mound for the fort could be in any form. But a fort had to have certain features—steps, an arched gate, a bastion, and a cave. The first three things were according to Aaji's science and the fourth was Dada's specialty. After soil was daubed on the neatly arranged stones and soil, the next step was to construct the steps. Initially, Dada would fill a matchbox with mud and form the square bricks for the steps. But this was slow going as he had to first make bricks and then arrange them into steps. Later, he started placing matchboxes on the mound and daubing them with mud. We needed several matchboxes for this, and I was the one who had to collect them a month before Dada started the work. The steps looked big as they were moulded on the empty matchboxes. They were, in Aaji's words, 'A pearl heavier than the nose.' As I said so, Aaji said, 'Let it be!' Once Dada suggested that we construct a road instead of steps. To this, she responded, 'Then, it would just be a hill. Shouldn't there be steps if it is going to be a fort? Would Shivaji merely walk on the road? He is the king, and the king should walk like a king.'

After the steps and the gate, building the bastions was our next task. There had to be a minimum of two bastions. There again, Aaji's science: there had to be a bastion on the fort. We call it a fort because there is a bastion. Otherwise, it would only be a hill. Dada would build the bastion at the top of the hill. His usual trick was to put empty paint tins upside down and daub them with mud. We wouldn't get these tins every year. That's why we would scrape the mud off the tins and keep them in our toy box. Also, Dada had an idea of pasting a piece of paper on the tins instead of daubing them with mud in order to build a fort wall. He would colour the paper grey and use white to draw the lines. The rest of the hill would be red, but the bastion would look like seasoned stone. This trick made Aaji very happy.

While Dada built the fort, Aaji would continue her chatter, sitting on the steps. Once when Dada was building the Raigad Fort, she made him build a Hirkani bastion—named by Shivaji after a woman who scaled down the walls of the Raigad Fort—on it. Though we knew the story of Hirkani, Aaji narrated it again. After telling the story, she said, 'Shivaji was great, but Hirkani was greater. Because of her, he learnt to build the bastion. If Hirkani had not climbed down the fort, would he have built one?'

There was no cave in Aaji's science of forts. But Dada would always make a cave. No one knew from where he got that idea. He would start thinking about the cave while planning for a fort. He would design a furrow with stones and dab soil on it so that the cave would be visible. If possible, he would make more than one cave. If there was space outside the caves, he would plaster them with mud and arrange small stones to sit on. Once Aaji told him to have Tukaram Bua sit inside. That year, he got the Tukaram Bua toy. I had also told him to keep a tiger inside the cave. We had a toy tiger. But Dada wouldn't do that. Sometimes, he would construct a tunnel-like opening for the cave from both sides.

Dada was fond of creating a river, which Aaji always supported. She would say that as all the forts of Shivaji were in hilly areas, there had to be a river and it should flow by the hillside. The question was: how to bring water into the river after it's made? For that, Dada would plunge a tin into the rear end of the fort and pierce a hole under it to hide a water tube. As we poured water into the tin, it would flow down like a river. Of course, it wouldn't be enough to flow like a river. Nevertheless, the patch would be wet. Before someone could ask us why there was no water in the river, Aaji would volunteer that the river has dried up, but that it would flood in the monsoon.

After all the soil was smeared on the fort, our first job was to sow garden cress seeds in it. Aaji would insist on doing this as early as possible because they took a couple of days to sprout. She would say that since the fort is on the hill, it has to be forested. Shivaji could fight all the wars because they happened in the woods. Aaji liked the fort looking green. We would fling garden cress seeds all over the fort so they would sprout everywhere. Even around Shivaji's throne. Shivaji Maharaj wouldn't be visible when covered with the greenery of the sprouts. But Aaji didn't care.

Once the fort was finally ready, Aaji would arrange toys on

it. The toys would be from previous years. A few new toys would be bought from the potters in the neighbourhood. If the toys were carefully wrapped in paper and stored, we could use them the next year. But the colour of some of the toys would fade and the noses of some others would wear away. Every year we had to discard a few such toys.

The mavale toys were not proportional to the fort. The colourful mavale toys looked funny on the grassy and red-black fort. One mavala toy was as big as an arched gate. Shivaji's idol on the throne would occupy the entire top portion of the fort. But no one worried about that. We had to place the toys there, that was all. Of course, the mavale toys were not the only ones we included. Later, the potter-artisans in the neighbourhood started making different sorts of toys. For example, a grocer woman, a fruit-seller woman, a woman carrying a pot and a jar, a farmer carrying her child, a woman washing clothes or pots, a coolie pulling his cart, men playing the drum and a pipani, and whatnot. I would love a mavala toy with a real sword. In his arm would be a small slot for the sword and on his face a luxurious moustache.

Actually, plastic soldiers were also available and Dada liked them more than the earthen ones. There were two types of plastic soldiers. One type was very small, made of celluloid. They would not even be visible on the fort. But those toys were more fitting for our fort. The other type were solid plastic ones. They were moulded and had their own base. Such soldiers were either in the sitting or prone positions. They were available in two colours: brown and green. So Dada always wanted to depict the war between India and Pakistan. But it never materialized. Aaji would say, 'Ours is Shivaji's fort. Where does this India–Pakistan thing come in? Arrange your plastic soldiers down there and not on the fort!'

Our fort would look beautiful with the toys arranged in the tall grass. Somewhere Dada had seen painted hills and blue skies at the background of a fort. Our fort also had the walls to support such an undertaking. But our landlord wouldn't allow us to paint the walls. Dada brought the used engineering drawing sheets from Raju, painted a blue sky on them and pasted them as the background of the fort. He drew a sun too.

'See how Shivaji's flag is fluttering in the blue sky,' said Aaji.

'Aaji, why do you address him as Shivaji all the time? Why don't you address him as "Shivaji Maharaj"?'

For a moment, she didn't understand my question.

She then asked, 'How do you address Ganapati?'

'Ganapati bappa!'

'And me?'

'You? Aaji.'

'Aai?'

'Aai.'

'Why?'

'Why means? That's how it has to be. It has to be the same for the king,' said Aaji. 'The person who is close to you and is our own has to be called that way. The king is also our own, therefore, we address him that way. "O king, get up. Take care of your people. See, it hasn't rained, dig a lake." We have to tell him like this. Understood?'

'Yes,' I said.

That year, Aaji hadn't been feeling well since Anant Chaturdashi. She was finding it difficult to breathe. The doctor had kept a machine in the house and she was on oxygen. She stopped walking about the house. She would remain in bed all the while. Gradually she stopped eating. She asked us to build the fort as Diwali was approaching. She would sit in a chair on the steps with a tube in her nose. That Diwali, she saw the completion of the fort; content, she passed away on Tulsi Marriage day.

After Aaji died, Dada never built a fort again.

Translated by Ashutosh Potdar

HARI'S LAUGHTER

JAYANT PAWAR

And at last Hari laughed. Laughed uproariously. The curator of the national zoo heard something like thunder in the dark of the midnight hour. He woke up with a start and ran like the wind to Hari's enclosure. It was hardly an enclosure. More like a small spacious park. It was covered all around in thick grass with a brimming pond in the centre for Hari to laze in. It was at the edge of that pond that Hari was standing and laughing uproariously. He had opened his massive jaws so wide that the entire earth would have fit inside it. His sharp white teeth sparkled inside that jaw. When Mother Yashoda ordered the butter thief, child Krishna, to open his mouth wide and saw the universe revealed in it, at first she was shocked and then delirious with joy. The shock and joy that the curator felt was no less than hers. He retraced his steps at a run and called the director of the zoo. When the director, annoyed by the strident ring of the telephone in the middle of the night, heard that Hari was laughing, he could not hold back his joy and broke into uncontrollable laughter in the darkness of his room. He broadcast the news with such consummate skill that within minutes it had reached the home minister's ears. The minister was engaged just then in revealing significant statistics in a meeting convened for an in-depth discussion regarding ways to raise the country's development rating. When he noticed the words, 'Hari is laughing uproariously' on the tiny screen of his mobile phone, he stopped all further discussion and showed the message to all present. The solemn mood of the meeting was instantly transformed into one filled with peals of laughter. The entire situation was about to undergo a sea change. The covert criticism directed at the government was going to cease instantly. The critics were going to choke on their words. The joke was going to be on those who had joked about the home minister. His status in the cabinet was going to rise and perhaps lead to more funds in his pocket. The reputation of the director of the national zoo was going to shine forth more radiantly. Expensive new projects were going to be sanctioned with trickle-down benefits at the grassroots. Not only was the zoo curator's job now secure, he could even look forward to a promotion. Most importantly, the nation was going to be happy. A wave of laughter was going to spread across its length and breadth. All because Hari was laughing. He was laughing uproariously with his jaws wide open.

It is time to reveal that Hari was a twenty-seven-year-old hippopotamus. Hari of the lustrous purple hide, short, powerful legs, and brown eyes filled with an expression of unbelievable tenderness, was originally Harrison, a handsome hippo who had been transported to the zoo a year before from the jungles of Congo to become the centre of the nation's attention. Harrison had become Harry and Harry had been Indianized to Hari. The one and only reason why he had become an object of such national curiosity and aroused such intense fascination was that he belonged to the very rare species of laughing hippopotami from the central African jungles. Few people know about these animals. Hippopotami are otherwise considered to be dangerously ferocious. When this creature, who can lift entire bales of grass lightly on the pointed hairs of his upper lip, crunching them to a mash, opens his jaws wide and roars, the mightiest animals in the jungle tremble in trepidation. We have seen this beast, who makes even lions quake, only from a distance, in zoos or in the circus or on TV channels like Discovery or Animal Planet. We have often seen him lazing peacefully in water or standing stock still on a grassy plain like a statue. There's nothing in his blinking, potato-like eyes to suggest his ferocity. But if you ask the people of the Congo valley, no other creature is as dangerous as him. You might guess at the cruelty that lies hidden behind his stony calmness if you have seen the video on Discovery Channel which shows a hippopotamus in the clutches of seventeen lion cubs. As he sits behind a bush lost in thought, the cubs, who have gone completely wild, leap onto his back, tearing at him with their little teeth and claws. He takes to his heels in a bid to escape them, but then, at one point, he spins around in mid-stride, opens his jaws wide, and crunches a whole cub between his teeth. Those who have seen the spectacle must surely have felt their hearts missing more than a beat. Herds of these menacing hippopotami are to be found wandering around the jungles of Congo's Virunga Park. However, the laughing hippos are a race apart. They also open their jaws wide, but when they do, the expression in their eyes is not murderous. Rather, the eyes turn into wide slits that express a mischievous merriment. That is what gives us the impression that their open jaws mean laughter. Perhaps it is that. At least the Hutu and Mai Mai tribes of the Congo jungles firmly believe it is. Even the officer in charge of Virunga Park assured our home minister that this breed of hippopotami was less aggressive than the others. It so happened that the home minister's wife had fallen in love with Harrison who was of this breed of laughing hippos.

This is how it came to pass. Our home minister had gone to Uganda to attend a Third World Peace Conference accompanied by his wife. After the conference, desiring to enjoy the pleasures of an African safari, they travelled around the Democratic Republic of the Congo and the neighbouring countries of Angola and Namibia, stunned by the richness of the wildlife they saw. They were driving around the Virunga National Park when Harrison appeared from nowhere and stood in front of their vehicle. He only had to open his jaws and narrow his eyes for the home minister's wife to break into delicious gooseflesh and exclaim delightedly from her seat. There Harry stood, his buttery smooth purplish hide sparkling, his massively billowing stomach curving in a lyrical line, his thick, strong legs rooted in the earth like columns, flaunting the pointed teeth in his laughing jaws. The home minister's better half cried, 'He's the one! He's the one!' She recalled having seen just such a laughing hippopotamus on a visit to the Great Russian Circus with her daughter, who was now doing a crash course at the University of Ohio. He had been the biggest attraction in the circus. The sight of him had sent a thrill down the spines of both the home minister's better half and the apple of his eye. Indeed the Great Russian Circus had advertised him widely: 'Come and see the laughing hippopotamus!' Little children screamed when he came on. Many could barely suppress the urge to put their hands in his jaws and feel inside them. The home minister's wife said to her lord and master, 'Do let's take this hippo home.' The demands of great people are also great. And they are always fulfilled, because fulfilling them is a sign of equal greatness. Did not Sita in the Ramayana insist on having the golden deer captured for her? But Mrs Home Minister's demand turned out to be for a larger cause. Sita wanted the golden deer to make a golden bodice for herself. Mrs Home Minister wanted the hippopotamus for the nation. The home minster cast an indulgent glance upon his wife and said, 'Done.'

The minister was a keeper of his word. A mountain of resolve. He was determined to import the African hippopotamus into the country as national wealth. It was not as though the national zoo lacked hippopotami. But here was a laughing hippopotamus. This made him unique. It had the potential of being the glory of an up-and-coming nation. The director of the Virunga National Park said, 'Sir, this species is on its way to extinction. Circuses from around the world have paid enormous sums of money and taken away our laughing hippopotami. This is a comparatively peace-loving species. The Tutu people from Rwanda take advantage of this and kill them. Their meat is very tasty. Since the law forbids their hunting, they are sold in a powerful pan-African black market. As for their teeth, the prices for which they go put the elephant's tusks to shame.' To which the home minister said, 'You have no need to worry about price. If we say we will buy this hippopotamus, it means we will buy it.'

'But how can you take just the male hippopotamus? Does he not need a mate? Without a mate he will go berserk. Forget laughter, he will create mayhem.'

The director was right. He then showed them a female hippopotamus. Messi. The deal was made. It is said that thousands of crores of rupees exchanged hands. Harry and Messi were loaded onto an enormous ship. Enough grass was also loaded to last them for two months. Even the cage that was constructed for them on the ship was gigantic. And so, rounding the Cape of Good Hope, the two hippos made their way to a faraway land.

The media had broadcast news of their arrival all over the country well before they reached our shores. The event had created a downpour of stories in the press. TV channels had run interviews with the honourable home minister, and informative programmes on hippopotami and their history. There had been a bumper harvest of Harry's photographs in government publicity outlets. The whole environment was alive with Harry. An expansive new space was created for the hippopotami couple in the zoo. A huge lake was built inside. Deep trenches were dug all around with the space within left open. Any suggestion of a cage was deliberately avoided. Every visitor would get an uninterrupted view of the hippopotami and be able to take snapshots of them. It goes without saying that the Opposition held up parliament for a few days over the extravagant expenditure on the hippopotami. But that only resulted in it becoming a prestige issue with the government. To have a laughing hippopotamus in the national zoo was vital as a symbol of a nation growing happier by the day. It was important that the country rise in global happiness ratings, even as it was soaring up an incredible graph of progress.

A happy people do not weep. Do not lose their resilience. They laugh, march aggressively forward, taking the nation with them. The laughing hippopotamus was going to carry precisely this message to the world. The home minister was garnering praise for his imagination.

 Harry and Messi arrived. They were accorded a huge welcome. An immense throng gathered to witness their ceremonial dedication to the nation. Many had to be turned away because the tickets ran out. People were overheard saying the hippopotami did indeed look different. Look at the female. How enormous she was. A truly well-matched couple. Everybody stood around gawping at them. But, surprisingly, Harry did not laugh that day. Nor did Messi. They did not as much as open their jaws. The crowd kept shouting 'Hari, Hari, cheer up, Hari' till they were exhausted. The curator threw whole bales of grass before them. But both kept their jaws tight shut. Harry had suddenly become grave. He looked at everybody with a fixed gaze. That day the public went away disappointed. The following day a new lot of visitors arrived but they too went away disappointed. Harry refused to laugh. The crowds continued to come for a few more days but Harry did not laugh. Messi did not laugh. Gradually the crowds coming to the zoo began to thin. The criticism against the government started to intensify in the same measure. A buzz grew. The laughing hippopotamus was a lie, a way to mislead the public, a huge scam involving big names. The media discovered that the African company which had mediated the sale of the hippopotami was itself bogus. The home minister was deeply dejected by the criticism. He sent out a mandate to his subordinates ordering them to do something, anything, to ensure that Hari laughed. The subordinates set to work.

 Actually an entire army set to work. The animal experts in the country sat thinking about why Hari was not laughing. They consulted psychologists to discover if he was confused, depressed, or nervous. His diet was changed. African music was played to lift his spirits. His two-inch thick hide was tenderly caressed with a spray of cool water. Hari continued to be quiet through it all. Messi too remained quiet. Since nothing seemed to move them to a show of spirit, the zoo bears were brought in to tickle them. Initially the bears cowered. But once they lost their inhibitions, they tickled the hippos as dedicatedly as they could. But Hari and Mausi, as she had now come to be known in the Indian way, were unmoved. Monkeys were brought to dance before Hari. He gave them a steadfast stare. Somebody suggested, 'Circus people have the key to these fellows. Bring on the clowns.' The clowns came with their red noses and their painted faces. They performed a series of silly tricks, did somersaults, let down their pants, lost their balance, fell about. The watching crowd split its sides laughing. But not Hari and Messi, whose faces showed not a wrinkle of amusement. Then some bright fellow said, 'Force open their jaws. We'll play some canned laughter.' But Hari opened his jaws just enough to eat grass. Nobody got to see the majesty of his fully open jaws. Hari was lost in himself. He sat around with a contemplative expression. He would lie in the water with Messi, but would not play around. Instead, he would lean his head on her back and lie quietly in the water. The home minister now began to wonder if he had been cheated. He called the director of the Virunga Park. The director said, 'This is the very hippopotamus that you saw. We Africans might kill but we never deceive.' He added another piece of information. He said there were some laughing hippos who tended to be solemn. They were given to thinking. They rarely laughed. But when they did, the very earth shook. He said these hippos were the rarest of the rare. Their ancestors' skulls had been discovered in the Zambian jungles. An investigative study was underway.

But we were not looking for thinking hippos. How could they symbolize a happy nation? It was certainly not thinking citizens who set a nation on the path to wealth!

After that, the zoo administrators decided to act. They took the curator into confidence. They sent for the mahout. They sat together all night in careful thought and that very night a radical change occurred in the treatment meted out to Hari. They began bombarding his thick hide with sharp bullets. He was thrashed with metal rods. Seeing that he still did not react, attempts were made to pull his teeth out of his jaws. Rods were thrust into his private parts. The same things were done to Messi. She would run berserk when she saw people approaching. Plunge into the water. Hide behind Hari. Hari would look around meekly. On one such night a strong electrical current was passed into the pond to get Messi to come out of her hiding place. The following morning her body was found lying at the bottom of the lake. Hari sat far apart, his face buried in the ground. The death of the female hippopotamus made national news. Hari grew even more quiet after this. He would stand for hours in the grass like a statue, looking at the sky with lacklustre eyes, deep in thought. The home minister, refusing to lose his peace of mind, spent the time conducting a Mahachandi yagya to make the hippopotamus laugh. He made an offering of twenty-one African alligators to the deity.

And then....

After then, one night, the zoo resounded to an ear-splitting clap of thunder, like an enormous flash of lightning. The curator woke out of a deep sleep, startled, and rushed headlong towards the explosion. What he saw was Hari standing before him laughing uproariously. He had opened his jaws wide enough to touch sky and earth and was laughing like thunder. He was laughing as though he had been pumped full of laughing gas. He was laughing without stopping.

Finally Hari laughed.

Hari laughed and the citizens of the country laughed with him. They came in throngs to see the laughing Hari. The zoo administrators advertised a great plan. The laughing citizenry were welcome to take selfies with the laughing Hari. People rushed to the zoo, standing in serpentine queues at the gate. They stood enthusiastically in the heat of the sun, in blowing winds, and crashing rain. They went up to Hari unafraid, laid their hands tenderly on his wounded purple head and took laughing selfies with him. Hari too laughed. Only, nobody saw the difference between their laughter and his.

Translated by Shanta Gokhale

ACKNOWLEDGEMENTS

I am grateful to Eknath Pagar, Randhir Shinde, Rafiq Suraj, Himanshu Smart, Anjali Nerlekar, Nancy Demerdash, Arvind Jadhav, Parineeta Dandekar, Pujitha Krishnan, and Karishma Koshal for their valuable suggestions in selecting the stories, writing the introduction, and supporting me in completing this project.

While every effort has been made to locate and contact copyright holders and obtain permission, this has not always been possible; any inadvertent omissions brought to our notice will be remedied in future editions. Grateful acknowledgement is made to the following copyright holders for permission to reprint copyrighted material for translation in this volume.

'What a Life!' by Shripad Mahadev Mate, included with permission of Continental Prakashan, Pune; translation included with permission of Jayant Karve.

'Divine Intervention!' by Chintaman Vinayak Joshi, included with permission of Continental Prakashan, Pune; translation included with permission of Keerti Ramachandra.

'I'll Be Right Back' by Digambar Balkrushna Mokashi, included with permission of Bimba Joshi; translation included with permission of Keerti Ramachandra.

'Manjula' by Arvind Gokhale, included with permission of Continental Prakashan, Pune; translation included with permission of Keerti Ramachandra.

'Gold from Graves' by Anna Bhau Sathe, included with permission of Savitri Sathe; translation included with permission of Jerry Pinto.

'Hymn of the Deceased' by G. A. Kulkarni, included with permission of Popular Prakashan; translation included with permission of Sachin C. Ketkar.

'A Faceless Evening' by Gangadhar Gadgil, included with permission of Popular Prakashan; translation included with permission of Keerti Ramachandra.

'Morning Glory' by Shankar Patil, included with permission of Mehta Publishers; translation included with permission of Jayant Karve.

'The Husband' by Bhau Padhye, included with permission of Arati Salunkhe; translation included with permission of Jerry Pinto.

'King Maruti' by Vyankatesh Madgulkar, included with permission of Mehta Publishers; translation included with permission of Shanta Gokhale.

'Sorrow' by Kamal Desai, included with permission of Popular Prakashan; translation included with permission of Shanta Gokhale.

'Revolt' by Baburao Bagul, included with permission of Speaking Tiger Books; translation included with permission of Jerry Pinto.

'The God of Brahmins' by Hamid Dalwai, translated with permission of Ila Dalwai-Kambli

'Vacancy' by Ratnakar Matkari, included with permission of Pratibha Matkari; translation included with permission of Jayant Karve.

'A Black Hole' by Jayant Vishnu Narlikar, included with permission of the author; translation included with permission of Anil Zankar.

'Relationships' by Asha Bage, included with permission of the author; translation included with permission of Jayant Karve.

'Continuity' by Shyam Manohar, included with permission of the author; translation included with permission of Rupali Vaidya.

'And Then It Poured' by Gauri Deshpande, included with permission of Surinder Singh; translation included with permission of Anjali Nerlekar.

'Kalluri's Radio' by Vilas Sarang, included with permission

of Shabdalay Prakashan; translation included with permission of Shanta Gokhale.

'Crows' by Yogiraj Waghmare, included with permission of the author; translation included with permission of Jerry Pinto.

'The Eclipse Shall Pass....' by Urmila Pawar, included with permission of the author; translation included with permission of Swatija Manorama.

'Red Muck' by Bhaskar Chandanshiv, included with permission of the author; translation included with permission of Jerry Pinto.

'The Dust of Vaikuntha' by Ranganath Pathare, included with permission of the author; translation included with permission of Anagha Bhat Behere.

'The Boss and his Dog' by Bharat Sasne, included with permission of Meena Bharat Sasne; translation included with permission of Rupali Vaidya.

'War' by Saniya, included with permission of the author; translation included with permission of Keerti Ramachandra.

'Once There was a Crow' with Rajan Gavas, translated by permission of the author.

'The Fort' by Milind Bokil, translated with permission of the author.

'Hari's Laughter' by Jayant Pawar, translated with permission of the author.

NOTES ON THE AUTHORS

SHRIPAD MAHADEV MATE (1886–1957) was a writer, professor, and social reformer engaged in the struggle against untouchability. He was born in the village of Shirpur in the Vidarbha region and educated in Satara and Pune. At the start of his career as a writer, Mate put together a volume entitled *Kesariprabodh* (1931), compiling writings from the Marathi newspaper *Kesari*, founded by Lokmanya Tilak. His other compilations include *Vidnyanbodh*, supplemented with an elaborate 200-page introduction which was later published as a book titled as *Vidnyanbodhachi Prastavna* (1948). Mate is also known for his radical work *Asprushyancha Prashna* (1933) that he wrote to create awareness among upper castes about untouchability. His short story collections *Upekshitanche Antarang* (1941), *Anamika* (1946), *Manuskicha Gahivar* (1949), and *Bhavananche Pazar* (1954) are well known.

CHINTAMAN VINAYAK JOSHI (1892–1963) was a professor of Pali, English, and Marathi. After starting his career as a teacher in Amravati and Ratnagiri in Maharashtra, he moved to a college in Baroda in Gujarat to continue with his teaching work. Later, he was called on to work as a director of the archive of the princely state of Baroda. After his retirement, he lived in Pune. Joshi was a scholar who collected and studied pauranik or mythological books in the Pali language. Influenced by the works of the scholar Dharmanand Kosambi and Buddhism, Joshi wrote introductory books for Pali, such as *Jatakatil Nivadak Goshti* and *A Manual of Pali*, as well as *Shakyamuni Gautam* (1935), *Buddhasampraday Va Shikvan* (1963), and a biography of Maharaja Sayajirao Gaekwad III. He achieved great popularity as a writer of humorous works such as *Erandache Gurhal* (1930), *Chimanravache Charhat* (1933), *Ankhi*

Chimanrao (1940), *Stationmaster* (1943), *Moru ani Maina* (1943), *Osadwadiche Dev* (1946), *Gundya Bhau* (1947), and several others.

DIGAMBAR BALKRUSHNA MOKASHI (1915–81) was born in Uran in Raigarh district, studied engineering, and ran a radio repair shop in Pune till his death. *Lamandiva* (1947) was his first collection of short stories followed by *Kathamohini* (1959), *Amod Sunasi Ale* (1960), *Vanva* (1965), *Chaplus* (1974), *Ek Hajar Gaayi* (1975), *Adikatha* (1976), *Mauli* (1976), and *Tu ani Mee* (1977) that cover different genres such as mystery, thriller, and horror. As a novelist, he wrote four novels including *Sthalyatra* (1958), *Purushas Shambhar Gunhe Maaf* (1971), *Dev Chalale* (1961), *Anand Ovari* (1974), and *Vatstsayan (1978)*. The last two are biographical works on the lives of Sant Tukaram and Vatstayan respectively. A versatile writer, Mokashi has travelogues, writings for children, as well as translations and a manual for radio owners to his credit.

ARVIND GOKHALE (1919–92) was born in Islampur in the Sangli district of Maharashtra. After publishing his first short story, 'Hair Cutting Saloon,' in the periodical of Sir Parashurambhau Mahavidhyalaya in Pune, he has committedly handled the literary form of the short story by writing hundreds of stories throughout his life, collected in thirty-five collections. He has also published five books of micro short stories and six collections of long stories. Some of his best known stories are 'Katarkhel', 'Manjula', 'Rikta', 'Cactus', and 'Vighnaharti'. Many of his stories have been translated into Indian and European languages. Besides stories, he has written several essays and a travelogue, and has translated American stories into Marathi and edited anthologies of Marathi story writers. Gokhale was the recipient of the special award from the Maharashtra Sahitya Parishad and the emeritus fellowship given by the cultural ministry of the Government of India (1984–86).

ANNA BHAU SATHE (1920–69) was a storyteller, novelist, poet, playwright, travelogue writer, and lyricist, well known for his sharp and extensive commentary on caste-based injustices in society. He was born in the village of Wategaon in Sangli district. He left his village with his father and went to Mumbai to earn a living as a porter and a mill worker. Eventually, he taught himself to read and write. After publishing his first story, 'Majhi Diwali', in the weekly *Mashal* in 1949, Sathe went on to publish several collections of stories. He has published a total of thirty-five novels. His works have also been adapted for films. Apart from his prose, Anna Bhau Sathe is also known for songs (Shahiri and Powadas)—such as the famous 'Mumbaichi Lavani'— that are popular even today. Throughout his life, Sathe participated extensively in labour movements, joined the Samyukta Maharashtra Movement, and also organized the first Dalit Sahitya Sammelan held in 1958. His writings have been translated into several Indian and European languages.

GURUNATH ABAJI KULKARNI (1923–87) is well known by his initials 'G. A.' to readers of fiction writing. He was born in Eksumba, lived in Belgaum, and taught English for thirty years at a college in Dharwad. A prolific writer, G. A. wrote short stories and a memoir, and had elaborate correspondences with several contemporaries that have been published posthumously in different volumes. He was also the translator of the novels of Conrad Richter and William Golding. G. A. is best known for his first published work, *Nilasavala* (1959). His other collections of stories include *Raktachandan* (1966), *Kajalmaya* (1972), *Hirave Rave* (1960), *Sanjshakun* (1960), and *Pingalavel* (1972). He received the state government awards for his collections *Nilasawala* and *Raktachandan*. Sahitya Akademi declared *Kajalmaya* the best work of art in Marathi literature in 1973, but he turned down the honour. Some of Kulkarni's short stories have been translated into English, Hindi, and Kannada.

GANGADHAR GADGIL (1923–2008) was born in Mumbai. He earned a master's degree in economics and history from the

University of Mumbai and taught economics at different colleges in Mumbai. As a prolific creative writer and an academician, Gadgil published fictional and non-fictional work including several stories, novels, travelogues, reviews, plays, children's literature, and essays on economics. Some of his notable collections of short stories are *Manaschitre* (1946), *Kadu aani God* (1948), *Navya Vata* (1950), *Talavatil Chandane* (1954), and *Palna* (1961). *Gopuranchya Pradeshat* (1952) and *Saataasamudrapalikade* (1959) are travelogues on his experiences in South India and Europe, respectively. He is also known for his critical writings, some of which have been published as collection of essays, including *Sahityatatle Maanadanda*, *Khadak ani Pani* (1960), *Panyawarhi Akshare* (1978), *Ajkalche Sahityik* (1981), and *Pratibhechya Sahawasat* (1985). His stories have been translated into several languages including Hindi, Gujarati, Urdu, Kannada, Malay, and Turkish.

SHANKAR PATIL (1926–94) was born in Pattankodoli and studied in Tardal, Gadhinglaj, and Kolhapur. After teaching in different schools of Rayat Shikshan Sanstha, he worked at All India Radio, Pune. In 1959, he studied rural life on a scholarship from the Asia Foundation and wrote the novel *Tarfula* (1964). He was appointed as a special officer for Marathi language in the Maharashtra State Textbook Production and Curriculum Research Board. From 1960 to 1968, his storytelling flourished. Patil's first collection of short stories, *Valiv*, was published in 1957. Some of his other collections are *Bhetigathi* (1960), *Abhal* (1961), *Dhind* (1962), *Oon* (1963), *Wavari Sheng* (1963), *Khulyachi Chawdi* (1964), *Pahuni* (1967), *Fakkad Goshti* (1973), *Khelkhandoba* (1974), and *Sarpanch* (1977). He has received a number of awards for his writing and his stories have been translated into Indian and Western languages. His vagnatye (plays) *Galli Tey Delhi*, *Katha Akalechya Kandhyachi*, and *Lavangi Mirchi Kolhapurchi*, among others, have become very popular. Besides short stories, Patil has written screenplays and dialogues for Marathi films.

BHAU PADHYE'S (1926–96) full name was Prabhakar Narayan Padhye. Born in Dadar in Mumbai, Padhye earned his bachelor's degree in economics. He was a full-time activist with a labour union from 1949 to 1951. He did various kinds of jobs at schools, a mill, and an insurance company. Later, he worked as a journalist and editor at newspapers and magazines. During his lifetime, Padhye endured a long, unending tussle regarding the publication of his books. Some of his novels are *Dombaryacha Khel* (1960), *Vaitag Vadi* (1965), *Vasunaka* (1965), *Barrister Aniruddha Dhopeshvarkar* (1968), *Rada* (1975), and *Jailbirds* (1982). Some of the collections of short stories are *Ek Sunehara Khwab* (1980), *Murgi* (1981), and *Thalipeeth* (1984).

VYANKATESH MADGULKAR (1927–2001) was a Marathi storyteller, playwright, screenplay writer, and novelist born in Madgul in the Sangli district. Despite not having finished school, he studied literature. He participated in the struggle for independence in 1942. After a short stint as a journalist, he came to Mumbai around 1950 and started writing Marathi screenplays, prior to which, his collection of short stories *Mandeshi Manase* (1949) was published. Some of his other short story collections are *Gavakadchya Goshti* (1951), *Hastacha Paus* (1953), *Sitaram Eknath* (1951), *Kaali Aai* (1951), and *Jambhlache Diwas* (1957). His novels are *Bangarwadi* (1955), *Vavtal* (1964), *Pudhach Paul* (1950), *Kovale Divas* (1979), *Karunashtak (*1982), and *Sattantar* (1982). Madgulkar also wrote plays, folk dramas, film stories, screenplays, and fine prose. He was also known as a nature lover, hunter, and painter, without having received any formal education in painting. Many of his books won the Maharashtra state awards and he has received several other awards for his writing—including the Sahitya Akademi Award for the novel *Sattantar* in 1983. His stories have been translated into various world languages such as Danish, German, Japanese, Russian, and others.

KAMAL DESAI (1928–2011) was born in 1928 in Belgaum,

Karnataka. She moved to Mumbai to pursue a master's degree in Marathi from Bombay University, and worked as a lecturer in Marathi in various colleges in Maharashtra. She began her writing career in 1955 and went on to publish two collections of short stories and novellas *Hat Ghalnari Bai* and *Ratrandin Amha Yudhacha Prasang*. Kamal Desai was equally interested in philosophy, visual arts, social sciences, films, theatre, and many other fields. She has translated Bernard Bozankit's *Three Lectures on Aesthetics* and Vandana Shiva's *Stolen Harvest* into Marathi.

BABURAO BAGUL (1930–2008) was born in Vihitgaon in Nashik district. He studied up to class eleven at Vihitgaon and Mumbai. Initially he worked as a marker in a laundry, then as an assistant to a compounder, he later worked for twelve years as a labourer, first at the Kohinoor Mill in Dadar and later at the railway machinery factory at Matunga. He resigned from the railway service in 1968 to devote his time to writing. The influence of Marx, Lenin, Mahatma Jotirao Phule, Dr Ambedkar, as well as the ideas and literature of Gorky, Chekhov, and Saratchandra Chatterjee inspired his literary work. Bagul's well-known literary works include *Jenvha Mi Jaat Chorli Hoti* (1963), *Maran Swasta Hot Ahe* (1969), and *Sood* (1970). He was one of the leading Dalit writers who stirred up post-1960 Marathi literature.

HAMID DALWAI (1932–77) was a writer, activist, and social reformer who lived and worked in Maharashtra. He was born into a Marathi-speaking Muslim family in the Ratnagiri district in 1932. He became known both for his reformist work in Muslim communities as well as his literary works in Marathi. Some of his most popular works include a collection of short stories called *Laat* and a novel, *Indhan*. Some of his unpublished work has been published posthumously by Sadhana Publication in Pune. He wrote thought-provoking books such as *Muslim Jaatiyateche Swaroop—Karane Va Upaay* and *Islamche Bharatiy Chitra*. He also wrote *Muslim Politics in Secular India* in English. In order to bring about an awakening in the Muslim community in India, he established the Muslim Satyashodhak Mandal in 1970.

RATNAKAR MATKARI (1938–2020) was a litterateur, theatre personality, director, producer, painter, as well as a writer of plays, one-act plays, plays for the young, short stories, and essays. He has, to his name, several one-act plays, twenty-three collections of short stories, three novels, and twelve collections of essays. His large body of work also includes his autobiographical book *Maze Rangprayog* that is a reflection on his own work in theatre. He has even written several television series. Matkari has been the recipient of numerous awards and accolades and was one of the rare personalities who was awarded both the Sangeet Natak Akademi Puraskar and Sahitya Akademi Puraskar. He is credited with establishing the occult genre of stories in Marathi literature.

JAYANT VISHNU NARLIKAR (b. 1938) is a renowned astrophysicist. For his accomplishments, Narlikar was conferred the civilian honour of Padma Bhushan by the Government of India at the age of twenty-six. He set up the renowned Inter University Centre for Astronomy and Astrophysics (IUCAA) in 1989 in Pune. Since his retirement in 2008, Narlikar has continued to live in Pune. His first book of science fiction stories, *Yakshanchi Denagi*, was published in 1979. His short stories and novels published since then have been very popular. He has also edited encyclopaedias and anthologies and written non-fiction books, which present the history and poetry of science in an engaging way. His books have been translated into many Asian and European languages.

ASHA BAGE (b. 1939) was born into a middle class family and studied Marathi literature and music for her post-graduation degree. Since the publication of her first story that appeared in the Diwali edition of *Tarun Bharat* in 1972, Asha Bage has created an enormous body of writing across twelve collections of short stories and six novels. Some of her short story collections are

Marwa (1984), *Pooja* (1989), *Darpan* (1997), *Rutuvegale* (1999), *Paani* (2003), and *Paulwatevarale* (2004). Her novels include *Manaswnini* (1978), *Zumbar* (1984), *Tridal* (1994), and *Bhoomi* (2004) that received the Sahitya Akademi Award in 2003. Apart from these, she has co-written *Vata aani Mukkam* (2009) that contemplates and comments on the process of writing. Asha Bage lives in Nagpur.

SHYAM MANOHAR (b. 1941) was born in Tasgaon in Satara district. He was a professor of physics in a college in Pune and is a short story writer, novelist, and playwright. After publishing his first short story 'Competition', Manohar went on to publish a number of stories that are collected in *Ani Bakiche Sagale* (1980) and *Binmaujechya Goshti* (1980). Some of his published novels are *He Ishwarrao, He Purushottamrao* (1983), *Sheetyudh Sadanand* (1987), *Kal* (1996), *Khoop Lok Ahet* (2002), and *Utsukate Mee Jhople* (2006). His plays are *Yakrut* (1986), *Hriday* (1987), *Yelkot* (1993), *Premachi Gosht* (1997), and *Darshan* (2004). He has received a number of awards for his writing including the Sahitya Akademi Award in 2008.

GAURI DESHPANDE (1942–2003) was born in Pune. She was a writer of stories, novels, essays, columns, and poems and a professor of English at Savitribai Phule Pune University and Fergusson College. She wrote in Marathi as well as English. She translated Richard Burton's *Arabian Nights* into Marathi. Some of her popular works in Marathi include fiction like *Ahe He Ase Ahe* (1986), *Ekek Pan Galawaya* (1985), *Niragathi Ani Chandrike Ga Sarike Ga* (1987), *Goph* (1999), and *Utkhanan* (2002). One of her most well-known works in English is the short story collection *The Lackadaisical Sweeper: Short Stories* (1970). She also translated remarkable writings from Marathi into English, including works like ...*And Pine for What Is Not* (translation of Sunita Deshpande's *Ahe Manohar Tari*...). Her published work also includes three volumes of poetry in English—*Between Births* (1968), *Lost Love* (1970), and *Beyond the Slaughterhouse* (1972).

VILAS SARANG (1942–2015) was born in Karwar, a coastal town in Karnataka. He secured a doctorate in English literature from Bombay University and then went on to secure a second doctorate in comparative literature from Bloomington, Indiana. He spent five years in Iraq (1974–79), where he taught English at the University of Basrah. Sarang was head of the English Department at Bombay University from 1988 to 1991, during which time he also edited the *Bombay Literary Review*. From 1991 to 2002, he taught at Kuwait University. As a bilingual writer, Sarang has stories, novels, and poetry in both languages to his credit. His Marathi short story collections are *Soledad* (1975) and *Atank* (1999) and translations of his stories in English are collected in *A Fair Tree of the Void* (1990) and more recently *The Women in the Cages* (2006). His other works include the English novel is *The Dinosaur Ship* (2005) and the Marathi novel *Enkichya Rajyat* (1983). His Marathi collection of poems is published under the title *Kavita* (1969–84) and his collection of English poems is published as *A Kind of Silence* (1978). He has also written significant criticism in Marathi.

YOGIRAJ WAGHMARE (b. 1943) was born in Yermala in Osmanabad district in Maharashtra. After a hard-earned school education, Waghmare completed his education in Ambajogai and Aurangabad in Maharashtra. He has worked as a secondary school teacher and retired as the district level primary education officer. Waghmare is a writer of short stories, novels, plays, and children's stories. He started writing stories when he was a student in college. His first story, 'Udrek' was published in 1970 in the quarterly *Asmitadarsh*. Some of his collections of stories are *Udrek* (1978), *Begad* (1980), *Guddani* (1983), *Horpal* (2008), *Bahishkar* (2008), and *Niyat* (2019). He has also edited a few anthologies.

BHASKAR CHANDANSHIV (b. 1945) was born in Hasegaon, Kalamb, in the Osmanabad district in Maharashtra. His name was established in the world of Marathi literature with his first collection of short stories, *Jambhaldhav*. After his college and university education in Ambajogai and Aurangabad, Chandanshiv taught Marathi at different colleges till his retirement. He started writing stories at the age of twenty. Influenced by Mahatma Jotirao Phule's views on agriculture, he wrote with great passion and concern about the issues of agriculture, farmers, agricultural labourers, various sections of the society dependent on agriculture, especially dryland farmers, their agricultural products, markets, guarantees, droughts and unemployment. His story collections are *Jambhaldav* (1980), *Marankala* (1983), *Angarmaati* (1991), *Navi Varul* (1992), and *Birad* (1999). He also has collections of essays, anthologies, and literary criticism to his credit.

URMILA PAWAR (b. 1945) grew up in a small village near Ratnagiri in the Konkan area. Her father's insistence on educating his children eventually led to Pawar's moving to the city of Mumbai to study. She went on to become an activist, involved in the issues of caste and gender, an award-winning writer with a widely read autobiography who continues to raise issues of caste and gender. Pawar's short story collections include *Sahav Bot, Chauthi Bhint*, and *Hatcha Ek*. Her autobiography, *Aaydaan* (2003), translated as *The Weave of My Life: A Dalit Woman's Memoirs* by Maya Pandit is well known among Marathi and English readers. An active member of the Ambedkarite movement, Pawar's writing has been included in the curricula of several universities.

RANGANATH PATHARE (b. 1950) was born in the village Javale in Ahmednagar district in Maharashtra. He taught physics at a college in Sangamner and retired in 2010. Pathare has written several novels, the most prominent among which are *Dive Gelele Divas* (1982), *Rath* (1984), Namushkiche Swagat (1999), *Tridha* (2004), *Dukkhache Shwapad* (1995), *Tamrapat* (1994), *Bhar Chaukatle Aranyaroodan* (2008). He has seven collections of short stories including *Anubhav Vikne Ahe* (1983), *Gabhyatil Prakash* (1998), and *Shankhatla Maanus* (2008) among others. His works also include critical analyses and translations of history, culture, and literature. He is the recipient of numerous awards including the Sahitya Akademi Award in 1999. His writings have been translated into various languages.

BHARAT SASNE (b. 1951) was born in Jalna district in Maharashtra. Sasne is known for his short stories, long stories, essays, plays, translations, novels, and writings for the young. He has several collections of short stories to his credit and some of them are *John and Anjiri Pakshi* (1980), *Laal Phulanche Jhaad* (1984), *Ayushyachi Choti Gosht* (2000), *Shubhvartamaan* (2008), and *Band Darwaja* (2014). Sasne is also known for writing long short stories that have been collected in nine volumes like *Chirdaah* (1986), *Aswasth* (2015), *Vistirn Raatr* (1986), *Anarth* (1989), and *Daat Kaala Paus* (2020). He has received a number of awards for his writing. He retired as the district magistrate of Beed district.

SANIYA (b. 1952) was born in Sangli and lives in Bangalore. After publishing her first short story, *Harvaleli Paulvat*, in 1968, she has published more than twelve collections of short stories: *Shodh* (1980), *Paratitee* (1989), *Bhumika* (1994), *Prayan* (1997), *Punha Ekda* (2015), and others. She also has three novels, *Sthalantar* (1994), *Avarthan* (1997), and *Avakash* (2001) to her credit. She has translated Shashi Deshpande's English novel *That Long Silence* into Marathi. Her writing has been translated into different languages including Hindi, Gujarati, English, Kannada, German, and Urdu. Saniya has won accolades and awards from various organizations and the Maharashtra government for her contribution to literature.

RAJAN GAVAS (b. 1959) was born in Atyal, a village in the Kolhapur district. He has published six novels, two collections of short stories, seven books on literary criticism, and a collection of poems. His work has been translated into Kannada, English, Hindi, and Gujarati. Some of his literary works are *Rivanavayali*

Mungi, Choundak, and *Bhandarbhog.* Gavas is a recipient of several awards such as G. L. Thokal, Bhairu Ratan Damani, and the Sahitya Akademi, for his novel *Tankat* (2001). He retired as a professor of Marathi literature from Shivaji College, Kolhapur.

MILIND BOKIL (b. 1960) is a sociologist with a PhD in social anthropology. He has undertaken several socio-economic studies of development projects and voluntary agencies. An activist, he has worked in tribal and economically backward areas. He writes both fiction and non-fiction and has more than a dozen books (short stories, novels, travelogues, and sociological studies) to his credit. Some of his books are *Zen Garden, Ekam, Udakachiya Aarti, Ran Durga, Samudraparche Samaj,* and *Sahitya, Bhasha ani Samaj.* He has received several awards including the Best Literature Award from the Maharashtra foundation. A Marathi movie based on his novel *Shala* bagged the National Award in 2012 as well as forty other national and international prizes.

JAYANT PAWAR (1960–2021) was born into a mill worker's family. Pawar was a playwright, short story writer, screenwriter, journalist, and theatre critic. He won the Sahitya Akademi Award in 2012 for his short story collection *Phoenixchya Rakhetun Uthala Mor.* He also won the best writer award at a competition organized by the Akhil Bharatiya Marathi Natya Parishad for his play *Kay Danger Vara Sutlay.* His other works include the plays *Adhantar, Darkveshi, Paulkhuna,* and *Majhe Ghar.*

NOTES ON THE TRANSLATORS

ANAGHA BHAT BEHERE is assistant professor of Russian at Savitribai Phule Pune University, Pune. She is the founder, and currently the editor, of *Kelyane Bhashantar*, a journal in Marathi dedicated to literary translations from various foreign languages into Marathi. She translates mainly from Russian into Marathi.

ANIL ZANKAR is a film-maker and a winner of two national awards for writing. He has taught scriptwriting, direction, and film history. He has written extensively on films and film history in Marathi and English. His recent work includes a documentary on Dr Jayant Narlikar for the Sahitya Akademi. He is currently working on a book on Mumbai.

ANJALI NERLEKAR is an associate professor at Rutgers University, New Brunswick, in New Jersey, USA. Her first book is *Bombay Modern: Arun Kolatkar and Bilingual Literary Culture* (2017). She has also co-edited (with Laetitia Zecchini) a special double issue of the *Journal of Postcolonial Writing* ('The Worlds of Bombay Poetry', 2017). Her other publications include translations of Arun Kolatkar's poetry and texts of Marathi short fiction, essays on modern Indian poets, and on Indo-Caribbean writing. Her ongoing project (in collaboration with Dr Bronwen Bledsoe at Cornell University South Asia collections) is the building of an archive of multilingual post-1960 Bombay poetry at Cornell University titled 'The Bombay Poets Archive'.

ASHUTOSH POTDAR is an award-winning Marathi writer of several one-act and full-length plays, poems, and short fiction. He also writes scholarly essays in Marathi and English and has co-edited a volume of essays on performance-making and the archive, and an anthology of art writing in Marathi to be published by Routledge India and Sharjah Art Foundation respectively. Ashutosh edits *Hakara*, a peer-reviewed bilingual journal of creative expression published online in Marathi and English. He is the recipient of several awards for his writing, including the Maharashtra government's Ram Ganesh Gadkari Award. Ashutosh teaches literature and drama at FLAME University, Pune.

DEEPALI AWKALE is a writer, translator, and performer. She writes and translates for the *Sadhana Saptahik*, a weekly established by Sane Guruji. Awkale is a practising counselling psychologist and a senior consultant in mental health projects, especially in the education sector.

JAYANT KARVE's translations have appeared in *An Anthology of Dalit Literature* and *The Oxford Anthology of Modern Indian Poetry*, among others. His translation of Vijay Tendulkar's *Ghashiram Kotwal* was performed off Broadway in New York by the Pan Asian Repertory. Karve lives in San Francisco.

JERRY PINTO is a Mumbai-based English poet, novelist, short story writer, translator, as well as journalist. Pinto's works include *Helen: The Life and Times of an H-Bomb* (2006), which won the Best Book on Cinema Award at the 54th National Film Awards and the collections of poems, *Surviving Women* (2000) and *Asylum and Other Poems* (2003). His first novel *Em and the Big Hoom* was published in 2012, for which Pinto won the Windham-Campbell Prize and was awarded the Sahitya Akademi Award in 2016.

KEERTI RAMACHANDRA translates from Marathi, Kannada, and Hindi into English. Some of her translations from Marathi include *A Dirge for the Damned* and *Mahanayak* (both by Vishwas Patil), *A Faceless Evening and Other Stories* (Gangadhar Gadgil), *The Song of Life and Other Stories* (Vijaya Rajadhyaksha) and *Of Closures and New Beginnings* (Saniya). Besides these she has translated short fiction by Joginder Paul and Premchand. From Kannada, she co-translated (with Vivek Shanbhag) *Hindutva or*

Hind Swaraj by U. R. Ananthamurty. She was the recipient of the Katha A. K. Ramanujan award for translation from more than two languages. Keerti has been an editor of fiction and non-fiction for almost all major publishing houses over the last twenty-five years.

RUPALI BHAVE is a theatre practitioner, facilitator, translator, and author. She is the founder of Jacaranda, an organization that brings theatre to children, and the co-creator of The Box, a black box theatre in Pune. She works as a programme manager with SMART: Strategic Management in the Art of Theatre.

SACHIN C. KETKAR is a Maharashtrian bilingual writer, translator, and critic based in Baroda, Gujarat. He has authored two collections of poems—one in Marathi and one in English—and has translated and edited an anthology of contemporary Marathi poetry, called *Live Update*. He has translated fiction and poetry from Gujarati and Marathi into English.

SHANTA GOKHALE is an accomplished translator and writer of novels, plays, short stories, film scripts, and innumerable newspaper articles. She has translated essays, short fiction, novels, autobiographies, and plays from Marathi into English and a play and a novel from English into Marathi. Gokhale has a volume on the history of Marathi theatre and edited books on the works of theatre directors Satyadev Dubey, Veenapani Chawla, and oral history experimental theatre in Mumbai to her credit.

SUHAS PARANJAPE has been associated with various people's movements. He retired as a senior fellow from Society for Promoting Participative Ecosystem Management, Pune, and is presently engaged in voluntary freelance translations.

SWATIJA MANORAMA is an active participant of Forum against Oppression of Women, an autonomous women's group in Mumbai, since the last thirty years. She is not a translator by profession but loves to reach out to people across cultures.